Shadows of the War

Kim Poovey

DG

To God, my rock and redeemer.

*And to the many women in history who weren't afraid to step
out of their comfort zone to serve in heroic ways.*

Prologue

December 1860

"I've been leading this fight for years," Mr. Rhett declared. "Tonight is the night we declare our independence!"

"Agreed!

"Here, here!"

"Independence for South Carolina!"

The voices roared through the lower level of the Craven Street home in Beaufort, South Carolina. With only five days until Christmas, the group of delegates representing the area were eager to sign the papers that would separate the state from the Union.

"No more of their ridiculous taxes!" one man cried out.

"Or ignoring the law!" another shouted.

"Gentlemen, the shadows of war are upon us! May we fight to protect our rights!"

"And repel their anti-slavery views!"

Glasses clinked and each man downed the shot of whiskey.

Mr. Rhett drew a pocket watch from his silk brocade waistcoat and checked the time. "Shall we make our way to Charleston?"

"Indeed," Mr. Barnwell replied.

The men stepped into the crisp December air and boarded the carriages lined along the dirt road in front of the Greek Revival mansion. After more than a decade of clamoring for self-government, it seemed as if the discourse was finally coming to fruition.

Chapter 1

December 1860

Maggie

Maggie swept Jane's silky brown locks away from her face, and with a few pins, fastened them at the crown of her head, allowing the tightly coiled ringlets to frame her porcelain skin. Late afternoon sunlight filtered through the gauzy curtains of Jane's room where she sat before the vanity mirror. The dress she would wear to the party later in the evening was draped across the multicolored quilt on her iron bed. December in the South Carolina Lowcountry was generally mild allowing for outdoor gatherings and light shawls.

Jane shuffled her feet against the braided rug beneath the stool on which she sat as Maggie slid a silver comb adorned with a delicate spray of lace at the top of her daughter's head and smiled. Leaning down, she rested her cheek against Jane's and gazed at their reflection.

"You're the loveliest young lady I've ever beheld," she said, softly. "Everyone at the Christmas party will be in awe of you."

"Thank you, Mama," Jane replied, her gaze shifting to the vanity. "May I ask you something?"

"Anything."

"Is it true there's going to be a war?"

As Maggie feared, Jane had been exposed to the rumors of impending conflict. "Where did you hear about that?"

"Caroline spoke of it when Elora and I were at her house the other day."

Maggie forced a smile, patting her daughter on the shoulder. "There's no need to concern yourself with such things," she said.

"Mama, I'm not a child anymore," Jane replied, sternly. "I'm almost thirteen and I want to know the truth."

Maggie blew out a breath. Her daughter was correct. It was time to treat her as more than the innocent little girl who'd been left in their care at the ripe young age of five. She was an intelligent child and capable of discussing some of the more serious events in life.

"There is talk of South Carolina leaving the Union. But it's only talk, nothing more. As for war, there's no need to worry about that now. Even if we were to secede it doesn't necessarily mean fighting will follow."

Jane pursed her lips. "You make it sound so simple when everyone else acts as if it's an exciting event like some sort of ball."

"Life has enough worries of its own without troubling yourself about things that may or may not occur. At this time, nothing has taken place except for a faction of gentlemen who want to break up the states and run things their own way."

"Would you tell me if there was going to be a war?"

Maggie nodded. "If the time comes, I'll discuss it with you. But not until there's reason to do so."

"Thank you, Mama," Jane replied with a slight smile.

"Now, let's get you dressed and focus on all the fun you'll have at the party this evening."

Maggie's stomach curdled. She hated that her daughter was

being exposed to the perils of the world at such a young age. Regardless, she'd shield Jane from as much as she could while being honest with her. It was hard enough carrying the burden of a possible conflict that could break apart the country Maggie had come to love.

Clamor about secession had been rampaging through town, sending the population into a frenzy. It seemed as if everyone was sliding down an unpredictable slope of speculation into a puddle of doom. Division reigned as many endorsed seceding from the Union while others stood firmly on the side of preserving the country formed less than a century earlier. The only thing Maggie wanted was peace.

The entire fiasco started when Mr. Rhett, a wealthy and well-respected businessman, made an impassioned speech beneath one of the massive oaks on the other side of town, inciting the community to support secession. Talk of seceding wasn't a new concept. Bluffton had been a hot bed of the topic for decades. Those in favor of dividing the country reached far beyond the town limits into every state. Thus, the name of 'Bluffton Boys" was applied to all who supported secession since the idea was born in this modest South Carolina township.

The notion of leaving the Union was a dangerous subject for Rose Hall Plantation, where Maggie and her family resided. Their small home was nestled along the river's edge, not far from the main house, beneath a canopy of live oak trees bedecked with tufts of Spanish moss. To the rest of the world, Rose Hall appeared to be like any other working plantation complete with acres of Sea Island cotton growing and a host of slaves. Unbeknownst to outsiders, Rose Hall was actually a safe house on the Underground Railroad. Free Negroes worked the land as paid employees, many of them serving the Railroad specifically. It was a delicate balance to keep this secret from others and all involved did an outstanding job of portraying their roles as the enslaved.

Elora Polk, daughter of Dr. and Mrs. Polk who owned the plantation, was one of Maggie's dearest friends and a staunch abolitionist. Elora's grandfather; however, was not. He was one of the most outspoken of the Bluffton Boys insisting the state secede from the Union in order to maintain their decision-making rights and to preserve their way of life. In other words, they wanted to keep their slaves. Although no law had been proposed by the federal government to dissolve the institution of slavery in the south, many in the southern states felt it was only a matter of time and thus action must be taken immediately.

Once Jane was dressed and on her way to the party at the Morgan's home in town, Maggie meandered to the main house to check the inventory of salves and ointments. She was responsible for mixing most of the herbal remedies for those residing on the plantation as well as passengers of the Railroad. Dr. Polk used Maggie's concoctions for many of his patients as well. She'd gained her knowledge and skills from Willa and Letty, two Negro workers at her uncle's farm in Pennsylvania when she was staying there. While the situation at her uncle's home was abusive, she'd managed to befriend some of his workers who helped Maggie maintain her sanity until she was able to escape.

Walking into the parlor of Rose Hall mansion, Maggie found Elora stitching a white Palmetto tree on a sea of red fabric.

"What are you working on?" Maggie asked.

Elora rolled her eyes. "A flag for Grandfather."

"A flag?"

Elora dropped the fabric to her lap and sighed. "Grandfather wants a flag to represent the secessionist efforts. Of course,

I had no choice but to accept his request." Her shoulders slumped. "I love my grandfather despite his beliefs about slavery. Nevertheless, we need to make sure he doesn't suspect what we really do here and agreeing to stitch this flag will help preserve our secret."

"That is a difficult endeavor."

Sighing, Elora picked up the fabric and began stitching again. "If he only knew that his own family was part of the Underground Railroad and doing so on the land he gifted them. He'd have a conniption."

"I'm sorry you have to continue this ruse with him. It can't be easy creating a flag for something you abhor."

"Being Grandfather's favorite grandchild takes the sting out of it, even if I would like to burn this blasted flag once it's done." She gave a slight smile and continued her sewing.

Maggie chuckled. "I've come to check the pantry and see what supplies are running low."

"Has Jane left for the party?" Elora asked as she drew the thread up through the bright red fabric.

"A few minutes ago. She looked so lovely, much like her mother did when she was younger."

"I hope she has a good time," Elora said. "She's such a dear girl with so much kindness in her."

"Indeed," she replied, pride welling in her chest. "I'd best get to the task at hand. I'll see you tomorrow."

Maggie traipsed down the back hall to the butler's pantry. Scanning the shelves, she noted they were running low on ointment for sore muscles and cough medicine. All the while her thoughts raced over the secession debate. Perplexed by the whole scenario, Maggie pondered how the situation would play out and how it would impact the Polk's efforts in helping the enslaved to freedom.

Regardless of the intensifying disputes flurrying about

town, the Polks continued their clandestine work with the Railroad while giving the impression they believed slavery was a nationally sanctioned right. Granted, the constitution of the United States had clauses that supported slavery. However, many northern states had already abolished the reprehensible practice of owning another human being. With all the farms and plantations in the south, slavery was an economic necessity. In the end, money drove all decisions whether moral or not. With the talk of secession gaining traction, it seemed drastic action would be taken one way or another. Maggie only hoped the rumors of war would fizzle before things progressed to a point of no return.

Several hours later, Jane returned to the cottage.

"How was the party?" Maggie asked as Jane stepped inside.

"Fine," Jane muttered, her eyes downcast as she bolted down the hall.

Sighing, Maggie followed her daughter to her room where Jane hurriedly slipped off her gown and slumped onto the bed.

Maggie sat next to her and took Jane's chilled hand into hers.

"My dear girl, what happened? Was there talk of war?"

Jane shook her head, refusing to meet Maggie's gaze.

"Then what has you in such a state?" she asked, tipping up Jane's chin.

"Caroline Belfair was there," she said, a tear trickling across her cheek. "She was bragging about her ancestors and asked about my family. When I told her I was adopted she laughed and said that was another way of saying my real parents didn't want me. Then she said well-bred parents didn't give away their children and I must be from poor stock."

Rage burned within Maggie's chest. How dare anyone treat

her daughter so cruelly? Her first instinct was to ride over to Belfair Plantation and demand an apology, even though she knew it wouldn't alter the hardened heart of Caroline Belfair. She'd always been a spoiled little girl with absolutely no consideration for anything but her own selfish views. Gathering her wits, Maggie exhaled. Comforting a hurt child was more painful than answering questions about a potential war. She could protect Jane from speculation but not the spitefulness of others.

"My dearest Jane, sometimes people aren't happy in their lives and go out of their way to make others miserable. In many cases, they're trying to hide their own insecurities. They actually have little confidence in themselves."

"Caroline doesn't seem insecure to me," Jane grumbled, rolling her eyes as her shoulders dropped. "She thinks she's the most beautiful and beloved girl in town."

"Try not to let her rudeness taint your judgment. It's important to look deeper, listen, and have compassion in order to understand a person's true heart."

"Why should I be nice to her when she's so hateful?" Jane asked with a scowl.

"Because Caroline might have an unhappy life."

"So, I should let her be mean to me? That doesn't seem fair." Her lower lip jutted out in a pout.

"Never let anyone treat you harshly but understand Caroline may have secrets that make her act the way she does," Maggie said resolutely.

"She said I'm the only one who doesn't live with her *real* family," Jane murmured.

"You do live with your real family. Remember, your mother was my cousin." Maggie draped her arm about her daughter's shoulders. "You have a rich history and are loved beyond words. You live at one of the finest plantations in the county, embroider better than most adults, and most importantly, you have a pure heart. What more could you possibly want? If Caroline can't accept you for who you are then it's her loss. The other girls like you."

Tears crested in Jane's eyes as she chewed her lower lip, a habit she'd picked up from Maggie. "I don't mean to be disrespectful, and you know how much I adore you and Papa, but I was wondering," she hesitated before continuing, "What do you know about my family history, specifically my father?"

Maggie's gut churned. She knew this topic would arise one day but had never worked out what she'd say when it did. Jane was everything she and her husband, Seth could ever want in a daughter. Susannah, Jane's birth mother and Maggie's estranged cousin, had brought Jane to Rose Hall after contracting a terminal illness. Despite their acrimonious parting years earlier, Maggie welcomed Susannah back into her life and cared for her until her last breath. One of Susannah's final requests was that Maggie and Seth adopt her daughter, Jane.

Jane had been a bit shy at first but quickly settled into the family routine, especially when it came to Joshua, Maggie and Seth's son. He was only a toddler at the time and Jane was instantly smitten. She seemed to adore his sweet face and curly locks as she coddled and played with him. After years of contentment and joy with her small family, Maggie had to face the question she'd been dreading, how to explain Jane's lineage. Due to the violent nature of Jane's conception, Susannah had specifically requested Maggie never reveal the circumstances to her daughter. Sadly, Jane's family history was tumultuous at best.

Maggie inhaled deeply before speaking. "I never knew your father."

"You and mother were close, were you not?" Jane asked.

"We were." Maggie wasn't lying exactly; they had been close in the beginning, and at the very end.

"Surely, she told you something about him."

"All I remember is that he was only in her life for a very brief time. We didn't discuss him much because it made your mother sad."

"Sounds like she really cared about him," Jane said with a tilt of her head.

"Undeniably. She had very strong feelings regarding your father," Maggie replied. At least she hadn't been dishonest.

"What about my mother? I remember so little about her. She'd always send me to stay with the neighbors while she was working."

"Your mother loved you more than anything in the world," Maggie said. "That's why she brought you here to live with us."

"I remember her being very sick."

"Yes," Maggie smiled, gently touching her daughter's cheek. "She knew she couldn't care for you any longer and that we'd provide for you."

"Tell me more about her."

"She was very pretty and one of the most talented needleworkers I've ever known. You favor her in that manner."

Jane grinned at the compliment. "And my grandparents?"

This was a tough question. How could she possibly tell Jane about the abusive people who drove her mother to a life of ill repute and then abandoned her and her child? Not to mention the cruelty and abuse they'd inflicted on Maggie.

"Your grandmother was an elegant lady, and your grandfather was...very tall."

Jane wrinkled her nose. "I didn't mean how they looked. What were they like?"

"Um," Maggie wavered, trying to find the right words.

"Your grandmother was also very talented at needlework and your grandfather, well, he loved animals, especially his dog."

The explanation seemed to pacify Jane's young mind as a smile spread across her face.

Once Jane had changed into her nightclothes, they said their bedtime prayers. Maggie sat with her daughter, smoothing her hair until she slipped into a restful slumber. As she left the room, Maggie rolled her shoulders. It was hard enough having to explain Jane's family background, but the shadows of a pending war made the situation more difficult. For the first time since being a parent, Maggie truly feared for her children's future.

Chapter 2

April 1861

Maggie

Birdsong skittered across spring breezes as the pungent aroma of the marsh mingled with the fragrant perfume of budding flowers. Maggie sat on the front porch pulling threads from the hem of one of Jane's dresses to lengthen it. Her daughter was growing so quickly. Maggie plucked at a stubborn stitch with the point of the needle, inadvertently stabbing her finger. She let out a yelp and sucked the bead of blood from her fingertip. The pinprick was enough to open the dam holding back Maggie's fears. A tear trickled down her cheek as she dropped the dress to her lap, bowed her head, and cried.

The uncertainty of impending invasion and inevitable hardships weighed heavily on her conscience. Even worse, how would they be able to get the enslaved to freedom with all the troops and blockades? Not every northern state was safe for those escaping bondage, especially after the fugitive Slave Act of 1850 had passed. This abominable law required slaves to be returned to their enslavers regardless of whether they were in a free state or not.

To make matters worse, President Lincoln proclaimed a blockade on the southern ports in an effort to force the south into submission. Maggie's gut churned over the repercussions of not being able to access supplies from outside sources. The impact on their life in the Lowcountry would be dramatic. Lack of food, cloth, and medical supplies would render them defenseless if the blockade was successful.

Setting Jane's dress aside, Maggie stood up, and paced the front porch, the worn boards groaning along with her withering hopes of peace. In addition to the unease about Underground Railroad activities, the idea of her children suffering was more than she could bear. Famine had forced Maggie and her father to flee their native Ireland years ago. They'd each suffered greatly before finding their way to Rose Hall where life had been pleasant and productive for them both. She was determined her children wouldn't suffer as she had. Maggie swiped at her tears, plopped down onto the chair, picked up the dress, and resumed her work. Now was not the time for dramatics. She had to be strong.

Maggie's mind kept flashing back to the headlines from the week before with news of the battle of Fort Sumter splashed in bold print across the front page of the paper. Rudy Taylor, long-time friend of the Polks and a staunch supporter of the Underground Railroad, was the owner of the *Homefront Herald* newspaper. On more than one occasion he'd saved the day with his savvy thinking and well coded wording in the periodical warning conductors of perilous situations.

Any hopes of avoiding war were dashed when the Confederate army fired on Fort Sumpter in the wee hours of the morning of April 12th. It came as quite a shock to learn the fighting was in nearby Charleston which meant it could arrive in Bluffton at any time. No doubt, the Union army was disgruntled over losing the first battle and would seek to redeem themselves sooner than later.

Maggie's skin prickled when she saw Miss Clara, housemaid for the Polks, rushing up the walkway. It was a rare occasion that Clara came to the cottage.

"Miss Clara, is everything alright?" Maggie asked, standing up. Her fingers tingled with trepidation. Every little announcement seemed to be steeped in doom.

"Dr. Polk wants everyone to meet at the main house at four o'clock," she said, concern veiling her expression.

"Thank you for letting me know," Maggie replied with a nod. "We'll be there."

Clara hurried back toward the house as Maggie sat down, her mind racing, and the hair on her arms bristling. Things must be dire if Dr. Polk was calling them together for a meeting.

* * *

Maggie, Joshua, and Jane gathered in the front parlor of the mansion with Elora and Mrs. Polk. Warm breezes carrying the scent of jasmine billowed through the room. A spray of roses in a porcelain vase perched upon the side table, a reminder of Mrs. Polk's green thumb in cultivating the fragrant flowers. Maggie settled on the velvet settee with her children on either side. Seth was still out scouting for more information about the current situation. He'd been known as *The Ghost* on the Underground Railroad due to his stealth movements and ability to thwart slave hunters. When he wasn't helping escapees, he worked around the plantation in a variety of duties to include carpentry and tending to animals. However, since he'd become a father, most of his time was spent near home.

Now his experience with the Railroad was serving him well in obtaining information about potential hostilities.

Elora's countenance was dismal as she sat silently picking at a loose thread on her dress. Even Mrs. Polk's amiable demeanor was subdued. It seemed everything Maggie had feared regarding the rumors of war was coming to fruition.

Dr. Polk entered the room, his countenance sullen. Dark shadows eclipsed his eyes and lines creased his cheeks. He seemed to have aged in the past week since news of the battle at Fort Sumpter broke. He took in a deep breath as if he were about to deliver bad news to a patient.

"I'm afraid the reports aren't good," he sighed. "Charleston is in an uproar, as you can imagine. At present, there hasn't been any sign of retaliation by Union forces, but I don't believe they'll stay silent for long. I fear the pot is simmering and about to boil over. Of course, the blockade could bring the entire situation to a rapid close."

He paused and rubbed his forehead. "Considering our *activities* with the Railroad, I think it's best we err on the side of caution and take an extended holiday north."

"Father, you don't actually believe the Union Army will come this far, do you?" Elora asked, her complexion paling.

"I don't know and I'm not willing to take that chance. If our neighbors discover we've been conducting runaway slaves to freedom, things could get ugly. If the Union Army arrives and believes us to be supporters of the rebellion, we could all be killed. Considering my father's involvement and stalwart commitment to secession, it wouldn't bode well for us should the battle lines extend to this area."

"Where will we go?" Mrs. Polk queried.

"I've been in contact with the Milners in Pennsylvania. They've agreed to house us until it's safe to return."

The Milners had saved Maggie when she was weakened

by starvation after running away from her uncle's abuse. She owed them her life. Because of their efforts, Maggie became part of the Underground Railroad which eventually led her to meet Seth. In a strange twist of fate, they later discovered the Milner's adopted daughter, Annalissa, was actually Seth's half-sister. It was through these connections that the Polks and the Milners became acquainted and forged a steadfast bond. Needless to say, the Milners were some of the most upstanding people Maggie had ever known and she adored them.

"When do we have to leave?" Elora's voice shook as she wrung her hands in her lap.

"We'll be leaving in phases. Maggie and the kids will accompany you and your mother to Pennsylvania along with Mr. McFarland. Seth and I will come at a later date once things are settled here."

Maggie chewed her lower lip. She wasn't comfortable leaving Seth behind even for a brief period of time. They'd worked as a team for years and could sense each other's needs effortlessly. Even though she knew Seth was capable of taking care of himself, she'd feel better if she was here to support him. Maggie had been on enough missions to know how to handle any confrontation that might arise not to mention she was one of the best shots in town.

"What about Heddy, Olive, and the rest of the workers?" Elora asked. "Will there be room at the Milner's farm for everybody?"

"I've spoken with all of them. Hatch and Davis will drive the carriages. Clara will accompany you all. Olive and Heddy will be going with Bertie to her family homestead outside of Boston. The others insist on staying. They said this is their home and they won't abandon it."

"They can't possibly stay behind! If it's too dangerous for

us, then it's too dangerous for them!" Elora was practically yelling.

"They're free people and can do as they please. This is their choice and I respect and support it. I, too, am concerned about their safety but they're intelligent, resourceful folks. If they choose to remain and face whatever happens here, they have that right."

Elora's shoulders slumped. "I'll worry myself sick about them."

"Worrying won't do them or you any good. We'll pray for their safety," Mrs. Polk said calmly, patting her daughter's hand. "It's the best thing we can do."

"Maggie, you've been awfully quiet," Dr. Polk said.

"I'm trying to absorb it all. I truly hoped it wouldn't come to this and yet here we are having to flee from our homes." Her chest constricted with the pain of it all. She wanted to cry out that this was her home too and refuse to abandon it. But her children were there, and she'd not add to their worries.

"It is disturbing but this conflict shouldn't last too long. Both sides are bound to come to their senses, and we'll be back here before summer's end," Mrs. Polk said with a reassuring smile.

Jane and Joshua sat quietly. Maggie rubbed Joshua's back, more to sooth her nerves than his. Just a few months ago Jane was attending her first formal function and had worried about the cruel comments of another girl. Now she was being uprooted. Despite her attachment to the Milners, Maggie wasn't comfortable taking her children away from the security of their own home for an undisclosed period of time.

Hoof beats pounded down the drive catching everyone's attention. Maggie peered out the window, breathing a sigh of relief as she watched Seth halt his horse, Phantom, at the front of the house. He'd been gone since early morning. Dismounting, Seth took the stairs two at a time, walked into the parlor, and removed his hat. His expression was somber. Maggie cringed when he didn't come over to sit with her, instead standing in the doorway fidgeting with his hat which meant the news couldn't be good.

"I've just come from Brimley Plantation. The local regiments are being called up. They leave within the week."

"This is outrageous!" Elora declared, sitting straighter. "Fort Sumter has been seized. The President has declared a blockade in an effort to starve us. Calling up troops will only worsen the situation. Why doesn't someone stop this before it goes any further?" Elora's gaze darted from Seth to her father. Her apprehension was palpable.

"This is a delicate situation.," Dr. Polk said. "Neither side wants to appear weak, and both feel their cause is justified, even to the point of fighting. I'm afraid this won't be resolved as easily as we would like. It seems both sides will have to battle it out in order to find a compromise."

Elora blew a breath across her lips and slumped back in the chair. "I don't like this one bit," she grumbled.

Seth walked over to Maggie and grasped her hand. "Take the kids back to the cottage and start packing. I need to speak with Dr. Polk and then I'll be home to help."

His deep blue eyes penetrated the fear pooling in Maggie's chest. Somehow it would all work out. She only prayed it could be done quickly with minimal repercussions.

* * *

Maggie walked with the kids along the sandy path to the cottage. Seagulls squawked overhead as breezes fluttered a loose strand of Maggie's auburn tresses. How could their world be crumbling when there was so much beauty surrounding them? She'd experienced famine, abuse, being disconnected from her family, nearly dying from childbirth, and perilous situations conducting the enslaved to freedom. None of it was as disconcerting as the war hovering on the doorstep of her life. The idea that a well-armed fighting force was vying to invade and battle to the death was distressing. She and her family and friends would be viewed as the enemy no doubt making them open targets for torture or death. Add in the potential for starvation from the blockade and the scenario seemed entirely hopeless.

"Mama," Jane said, clutching Maggie's hand. "Why do we have to go to Pennsylvania?"

"Because the war is very close, and we need to go somewhere safe." Maggie and Seth had agreed never to downplay serious situations with their children. They wouldn't necessarily give all the details, but honesty was the best approach, in their opinion.

"Won't the war be there too?"

Maggie hesitated before responding. "Hopefully not. For now, it's the safest place for us to go. Think of this as a great adventure. The Milners will have plenty of fun things planned and you'll get to spend time with your Aunt Annalissa when she comes home from college."

"Oh goody!" Joshua declared. "She takes me out at night to listen to the hoot owls!"

"And I know she'll be happy to do so again." Maggie smiled at her son's enthusiasm. If only she could be as carefree. His age made him oblivious to the gravity of the situation.

Jane kicked stones as she trod next to her mother, her face downcast.

Maggie squeezed her daughter's hand. "Are you alright?" she asked.

"I'm fine, it's just..." Jane paused and gazed out over the

marsh. "I love the Milners and have great fun when we visit but I'd rather stay here. This is home."

"I know exactly how you feel. Hopefully, we'll be back in a couple of months."

Even as Maggie said the words, she knew in her heart it wouldn't be that simple. This was war and there was no telling how long it would go on or how far it would reach. Yet something else niggled at her conscience, something she knew wouldn't settle well with Seth. She couldn't sit idly by and do nothing when so much was at stake at Rose Hall. If Seth and Dr. Polk were staying for a brief period before heading to Pennsylvania, then she wanted to remain too. Regardless, Maggie needed to be brave for Jane and Joshua's sakes. If she was going to send them north without her, it was imperative they feel secure and not concern themselves with her welfare.

As they approached the cottage, Maggie asked Jane to keep Joshua occupied by the marsh. She needed time to think. Slipping inside, she paced the room, trying to decide how to broach the subject of staying at Rose Hall with her husband. Moments later Seth came through the door.

"I need to speak with you," she said, walking over to him.

"About what?"

"I want to stay here with you," she replied, her gaze locked on his.

"No, Maggie." Seth stepped back shaking his head. "Dr. Polk and I will only be here temporarily until things are secured. Since many of the workers have chosen to stay behind, we need to make sure they're provided for and that valuables are well hidden. We have no idea when the Union will arrive or what they'll do. I need you to go with the children. It's safer."

"Safer for whom? You're staying behind with Dr. Polk."

"Yes, but we're men." He sucked in a breath as soon as the

words left his lips. His gaze shifted away from hers as he rubbed his forehead. Obviously, he knew he'd crossed a line.

Maggie planted her hands on her hips, her Irish spirit coursing through her veins and tinting her cheeks. "I've faced capture and death while helping the enslaved escape bondage. I've killed a man, and I'm a darn fine shot. Give me one good reason why I shouldn't stay and help."

"I'll give you two. Jane and Joshua," he replied, squaring his shoulders.

His words pierced her heart like an arrow. Taking a deep breath, she weighed her response.

"Jane and Joshua will be fine with the Milners. The worst thing they face is being spoiled. Elora and my father will be with them for the journey up there. They'll want for nothing."

"Except their mother."

"*And* their father," Maggie shot back.

Seth rested his hands on Maggie's shoulders. "Don't be so defensive about this. We both have responsibilities that will take us in different directions. Please do this for me, Maggie. I can't bear the thought of you being in harm's way."

His pleas only strengthened Maggie's resolve. "It didn't bother you when we were transporting runaways."

"It did but I knew better than to express my concerns. When you almost died after Joshua was born...." he said, his words fading. "I thought I would cease to exist if you didn't make it. I don't want to go through that again. If you and the kids are with the Milners I won't have to worry as much."

"But I will," she said sternly. "You act as if you're the only one with something to lose."

Her words seemed to hit him with the force of a tidal wave. He looked down and exhaled. "I can't argue with your logic," he said, rubbing the back of his neck. "You can stay here and help. But if things get *too* dangerous, I insist you join the others. Agreed?"

Maggie grinned. "Agreed."

Seth pulled her into a tight embrace and whispered in her ear. "I love you, Maggie."

"Love you, Seth," she replied, nestling her head against his chest. She'd won this battle yet suspected there'd be many more to come.

Maggie prepared everything the kids would need for their stay with the Milners in Pennsylvania. Once their things were packed into a large camel back trunk and the leather straps secured, Maggie sat on the bed, wiping a tear from her cheek. The children would be leaving the following morning. Her heart broke over sending them north, but she knew they'd be well cared for with Elora, Mrs. Polk, and their grandfather accompanying them. At least she and Seth would be there in a few weeks.

The next morning, everyone gathered in front of the main house. Two carriages waited, the horses pawing the sandy ground and tossing their heads seemingly sensing the tension in the atmosphere. Mist hovered above the marshes as Maggie, Seth, Mrs. Polk, and Elora exchanged well wishes for safe travels. After saying their goodbyes, Elora and Mrs. Polk boarded the first carriage. Seth and Maggie turned to their children.

"Why aren't you coming with us?" Joshua moaned, his eyes red from crying.

"I have things to do here. But not to worry, Papa and I will join you as soon as we can."

Jane took Joshua's hand. "They'll be fine. There's no need to fret."

Maggie's heart swelled at Jane's bravery. For such a young

person she was incredibly wise. She hated that her daughter had to face such a trial but knew she was bold enough to do so with dignity and grace.

Brushing Joshua's cheek with her hand, Maggie conjured up her best smile. "It's been some time since you visited the Milners. The Pennsylvania countryside is delightful at this time of year." Maggie hoped her feigned enthusiasm would alleviate any worry for her son. "You'll get to ride horses through the pastures and swim in the creek."

"I remember the creek!" Joshua squealed. "That's where I caught my first fish!"

"Indeed, you did. So, you see, you've nothing to be upset about. You know the Milners will be good to you." Maggie winked.

"That means we can have an extra cookie after supper," he said with a sideways glance and a crafty smile as he rubbed his belly. "Miss Darla makes the best sugar cookies."

Arching her brows, Maggie leaned over and tilted up her son's chin. "I expect you to be on your best behavior and mind your sister when you get to Pennsylvania."

"Promise," he said with a sheepish grin, his hands behind his back.

"Mama, he's got his fingers crossed," Jane announced.

"Joshua Daniels," Maggie said sternly.

Ducking his head, Joshua smirked. "Oh alright, I'll be good."

Maggie kissed him on the cheek. "Your father and I will travel to Pennsylvania as soon as we can," she said.

"Love you, Mama."

"Love you," she replied.

Joshua ran into his father's arms for a farewell hug.

"Make me proud," Seth said, tousling his son's hair before helping him into the carriage.

Jane smiled at her mother before kissing her cheek. "Goodbye, Mama."

"Goodbye, my dearest Jane." Maggie scooped her daughter into an embrace and whispered in her ear, "Love you more than all the stars in the sky."

Jane stood back and smiled. "Love you more than apple pie."

They'd been saying the same phrases since Jane was six years old. Maggie couldn't remember how those two particular sayings came to be, nevertheless they'd stuck.

"Bye Papa," Jane said in her little girl voice letting Maggie know she was feeling vulnerable behind her brave façade.

Seth hugged his daughter tightly. "Make sure your brother behaves," he whispered in her ear.

Jane looked up at her father with a smirk. "You know he doesn't listen to me when he's up to mischief, but I'll do my best."

When the children were nestled into their seats, Maggie turned to her father.

"'Tis hard to leave my lassie again," her Da said as he pulled her into a bear hug.

"I'll be fine, Da," she replied, her throat dry as she fought back the sob threatening to burst forth. "It won't be long before we're together again."

Stepping back, Maggie's father gave a nod to Seth. "Be careful, both of you," he said before disappearing into the carriage.

Maggie's chest tightened. The thought of being away from her children pained her; however, the pull for her to stay was strong. Her kids would be fine. They'd have so much fun they'd hardly miss her. At least that's what she told herself as she brushed tears from her eyes. She wanted to maintain a strong decorum but was failing miserably.

Sunrays splashed over the horizon in waves of mango and lavender as the scent of jasmine perfumed the air. Maggie and Seth watched the carriages carom down the drive with their children, family, and friends. When the carriages had disappeared, she and Seth walked along the sandy path toward their cottage in silence. Maggie's nerves were raw with worry for her children's long journey to Pennsylvania as well as the tensions building around the area.

Seth held the door open as Maggie stepped inside their cottage. Tears crested in her eyes as she glanced around the space. Joshua's boots stood by the door and one of Jane's hair ribbons was crumpled on the side table by the green brocade chair. The best thing she could do was to stay busy, she told herself, and tidying the place seemed to be a good start. Seth came up behind her, wrapped his arms about her waist, and pulled her to him.

"They'll be fine," he whispered in her ear temporarily distracting her from her thoughts. His lips brushed the back of her neck sending a shiver down her back. After years of marriage, he could still make her body quiver.

She turned to face him taking in his sultry blue eyes, strong jawline, and wavy hair. "We're on our own for a while," she said, her lips meeting his.

"So we are," he muttered.

Taking Maggie's hand, Seth escorted her to their bedroom and closed the door.

Chapter 3

Spring 1861

Maggie

While Seth and Dr. Polk prepared for possible intrusions from the Union army, Maggie worked on restocking the larder with medicinal salves, balms, and ointments for the workers who'd chosen to stay behind. By the end of the day, her hands were raw from pummeling herbs for the mixtures.

Although she and Seth missed Jane and Joshua, they took advantage of their time alone. They enjoyed long walks by the marsh at night, dancing in the parlor, even taking turns soaring on the old tree swing and splashing into the cool water of the river. Despite the war raging around them, they found ways to quell their fears, at least for the time being.

A couple of weeks after the children had left, Seth, Maggie, and Dr. Polk, were pleased with all they had accomplished. At this rate, they'd soon be able to join the others in Pennsylvania. With the fighting inching closer every day, Maggie was anxious to escape and have her family reunited despite the pang of uncertainty that reverberated through her chest about leaving.

The sun's heat sent pearls of sweat across Maggie's head and neck as she turned the soil in the garden beds beside the house for fall planting. Surely, they'd be home by then. She straightened up, removed her straw bonnet, and wiped the perspiration from her brow. A smile creased her eyes when she saw Dr. Polk and Seth coming up the path. It was odd to see them at this time of day. Perhaps they had news that the fighting had ceased. Maggie dusted her hands on her apron and started toward the cottage. That's when she noticed Seth's gait was off and he was leaning on the doctor. She watched as Seth stumbled up the front steps with Dr. Polk gripping his arm to steady him. Maggie's breath caught. Seth was hurt. She bolted in the back door where she saw Dr. Polk ease Seth into a chair.

"What's going on?" she asked, racing to her husband's side.

"Took a tumble from the ladder. It's nothing serious," Seth huffed, propping his foot on the stool.

Dr. Polk's gaze met Maggie's. "It appears to be a nasty sprain. He needs to stay off his feet for several days and keep the leg elevated."

"I appreciate your concern, Doc, but there isn't time for rest. We have work to do," Seth replied.

"As I said, it's a bad sprain. If you don't rest the ankle, it'll get worse and you won't be of any use," Dr. Polk said with a stern look.

"I'll make sure he stays off of it," Maggie said, secretly relieved for his injury. It would prevent him from being forced into service as so many locals had. She felt guilty for her selfishness in wanting to keep him with her when others were sending loved ones off to fight. But this wasn't a cause she believed in and sacrificing her husband was more than she was willing to give.

Seth sighed, shaking his head. "I'll rest for this evening and be good as new by morning. I'm a grown man, I don't need to be coddled."

"Then act like an adult and follow the doctor's orders." Maggie gave the doctor a knowing glance. "I'll tend to him Dr. Polk."

With a nod the doctor left the cottage. Seth started to stand when Maggie pushed him back into the chair.

"What are you doing?" she queried.

"Getting back to work."

"No, you're not. You heard what Dr. Polk said. You're going to stay right there and keep that leg elevated."

Seth rolled his eyes and blew out a breath. "Please don't do this Maggie. I'm perfectly capable of...."

"Making your injury worse?" she interrupted. "Now is not the time for bravado. We need you at your best. Further trauma to the ankle will only delay your recovery. I can do your chores as well as my own. I'll not hear another word about it."

Her tone of voice was stern letting Seth know she meant what she said. After years of marriage, he was wise enough not to quarrel when her Irish spirit took hold. Closing his eyes, he slumped back in the chair.

Days passed and Seth was no better. Further examination revealed his injury was more serious than originally thought. Apparently, he'd torn something in his ankle, extending his recovery time over the course of the summer. He was able to do a few things at the cottage while Maggie and Dr. Polk worked around the plantation. Thankfully, Maggie was hearty and capable of taking on some of the more strenuous duties allowing Seth the time he needed to recuperate.

Although Maggie had the physical ability to perform many of Seth's chores, she found her back and shoulders aching at the end of each day. Shoveling dirt, cleaning stalls, and hauling hay weren't her favorite activities, but she was thankful for the distraction from her daily worries regarding a Union invasion and missing her children. Of course, Maggie would never let Seth know about the strain to her muscles and spine. Each morning after she left the house, she'd rub liniment on her aching joints and muscles. She couldn't do this at home as the strong odor would give away her secret. While the ointment didn't alleviate all the soreness, it did keep her a bit more comfortable throughout the day.

Maggie made her way to the barn shortly after sunrise, her muscles screaming from the previous day's work. A great white egret took flight as she walked along the edge of the marsh, the grasses glimmering in the early morning light. The rope swing dangled from the massive live oak tree, reminding her of past summers where the kids would sway over the water squealing with delight. It seemed like an eternity since she'd read to Joshua or braided Jane's hair. She missed her children and the life they'd built at Rose Hall.

A sob burst forth as her knees buckled. Crumpling to the ground, Maggie buried her face in her hands. She was tired of always being strong. Just once she wanted to run from responsibility and be free of the turmoil swirling around her. Hadn't she endured enough already? Why couldn't she and Seth just live a simple life with their children?

Thus far, the Confederate Army had been able to stave off the enemy; however, that would likely change sooner than later. The Union Army had better resources and more men. Even worse was watching Seth struggle between wanting to preserve the country and defend his home state of South Carolina. Many were in the same position. Most southern men had already been pressed into service. Seth's injury had delayed that situation. But it was only a matter of time before he'd have to choose or risk the decision being made by others. That frightened Maggie more than anything.

She dried her tears and struggled to her feet, brushing sand from her skirt. "Stop it," she scolded herself. "You're an Irish woman who has survived more than most people. Now is not the time for weakness. Now is the time to stand firm and fight."

Chapter 4

August 1861

Elora

Elora clutched the needle in her fingers as she pulled the silky pink thread up through the canvas. She'd immersed herself in her embroidery since arriving in Pennsylvania months ago. Annalissa's return from Oberlin College had been a boon as it gave Elora someone close in age to talk to. The better she got to know Annalissa, the more she could see traces of Seth. They may only be half siblings, but they shared the same quiet demeanor and strong will.

Although things were pleasant at the Milner's farm and Elora enjoyed Annalissa's company, her heart was rooted in thoughts of home. Maggie had written of Seth's injury and all the work being done around the plantation. The Union army had yet to arrive there for which she was thankful. However, it was only a matter of time. Elora's mind was troubled by her lack of involvement. Even with Railroad activities, she'd been on the cusp, only aiding from a distance. Except for that one night with the dogs. She shuttered at the memory pricking her finger in the process.

Granted, she was helping in a small way by looking after

Jane and Joshua. Each afternoon, Elora and Jane sat in the front parlor of the Milner's farmhouse embroidering or reading while Annalissa took Joshua around the farm to help with the animals. He had a natural inclination for any creature and rode with the same confidence as his father. Joshua vowed that when he grew up, he would be a veterinarian, and no one doubted he'd achieve his goal. Jane was self-sufficient. However, Elora could tell that she was worried about her parents despite her putting forth a strong façade.

While the August climate in Pennsylvania wasn't as sticky as the Lowcountry, the temperatures were brutal, nonetheless. Without marsh breezes, the air was stagnant, creating a suffocating heat. Early one morning, Elora meandered across the grassy expanse behind the house to the shade of a towering maple. The milder temperatures of daybreak coalesced with the soft glow of the sun and twittering of songbirds. She settled beneath the tree enjoying the day before the mercury began to rise. Cattle grazed in lush pastures, chickens pecked the ground nearby, and a rooster strutted around the coop. Inhaling, she took in the sweet fragrance of a summer morn.

Absorbing the peacefulness surrounding her, Elora pondered how things could be so tranquil in the Pennsylvania countryside while a war raged in the southern states. She wasn't glad Seth was injured but there was a tinge of relief that it prevented him from going into battle, at least for now. Seth had been like an older brother to Elora since she was a little girl. She was aware of his dedication to South Carolina. It was his home state. However, she also knew he believed the country should remain united. Having his half-sister living in Pennsylvania added another element to the convoluted decision he faced. Deep in her heart, Elora hoped Seth, and her own father, would be able to avoid enlistment. Her nerves were raw at the idea of them fighting or worse, being wounded or killed. Bile burned her throat at the thought.

Shaking off her trepidation, Elora reached into her pocket and removed the latest issue of *Harper's Weekly*. The front page showed a sketch of two ladies riding in a carriage guarded by Union soldiers on horseback. Her eyes widened and her hand covered her mouth as she read the account of two Confederate women who had captured a Union Captain from a Connecticut regiment. In a bizarre turn of events, a few men who'd been separated from the same unit, arrived at the house where the women were hiding the captain. The soldiers tricked the homeowner into believing they were southern sympathizers leading the old man to reveal the schemes of the two ladies as well as the location of their captive. The Scott sisters were taken prisoner and brought to the Union encampment at Falls Church, Virginia for their crimes.

Dropping the paper in her lap, Elora slumped back against the tree trunk. Never in her life would she have imagined ladies being so bold as to capture a soldier. Then again, the things Maggie had done in service for the Underground Railroad over the past few years were beyond what a typical woman would do, such as transporting escapees, hiding in the filthiest of conditions, traveling alone, and on one occasion, shooting a man. In light of all these things, Maggie was still viewed as a lovely woman who kept house and a garden for her husband and children while creating remedies for a multitude of ailments. Yet, Elora was expected to be prim and proper.

Elora resumed her reading, exasperated by the paradox between a woman's societal expectations and the things she was capable of accomplishing. Ladies were viewed as delicate and fragile, yet they could be powerful and influential in the most discreet manner. A slight flush, fluttering eyelashes, a simper, or a well-worded compliment by a refined woman could detach a man from his senses. Feminine wiles were more powerful than any weapon when applied correctly. If only she could find a way to contribute something meaningful to the war efforts, perhaps she wouldn't feel so inept.

Later that afternoon, Jane and Elora sat in the front parlor stitching a set of seat cushions patterned with an array of colorful blooms. Mrs. Polk sauntered into the room and peered over her daughter's shoulder.

"It's coming along splendidly," she said.

"Thank you," Elora replied.

The sun cast a golden glow across the space as warm breezes drifted through the open windows caressing Elora's cheeks. Mrs. Polk sat in a wing chair next to her daughter, her broad smile and sparkling eyes catching Elora's attention.

"Mother, you look as if you have good news," she said. Her heart beat with anticipation as she sat straighter, resting her needle on the canvas. Perhaps there was word the fighting had ceased and they'd be returning home. As much as she was enjoying her stay with the Milners, she was ready to resume her regular routine.

"I do have some exciting news," she replied.

Jane stopped what she was doing to listen, obviously eager to hear the announcement too.

"I've been able to make arrangements for you to attend Oberlin College. It appears we may be here longer than we expected. Since you were supposed to start your studies this fall anyway, Oberlin seemed a good choice."

Elora inhaled. She'd planned on attending school in South Carolina. Not that she was opposed to studying at Oberlin, but it confirmed their stay had been extended for an undisclosed period of time.

"That sounds wonderful," she said, resuming her stitching.

"You don't seem very happy about it. Do you have some objection to Oberlin? Annalissa will be there to show you around."

"Not an objection so much as disappointment. I'd planned on attending Columbia College. And then there's the war." Even as she said it, Elora knew that wasn't the real reason for her reluctance. She wanted to be part of something more important than embroidering cushions and attending college. She wanted to be at Rose Hall helping Maggie and Seth.

"I realize things aren't going as we'd planned. But college will occupy your mind, so you won't worry as much about the ongoing conflict."

"Actually...." she hesitated. "Perhaps we could discuss it later." Elora noticed Jane watching their interaction intently. This was not a conversation she needed to hear.

Mrs. Polk gave her daughter a skeptical look as she stood. "Very well. We'll talk later." Turning to Jane, Mrs. Polk smiled. "Your work is lovely, Jane. You have a gift for needlework."

"Thank you, Mrs. Polk," Jane replied, a blush coloring her cheeks.

Mrs. Polk exited the room leaving the two young ladies to their stitching.

"How thrilling that you'll be attending college with Annalissa," Jane said.

"I suppose," Elora shrugged.

"Aren't you excited?"

"In a sense. I guess I'm a bit homesick."

"I understand," Jane sighed. "I miss home too but most of all Mama and Papa."

Inhaling, Elora pulled the colorful strands through the linen as her mind teetered between wanting to return to Rose Hall and making her parents happy by going to college. No doubt they'd gone to a great deal of trouble to get her admitted so quickly. Her parents allowing her to return home seemed unlikely, then again, she wouldn't know unless she asked. She was ready to step into the world and do something a bit unconventional. Now all she had to do was persuade her mother and father.

After dinner, Jane and Joshua gathered with the Milners in the front parlor. Elora realized this was the perfect time to speak with her mother in private about her plans. Reaching out, she touched her mother's arm.

"Mother, could we take a stroll about the yard? There's something I need to speak with you about privately," Elora said, raising her eyebrows.

"That sounds like a lovely idea."

Mrs. Polk followed her daughter out the back door. They meandered along the path around a large red barn and various outbuildings. Cows grazed in a nearby pasture as the sun began its descent, rippling the clouds in ribbons of vibrant orange, red, and gold. Elora looped her hand through the crook of her mother's elbow as they walked side by side.

"So, tell me what's bothering you," Mrs. Polk said.

Elora's head drooped as she took in a deep breath. "I don't want to go to Oberlin in the fall." There, she'd said it. Her muscles tensed as she prepared for the fallout.

"What's your opposition to Oberlin? I know you had your heart set on Columbia but that's not feasible right now. Oberlin is an outstanding institution with a fine staff of professors. Once the war is over, you can transfer if you'd like. At least this way you won't be delayed in your studies."

"I want to go home."

Mrs. Polk stopped and stared at her daughter. "I know

you're homesick but it's impossible for you to return at this time."

"It's not about being homesick, although I do miss the plantation," she sighed. Her mind wandered back to the Spanish moss swaying gently from the crooked branches of live oak trees and breezes carrying the pungent aroma of the marsh. "I want to be a contributing part of the war."

Mrs. Polk's eyes widened. "Are you suggesting that you return home to help with the conflict?" she asked. "In what manner do you propose to do this?"

"I haven't figured that out yet. Maybe serve with one of the regiments as a nurse, or something," Elora replied, more meekly than she'd intended.

"Out of the question!" Mrs. Polk declared. "War is no place for a young lady."

"Maggie is helping," Elora retorted.

"Maggie is a grown woman who can make her own decisions and she's more capable of handling the situation."

Fury pulsed through Elora's limbs making her hands tremble. She was tired of being viewed as a helpless child. "I'm capable too! I can shoot and ride. I know the trails along the marshes better than most people," she hollered. "You had no problem letting me help with the escapees."

"That was different. Your father and Seth were there to oversee things. You were never directly involved."

"I was the night of the dog attacks!" Elora squalled, tears cresting in her eyes at the memory. It had been the most horrific experience of her life. Even though she didn't witness the attack firsthand, the screams of the escapees as dogs tore flesh from bone still haunted her.

Mrs. Polk stood straighter and touched her daughter's arm. "Which is precisely the reason why we protect you now. You should never have experienced such a violent situation, and your father hasn't forgiven himself for exposing you to it."

"Maggie witnessed it and she survived. No one was concerned about her well-being," Elora snapped back.

"Elora Polk, how dare you! We were mortified that Maggie was involved. If we'd had any idea what was going to happen, we never would have sent the two of you out that night." Mrs. Polk's face flushed as she looked away.

Elora exhaled. Upsetting her mother wasn't helping her case. "Mother, I'm not trying to oppose you, only to convince you that I'm a mature woman and able to contribute," she said softly. "I want to help, not sit by and do nothing when so many others are sacrificing all they have."

"The answer is no. That's my final word on the subject." Mrs. Polk turned toward the house.

"What about Father?" Elora called out, her pulse racing at her mother's refusal to consider her request. "Doesn't he have a say in this?"

Mrs. Polk spun around, anger radiating from her eyes. "I don't need to consult your father on this matter! I know he'd agree with me!"

"Perhaps we should write him and find out!"

"There's no need," Mrs. Polk exclaimed. "He should be here in a few days, and I assure you he'll forbid your involvement in the war."

Mrs. Polk started back to the house with a determined pace. Elora had never seen her mother so incensed and for a moment, it rattled her fortitude. All she wanted was to be treated like an adult. Why was it such a problem for a woman to assist in times of war? Defeated, Elora headed for the house. The last thing she wanted to do was argue with her mother during such a diffi-cult time. Not in the mood to socialize, she slipped in the back door, climbed the stairs to her room, and changed for bed.

Crawling between the cottony sheets, Elora rested her head against the pillow, her mind buzzing with all that had transpired. As she lay in bed with the serenade of cicadas resonating through the open window, she noticed the Harper's Weekly she'd been reading that morning sitting on the night table. Her thoughts drifted back to the article she'd read earlier about the Scott sisters capturing a Union officer as well as conveying secret information. All this was done clandestinely while the world believed the sisters to be two delicate and harmless southern ladies.

Elora bolted upright, a smile creasing her cheeks as her determination resurfaced. If her parents wouldn't permit her to help openly, then she'd do so covertly. She was tired of being fawned over like some sort of china doll. Over the years, she'd successfully helped with the workings of the Railroad and felt skilled enough to assist with the war. With some careful planning she'd find a way to participate without being discovered. The question was how to accomplish it before she was shuffled off to college.

Chapter 5

August 1861

Elora

D r. Polk arrived at the Milner's farm a few days later. Maggie and Seth would be traveling at a later date once Seth's leg was completely healed. Elora didn't dare mention her plans since she knew her father would probably side with her mother. Regardless, she'd find a way to accomplish her goal to join the war efforts.

Sitting before the vanity mirror, Elora gazed at her reflection as she ran the silver handled brush through her coffee brown tresses. Her stomach churned at the idea of deceiving her parents but what other choice did she have? The journey to Ohio would be long and she'd have to keep up the charade of willingly going to school. Annalissa was highly intuitive and able to pick up on the slightest change in demeanor or facial expression. Elora couldn't risk exposing her secret to anyone.

From the time Elora and her mother had argued about her assisting with the conflict, she'd been plotting. It had been difficult to steal away to do what was needed to prepare but somehow, she'd managed. For two weeks Elora spent time in the woods for target practice with her father's spare pistol. Luckily, he'd been too busy treating a sick woman from Reverend Milner's congregation to notice the missing firearm. Elora had also stitched some trousers and worked on altering her appearance to that of a man. If all went well, once she was in Ohio away from her mother's watchful eye, she'd be able to implement her plan with little interference.

The day of their departure arrived beneath a herd of fluffy clouds parading across a canopy of blue. The trunks were affixed to the boot of the carriage as the Polks and Milners gathered to send Elora and Annalissa off. Mrs. Polk embraced her daughter and whispered in her ear.

"I'm proud of you for doing this. I know it's not what you wanted but I believe you'll be very happy at Oberlin."

"Thank you, Mother. I'm certain this will be an experience I'll not soon forget." Guilt formed a lump in Elora's throat preventing her from saying anything else.

"Study hard my dear and write as often as you can," Dr. Polk said, pulling her into a strong hug.

"I fear I'll be so engrossed in my studies that letters may be few and far between," Elora said, conjuring the most convincing smile she could. Lying to her parents was one of the hardest things she'd ever done but there was no other way. The less they knew the better. They'd lock her away if they had an inkling of her intentions.

Once the farewells and hugs were complete, Elora and Annalissa stepped into the carriage and shut the door. The vehicle lurched forward as both ladies waved and watched their parents fade into the distance.

Elora sighed heavily as she shifted in her seat.

"Are you nervous about something?" Annalissa asked.

"In a manner of speaking," Elora replied, averting her gaze. "Father said something about going to Washington D.C. to provide medical support should it be needed."

"My father will be going with him. He assured me they'd be safe and far from the fighting."

Elora nodded and stared out the window. How she wished she could discuss her plans with Annalissa. She felt as if she might burst if she didn't tell someone. Silence ensued as the carriage jostled down the road rocking its passengers like a boat on stormy seas. Elora could feel the weight of Annalissa's stare. Daring to meet her gaze, Elora gave a weak smile as she fidgeted with the cuff of her undersleeve.

"Tell me what's really troubling you. Perhaps I can alleviate some of your unease," Annalissa offered.

"I'd rather not discuss it if you don't mind. I feel rather silly about it."

"There's no need to feel uncomfortable about embarking on a new venture. If you decide you'd like to talk, I'll happily listen." Annalissa replied.

With a nod, Elora looked out the window. Thank goodness, she thought, Annalissa only suspected her of being nervous about attending college. Elora took in the landscape with its trees cloaked in an artful display of summer greens fading to early autumnal hues of yellows and reds. This was one of the things she adored about the north. The fall colors couldn't be rivaled. The Lowcountry offered a change of season but not like the vibrant exhibition of the Pennsylvania terrain. Fall was the one time of year Elora preferred the northern climate.

They rode for what seemed an eternity without speaking a word. Elora's nerves were taut. She needed to talk about something to ease the tension gripping her muscles. Finally, she started up a conversation.

"Are you excited about returning to campus?"

"Very much. I love it there." Annalissa's eyes twinkled and her dimples deepened. "I feel certain you will too."

"What do you like best about it?"

Annalissa paused for a moment, tilting her head. "Probably the professors. I've never encountered such a fine group of intellectuals. They're open to discussions regardless of your personal stance and their breadth of knowledge is extensive."

"That's wonderful to hear," Elora sighed. And it did sound wonderful. Too bad she'd not be there to enjoy it. As soon as she saw an opportunity to flee, she'd be gone.

"Please forgive me for asking again, but you seem distracted. Are you certain there's nothing you'd like to discuss?"

Elora glanced at Annalissa whose gentle demeanor touched her heart. Maybe she should tell her. Then again, she might say something to her parents. Elora bit her lower lip and gazed out the window.

Annalissa leaned forward and touched her arm. "Now I know something is amiss. Please tell me what's bothering you."

Elora looked down at her hands, her eyes moistening. "I can't say," she responded.

Annalissa slid onto the seat next to Elora. "I implore you to tell me. Whatever is troubling you, I want to help."

Gazing at Annalissa, Elora noticed the eagerness radiating from her dark eyes. If Maggie had trusted her when she was running from her uncle, perhaps she could too. "Can you keep this between us?"

"I promise," she replied, squeezing Elora's hand.

Elora took in a deep breath. "I'm not going to stay at Oberlin."

"Whyever not?" Annalissa said, her eyebrows arching.

"I'm going to help with the war. And before you give me a lecture about the dangers, I'm well aware of them. I need to do this." Elora exhaled. Having disclosed her secret to someone made her feel lighter as if she'd been carrying a fifty-pound feed sack on her shoulders.

"What are your plans?" Annalissa asked, sitting straighter.

Elora paused. "Forgive me but I'm a bit surprised you aren't fussing at me. My mother had a fit when I told her I wanted to contribute to the war."

"Of course, she did. You're her daughter and she wants to protect you."

"Coddle me is more like it," Elora huffed. "She thinks I'm still a child."

Annalissa grinned. "Your mother will always view you that way. Parents have a difficult time seeing their children as adults. So, tell me what you intend on doing."

Elora hesitated, her courage waning at the idea of sharing the extent of her plans. Would Annalissa accept her desire to enlist in the army and if she didn't, would she alert Elora's parents of her intentions? Once again, she thought about the secrets Annalissa had kept for Maggie and decided it was better to have at least one person aware of what she was doing in case she needed help.

Over the course of an hour, Elora shared her idea of dressing as a man and enlisting with a regiment. When she finished presenting her plan of action, Annalissa sat in silence, a worried expression furrowing her brow.

"Do you support my decision?" Elora asked, her heart pounding as she waited for a reply.

"I understand your desire to go into the world and make your mark. However, putting yourself in harm's way may not be the most prudent manner in which to do so. This is a very daring proposal," Annalissa said, concern erasing her dimples. "Do you really believe you can accomplish this?"

"I'm certain of it," Elora replied, although she didn't feel as confident as she let on.

"Then you must do what you feel is right. You're an intelligent and capable young woman." Annalissa hesitated. "What if you're injured?"

"I'll take extra precautions to avoid detection. There's no guarantee I'll not be hurt but I'll have to deal with that if the time comes."

"You're truly determined to do this, aren't you?" Annalissa asked.

"Yes, I am," Elora replied, lifting her chin.

Annalissa chewed her thumb nail before responding. "I understand your need to do this. I, too, would like to do something to help with the war but being half black the color of my skin limits my involvement."

Elora squeezed Annalissa's hand. "Then help me do this."

A slight smile curled Annalissa's lips as the sparkle returned to her eyes. "What can I do?"

"I'll need you to mail letters to my parents. I'll write them ahead of time with the typical stuff about studying and meeting new friends. Then you post them every so often and it will seem like I'm actually at school.

"What if they want to visit?"

"I hadn't thought about that," Elora paused, scrunching the right side of her lip. "If they ask to visit, I'll tell them I'll be doing mission work elsewhere and not to come."

"I know others who have worked off-campus so it's not an implausible excuse."

Elora smiled. "Thank you for helping me with this."

"Absolutely. If I can't help first hand then I'll help from the shadows," Annalissa said with a rebellious grin.

Chapter 6

November 3, 1861

Maggie

Maggie's duties had increased in the months since Dr. Polk had gone north. Between treating minor injuries on the plantation, doing chores, and tending to Seth, she was worn out. To make matters worse, Seth's recovery had been slow. While he was able to walk on the ankle, he still had a slight limp. Maggie worried for him. Now that he was healing, he faced the inevitable decision about which side to serve on in the war. Sadly, the decision as to whether he should fight wasn't an option. All able-bodied men were expected to enlist, whether driven by personal duty or by pressure from others.

Rumors of beatings and torture to those who refused to join the army were making their way around town. Maggie was thankful Seth's injury had given him time to contemplate what he would do. Of course, everyone they knew had signed up on the southern side but Seth and Maggie's ties to the north provided options not available to others.

Despite his injury, Seth, Maggie, and those who remained had managed to prepare for the impending invasion. They'd also helped several escapees traveling by way of the river on their way to the next Underground Railroad stop at Oak Point Plantation outside of Charleston. The route had been drastically altered due to the presence of soldiers on both sides, making transport more treacherous than ever.

November nipped the Lowcountry air with a slight chill that made the atmosphere feel forlorn and barren. Storms darkened the skies as wind whipped the trees into a frenzy. A foreboding feeling niggled at Maggie's nerves, shrouding her in a sense of unease. They'd done all they could to prepare the plantation should the Union Army make it this far. Reports suggested the invasion was inevitable. It was time to head north, and Maggie was packing her trunk while Seth was at the stables making preparations. Hopefully, they'd be able to leave first thing in the morning, but the strength of the winds and the thunderous clouds suggested they could be delayed. It was unusual to have a storm of this magnitude so late in the season. Then again, nothing in the world seemed normal any more.

A shiver rattled her body as rain cascaded down the paned windows. In the distance, thunder rumbled and lightning flashed. Something menacing resonated deep in Maggie's soul. This was more than disquiet over an out of season storm. She continued packing when she heard the cottage door slam shut. Running to the parlor, she stopped and stared at Seth who was shaking the water from his wavy locks. His shirt was soaked and his boots were caked with sand.

"Everything alright at the barn?" Maggie asked, handing Seth a towel.

He rubbed the droplets from his hair and blotted his face before handing the dampened towel back to her. "Just got the horses into the barn when the sky opened up. I don't ever remember a storm like this in autumn."

"It's like a bad omen," she said flatly.

"Don't be so dramatic. You're only nervous about the journey being delayed. Once the storm clears, we'll head out," he said, drawing her to him.

"I can't explain it, but I have a terrible feeling about this whole thing," she replied, snuggling her head into his chest.

"It's the upheaval. You're missing the kids, the Union Army is getting closer, and we have to leave our home. It's only natural you'd feel addled."

Pulling back, she stared into his steely blue eyes. "It's more than that. I'm worried about...." She looked away unsure whether to say what was on her mind or not.

"About what?" He caressed her cheek, his expression softening.

"About what you and I are going to do when we get to Pennsylvania."

Seth took her hand and led her to the settee where they sat down. "I've done a great deal of thinking about this and have finally made my decision." He paused as Maggie leaned forward, her shoulders tense as she waited for his declaration.

"As much as I love my home state of South Carolina, I cannot join the rebellion. My heart belongs to this country as a whole. I don't believe division is the answer. I've read the Confederate constitution and it's written in such a way that abolishing slavery is improbable." He ran his hand through his sandy curls and looked at his wife. "I've spent a good portion of my life helping to free those in bondage. I can't do anything that would further inhibit their liberty."

Tears crested in Maggie's eyes as she contemplated his decision. He was going to fight with the Union. Even though she always knew he'd have to enlist, it hadn't seemed real until now. Her insides quivered like freshly made jam and her head felt as light as a feather.

"Maggie, are you alright?" Seth asked, placing his hand on her shoulder.

"I'm as good as can be expected," she muttered.

"You look pale."

"How should I look?" she snapped. Her annoyed response shocked her. "I haven't seen my children in months, I'm leaving my home, and my husband is going to war!" A sob escaped her lips as she buried her face in her hands, her shoulders shaking.

Seth wrapped his arms around her and held her close. He kissed the top of her auburn locks before whispering in her ear. "It's going to be okay. The war can't last too long, and we'll be back here before you know it."

Maggie shoved him away, her vision blurred by tears as she squalled. "How can you sit there and tell me everything will be fine? You don't know that! What if you're injured, or worse?" she gasped, her words fading into a whimper.

Seth inhaled. "I can't guarantee anything. But I've been fighting a silent war for years. On more than one occasion I've faced death and injury transporting escapees to freedom. I'm good at scouting and finding solutions to impossible situations at the drop of a hat. I realize this war is disconcerting but I'm more than capable of handling dangerous conditions and staying safe under unusual circumstances."

Maggie wiped the fear from her cheeks and took a few deep breaths before speaking. "I know you're right but that doesn't take away the worry." Her green eyes locked onto his. "I love you more than you know. If anything were to happen to you, I couldn't go on."

Seth cupped her face in his hands. "I love you too, but don't underestimate your strength, Maggie Daniels. You can handle anything that life offers up. You've proven it over and over."

Another tear trickled down her cheek and she sniffled. "I don't want to lose you."

"You'll never be rid of me. I'll haunt you if I have to."

Maggie chuckled and looked away. Naturally, she was scared but she needed to have faith in Seth's abilities and hope the war ended quickly.

"I'm sorry for being so emotional. The separation from the kids and knowing you'll be fighting is distressing."

"It's not easy for me either. A man has no other option but to serve. Just know I will do everything possible to stay safe and come home to you. You're my world Maggie, and I don't want to be away from you or the children any longer than I have to be."

His lips brushed hers, sending a chill bumping across her skin. She leaned into his embrace as his kiss intensified. Maggie stood up and grasped Seth's hand, leading him into the other room.

November 7, 1861

Maggie's heart raced as she rushed through the room packing the last few items in her trunk. The storm had finally moved through leaving behind an eerie stillness that stabbed at her heart. As she placed her woolen shawl and gloves in the trunk, an explosion shook the floors and rattled the window-panes. Slamming the trunk lid shut, she ran across the room and gazed out the window when another blast sounded. Her lungs constricted and her limbs quaked as dread filled her soul. It seemed the war had finally arrived.

Seth bolted through the door, out of breath.

"Have you got everything packed? By the sound of the cannon fire the Union Army isn't far. We need to leave now."

Maggie stood and nodded. "The trunk is ready and so am I."

Her words were firm, but fear gripped her body. The idea that the fighting was so close sent adrenaline rushing through her veins. Would they make it out of town before the army arrived?

"The carriage is out front and Phantom is tacked and ready. Once we load everything, we'll be on our way."

He rushed from the room, leaving Maggie staring after him. She glanced around the space, her chest tightening. This was her home. It was the place where she and Seth spent their wedding night. It was the place where she gave birth to Joshua. It's where her life happened. The lump in her throat threatened to choke her. When would she return and would it be the same life she'd loved so much?

Taking in a deep breath, Maggie conjured all her courage. She needed to be strong, not only for herself but for Seth and her children. She'd survived abuse, starvation, and extreme danger. A war might be the pinnacle of her challenges but somehow, she'd manage that too. With one last glance around the room where so much of her life had occurred, she exhaled, grabbed her satchel, and walked out. With each step her fortitude strengthened. Seth grabbed the trunk and secured it to the boot of the carriage before helping Maggie onto the driver's bench.

Swinging into the saddle, Seth gathered the reins and looked at his wife. "You ready?" he asked.

With a nod, Maggie shifted in the seat and launched the horses forward. Driving down the sandy lane, she swallowed the anguish wedged in her throat as her home faded into the distance.

Chapter 7

November 1861

Seth

Thankfully, the trip to Pennsylvania had been uneventful. They'd stayed with friends of the Railroad along the way making the journey less taxing. The war had everyone on edge and seemed to be the only topic of conversation. Seth was worried about his wife. He could tell she was struggling with the situation and what his role would be once he joined a regiment.

Even he wasn't sure how things would play out. What he did know was that he had to enlist. On the trip north, he'd spent a great deal of time mulling over how that would look. With his scouting skills and ability to outmaneuver most trackers, he'd be of good use. Deep in his heart, though, he knew the reality of the situation would most likely land him in the infantry facing the front lines. Not much in his life had scared him, except when his family was in danger, but the idea of facing the enemy was disconcerting.

Men never discussed their fears and generally didn't admit it to themselves. Fear could cripple your instincts and make you second guess yourself which in a battle situation could get you killed. This was something that had kept him sharp when escorting the enslaved on their quest for freedom. Seth had too much to live for to hinder his fortitude with emotions. He'd done well with the Underground Railroad and would likely be successful as a soldier.

Maggie's words echoed through his mind piercing his heart. *You act as if you're the only one with something to lose.* The anguish in her eyes as she reminded him that she too would fret about his safety as he did for hers, pained him. The last thing he ever wanted to do was hurt her but as a man he had an unspoken duty to defend the country in which they lived. In essence, he was protecting them by safeguarding their way of life. At least that's how he justified it to himself.

Seth rode Phantom to the barn behind the Milner's house, cleaned him up, and settled him into a stall with hay and fresh water. Shutting the stall door, Seth watched Phantom pulling at tufts of hay and crunching it with a shake of his head. His ebony coat held a blue luster in the dim light of the barn. Phantom had been his steed for years and had seen him through many a mission with the Railroad. But could he endure the ferocity of a war? There wasn't time to find a new horse and train him to the level of Phantom. At that moment the decision was made; Phantom would go into battle with him. There was no other being in the world Seth trusted more with his life.

He exited the barn and strode toward the house. The back door flew open, and Joshua bolted toward his father with a squeal of delight and arms open wide. Seth scooped up his young son and held him tight against his chest as Joshua's feet dangled a couple of feet off the ground.

"I missed you, Papa!" he said, squeezing Seth's neck. "There's too many girls here and Mr. Milner is always at work."

Seth chuckled at his son's words. "Someday you'll like being surrounded by women," he said, lowering his son to the ground.

"Eww, why would I want to be around girls? They're always so fussy and talking about their dresses," he said, rolling his eyes. "And you can't burp around them, or they get upset and tell on you." Joshua huffed and folded his arms across his chest.

"It can't be all that bad," Seth replied.

"I suppose Annalissa's not so bad. She lets me feed the cows and the horses." His eyes brightened as a smile revealed a missing tooth.

Seth tousled his son's auburn curls and grinned. "See, you like being around Annalissa."

"But she's gone off to school with Miss Elora. Now I have to spend time with Jane, Mrs. Milner, Mrs. Polk, and Darla. Not that I mind Darla either, she sneaks me an extra cookie or brownie when no one is looking." Joshua grinned, scraping the dirt with the toe of his boot.

Seth shook his head, amused by his son's innocent view of the world. If it didn't involve animals or food, he wasn't interested. Typical little boy. A pang reverberated in Seth's chest at the idea of leaving Joshua, and Jane. He loved his children but knew he had to do this for their sake. Maggie would be here which gave him the strength to venture into such dire circumstances.

Walking to the house, they stepped through the back door into the kitchen where the smell of roast beef wafted through the air making Seth's stomach grumble. Miss Darla, the Milner's housemaid, stood over a simmering pot at the hearth. She turned with a smile, her eyes bright and her gray hair tucked neatly at the nape of her neck.

"Hello, Mr. Daniels, it's good to see you again," she declared, brushing a silver lock from her forehead.

Joshua ran to her side and looked up with a smile. "Now that my papa is here, Mr. Milner, Dr. Polk, Grandpa, and I won't be the only men in the house. Of course, they don't need extra cookies like I do since I'm a growing boy and all," he declared.

"I agree," Darla whispered back.

"Joshua, don't bother Miss Darla, she has work to do."

"He's no bother, Mr. Daniels. He keeps me company while I cook and sometimes, tells me stories." The right side of her mouth curled as she turned back to the steaming pot.

"Please call me Seth. Mr. Daniels makes me feel, well, old," he grinned. "If you'll excuse me, I need to get some things done before supper," he said, leaving the kitchen.

Seth climbed the stairs to the room he normally shared with Maggie when they visited and found her unpacking. Walking up behind her, he turned her toward him, wrapped his arms around her waist, and pulled her closer. She leaned into him and looked up, meeting his gaze.

"How are you doing?" he asked, planting a kiss on her forehead.

"Stiff from days of driving the carriage, but well."

"I'd offer to loosen you up, but Joshua will probably be looking for me any minute," he said with a sly smile.

Maggie grinned, her green eyes shimmering. "I think our carefree days of togetherness are on hold for a while," she replied, kissing him.

His pulse quickened as he held her close and returned her kiss. He was glad to be back with the kids but all he wanted right now was Maggie. He stepped back and caressed her cheek.

"I did a lot of thinking on the way up here," he said, taking in a breath. "Tomorrow I'll see about joining a regiment."

Maggie's eyes dropped.

"You know I don't have a choice in the matter," he muttered.

"Except you do have a choice. We're in Pennsylvania now. It's not like it is in the south where everyone is expected to fight. Surely, you could find something substantial to do that wouldn't involve joining the army."

Seth's chest felt like it was being squeezed by a boa constrictor. How could he make her understand that a man had certain obligations in life and defending his country was one of them?

Tipping her chin up, he met her tear-stained gaze. "You always knew I'd fight for one side or the other. This has been an agonizing choice for me, Maggie. Having to choose between my home state and the country, not to mention leaving you and the kids, has been one of the most difficult decisions of my life."

"I know but part of me hoped it wouldn't come to this."

He drew Maggie to him and kissed the top of her head. "We'll be okay. This war can't last too long and then I'll be back with you and the children."

Days later, Seth was packed and ready to head out. Phantom was tacked up and waited at the front of the house. Jane had her arm draped around Joshua's shoulders as he sniffled and wiped his eyes. Mrs. Milner and Mrs. Polk had bid their good-byes after breakfast and stayed inside the house to give the family privacy for their farewells.

Maggie hugged Seth tightly, nestling her head against the dark blue wool of his uniform. Leaning in, he whispered in her ear.

"I love you, Maggie Daniels, more than anything in this world. I'll do everything in my power to come back to you and the kids."

His words seemed to release the pent-up anxiety which now trickled across her flushed cheeks. He held her a minute more before stepping back and wiping away her tears. Seth turned to Jane and Joshua who were huddled on the front stoop watching.

Joshua bolted to him, throwing himself against his father in a strong embrace. "I'll take care of all the women while you're away Papa, promise. And I won't cause any trouble either."

Seth kneeled down and held his son. "I know you'll do a fine job taking care of your mother, sister, and all the animals. I'll be home when I can." His voice cracked as the last few words left his lips. Joshua's small frame shook in his arms like a tree branch in a hurricane. Seth released him and gave the strongest smile he could muster. As if the scene weren't painful enough, Joshua squared his shoulders and offered his hand.

"Be brave, Papa. I'm proud of you."

Clutching his son's hand, Seth felt as if his heart might explode. With all the upheaval and uncertainty in their future, his young son was trying to be strong for his father. Pride filled Seth's chest at Joshua's courage.

Jane trudged over to him and hugged him tightly. "Love you, Papa. Please take care and don't get injured or shot."

He held her slender form against him and planted a kiss on top of her burnished locks.

"Love you my dearest Jane."

She stepped back, allowing Maggie and Seth to embrace once more. He held his wife firmly against him wanting to sear the feeling into his mind for the moments when things would be unbearable. She'd been the center of his existence for so long. He took comfort knowing she and the children would be safe here although the pain he was inflicting on them wounded him to his core.

Seth released Maggie with another "I love you," and mounted Phantom. Tipping his hat, he spurred Phantom forward and cantered down the drive leaving his heart at the front stoop of the Milner's home.

Chapter 8

November 1861

Elora

It had been a couple of months since Elora had settled into her dormitory and started classes. While trying to figure out the logistics of joining the war efforts, she was spending time enjoying her studies. A part of her was sad she'd be leaving Oberlin as she'd come to appreciate the campus and her professors. But she was determined to follow through on her plans as soon as she figured out how to do so.

It wasn't surprising that Elora's English class was her favorite being she had an extensive library at home which she'd inhabited for a good deal of her childhood. She loved everything Jane Austen had written but was enamored with a modern writer, Charles Dickens. Something about his prose made her feel as if she were sitting before him as he told the story. Professor Brown, her English teacher, was an animated instructor with Shakespearean attributes in his manner of presenting material. Every tome he assigned seemed like the most interesting story ever printed. Elora actually looked forward to each class even though it started at 8:00 a.m. sharp. Of course, his dark eyes and silvery hair made for an attractive package leading many of the girls to arrive early in order to gawk at the dapper professor. Even Elora was a bit smitten with his handsome face and debonair mannerisms.

The best thing about Professor Brown was his willingness to challenge the female mind. He didn't assign the usual romantic dribble reserved for women. He exposed his students to a wide array of literature. The most shocking of her assignments was *Frankenstein* by Mary Shelley. Elora wasn't certain what made it such a controversial read, the writer being female or the subject matter. Regardless, the theme of the book as it related to human rights struck her heart, especially after her years affiliated with the Underground Railroad.

Mary Shelley's work had impacted Elora so deeply that she chose it as the subject for her first paper. Apparently, she'd impressed Professor Brown with her interpretation and prose. One morning following class, he asked to speak with her.

"Miss Polk," Professor Brown called as Elora was gathering her books. "May I have a word with you?"

Some of the other girls hesitated, envy masking their expressions as they left the classroom.

Elora approached his desk, her palms sweaty and her lips dry. Had she done something wrong?

"I wanted to discuss your paper," he said, his dark stare piercing her heart.

"Is there a problem?" she asked, concerned she may have been too forward in her opinions.

"Not at all. In fact, I was rather impressed with your analysis of Shelley's work. Not many people would have taken that stance."

"Thank you, sir," she replied, a warmth spreading up her neck and across her cheeks.

"Have you considered being a writer?"

"A writer?" Elora was stunned. No one had ever mentioned writing to her before. "No, sir."

"Well, you should," he said, handing her the paper. "You have a way with words and your power of persuasion is exemplary."

"Thank you," she mumbled, glancing at the large "A" scrolled at the top of the front page.

Elora hurried from the room, her head swimming at the compliment. She'd never received praise as worthy as this, especially from such a debonair and erudite gentleman. The idea of being a writer was intriguing although as a woman she knew her publishing opportunities would be limited.

Professor Brown's classes nearly led Elora to abandon her quest to serve in the army while at the same time strengthening her resolve to help humanity in some way. She loved the country and fighting to preserve it seemed more important than remaining at the college just because she was enamored with a professor.

In her history class they were studying Joan of Arc which led Elora to spend hours in the library researching other women who'd contributed more to the world than sewing, cooking, and birthing children. She discovered Semiramis, queen of the Assyrians, Boadicea, a British queen, and Bona Lombardi, a peasant girl in Italy. The more she read, the more empowered she became. She could do this; she was certain of it.

While concentrating on her studies, Elora had also been working on developing her persona for enlistment in the army. She'd almost lost her nerve several times but realized she'd regret her choice if she stayed on campus. No matter how tempting it was to continue her education, Elora knew there'd be plenty of time for that later, assuming she survived the war. Shaking off her trepidation, she prepared to meet Annalissa for the evening meal.

As the dinner hour neared, Elora pulled her hair into a pony tail, careful to keep it as neat and tight as she could. She slipped on a pair of trousers, a baggy cotton shirt, and a tweed coat she'd fashioned each evening before bed. With a small rag she blotted dark shoe polish around her jaw line to look like stubble and topped her ensemble with a bowler hat. Gazing at her reflection, Elora furrowed her brow, stood straighter, and squared her shoulders. Perfect, she thought.

Making her way across campus, Elora adapted her stride to longer lengths, adding more of a flat-footed step like she'd practiced. She made sure to arrive early to catch Annalissa before she entered the dining hall. It wouldn't be proper for Elora to join her friend for dinner in her current state of dress.

She arrived and stood in the chilly air as ladies sauntered past, tipping her hat at each one while keeping her posture as straight as possible. When she spotted Annalissa coming toward her, Elora squared her shoulders and put forth her sternest expression.

"Excuse me, Miss," Elora said in a gruff voice. "I'm looking for the dining hall."

Annalissa stepped back; her countenance cautious. "It's right there," she said, pointing to the steps, "but gentlemen aren't permitted to dine with the ladies."

She started for the building when Elora grasped her upper arm and stepped closer. "Then I suppose we need to dine elsewhere."

Yanking her arm free, Annalissa gazed at the outlandish gent. "I don't mean to be rude, but I've no intention of joining a strange man for dinner. "If you'll excuse me, I'll be on my way," she said firmly.

"Miss Milner, is that anyway to address a dear old friend?" Elora asked with a deepened voice.

"Who are you and how do you know...?" Before she could

finish her sentence, Annalissa gasped. "Elora, is that you?" She leaned in, scanning the person before her from head to toe.

"Indeed, it is," she giggled, removing the hat from her head.

"Why are you dressed like that?" Annalissa queried.

"I'd like you to meet Walter Polk. Lieutenant with the first Ohio Volunteer Army," she said with a low bow. "I signed up with my new identity a few days ago."

"I'm flabbergasted. You actually look like a man."

"Thank you," Elora said, pride lifting her chin. "Shall we go for a stroll before dinner?" she asked, offering her arm.

A hearty burst of laughter rolled from Annalissa's lips as she slipped her hand through the crook of Elora's elbow. Winter's bite cut through the tweed coat and reddened Elora's cheeks and nose. November in Ohio was much brisker than the milder temperatures she was accustomed to in the Lowcountry.

"I can't believe you've done this," Annalissa said as they strolled down a long walkway beneath partially barren trees.

"Many of Oberlin's students have enlisted so it wasn't difficult to accomplish. The army is in such dire need of soldiers they actually signed people up on campus. I dressed as Walter Polk to test out my new image and voila, it worked. I'm supposed to start drilling with the regiment next week."

"What about the holidays? It's one thing to convince your parents you're too busy to write but to be absent during Thanksgiving and Christmas would be nearly impossible to explain."

"I've taken care of everything," Elora said with an impish grin. "I wrote to my parents explaining that I'd signed up to do mission work out west. Then I sent a private letter to my mother reminding her how I'd wanted to contribute to the war efforts and since I was denied that opportunity this would allow me to do my part in a manner befitting a lady."

"And?" Annalissa asked, her eyebrows arched.

"She agreed to it. My mother isn't a prude by any means. She believes women should be permitted to do more than what society deems appropriate. However, she does have her limits and apparently serving in the war is outside her scope of approval."

They walked in silence for a few moments before Annalissa spoke.

"Are you sure you can keep up this identity with a group of men? I mean, this is fine for now, but it will take a lot to maintain this guise."

"It won't be easy, but I know I can handle it," Elora replied confidently.

Annalissa stopped and looked at her friend. "What about your jawline, how did you darken it?"

"Shoe polish."

"And if it rains and washes away?"

"I'll keep a jar with me and reapply it when I get a chance," Elora said.

"I think you could get away without facial hair if the rest of you was more, manly."

"What do you mean exactly?"

"You need to cut your hair instead of wearing it in a ponytail."

Elora reached back and stroked the long lock bound at the back of her head. She'd always loved her hair. In her opinion, it was one of her finest features. But Annalissa's suggestion made sense. She'd be more masculine with a shorter cut, but her heart sank at the idea.

"I think you may be right about that. I really hate to cut it, but I may not have a choice."

"I feel it would help camouflage your femininity. Speaking of which, how do you plan on concealing, um...," Annalissa paused, looking away.

"What?"

"You know...your chest."

Elora chuckled. "Already thought of that. I'll use bandaging to flatten everything. It can't be any more uncomfortable than a corset."

As they continued their stroll, Elora's head hung a bit lower as she contemplated Annalissa's suggestions. She'd planned everything so carefully, and yet there were still glitches.

Once they circled back to the dining hall, Annalissa faced Elora, concern shrouding her countenance. "I don't mean to diminish your ambitions, but are you certain you want to take this risk? It's one thing to assist with the war and an entirely different situation to fight in it. Do you really believe you're prepared to serve in such an extreme manner?"

Elora glanced at the ground, pondering her answer for a moment. Looking at Annalissa, she exhaled. "I'm absolutely positive about this. I've been target practicing for months and I must admit I'm a fine shot. My horsemanship skills are exceptional as is my sense of direction. I spent my life riding the trails at home and know how to find my way anywhere."

"That might be so, but you didn't have hundreds of men shooting at you with rifles and cannons."

"I appreciate what you're saying but if I think too deeply about it, I'll lose my nerve. I can handle this, of that I'm certain. I'll just have to be judicious in everything I do. There's just one problem."

"Which is?"

"Communicating with my mother. I don't know how reliable the mail will be in a war zone." Elora shrugged.

"How do you plan on handling it?"

"I told her mail delivery would be erratic where we're going, especially with our group moving around. All the same,

I've pre-written a few letters that I need you to mail periodically."

Annalissa nodded. "If you're determined to see this through, I'll support you any way I can."

Elora grasped Annalissa's gloved hand. "Thank you for believing in me. I need to do this and prove to myself that I'm capable of accomplishing more than embroidered seat cushions."

"Elora, you're capable of accomplishing anything you set your mind to. I just don't want to see you lose your life trying to show how much you can do with it." Annalissa smiled. "Are you going to join me for dinner?"

Elora nodded. "Let me change and I'll be back shortly."

"See you then," she said.

Annalissa slipped inside the dining hall as Elora strode back to the dormitory to resume her female persona. Despite all her practicing and planning, she suddenly felt unprepared, doubt crowding her thoughts. Annalissa's words seemed to magnify her reservations, something she needed to squelch before engaging in the most dangerous endeavor of her life.

Chapter 9

Winter 1862

Maggie

Seth had been gone for three months now and Maggie had settled into a routine with the kids and the Milners. She continued her work mixing salves and ointments for the farm workers, mended clothing, and schooled her children in between. Since Maggie had been trained in herbal remedies while living at her uncle's farm in Pennsylvania, she was able to blend exactly what was needed with little study. Mostly, she prepared primrose ointment for burns, hyssop cough syrup, spring tonic for digestion, and her standard lobelia and cayenne liniment for cuts and bruises. With frigid temps and snowy days, the need for remedies to treat cold-weather related ailments was greater than usual.

Maggie had received a couple of letters from Seth letting her know his skills with the Railroad were highly regarded by his commanding officer who'd put him in a position of scouting. Scouts were skilled horsemen with experience infiltrating dangerous situations and collecting intelligence. It was the perfect role for Seth with his years on the Underground Railroad seeking out information in order to transport escapees safely to freedom. Although still a dangerous job, Maggie took some comfort in the fact he wasn't on the front lines with the infantry.

Despite the ongoing news of battles and the thousands of lives being lost each day, Maggie managed to keep her demeanor positive for Joshua and Jane. Deep down she was fearful of whether the fighting would remain in the southern states or make its way north.

Maggie, Mrs. Polk, and Mrs. Milner sat around a small wooden table beneath the window in the front parlor with a sewing basket resting between them. Maggie stared through the wavy glass panes at the snow blanketing the landscape, her emotions swirling like a cyclone. How she longed for peace.

"Have you read the paper today?" Mrs. Milner asked Mrs. Polk. "I didn't get a chance to look it over this morning. I needed to take some soup to Mrs. Tanner. She has a terrible cold."

"There's quite a lot going on," Mrs. Polk replied, snipping a lose thread. "Edwin Stanton has been appointed by the U.S. Senate as Secretary of War to replace Simon Cameron."

"I'm sorry to hear Mr. Cameron has been dismissed. He was a Pennsylvania senator before his appointment to Secretary of War," Mrs. Milner said. "Did it say why he was removed?"

"Apparently, his effectiveness was in question due to the ongoing conflict. Many believed the war would only last a few weeks and here we are more than a year later."

"Let's hope Mr. Stanton will be more successful," Mrs. Milner responded, rethreading her needle.

"I also read that Grant and Foote have taken over Fort Henry in Tennessee," Mrs. Polk added.

"What about South Carolina?" Maggie queried, her head beginning to ache from the bleak topic of conversation. She just wanted the war to end so Seth, Dr. Polk, and Reverend Milner could come home.

Mrs. Polk looked up from her sewing and sighed. "Unfortunately, the news reports speak of devastation and starvation in the southern states. I worry for our folks who stayed behind, but I also know them to be intelligent, resourceful people. I pray for them every night."

"The election of Jefferson Davis as president of the Confederate States seems to have consummated the disunion of the country," Mrs. Milner said.

Maggie's stomach roiled. If the south won the war and the country was split into two separate entities, they'd never be able to return to Rose Hall. Their neighbors would view them as traitors for fleeing to the north. Even worse, if their work with the Railroad came to light it would be a death sentence should they go back. Starting over in the north wasn't necessarily a bad thing but she'd miss the Lowcountry life, especially the soft caress of marsh breezes against her skin, sitting on the porch swing watching Spanish moss billow from ancient live oaks, and crabbing from the dock behind their cottage. The Union must be preserved if Maggie hoped to resume the lifestyle she'd come to love.

"Have you heard from Seth lately?" Mrs. Milner asked as she mended a pair of slacks, interrupting Maggie's thoughts.

"Not in the past couple of weeks," Maggie replied, her heart thumping a bit harder. She knew Seth's ability to write would be greatly hindered by the demands of scouting. He'd said as much in his last letter. However, in the past when he was on missions for the Underground Railroad, he'd been able to communicate through the *Homefront Herald*, a newspaper owned by Rudy Taylor. Whenever secret information needed to be passed along regarding the transport of escapees, Rudy would post coded adverts so conductors would know which routes to avoid should slave hunters be in the area. But communication through the paper wasn't an option now, making the extended time between correspondence distressing.

"I'm sure the mail has slowed with everything that's going on," Mrs. Milner said. Changing the subject, she asked, "Is Joshua still at the barn with your father?"

Maggie grinned. "Yes. Poor Da has to escort him there several times a day to check on Peaches. Since Mr. Milner tasked Joshua with caring for the pony while he was away, the child is obsessed with making sure nothing happens to him."

"Joshua seems quite attached to his grandpa," Mrs. Milner smiled.

Hoofbeats pounded, diverting Maggie's attention. Glancing out the window, she saw a horse and rider galloping to the front of the house. Her heart seized. Please don't let this be bad news, she thought. Any unexpected guests could bring word that something terrible had happened to Seth. She exhaled when she realized it was the postman.

"Mr. Johnson is here with the mail," she announced, starting for the foyer.

"Maybe you'll have a letter from Seth," Mrs. Milner called as Maggie opened the front door.

"Good day, Mrs. Daniels," the postman said with a nod as he handed her a few letters. "Got one in there for you. Have a good afternoon."

"Thank you, Mr. Johnson," she replied, hurrying inside. Her pulse quickened at the thought she'd received a letter from Seth.

Maggie plunked down in her seat and started sorting through the envelopes, her fingers trembling with anticipation.

Mrs. Milner looked up and smiled. "I heard Mr. Johnson say something about a letter for you. How exciting." Her eyes sparkled as she watched Maggie flip through the letters.

Maggie's hope faded as she gazed at the last one.

"Is something the matter?" Mrs. Polk asked, leaning forward.

Maggie shook her head. "The letter isn't from Seth. It's from Dr. Towne."

Dr. Laura Towne was a staunch abolitionist who had taken in two of Maggie's dearest friends, Willa and Letty. They were the ones who'd taught Maggie all about herbal remedies and concoctions when she was living at her uncle's farm. When his farm was sold, Willa and Letty found work elsewhere. Willa's bad back and aging joints weren't holding up as a laundress, so Dr. Towne hired her to continue with her herbal remedies. Thankfully, she was able to hire Letty as well, bringing the two close friends back together with employment that suited their talents.

Maggie broke the seal on the envelope and unfolded the parchment. Hopefully, Willa and Letty were well. She couldn't bear the idea they might be in poor health. There was enough sadness in her world, and she didn't want any more added to her burdens.

Mrs. Milner stopped stitching and peered over her spectacles. "Is everything alright?"

Maggie read through the letter before responding. Her jaw dropped as she finished.

"Maggie?"

Placing the letter on the table, Maggie took in a deep breath trying to process what she'd read. "Dr. Towne has been enlisted as an agent of the Freedmen's Aid Society of Pennsylvania."

"That sounds interesting," Mrs. Polk said.

"Indeed. She wants me to join her in the endeavor."

"What exactly would you be doing?" Mrs. Milner asked, setting her sewing aside.

"She's requested that I accompany her to the Sea Islands of

South Carolina to help with the newly freed slaves," Maggie muttered, her spirit soaring at the idea of returning home. "Most of the enslaved were left behind when their owners fled right before the Union Army took over Beaufort."

"Oh my," Mrs. Milner declared. "Is that safe?"

Maggie shrugged one shoulder. "She says Beaufort and the surrounding areas are Headquarters for the Union Army and that we'd be well protected."

"Do you think Seth would approve?" Mrs. Polk queried.

Maggie's heart lurched within her chest. She hadn't even considered what Seth would say if she told him. "I don't know," she replied in a whisper.

"What would be your role?"

"I'd be assisting her with herbal remedies for the medical needs of the Negroes. Her friend, Ellen Murray, will be teaching them. She feels my knowledge of the area and its plantings would be of great benefit to their efforts," Maggie said, refolding the letter and sliding it into the envelope.

"I understand that you want to help, but I feel you should write Seth before making a decision. Union headquarters or not, it's still a war zone," Mrs. Polk said.

Maggie's mood sank. Even though she knew Seth trusted her instincts and ability to defend herself, he probably wouldn't be thrilled about her going south under the current state of affairs.

"I haven't time to write him about it. I don't even know where he is right now. It's the end of February and Dr. Towne is set to sail aboard the *Oriental* from New York to Charleston on April 9th. She wants me to come to New York and travel with her."

"When does she want you to meet her?"

"Immediately, so she can prep me on what's to be done."

Mrs. Polk straightened in her chair. "I don't mean to interfere, but I truly believe you need to discuss this with your husband. It's a serious endeavor and one that could be dangerous should the tide of the war shift. What if the Confederates retake Beaufort and the surrounding areas. Would you be safe then?"

Maggie wrung her hands like a wet rag. She didn't want to do anything that would upset Seth and the thought of leaving her children rankled her nerves. But she felt like a shell of herself walking around the Milner's farm doing ordinary things. So much of her life over the past few years had been spent in the service of others. It gave her purpose.

Shaking her head, she met Mrs. Polk's steady gaze. "I appreciate your concerns, but I feel strongly about accepting Dr. Towne's offer," she said, reaching across the table and squeezing Mrs. Polk's hand. "Please don't be upset with me. I'm going to need your support."

Mrs. Polk sighed. "If you're determined to do this, I'll support you any way I can."

"You're welcome to take our carriage," Mrs. Milner offered. "We've not had much use for it as of late with Mr. Milner being in Washington D.C."

"Thank you, that would be helpful," Maggie replied, chewing her lower lip. There was so much to be done if she was to travel in the next day or two. "Would you be willing to instruct the children while I'm away? Da doesn't have the patience for those things which is why he hired a private tutor to teach me when I was younger."

"I'd be more than happy to teach them," Mrs. Milner replied, resuming her sewing. "I adore them both as if they were my own."

Maggie grinned at her statement. Mrs. Milner could have filled the house with dozens of children and still provided all the love each of them needed. Her heart was just that big.

"How long do you think you'll be gone?" Mrs. Polk asked.

"Dr. Towne didn't say," Maggie replied. "I'm going upstairs to pen a response for tomorrow's post."

As Maggie climbed the stairs, her mind raced with the possibilities of Dr. Towne's offer and how Seth would react if he discovered she was going back to the Lowcountry. He'd likely be upset. The last thing she wanted was to distract him from his duties and worrying about her safety would do just that. She had to find a way to do this without being dishonest to her husband or adding any undue concern to his already stressful situation. But how?

After an hour of ruminating on Dr. Towne's offer and how to deal with Seth on the subject, Maggie had come up with a solution. Granted, it hinged on her father's willingness to help but she felt certain with a bit of persuasion he would acquiesce.

She found the kids in the front parlor drawing while Mrs. Polk, Mrs. Milner, and her Da sat nearby reading.

"Did you have fun at the stables this morning?" Maggie asked her son.

He looked up from his artwork and smiled. "We did. Grampa let me ride Peaches."

"That does sound like fun," she replied, looking at her father. "Da, may I speak with you in private?"

Mr. McFarland placed his book on the small round table and followed his daughter into the kitchen. Darla had gone to the market, so they had the room to themselves. The fire in the massive stone hearth warmed the space as they gathered at the pine table. Maggie poured two cups of tea and sat across from her father.

"What's so important that ye needs to speak with me alone?" he asked, taking a sip from his cup.

"I've been given an opportunity to serve the newly freed slaves," she said, planning her words carefully. She needed her father's support if she hoped to accompany Dr. Towne south.

As if sensing she was holding back, Mr. McFarland raised an eyebrow and spoke. "And by any chance does this opportunity have a risk to it?"

Maggie nibbled her lip. "Perhaps a bit," she said, glancing down at her mug of tea.

"Out with it, Lassie. Tell me what's really goin' on."

Maggie explained what she'd be doing and where. "I don't believe Dr. Towne would put me in extreme danger." Maggie reached across the table and took her Da's weathered hand into hers. "Please help me with this. I need to do something more than mend clothes and instruct the children."

"What about Seth? Do ye think he'd agree to this?" he asked, quirking his brows.

"Seth needn't be worried with it. He's got enough to do without being burdened with my activities. Which is where you come in."

Mr. McFarland removed his hand from hers, leaned back in the chair, and crossed his arms over his chest. "What exactly is it you're wantin' me to do?"

"Forward all of Seth's letters to me in South Carolina. I'll read them and answer them from there."

Her father's eyes narrowed. "Not sure I like bein' a part of something that deceives my son-in-law."

"There's no deceit. I'm protecting him. He doesn't need to be worrying about me. Trust me on this, I know what I'm doin'," she replied, her Irish accent tinting her words.

"And if you should be hurt? What am I to tell 'im then?"

"Like I said, I'll be with Dr. Towne and surrounded by the Union Army. Nothing will happen."

"What about Jane and Joshua?" he asked.

"Mrs. Milner and Mrs. Polk will watch over them and continue their lessons. I'll tell the kids I've been asked to help those who've recently been freed from slavery. They'll miss me but won't question my efforts."

"These are bright children. Don't you think they'll be upset over you leavin' and wonder why you're puttin' yourself at risk?"

"Not at all," she replied. "While Seth and I didn't go on as many missions once we had the children, we did do some overnight work with the Railroad. As I said, they won't question my absence."

"This is more than an overnight excursion."

"I'll explain that I need to go away for a while and return when the war is over. It won't be much longer, I'm certain."

"Very well," he sighed. "But I still think ye should tell your husband.

Relieved she had the support of Mrs. Milner, Mrs. Polk, and now her Da, Maggie only needed to inform Jane and Joshua. Despite telling herself that the children would accept her decision, deep down she dreaded their reactions most of all.

Later that night, Maggie escorted the kids upstairs. Jane and Joshua were sharing a room that overlooked the barns at the back of the house. Joshua loved being able to wake early and watch the horses trot around the pasture in the morning mist.

"I need to discuss something with you both," Maggie said, perching on the edge of Joshua's bed as Jane sat on hers.

"Is Papa okay?" Joshua gasped, fear clouding his bright blue eyes.

"He's fine," Maggie replied, praying it was true. "A friend has invited me to help her with some things and I've accepted."

"Does she live here?" Jane asked.

"No, she doesn't. I'll have to go to her."

Tears puddled in Joshua's eyes. "Why do you have to go?" he moaned.

"Because a lot of people are counting on me," she replied, her heart wrenching at her son's discomfort.

"We're counting on you too," Jane added with a disgruntled look.

"I realize that, but you have Mrs. Polk and Mrs. Milner here as well as your grandpa. Please understand, I need to do this."

Jane crossed her arms over her chest and flopped back on her bed.

"Please don't be upset with me, Jane. I couldn't bear it."

Sitting up, Jane's expression softened. "I'm not upset, it's only...we're already missing Papa. And now you're leaving too."

Maggie walked over to her daughter and hugged her. "I know this has all been hard on you but there are others who are suffering much worse than we are. They need my help."

Jane pulled away. "Where will you be going?"

Maggie weighed her answer carefully. Jane was a bright young lady who would recognize the danger of her mother going south. As much as she hated to do it, Maggie had no choice but to bend the truth. After all, she was protecting her children.

"I'll be traveling to New York," she said which wasn't exactly a lie.

"Can we write to you?" Joshua asked, sniffling as he wiped a tear from his cheek.

"I would like that very much."

"Will you write us too?" Jane asked.

"I'll do my best, but I'll be quite busy."

Jane nodded and slipped beneath the covers. "How long will you be away?"

Maggie shook her head. "I don't know exactly, probably until the war is over. But not to worry, it can't last much longer."

Jane turned over in the bed, her back facing Maggie.

"Jane, please don't be this way."

"I'm fine," she murmured. "Only a bit tired."

Maggie could hear the tears in Jane's voice and decided to let her daughter sort through things on her own. They could discuss it further in the morning after Jane had a chance to process everything.

"I love you both," Maggie said.

"Love you, Mama," Joshua replied, holding out his arms.

Maggie embraced her son, his tears seeping into the fabric of her bodice. Her chest constricted. She hated putting them through this but like her husband, she had a duty to serve. Kissing the top of Joshua's curls, Maggie released him and cupped his face in her hands. "You'll be so busy with grandpa, Mrs. Polk, and Mrs. Milner that the time will fly by and then I'll be back."

With a snuffle, Joshua rested his head on the pillow and pulled the quilt over his shoulders. Jane still had her back to Maggie as she blew out the candle on the night table and left the room, closing the door behind her.

Apprehension gripped her heart. Was she really doing the right thing? Slipping into her room, Maggie sat on the edge of the bed, buried her face in her hands, and sobbed. She cried about leaving her children, missing Seth, and the helplessness of waiting for the war to end. When her tears ran dry, she exhaled, her shoulders slumped. Her body felt numb. Maybe being occupied with Dr. Towne would keep her mind from dwelling on the turmoil swirling around her. She had to do this, no matter how distressing.

On the day of Maggie's departure, Jane and Joshua stood

with Mrs. Milner and Mrs. Polk on the front stoop, tears trickling down their rosy cheeks.

Mr. McFarland embraced his daughter in a bear hug and whispered in her ear. "Don' make me regret this, Lassie. Your ole Da needs you to stay safe."

"I'll be careful, promise," she replied, hugging him tighter. The scene from the docks in Ireland flashed through Maggie's head. He'd embraced her like this when he sent her to America to stay with her uncle. Except this time, she'd be fine. No one would harm or abuse her.

Stepping back, her gaze met his greenish gray stare. "Love you, Da."

"Love you," he replied, brushing the tear from her cheek.

Climbing into the carriage, Maggie adjusted her skirts and stared out the window. As the carriage launched forward, she watched her family grow smaller and smaller as she was jostled to and fro down the tree-lined drive.

Two weeks later, after days of being tossed about, Maggie was relieved when Dr. Towne's residence came into view. The carriage halted and the driver came to the side, opened the door, and handed Maggie from within. Clouds hung low in the sky and a damp chill saturated the air. Oh, how she missed the mild Lowcountry winters where spring made its appearance as early as March. Apparently, New York was still in the throes of winter. At least it had stopped raining. There was nothing worse than a cold rainy day in the north. It always made Maggie feel like she was trapped in a cave.

A host of three-story brick homes with barren trees in front, lined the street. Wrought iron fencing edged the hibernating greenery adding a delicate touch to the stark wintery scene. Maggie thanked the carriage driver and scurried to the front door. Before she could knock, the door opened. Willa's broad smile wrinkled her dark eyes as she pulled Maggie into a firm embrace.

"Miss Maggie, I's ever so glad to see you!"

Maggie returned the hug as her friend rocked her back and forth. "I've missed you too, Willa." Maggie drew back, a smile lifting her cheeks. "Where's Letty?" she asked, looking behind her old friend.

"You know she don't do sentimental scenes," Willa scoffed. "She's in the kitchen preparing coffee."

They stepped inside where a fire sputtered and crackled in the entryway hearth. Willa led Maggie down a long hall simply adorned with a couple of paintings depicting pastoral scenes and a woolen rug warming the heart pine floors. They entered the kitchen where Letty was placing a pot of coffee and four mugs on a silver tray. She looked up at Maggie, her eyes misting as she approached.

"It's good to see you, Miss Maggie," she said with a smile as she patted Maggie's shoulder.

"I'm glad to see you too, Letty."

Letty stepped back and grabbed the tray. "Dr. Towne's in her office. She wants to speak with all of us."

Maggie nodded and followed her two friends to a cozy area off the back of the house. Obviously, this was the doctor's private office as it housed a mahogany desk with shelves of medical volumes lining the far wall. Green and gold curtains framed windows that overlooked the gardens in the back. Maggie surmised the other door must lead to the examination room.

Letty placed the tray on a small round table with carved legs and poured the coffee. As Willa and Maggie took their seats, the door opened and Dr. Towne entered.

Dr. Laura Towne hadn't changed much since the last time Maggie had spoken to her. Her brown hair was neatly gathered in a bun at the back of her head, her dress was simple yet perfectly tailored, and her countenance exuded confidence.

"Maggie, it's lovely to see you again. Thank you for agreeing to my request," she said, grasping Maggie's hand.

"I'm honored you asked me, Dr. Towne."

"Please call me Laura. You know I don't stand on ceremony with colleagues." Adjusting her skirts, she sat in the chair across from Maggie. "I've tried to convince these two ladies to do the same, but they insist on formality." Dr. Towne grinned warmly at Willa and Letty who sipped coffee.

Maggie gave a sideways glance at Willa and winked. "I remember trying to add Miss in front of their names when I first met them, and they fussed at me."

Willa chuckled while Letty smirked. Nothing had changed. Willa was still the bubbly personality and Letty was still her no-nonsense self. It warmed Maggie's heart to know that no matter the time span, some things remained the same.

"If you don't mind, I'd prefer to address you as Dr. Towne," Maggie added.

"Very well," Dr. Towne said, setting her coffee on the side table. "Our undertaking is one of great significance. I've been tasked with opening a school for the freed slaves on St. Helena Island off the coast of Beaufort, South Carolina. When the plantation owners fled at the start of the war, they left their slaves behind, inadvertently freeing them. Of course, the Union doesn't recognize them as people but as contraband," she said with a disgruntled sniff. "Nonetheless, opening a school to educate them is a step in the right direction."

"It all sounds amazing," Maggie replied, sitting on the edge of her chair. The idea that the Negroes were not only free but would be educated was astounding.

"As I told you in my letter, my dear friend Ellen Murray will join us in early summer. She's one of the finest teachers I know. When the government decided to embark on this endeavor, and asked for my support, I knew Ellen was the one to help me. My next thought was of you. With your knowledge of the Lowcountry region and climate as well as your ability to concoct herbal remedies, I decided you were a necessary choice for my staff."

"Thank you for the kind words and your confidence in my abilities. Please know, my familiarity with St. Helena Island is limited. I've only been there once and that was at night. We were rendezvousing with a conductor to transport a young, enslaved woman and her sister."

Dr. Towne waved her hand in the air. "It's of no concern. What I need is your knowledge of the area and experience with herbal remedies."

Maggie sat straighter, listening to Dr. Towne explain all they'd be doing. Her heart palpitated at the thought. She'd be back in the Lowcountry helping the people she'd worked for years to free.

"As you know, the Union Army took control of Beaufort, utilizing its homes and churches as hospitals, headquarters, and housing for the men. There have been a few skirmishes in the region but nothing major within the Beaufort and Sea Island areas," she said. "While we'll be well protected, there are some risks. I'd understand if you changed your mind and decided not to go."

Maggie shivered at the memory of explosions and impending occupation by the army the day she and Seth fled Rose Hall. Since the Union had taken over Beaufort as its headquarters, the danger would be minimal. Most importantly, she'd be contributing to the betterment of the freed slaves. She desperately wanted to do something useful. It all seemed so simple until her mind drifted to Seth and his reaction if he discovered what she was doing. Granted, it shouldn't be an issue since it seemed much safer than her previous endeavors on the Railroad. Having come this far, she wasn't going to turn back now.

"I'm well aware of the dangers," Maggie said. "It can't be any worse than what I faced when transporting escapees to freedom."

"Very good. Once we arrive at St. Helena Island, we're to report to The Oaks plantation."

"I'm honored to serve alongside you, Dr. Towne."

The doctor smiled and reached for Maggie's hand. "I'm glad you'll be accompanying us. You'll be a boon to our efforts."

"Us? I thought Miss Murray wouldn't be there until summer."

Dr. Towne's smile broadened. "Willa and Letty will be assisting you. They're well versed in gardening and mixing the remedies. This way we'll have plenty of capable hands to help the Negroes adapt to their newfound freedom."

Maggie looked at her two friends and grinned. Not only would she be returning home but she'd have two of the dearest people she knew by her side. While she'd miss her children, she knew in her heart they'd flourish beneath the love of her Da, Mrs. Polk, and Mrs. Milner. If the war ended soon then Seth and the kids could join her. Once the fighting was over, she knew Seth would forgive her for keeping her activities from him. More importantly, the efforts of educating the freed slaves wouldn't end with the war. It was an ongoing task that would last well past the conflict, and she was proud to be a part of it.

Chapter 10

Winter 1862

Seth

Seth pressed Phantom forward through the woods in an effort to make it back to camp before dark. He'd been honored to be appointed as spymaster for the regiment meaning he now directed the unit spies as well as spying himself. Currently, he had vital information for the colonel and couldn't waste any time.

As he dodged and ducked through low lying tree branches, his heart pounded in rhythm with Phantom's hoofbeats. He was still wearing his Confederate attire, having left a southern unit where he was able to glean their coordinates for the next attack. Being southern himself allowed him to blend in without suspicion. Southern men were different than their northern counterparts, giving him an advantage that allowed him to garner information most others could not. In the event he was captured by Union forces while dressed as a Confederate, he was to use a code word along with his commanding officer's name that would alert them to his position as spymaster. Thus far, he'd not had to use it and hoped it would remain that way.

The smell of smoke permeated the air as he slowed

Phantom to a walk. They exited the wooded area and headed for the colonel's tent. Thankfully, his unit knew Phantom well and would overlook the fact he was donning the gray rebel uniform.

"Hey, Daniels," one of his comrades hollered. "You're just in time for chow."

"Need to see the colonel first," he hollered back, his breath steaming from his lips.

When he reached Colonel Pennington's tent, he dismounted and pulled a piece of paper from his coat pocket. Although a temporary shelter, the Colonel's quarters were comfortable. A small wooden desk with an inkwell, pen, and maps was placed in the center of the space. To the left was a cot covered in a wool blanket with a large trunk resting at the foot of it.

"Daniels, good to see you," the Colonel said, motioning for Seth to sit in the chair across from his desk.

"I've word about a potential assault south of here," Seth replied, handing the coordinates to his commanding officer.

Pennington studied the paper and rubbed his forehead. "Sneaky little Rebs thought they could pull this off," he huffed. "I'll send out a group to intercept. How many men are there?"

"Not many, maybe a hundred."

The Colonel nodded. "We can take care of this without breaking camp. Leave at sunrise and tell the Rebs we're preparing to come their way. If they think they can trap us, we'll have the advantage."

"Yes, Sir." Seth walked from the tent, grabbed Phantom's reins, and led him to a small makeshift paddock where he untacked and cleaned him up. He tossed several flakes of hay to the ground and turned him out before joining his fellow soldiers for the evening meal. His shoulders were stiff and his back ached from hunching over during his ride through the woods. He hated betraying fellow southerners but Seth's belief in preserving the Union was strong. He hadn't a choice, at least in his opinion.

After a dinner of beans and pork and a few shots of whisky, Seth retired to his tent. He'd had an early start to the morning and needed to get some sleep. As his head rested against the pillow, his mind wandered to Maggie. What was she doing right now? The right side of his mouth curled. She was probably sitting in front of the vanity mirror running a brush through her hair, the long auburn locks cascading over her cotton gown. The memory of Maggie's ivory skin pressed against his as they slept beneath the quilt they'd been gifted for their wedding warmed his heart. Once he drifted off, his mind wandered to distressing scenes of defeats and failed missions making for a fitful night's sleep.

Chapter 11

Winter 1862

Elora

Elora had saved a great deal of money from her allowance in addition to some sewing work she'd done for a seamstress in town, enough to purchase an extra pistol, ammunition, a saddle, and a horse. She kept the bay gelding, Jasper, at a small stable just off campus and had been taking long rides to get acquainted with his quirks and habits. Thus far he'd been as solid as any horse she'd ever ridden, and she had full confidence he would serve her well.

She'd already sent a letter to her mother saying she and the mission group were finally leaving for Oregon. Elora gave several more letters to Annalissa who would mail them over the next couple of weeks, the last one explaining the work was so demanding she probably wouldn't be writing for a while. The beauty of her plan was that the college was actually sending a missionary group to Oregon to establish a church so if her mother contacted administrators the story was viable.

Glancing around her dorm room, Elora inhaled and slumped onto the bed. She knew sleeping on the ground, eating food cooked over a campfire, and using the woods to relieve herself would be less than ideal. The idea of facing guns and cannons was even more alarming.

Stop it, she thought. She couldn't let her imagination wander to the dangerous circumstances she was about to embark upon. All her planning was coming to fruition and Elora knew she was as ready as she could be.

A knock startled her from her musings. Opening the door, she found Annalissa standing in the hall.

"Come in," she said, motioning her friend inside.

Annalissa took a seat by the hearth while Elora sat on the edge of the bed. For a few moments the two ladies sat in silence until Annalissa smiled and pulled something from her coat pocket.

"I wanted to give you something to carry with you, a kind of good luck charm." She handed the small garnet crested flower brooch to Elora.

Taking the delicate pin, Elora gazed at its faceted gems sparkling in the candlelight.

"This is the brooch Maggie used to wear," Elora said, turning it over in her hand.

"Indeed. I gave it to her when she had to leave our farm to go live with you. It kept her safe and I hope it will do the same for you."

"Didn't this belong to your mother?" Elora asked.

"It did. She pinned it to my clothing when she sent me with the other escapees. It kept me safe in extraordinarily dangerous circumstances," she replied. "When I gave it to Maggie it was with the understanding she'd return it when we met again. As you know, she did just that. I'm giving you the same instructions. Wear it beneath your uniform and return it when you come home after the war."

Tears crested in Elora's eyes. With a nod, she met Annalissa's gaze. "I promise to give it back, unharmed, when I return."

Rising from the chair, Annalissa embraced Elora. "May the Lord be with you and keep you safe."

"Keep praying that every night," Elora whispered in her friend's ear.

Annalissa released her, walked to the door, and paused. "Until we meet again," she said before hurrying from the room and shutting the door behind her.

Elora stared at the brooch, tears cascading across her flushed cheeks as she placed it on the dresser. Swiping at the tears, she changed for bed and slipped beneath the downy quilt, unable to quiet her racing thoughts. There was still time to change her mind and stay at Oberlin. No one would be the wiser except for the regimental leaders when Walter Polk failed to arrive.

Curling deeper beneath the warmth of the covers, Elora considered her options. While others would be unaware of her cowardice, it was something she couldn't live with. She closed her eyes and took in a few deep breaths until her body released the tension holding it captive. In the morning, she'd rise early, pack her things, and get Jasper from the stables. She needed to leave as soon as possible before her confidence faded and she lost her nerve.

Chapter 12

April 1862

Maggie

M aggie, Willa, Letty, and Dr. Towne boarded the *Oriental* on a brisk spring morning bound for Charleston, South Carolina. Memories of her last voyage when her father had sent her to the Pennsylvania countryside to escape the famine in Ireland wafted through Maggie's mind. At least this steamer was more accommodating than the one from Ireland. The *Oriental* boasted nicely furnished quarters and palatable food, not to mention, she was traveling with three incredible ladies. Nevertheless, she spent the first day in a state of wooziness.

During the voyage, Dr. Towne discussed her plans for the new school while Maggie shared her knowledge of the climate, herbs, and other plantings available in the region. The trip was keeping Maggie's mind busy, something she desperately needed. Worry for Seth plagued her every day. A momentary pang of guilt plucked at her chest for keeping her venture from him, but she knew it was for the best.

One morning over breakfast, Dr. Towne shared recent news reports regarding the war.

"The conflict seems to be intensifying. Hard to believe it's been a year since Fort Sumter was fired upon," the doctor said, taking a sip of tea.

"Hopefully, it will end soon," Maggie replied, her heart sinking at the thought it was nowhere near an end. "At least we'll be busy caring for and educating the newly freed slaves."

"Indeed," Dr. Towne replied with a smile.

Maggie took in a deep breath. Education was the key to true freedom. She was thrilled to be embarking on a new adventure that allowed her to continue serving those who'd been held in bondage, something she hoped to continue after the war came to a close.

A little over a week later, the ship landed in Charleston, and they traveled by coach to the ferry dock at the waterfront in Beaufort, South Carolina. As they jounced along dirt roads, Maggie took in the familiar scent of home with its pungent aroma of pluff mud, the sticky sludge left exposed when the tide went out. The oyster beds were full and the salty marsh breezes brushed Maggie's cheek.

"It's hot as an oven down here," Letty complained, fanning herself. "How you stand this heat, Miss Maggie?"

"Stop all your fussin,'" Willa scolded. "You haven't been here an hour and you're already findin' fault with the place."

Dr. Towne smiled as they bumped along. No doubt, she was used to their bickering after working with them for a few years.

"We have ways to cope with the heat," Maggie replied, with a chuckle. "We wear thin, sheer fabrics and spend a great deal of time on the porch. There's almost always a breeze coming off the water which helps."

"Humph," Letty grumbled as Willa elbowed her friend.

The town was much changed since the last time Maggie had visited. Everything was chaotic and disheveled. The once tidy and well-kept store fronts were now run-down and disordered. Soldiers crowded the streets and loitered outside of buildings leering at ladies who passed by. The only comfort was seeing the Negroes walking about freely. Of course, the Union Army considered them contraband of war, which in Maggie's opinion still wasn't an acceptable situation.

When they reached the landing, the driver helped them from the coach and unloaded their things. Maggie shielded her eyes as sunlight glinted across the water. She watched as the ferry, a flat-bottomed wooden structure with no railings or seating, made its way to the dock and stopped for all to board.

"We're not getting on that thing, are we?" Letty declared, her eyes widening.

"It's perfectly safe," Maggie said. "It goes across the river several times a day."

"I'm beginning to miss home." Letty mumbled. "Don' know how I got talked into this."

"Hush now and give the place a chance," Willa said. "This is Maggie's home, no sense bein' disrespectful."

Letty grunted and gave Maggie an apologetic glance.

The ferry driver, a colored man in worn clothing, secured the vessel, and began loading the trunks with Dr. Towne and Maggie helping. Stepping onto the rocking vessel, Maggie steadied herself as best she could, followed by Dr. Towne, Willa, and Letty.

Once everyone had boarded, the ferryman pushed off the dock. Maggie's stomach lurched with the rocking of the ferry over rippling waters. She sat atop one of the trunks since there was nothing to cling to. The last thing she wanted to do was lose her balance and topple into the river. Dr. Towne and Willa did the same. Letty sneered as she glanced around before plunking onto her own small box, her bony knees jutting up to her chest as she sat.

After an hour of wavering across choppy tides, Maggie was thankful when they reached the shore of St. Helena Island and her wobbling legs stepped onto solid ground. With a few deep breaths to settle her wooziness, Maggie looked up and saw a stout colored man sitting on the bench seat of a wagon, a wide brimmed hat shading his round face.

"You mus' be de doctor," he said, a broad smile revealing a few missing teeth. "I's Henry. I's come from The Oaks to fetch you all."

He alighted to the ground and helped the ferryman unload the trunks.

"It's good to meet you, Henry," Dr. Towne said, putting her travel bag in the back of the wagon. "These are my assistants, Maggie, Willa, and Letty."

"We's been awaitin' your arrival," he puffed, loading the last trunk in the back of the wagon where Maggie sat with her friends.

"We're glad to be here," the doctor replied, sitting on the bench next to Henry.

"Speak for yourself," Letty grumbled.

Willa shot her a stern look while Maggie laughed. It was wonderful to be back in the Lowcountry with some of the dearest ladies she knew. If only it were under more pleasant circumstances, and with Seth by her side, she could enjoy it more.

Henry clucked to the horses and slapped the reins against their haunches, launching them forward. The wagon rocked and tottered along the rutted sandy road while Maggie took in the gentle sway of palmetto fronds and marsh grasses. A blue heron took flight when they passed by, its grand wing span floating on the warm breeze with its gangly legs drifting behind.

They turned down a narrow road canopied by towering Live Oaks with Spanish moss swaying gracefully as if waving them home. A modest two-story clapboard house appeared at the end of the lane, its double verandahs greeting them. Henry halted the horses and jumped to the ground. Maggie hopped down and took in her surroundings. Jasmine crawled across a trellis at the side of the home and a series of small outbuildings spotted the yard. The marsh abutted the property only a few feet from the house. Four wooden rockers swayed in the breeze on the first-floor verandah, pinching Maggie's heart. How she longed to rock on the porch of Rose Hall mansion with Elora, Seth, and the kids. Closing her eyes, she inhaled the mix of brackish marsh air and flora as her mind drifted back to that long ago memory.

Willa and Letty disembarked with Henry's assistance. A couple of men emerged from the house and helped Henry with the trunks. Maggie, the doctor, Willa, and Letty followed them inside. The place was modestly furnished and most of the worn pine floors were bare. Although not as grand as Rose Hall, it was homey.

"I've been told there are three rooms on the second floor. Choose where you wish to stay and take some time to get settled," Dr. Towne said. "We'll have tea in the front parlor in an hour."

Climbing the stairs, Maggie noticed the faded wallpaper and the occasional creak of a loose board. When she reached the top, she peered in the first room on the left.

"I'll take this room, if that's alright," Maggie said to Willa and Letty.

"That be fine," Willa replied, checking out one of the rooms across the hall.

Letty walked into the third room. "This place sure is big," she announced, shaking her head.

Maggie plunked her bags on the bed and scanned the space. An oval braided rug was to the side of the iron bed along with a small pine night table. A wardrobe and wash basin stood on the opposite wall. Windows at the front and side of the room allowed for a refreshing cross breeze.

Unpacking, Maggie placed a sepia photo of Seth, the silver locket that held locks of her parents' hair, and her Bible on the night table. After putting her clothing in the wardrobe, she washed her face and hands and headed downstairs.

Dr. Towne sat on a silken brocade chair and poured tea. Willa and Letty occupied the settee. Maggie took a seat in the chair next to the doctor, accepting the cup and saucer offered.

"I hope you don't take sugar in your tea since we haven't any at the moment. Luxuries such as those are rare with the blockades in place."

"I never use sugar, so I'll be fine." Maggie took a sip and placed the cup gently into the saucer. "I'm surprised you were able to get tea."

"I have a few resources that will keep us well stocked in certain things. Tea and coffee being two of them." Dr. Towne gave a modest grin before lifting the cup to her lips.

"Good to know. I needs strong coffee to get me moving in the morning," Letty announced.

"Speaking of that, we should discuss a few housekeeping things before we get started," the doctor said.

"Dr. Towne," Willa interrupted. "Letty and I been discussin' the livin' situation and we ain't comfortable in this house. If we're gonna work with these folks, we need to be near them."

The doctor rested her cup on the table and straightened in her chair. "What are you proposing?"

"Is there a place we could stay that's closer to the colored folks?"

"I believe the overseer's cottage is empty. Are you certain that's what you want?"

Letty and Willa nodded.

"We appreciate you offering for us to stay in the main house but we regular folks and prefer something that let us be with the people we're here to help."

"Alright, I'll make the arrangements. If there's anything you need at the cottage, please let me know and I'll do my best to get it. It's hard to tell how much damage the soldiers have done so some things might not be obtainable."

"We don't need nothin' fancy," Willa said with a simper.

Maggie's heart swelled. These were the things that made Willa and Letty so special. They were always thinking about others and content with the modest aspects of living.

Dr. Towne took another sip of tea and began. "Over the next few days, we'll get acclimated to our surroundings and begin our work as soon as possible. These people are in need of assistance, and we must be diligent." For the next hour, she detailed some of the expected duties for their time on the island.

As the dinner hour approached, Maggie, Letty, and Willa helped with preparations while Dr. Towne met with one of the commanders responsible for the island. Willa was in the kitchen and Maggie and Letty were setting the table. A scream pierced the air, as Letty jumped back, nearly knocking over a chair.

"What's the matter?" Maggie asked, grabbing her chest.

The slender black woman pointed with a shaky finger at the floor.

"It's alright, Letty," Maggie chortled. "It's only a Palmetto bug. They're harmless."

"What you call that nasty thing?"

"A Palmetto bug."

"Look like a giant cockroach to me," she scowled.

"Actually, it's a water bug. They fly."

"What?" Letty screeched. "You's tellin' me that creature can fly at me?"

"Yes," Maggie replied sheepishly.

"That does it! I's goin' home!" she declared. "Ain't no way I's stayin' in a place with flying cockroaches the size of my foot!"

Willa lumbered into the room, planting her hands on her ample hips. "What is all this squawkin'?" she huffed. "Sounds like the war done made its way into the house."

"Letty discovered a Palmetto bug," Maggie said, pointing at the sizable brown beetle tottering across the wood floor.

Willa gasped. "Ain't never seen a cockroach that big before!"

"Exactly," Letty said. "Which is why I's not staying another minute. Them monsters can fly!"

Willa's eyes grew as big as marbles. "That true, Miss Maggie?"

"I'm afraid so. But they're harmless. They don't bite."

"Ain't nothing that big harmless," Letty retorted. "If that thing fly at me and stick in my hair, I gonna drop over dead of a heart attack."

Maggie chuckled. "You'll get used to them; I promise."

With a shiver, Letty brushed past Willa toward the kitchen mumbling about not liking the south one bit.

"Is she going to be okay?" Maggie asked Willa.

"Don' know," she replied, still eyeing the crawling bug. "I

tell you one thing, if one of them fly at me, I might just be joinin' her on the next ship north."

Shaking her head, Maggie continued setting the table as Willa returned to the kitchen. She could hear Letty and Willa discussing the monstrous flying cockroaches, as they called them, amongst the clatter of dishes.

Another scream followed by the crashing of a plate let Maggie know they'd found another one. It seemed this was going to be a trying adjustment for them.

Dinner discussion revolved around getting settled and beginning work as soon as possible. Willa and Letty would spend the night at the main house and move to the cottage the following day.

Dr. Towne was a remarkable person. Not many women held a medical degree and, more or less, took on the responsibility of entering a war zone to educate newly freed slaves. Her intellect and courage were admirable.

Maggie's duties primarily involved creating remedies and ointments, growing herbs and vegetables, some canning, and possibly tending to those with minor medical needs. A thriving garden where she'd grow what she needed was situated between the house and the shed at the far end of the yard. Outside sources were practically impossible to depend upon with the blockades in place so they'd need to be self-reliant.

The most disturbing part of the conversation with Dr. Towne had been the rules regulating the area. There were curfews in place and credentials needed when traveling to town. The carefree existence Maggie had known in the Lowcountry before the war was drastically altered. The soldiers occupying the area were not always polite, so they needed to be on guard when in town. They were told not to engage with them unless necessary. Some of the men were gentlemanly while others were crude and, at times, obscene.

"I'll not be sending any of the colored women or children to town without an escort," Dr. Towne told them.

"Is it really that bad?" Maggie asked, shocked soldiers could be so unruly.

"I've heard tales of irresponsible and violent behaviors within the township. As I've said, the soldiers are occupying churches and houses. They've taken the liberty of destroying the furnishings and art in the finer homes. I won't even tell of the treatment of the freedmen. The army considers them contraband and treats them as such."

Exhausted from days of travel and the bleak description of the town's current state, Maggie made an early night of it. As her head rested on the pillow, she ruminated on everything the doctor had shared over tea and then dinner.

A soft breeze ruffled the cottony curtains as bullfrogs serenaded from the nearby marsh, rustling Maggie from her thoughts. As she lay in bed, the jasmine scented air lulled her into a peaceful slumber as visions of Seth with his sandy locks and cerulean blue eyes, followed her to dreamland.

The following morning, Maggie met with Dr. Towne in her office.

"Would you like to see your work space?" the doctor asked.

"Very much."

Dr. Towne escorted Maggie out the back door, across the yard, past a small patch of herbs soaking in the sunlight, to a whitewashed building with a tin roof. Stepping inside, Maggie looked around. It was smaller than her work space at Rose Hall but had all the things she'd need to mix remedies. Windows on either side allowed for breezes to filter through providing a respite from the sweltering Lowcountry heat.

"This will do just fine," Maggie said with a smile.

"Splendid. Can you start tomorrow?" Dr. Towne asked.

"I can begin today if you'd like."

"Take some time to get re-acquainted with the area. Once you get started, you'll find little time for anything else."

Dinner was a joyful event. Willa and Letty joined them at the long table in the dining room where they laughed and chatted throughout the meal. It was an amazing experience for Maggie to be sitting alongside two of her oldest friends again. Willa and Letty would always hold a special place in her heart. Had it not been for their strength and support when she was living with her abusive uncle, she'd have crumbled beneath his cruelty. Add all the things they'd taught her about herbal remedies and salves, and she could attribute her life and livelihood to them.

After supper, Dr. Towne went to her office to work while Willa, Letty, and Maggie swayed in the rockers on the front porch.

"This sure is some fine livin', ain't it?" Willa said, a smile plumping her cheeks.

"Indeed, it is," Maggie replied, as pungent marsh breezes rippled across her skin. "It's even better with you ladies here."

"These bugs ain't so good," Letty grumbled. "The mosquitos are likely to haul me off before long. Ain't never scratched so much in all my days."

Willa slapped Letty's upper arm. "Stop being so negative. So, there's a few more bugs, it's still a nice place."

"Humph, if you think cockroaches the size of mice and itty-bitty gnats that leave welts makes a place nice, then yes, it's wonderful," Letty said dramatically, rolling her eyes.

"Maybe we can mix something to repel the bugs," Maggie offered.

"I'm thinkin' a wooden bat would do the trick," Letty grumbled.

Willa huffed. "Ain't it good to know some things never gonna change?"

"Actually, it's splendid," Maggie replied as she closed her eyes and leaned her head against the rocker listening to the cicadas chirp a nightly serenade. It was good to be back in the Lowcountry, even if it wasn't at Rose Hall.

Chapter 13

July 1862

Maggie

It was a sweltering day in early July when Maggie took the ferry to town to pick up supplies for the school. She'd been looking forward to the trip after being on the island for so long. Dr. Towne was supposed to accompany her but had an emergency at the last minute. Not wanting to cancel the outing, Maggie decided to go on her own.

Months had passed since she'd arrived, and she'd worked from sun up to sun down. Maggie kept the herb gardens weeded and watered, created whatever medicinal remedies were needed, and occasionally helped teach a lesson or two with Dr. Towne. The men, women, and children who'd once been enslaved and denied the right to an education were dedicated to their learning. For some it was difficult to put aside work for lessons as they seemed bound to their former roles. Hopefully in time, they'd adjust to their newfound liberty and accept the things whites had taken for granted for so long. After years of helping escapees, Maggie enjoyed watching the newly freed folks being given the opportunity for an education.

The overgrown foliage, weed ridden landscape, and weathered buildings wrenched Maggie heart as she ambled down the main street of town, making her wonder how Rose Hall was faring. Was Bluffton also teeming with groups of soldiers gathered in alleys leering at the women who passed and calling out indecent propositions? Maggie held a hankie to her nose in an effort to block the stale scent of body odor and alcohol. All of a sudden, she was thankful to be staying on the island where breezes were fragranced by the brackish wetlands and budding flowers.

Maggie had been to Beaufort a few times in years past and knew a shortcut to the general store where she was heading. Her skin baked beneath the afternoon sun as sweat trickled down her neck and back. She scooted down an alley behind the store fronts where towering oaks provided a respite from the sun. She wiped the perspiration from her forehead when she heard someone crying.

Following the sound, Maggie came upon a small, wooded area behind the buildings. As she crept closer, the pleas became clearer. That's when Maggie noticed a soldier holding a young Negro woman down on the ground. The woman squirmed against him as his hands held her arms. She begged him to release her as he tried to maneuver himself between her legs.

Maggie's Irish spirit fueled her anger. She marched over to the man, grabbed the collar of his coat, and yanked. Apparently, her stealth approach startled him as he fell to the ground amidst a chorus of expletives, his trousers unbuttoned. The young colored woman leapt to her feet and ran the other direction, disappearing between the buildings.

"Stupid wench," the man said, getting to his feet. He swung his arm back and landed a slap across Maggie's face knocking her to the ground.

Stunned by the attack, Maggie's head spun as she tried to stand. The soldier kicked her side knocking the air from her lungs. Within seconds he was on top of her. She could feel the handle of her gun dig into her left hip where it was tucked into her waistband. The soldier pinned her arms over her head, his face inches from hers and his breath hot against her skin.

"Stupid little wench, you shouldn't have interrupted my date."

"Attacking a helpless woman isn't a date," Maggie spat back.

"She wasn't helpless, she's a stupid darky. They're happy to oblige us soldiers." Malice glimmered in his eyes as he leaned his body against hers, so she was unable to catch her breath or squirm free. "Guess you're my date now," he crooned, a wicked smile crinkling his eyes.

Fear raced through Maggie's body, her heart pounding as the soldier pressed his lips against hers. She struggled to move her arms, but his hold was strong as he maneuvered his legs in an attempt to separate hers. Panic gripped her chest. His kisses were violent and deep, and she feared she'd lose consciousness for the lack of air getting to her lungs.

She tried biting down on his tongue, but he drew his head back and smiled down at her. "Don't even think about it little lady. I got no problem gagging you if I have to."

Sweat dripped from his forehead onto her cheek mingling with the angry tears cascading down her face. She tried once more to jolt her body upward and push him off, but he was too heavy. All of a sudden, she felt his right knee shift her skirt. At that moment a shot rang out sending the soldier toppling backwards releasing his hold on her.

Scurrying to her knees, Maggie gasped for air. The soldier stood up and faced another man in uniform who sat atop a bay horse, the barrel of his gun still smoking.

"What are you doing, Sergeant?" the man on the horse demanded.

"Just havin' a little fun, sir," he replied, buttoning his trousers. "This little filly chased away my date, so she agreed to oblige me and have some fun."

Maggie managed to stand despite her wobbling legs.

"This man didn't have a date, as he claims," she said angrily. "He was forcing himself on the woman. She was trying to free herself and pleading for him to stop when I walked up."

"It weren't nothing more than a stupid darky," he replied, giving Maggie a sideways look, anger percolating in his stare.

"Be on your way, Sergeant. And don't let me catch you harassing another white woman again or I'll have you written up."

The sergeant shot a disdainful glance toward Maggie, before placing his cap upon his head. He strode off, cursing under his breath.

"Are you alright?" the man asked, still sitting on his horse.

"I most certainly am not!" she hollered. "That soldier meant to force himself on me and you let him walk away as if it were nothing!"

The man blew out a breath and met Maggie's angry glare. "You shouldn't have interrupted him. These men are under a great deal of stress and need some downtime."

"If down time means assaulting women, then you need to learn a few things," Maggie huffed, barely able to speak for the rage choking her words.

"He wasn't assaulting a woman; it was a darky. They don't know any better."

Fury coursed through Maggie's veins; her fists clenched at her sides. "How dare you say such a thing? They're human beings for goodness' sake!"

"It seems you and I have a different opinion." Reholstering his gun, the man gathered up the reins. "Are you going to be alright? Can I escort you somewhere?"

"I'd rather take my chances swimming with an alligator than spend another moment with a narrow-minded dolt such as yourself," she said, her limbs trembling.

Maggie turned on her heel and stormed back to the main street, too nervous to be out of public view. She made her way to the general store where she slumped down on a bale of hay by the front door in an effort to calm her quavering nerves. Fear and anger battled within her. She'd barely escaped the attack but the man's flippant attitude toward the colored folks was repulsive. She rested a bit longer until her breathing steadied and the trembling abated.

Standing up, she went into the store, gathered the necessary items she'd come for, and hurried back to the ferry. When she arrived at The Oaks she stormed inside where she crumpled onto the settee and wept. Violet, the cook, walked into the parlor and approached her.

Touching her arm, she spoke softly. "Is you okay, Miss Maggie? Can I gets you somethin'?"

"No, thank you, Violet," she replied, her eyes puffy and red.

"Let me bring you some herbal tea. I makes my own blend and it'll fix you right up," she smiled, rubbing Maggie's shoulder.

"That would be nice, thank you."

With a nod, Violet hurried from the room. Maggie rubbed the back of her neck trying to unknot the tension from the afternoon's events. Something had to be done about the soldiers inhabiting the town.

Maggie had been pacing her room for over an hour trying to figure out how to broach the topic with the doctor. Now she understood the warning about not going to town unescorted. Her emotions swayed from anger to terror to nausea. She'd come so close to being victimized. How could men behave so indecently, and in uniform?

Maggie's hands shook and her heart raced as if she'd been running for her life. In a sense she was fighting to maintain the life she'd known, one where she could go places without fear of being leered at or assaulted. She was aware of the abominable treatment showered on the newly freed slaves but to witness it by a man who was supposed to be defending the area was beyond comprehension. A small part of her wanted to go back to town, hunt the man down, and put a bullet in his head.

She stopped in the center of the floor, her hand covering her mouth as she contemplated the thought. When had she become so violent in her reactions? Then again, she'd felt this way on more than one occasion when transporting escapees. This was no different, except this time the man had turned on her as well. He was a menace to society and needed to be stopped. The ire of it all burned her throat as she resumed her pacing. When Dr. Towne returned to the house, she'd discuss it with her. Since the government had sent her here surely, she knew someone with the power to help.

The floor rattled with the closing of the front door below. The doctor was home. Maggie hurried down the stairs and nearly ran into Dr. Towne.

"My goodness, Maggie, what has you in such a rush?"

"Forgive me, Dr. Towne, but I need to speak with you about something of a disturbing nature."

"Come with me," she said, leading Maggie to her office. "Have a seat and let's discuss it." She motioned for Maggie to sit in the chair beside her. The doctor's dark brown eyes radiated concern.

Maggie took in a deep breath to steady her rapid pulse. "Today when I was in town, I stumbled upon a soldier trying to force himself on a young colored woman."

"Is she alright?" Dr. Towne asked, straightening in her chair. "Did you bring her here?"

Shaking her head, Maggie exhaled before sharing the rest of the story. "I pulled the man off and she ran away."

"Thank goodness," Dr. Towne replied, leaning back in her seat. "I'm glad you were able to help her. These men can be animals at times."

"It didn't end there. The soldier was so enraged over my interference that he knocked me to the ground and attempted..." Maggie's words dropped off as the memory of the incident blocked her ability to speak.

Dr. Towne reached across and took Maggie's hand. "Are you alright?" she asked softly, her gaze resting on Maggie's flustered expression.

Maggie nodded. "Another soldier rode up and fired his weapon scaring the man off me." She swallowed hard as she twisted her hands in her lap. "The beast blamed me for interrupting his actions and said I needed to pay for what he'd missed out on." Maggie paused and wiped a tear from her cheek. "I expected the miscreant to be charged but instead the other soldier released him and told him not to harm another white woman or he'd be reprimanded. Then he told me I shouldn't have interfered because the Negroes were too stupid to know any better." A sob fell from Maggie's lips as anger and frustration shook her shoulders.

Dr. Towne held Maggie's hand until she'd calmed a bit.

"I'm terribly sorry you experienced something so horrible. As I said, these men seem to think they have the right to do as they please because they occupy the area," the doctor said. "I don't mean to berate you, but this is why I cautioned you from going to town on your own."

"I'm sorry to disobey your wishes. I only wanted to get the supplies we needed."

"I appreciate that and I'm glad you weren't injured. We have a guest coming to dinner this evening. He has a great deal of influence here. I think you need to share this with him, unless you're uncomfortable doing so. Otherwise, I'll gladly address it with him myself."

Maggie breathed a sigh of relief. The doctor wasn't going to sit by and allow women to be treated in such a manner, regardless of their skin color. It was one more aspect that bolstered Maggie's admiration for her.

"I'm willing to tell him what happened. Thank you, Dr. Towne." Maggie released her hand and stood. "I probably need to get some work done before supper. I was too upset when I returned so I'm behind on some of my duties."

"Nonsense," Dr. Towne replied, "You've been through a shock and should relax. Whatever needs to be done can wait until tomorrow."

"With all due respect, I'd feel better if I kept busy."

"Of course. But if you need to rest, take the time to do so. I need you at your best which means you have to take care of yourself, not just those around you."

With a nod, Maggie started for the door when Dr. Towne called out.

"Maggie, thank you for saving that woman today. That took a lot of courage."

With a nod, Maggie left the room and went back to work in the shed where she pounded out her frustrations as she pummeled herbs.

At seven o'clock, Maggie made her way downstairs for supper. She'd changed into a clean frock of green gingham and had her auburn hair pulled into a twist. She wanted to appear refined for the dignitary coming to dinner. Maggie hadn't thought to ask if he was assigned to the area or visiting from Washington. Regardless, she'd find out soon enough and wanted to put forth a good impression, if not for herself then for Dr. Towne. Too often men viewed women as hysterical and ridiculous. Maggie's heart fluttered as Seth's face entered her mind. He'd never treat a woman of any color with indignity. He accepted Maggie's independence and intelligence without reservation. It was one of the things she loved most about him. He was always kind, gentle, and respectful.

Voices drifted from the parlor catching Maggie's attention. She could see the back of a soldier who was speaking with Dr. Towne. Dressed in a blue uniform with a firearm holstered at his side, he was tall in stature with light brown hair curling at the base of his neck. Perhaps he was the escort for the gentleman who was coming to dinner.

Dr. Towne looked up and smiled at Maggie.

"Mrs. Daniels, please come meet our guest, Major James Brunson," she said, waving Maggie over.

Maggie entered the room as the man turned. Her heart caught when his deep brown eyes met hers. Rage bubbled in her gut as she fought to keep her emotions under control. The wretched soldier who'd come to her aid earlier in the day stood before her. He took in a deep breath, his cheeks coloring slightly as he stood tall in his Union blue. While he may have saved her from an unconscionable act, his narrowminded views were still repulsive to her.

"Major Brunson, this is Mrs. Maggie Daniels."

"We've already met," Maggie said.

The major's eyes darted to the floor momentarily before he spoke. "Indeed, we have."

"When did you meet each other?" Dr. Towne asked, cocking her head.

"Earlier this afternoon," Maggie replied, lifting her chin.

"I see," Dr. Towne breathed, moistening her lips. "Perhaps we should go to the dining room and be seated. Dinner will be served in a few minutes."

Major Brunson held out his hand directing the ladies to proceed him. Entering the dining room, Maggie sat in her usual place while Dr. Towne sat at one end of the mahogany table and the major at the other.

Violet hurried into the room and placed a tray with biscuits, a small roasted chicken, and potatoes in the center of the table.

"Violet, please be sure to serve the madeira wine the Major was kind enough to bring," Dr. Towne said.

The major shook his head and smiled. "That was a gift for you to enjoy," he replied. "I've got access to plenty more should I desire it."

"Very well. Thank you for your thoughtfulness."

All lowered their heads as the doctor said grace. Maggie's jaw clenched as Violet proceeded to serve the meal. An uncomfortable silence blanketed the room as silver clinked against china. Finally, Dr. Towne spoke.

"It seems we have something of a dilemma this evening. Shall we discuss it over dinner or wait until after?"

Her no-nonsense approach unlocked the tension holding Maggie's shoulders hostage. The major put his fork down and folded his hands.

"I came upon an unfortunate incident today behind one of the downtown buildings. I don't want to rehash the details of the situation in order to prevent any further discomfort to Mrs. Daniels, as it was of a sensitive nature."

Maggie dropped her utensils onto her plate, her Irish temper flaring in her eyes.

"Sensitive is an understatement. That man meant to force himself on me after I prevented him from doing the same to another woman," she said, her voice quaking with rage.

"A darky," the major corrected, "not another woman, per se."

"How dare you?" Maggie uttered through gritted teeth.

Dr. Towne intervened. "Obviously, Major, you've hit a nerve with Mrs. Daniels, and with me. We are all God's children, regardless of our skin color, and deserve the same dignified consideration and treatment."

"Forgive me, Dr. Towne, but we will have to disagree on that particular point. I've been around these people all my life. They haven't the intellect or cognizance to know any better."

Dr. Towne gave a stern look to Maggie, who'd opened her mouth to speak, letting her know she needed to let her handle this. Maggie bit her lower lip and stared at her plate in an effort to thwart her tongue from loosening.

"Major Brunson, Mrs. Daniels and I have worked closely with the freedmen and have garnered a much more favorable impression of their capabilities. They are every bit as intelligent and caring as any other group of people I've encountered in my travels. In fact, I have several who work with me creating herbal remedies and other vital concoctions for my work. If any harm were to come to them, I would have no problem alerting my contacts in both Pennsylvania and Washington." She lifted the crystal goblet to her lips and delicately sipped her drink.

The major ran his tongue across his teeth. "I understand completely, Dr. Towne, and I appreciate your candor. I'll take what you've said under consideration. While I cannot guarantee what the men do out of my sight, I will attempt to be equitable should I catch them doing anything untoward to any of the females in the area."

"Thank you, Major. I knew we'd find a way to rectify the situation. Now let's enjoy the rest of our supper before it gets cold, shall we?"

Although pacified by Dr. Towne's ability to work toward a

solution, Maggie doubted the major would see it through. His inaction earlier in the day was deplorable and she considered him as much the enemy as those who'd held the Negroes in bondage. Whether he owned slaves or not, his indifference for human beings based on their skin color was disgraceful. Maggie ate the rest of the meal in silence as Dr. Towne and the major discussed other concerns regarding supplies and her mission to educate the freedmen and women.

When the plates were empty, they escorted the major to the front door.

"Thank you, Dr. Towne, for a lovely evening. Your cook is exceptionally talented. Not many people could make such meager offerings so delicious."

"You're quite welcome, Major," the doctor replied with a smile. "I will share your compliments with Violet."

"Mrs. Daniels, please accept my sincerest apologies for your encounter earlier. I truly did not mean to offend you. My duties here are perilous. I fear my lack of response was indefensible," the major said with a bow.

"I accept your apology but still find your views of the Negroes disgraceful."

A slight smile wrinkled his eyes. "Perhaps you can help alter my views."

"Perhaps," she replied.

"I look forward to your attempts," he said, his smile broadening as he placed his hat upon his head and marched across the yard for his horse. Maggie closed the door behind him, relieved he was gone. It had been some time since anyone had stoked her anger as he had, and she found it oddly satisfying.

Maggie and the doctor walked to the parlor and sat down. Dr. Towne poured them each a glass of madeira wine.

"So, your first impression of the major was less than stellar, I take it," Dr. Towne said, handing the glass to Maggie.

"You could say that," Maggie replied, sitting straighter. "How can you keep your anger under control? I know you don't agree with his views."

"He's a man with a great deal of influence and I feel certain he'll be able to deal with the situation. While I do not agree with his perspective, alienating him won't help our cause. My duties here include being able to intermingle with the military leaders as well as tending and teaching the freedmen and women. I owe it to them to handle things in the most diplomatic manner possible," she said, raising her eyebrows.

"I'd like to be as composed and yet every time I think of him my blood boils."

"Understandable, considering all you've been through today. You were violently assaulted, Maggie. Don't belittle what you've suffered. Keep in mind, that although his view of the freedmen is repulsive, he did come to your aid."

Maggie swallowed hard. Being a woman was degrading at times. She was expected to thank a man who did nothing to prevent her attacker from repeating his deeds. As if she could read Maggie's thoughts, Dr. Towne spoke.

"Don't dwell on the unfairness of the situation. We have a long way to go for equitable treatment not only for those with a different skin color but for our gender as well. I can attest to that. Medical school is not considered a favorable choice for a lady. But I persevered and have shown myself to be competent as well as compassionate which is more than I can say for many of the gentlemen in my profession." Dr. Towne leaned back in the chair and sipped her wine.

"I understand what you're saying, and I agree with you. There were times when we were transporting escapees and I had to act like I was weak and vulnerable in order to blend in despite the degradation of it." Maggie blew out a breath. "I'll do my best to be civil to the major, but I fear that's as much as I can promise for now."

"That's all I can ask of you."

Maggie rose from her chair, her back stiff from being thrown to the ground earlier. "I'm going to bed," she said, setting the wine glass on the table.

"Goodnight, Maggie. I'll see you at breakfast."

Maggie trudged up the stairs, her legs weighted with fatigue. Once inside her room, she changed into her night gown and slid between the cottony sheets. Marsh breezes floated through the room caressing her cheek as she closed her eyes. She focused on Seth and her children in an effort to distract her weary heart from the trauma and unfairness of the afternoon. Thankfully, slumber escorted her to dreamland in a matter of minutes where visions of Rose Hall with family and friends filled her mind.

Chapter 14

Late Summer 1862

Elora

Taking in a deep breath, Elora closed her eyes and reclined on her cot. It had been an exhausting few days and now more than ever, she was missing the comforts of home. Between riding over hilly terrain with little time to eat or rest, her muscles ached and her once flawless hands were weathered and blistered. She'd just drifted off when one of the soldiers barged into her tent.

"Lieutenant!" he hollered.

Bolting upright, Elora rubbed her eyes. "Yes, Corporal."

"The captain needs to see you. It's urgent."

Elora jumped to her feet. "I'll be there directly." Thankfully, her voice was always scratchy and deep after awakening.

Three months had passed since Elora had cut off her coffee brown tresses, donned a blue uniform, and joined the Union Army. She'd been fearful about how well she'd be able to blend in and was pleasantly surprised to find it was easier than she'd anticipated. In fact, she was such a good shot and solid rider that her commanding officer had taken a shine to her. Captain Dixon was a hard driven yet fair man who was a brilliant strategist. Of medium build with gray-blue eyes and light brown hair, he was an exceptional equestrian and had gained the respect and devotion of his troops. Most importantly, he was in favor of dissolving slavery from the country.

All these factors made it easier for Elora to serve under him. Even better, the captain had her scouting due to her strong riding skills and her ability to surveil enemy movements without detection. Her duties as a scout kept her from the front lines for which she was thankful. While prepared to do battle, Elora was hoping to avoid direct confrontation as much as possible. The strain of hurting her parents should she be wounded, or killed, was a burden she carried every moment of every day. Of course, soldiering was constant, leaving her little time to dwell on the 'what ifs.'

The most difficult part of her subterfuge was tolerating the crude behavior and disgusting habits of the other men. Spitting, belching, and passing gas seemed to be a form of entertainment for them. In order to blend in, she laughed along with them and at times participated in their antics.

The food was edible albeit simple. What she wouldn't give for some of Miss Clara's scones. Not that she'd expected gourmet meals, feather down pillows, or soft sheets, but her current living conditions were deplorable compared to what she'd known at Rose Hall. The most challenging aspect of her situation was using the facilities. Her ability to urinate was greatly restricted by her anatomy thus she had to make sure to do so when no one was around.

Sometimes at the end of a particularly stressful day, she'd contemplate all the things she wanted to do when the war was over. First and foremost, was to swim in the river that ran behind her home without worry about how she was dressed. Secondly, she wanted to sit at a table for dinner and eat off of fine china using utensils. Finally, she longed to curl up in her own bed and doze off to the serenity of croaking bullfrogs, cicadas, and the salty breath of the marsh.

Tearing her mind from her ruminations, Elora pulled on her coat and boots and ran for the captain's tent. She'd made a habit of sleeping in her clothes for this very reason. While uncomfortable having her chest bandaged for so long, she couldn't risk being discovered in situations such as this. The only time she could get a break from the constrictive nature of hiding her curves was when she was out scouting and could take a quick dip in a river or creek.

Entering the captain's tent, she stood at attention.

"At ease, Polk. Have a seat."

"Yes, sir," she replied in her surliest voice, sitting on the chair across from his desk.

Glancing around the tent, she took in the orderly manner of the space housing all the things necessary for the captain to carry out his duties efficiently. The desk where she sat was near the tent flap allowing outside light to stream across maps and papers. His cot was nestled on the opposite side with an oil lamp perched on a small round table. A wool blanket covered the straw stuffed mattress with a patchwork quilt folded at the end. Odd, Elora thought. The quilt looked out of place with its pastel-colored squares. It gave a feminine touch to the captain's quarters making Elora wonder who had made it and why the captain chose to carry it into battle.

"I've just received word that my aide-de-camp has been shot."

"I'm sorry, sir. How long will Hendrickson be recuperating?"

"He won't. He's dead."

Elora nodded. He was a good man, and she was sorry he was gone. Clearing her throat, she met the captain's stare, awaiting his instructions. No doubt, he was sending her out to locate whoever had killed Hendrickson.

"Polk, I'm assigning you to the position immediately."

Elora sat up straighter, shock pulsing through her limbs. "Thank you, sir."

"Get some rest. We've got a busy day tomorrow."

"Yes, sir," she declared before leaving his tent. Her heart palpitated in rhythm with the swiftness of her gait as she marched across the field to her quarters. "Aide-de-camp to the captain," she muttered as she removed her coat and boots. She'd be writing and delivering orders for him. Obviously, the captain saw something in her, especially since there were other men with more experience. Nevertheless, it would keep her from being put on the front lines. On the other hand, she'd be doing a lot of stealth and dangerous errands. But she could handle it. She'd done well thus far and planned on continuing with her efforts. The thrill of contributing to the war alongside men who didn't suspect her true gender was like a jolt of adrenaline. The more she experienced it the more she wanted to continue.

A few months later, Elora was traveling with a message for a nearby regiment. Dark clouds loomed overhead shadowing the underbrush as she rode Jasper through the woods. Laughter drifted through the trees, catching her attention. Following the sound, she came to the edge of a clearing where a two-story farmhouse, in a state of disrepair stood just beyond the edge of the wooded area. A man and two ladies sat on the front porch chatting and laughing as if it were a peaceful Sunday afternoon.

She'd have no choice but to ride past them to get to her destination. Normally that wouldn't have been an issue except she caught a glimpse of something interesting in the older woman's lap. Obviously, their allegiance was with the south as Elora recognized the pattern of the flag the woman was stitching. She'd heard rumors there were southern sympathizers in the north and border states but she'd yet to encounter any. All of a sudden, an idea popped into her head. She shed her coat and hat and stashed them in the woods. She mussed up her hair, wiped her face, and pinched her cheeks. Concern niggled at her nerves over her trousers but there was nothing she could do about that. Hopefully, she'd come up with a clever excuse should they ask about her attire, which they likely would.

She rode Jasper leisurely to the front porch where three sets of eyes scrutinized her appearance. The woman had slipped the flag into her sewing bag right before Elora halted at the porch stairs.

"Good day," she said, shocked to hear her own female voice for the first time in months. "I hope you don't mind but I seem to have lost my way."

The man clutched a corn cob pipe between his jagged teeth and leaned forward. "Don't believe I know you. Where'd you come from?" His glare sent a shiver through Elora's body.

Putting forth her best portrayal of a helpless lady, she fluttered her lashes and frowned. "I'm from the neighboring town but fear I've gotten well off track. Those blasted Yankees were in the woods, and I didn't want to encounter them, so I took a different route," she gasped, feigning tears. "I can't stand those wretches and was too afraid to let them see me. I've heard what they do to southern ladies."

The woman who'd been sewing pushed her lower lip out a bit. "You poor thing. They are scoundrels!"

The other woman, who seemed considerably younger than her counterpart, chimed in. "What happened to your hair? It's awfully short for a girl," she said, narrowing her eyes.

Elora's heart thumped against her ribs. This woman wasn't

as easily fooled, and her short hair was a beacon that something was amiss. Elora conjured up a sob.

"Those horrid Yankees came to our house weeks ago. They beat my pa and took all our chickens. My ma is sick in bed. When I tried to fight them off, they said I was more of a man than my pa so they held me down and cut my hair." Elora rubbed at the nonexistent tear on her cheek. "I left early this morning to search for food when I heard a group of them. I was so scared; I took a different route. I'm from Butler."

"Butler?" the man declared. "That ain't the neighboring town, that's miles from here. How'd you get so far off track?"

"I'm that far away?" she cried. "Wow, I really did panic." All those years of playing make-believe with Seth when she was younger were paying off. She could tell by the old man's demeanor that he was buying everything she was peddling.

"Your clothes are odd," the seamstress noted.

"They burned all my dresses. The final insult. All I got to wear now are my brother's clothes. We ain't got no money and hardly any food. My pa can't work after the beating he took."

"Come on inside, honey," the seamstress said. "I gots an old dress that'll fit ya."

Elora dismounted and followed the woman into the house. The interior of the home was musty and drab but well kept. She waited as the woman looked through an old trunk at the foot of her bed and removed a homespun checkered cotton dress in varying shades of brown and purple.

"This oughtta fit," she said holding the dress up to Elora's chest.

"I believe it will, thank you." She took the dress and draped it over her arm.

"Would you like to change in the next room?"

"Thank you but I'd feel more comfortable changing when I get home. I cannot thank you enough for your generosity."

The seamstress pulled Elora into a hug and whispered in her ear, "We southerners gots to stick together."

"Yes, we do," Elora responded, following her to the front porch where she took her seat.

"A few miles west we gots a small group of men waitin' on this here flag," she said, pulling the cloth from her basket where she'd stashed it when Elora had ridden up. "Their numbers are low, but they still got a lot of fight left in 'em. I'm just sorry the only thing I can offer is to sew a new flag, but at least I'm doin' my part to support the cause," she said with a determined nod.

"I understand completely," Elora responded. "Wish there was something I could do to help."

The seamstress's head tilted back as a laugh erupted from her lips nudging a chuckle from the old man and the other lady.

"There's plenty you can do. This group of soldiers is headin' for Butler tomorrow. There's a Yankee group supposed to be in that area, and they got their sights set on revenge for the last battle." She grinned at Elora. "If you're able to locate some food, maybe you could find a way to get our men something to eat. I know they'd be much obliged."

Before Elora could answer, the old man spoke up. "No one would fault you for not wanting to get involved. If you get caught it won't be pleasant for you or your kin. Them Yankees done some bad things to women."

"I already survived them once and I'm certain I can handle any Yankee that crosses my path again," Elora said, patting the pistol at her side.

The seamstress sat straighter and smiled, revealing a couple of missing teeth. "You're a brave little thing. Bet your mama's mighty proud of you."

"She is very proud, thank you."

Elora continued her charade of being lost and asked for the shortest route back to Butler. After they gave her directions, she bid them goodbye, stuffed the dress in her saddle bag, and took the route they'd suggested. Once in the woods, she doubled back to get her coat and hat and completed her original mission.

Her mind raced with the possibilities of her recent encounter. She'd been able to glean valuable information by posing as a southerner who'd been mistreated by the Yankees. Even better, her feminine manner and southern accent seemed to lend credence to her persona making those supporting the Confederacy believe she was like them. She smiled to herself as she realized she'd found another way to support the war efforts. And just like that, a new identity was born.

Jasper's hooves pounded the ground as Elora rode back to her regiment. She ducked and dodged all manner of low-lying limbs, her pulse racing as fast as her horse's galloping legs. As she neared the encampment, the smell of campfire smoke floated on the air. She slowed Jasper to a walk and considered how she would deliver the information to the captain. When she had the story straight in her head, she nudged Jasper into a trot and went straight for the captain's quarters. Dismounting, she draped the reins over a tree limb and stood in the tent opening, her heart beating with the speed of hummingbird wings. The captain looked up from his desk and leaned back in his chair.

"What news have you got, Polk?" he asked, motioning for her to sit in the chair across from him.

"I've important information sir," she replied, sitting down. She proceeded to tell him about the small group of Confederates planning to attack the nearby town of Butler.

The captain rubbed his forehead. "You sure about this, Polk? I've had different reports about that group. Their numbers are low but they're dangerous. They'll use any tactics necessary to win."

"My source is reliable."

"Care to share the name of that source?" he asked, arching his eyebrows.

"Her name is Laura, and she supplies information to the Union. I trust her as much as I trust myself, sir." Using a variation of her own name seemed fitting as her secret identity.

His head bobbed several times. "Good enough for me. If you find her reliable then I'll take you at your word."

Leaning his elbows on the desk, the captain sat quietly for a few moments. "Polk, tell Jansen and Briggs to come in here. I have a mission for them," he said, a half-smile curling the right side of his mouth.

After sending Jansen and Briggs to the captain, Elora untacked Jasper, rubbed him down, and carried her saddle bags back to her tent. She pulled out the dress and smiled. When her stomach protested its empty state with a rumble, she stuffed the frock back into the saddle bag, and stashed it under her cot. Another round of grumbles and groans rolled through her gut reminding her she'd not eaten since morning. Feeling haggard, Elora made her way to the fireside where several men devoured whatever concoction the cook had thrown together for supper. She fixed a plate of rice and beans, grabbed a cup of coffee, and joined her fellow soldiers.

Chapter 15

September 1862

Maggie

Maggie pummeled away at a diuretic concoction of dandelion, burdock, sarsaparilla, and blue flag root as a breeze drifted through the door of the shed. Sweeping her hand across her brow, she continued crushing herbs in the well-worn stone bowl when hoofbeats pounded up the drive. She put the pestle down, wiped her hands on her apron, and stepped from within the shed. Her heart sank as she watched Major Brunson dismount his horse and walk onto the front porch of the house. Maggie was tempted to go back to work and ignore his arrival but thought better of it. Dr. Towne had made it clear that he was an asset whether she agreed with his personal views or not. Regardless of her dislike for the man, she had to play nice, at least for now.

Maggie made her way across the lawn and greeted him on the porch.

"Good afternoon, Major. Can I help you with something?"

Removing his hat, he stepped toward her. "I came to speak with Dr. Towne. Is she here?"

"She's tending one of the children who was injured at

school today." Maggie delivered the statement curtly. No doubt, he'd think the doctor was wasting her time tending to the Negroes. The idea fueled Maggie's indignation, making her want to say something snide. Instead, she bit her lower lip to prevent the words from tumbling out of her mouth.

"Perhaps you could help me," he said, glancing down at the ground. His light brown hair was cut just above his broad shoulders and his hazel eyes revealed a hint of sadness. He was a tall man with a commanding presence that seemed to whither at this particular moment as his shoulders slumped.

"What is it you need?"

"It's a bit...embarrassing."

Maggie furrowed her brows. "I can't imagine it could be all that bad."

He inhaled. "I seem to have some sort of rash."

Maggie's nurturing side took hold, temporarily dwarfing her anger.

"Come with me to the shed and I'll have a look at it."

He followed her to her workspace, removed his coat, and rolled up his sleeve. The skin around his wrist and forearm was welted and red.

"My goodness, that is nasty," she said, reaching for a jar of salve on the shelf behind her. "Why are you embarrassed about this?"

"I was foraging around the woods the other day and sat beneath a tree to rest. I didn't pay attention to where my hand was until the ants started biting. Apparently, I disturbed a rather large ant hill." He scrunched his lips as his cheeks colored.

Maggie stifled a laugh. "Ant bites are problematic around here. Have you had a reaction to them before?"

"Never. Then again, the ants in the northeast aren't as vicious as the southern ones."

"I'm sure you'll find a great many things in the south distasteful." She regretted the words as soon as they left her lips. The doctor had told her to be pleasant. "I'm sorry Major, that wasn't very considerate of me."

"No need to apologize. I appreciate your candor," he said softly, watching as she cleansed the area and applied the gooey balm.

"My candor, as you so eloquently put it, tends to get me into a great deal of trouble at times."

"Like when you're trying to save someone else?" he said, arching his brows as he rolled his sleeve back down and slipped on his coat.

"Exactly," she replied. Maggie wanted to stay angry with the major but there was something gentle in his eyes, not to mention his sudden timidity, that softened her feelings toward him.

"Mrs. Daniels, I want to apologize for my insensitive behavior the other day. I should have been more...accommodating to your situation."

Maggie glanced out the window. "Thank you." Looking back at him, she noticed his demeanor was much altered from their previous encounters. He seemed kinder and more human. "I'm sure your job puts you in a precarious position when having to lead and discipline your men."

He nodded. "It is a delicate balance and one that doesn't always allow me to be impartial. We're at war. These men wouldn't necessarily be my first choice of comrades in other circumstances, yet we're forced into service together. We're armed, far from our homes and families, and under constant alert. It's a dangerous combination."

Maggie resealed the jar and handed it to the major.

"Take this with you and apply it three times a day. But

cleanse the area first. If it isn't better in a couple of days, come back and let Dr. Towne have a look at it."

"Thank you, Mrs. Daniels. It feels better already."

"I'm glad," she replied with a slight smile.

The major placed his hat upon his head, gave a nod, and left.

Maggie returned to her work, surprised to find the hard feelings she'd been harboring toward the major begin to crumble. War did make for difficult times. Maybe Dr. Towne was correct. With a bit of her influence, Maggie might be able to help the major see the Negroes for the amazing people they were and that they deserved liberty as much as anyone else in the country.

Later that evening, Maggie swayed in the rocker on the porch, listening to the crooning of bullfrogs and cicadas. The creaking of the rocker rungs against the floorboards soothed her weary soul as her mind drifted back to the day's events, specifically the major's visit. The screen door screeched as Dr. Towne stepped from the house and settled in the chair next to Maggie.

"How was your day?" she asked.

"Interesting," Maggie replied with a sigh.

"How so?" the doctor said, leaning her head back as she rocked.

"The major came by to see you."

"About what?"

"He had an unfortunate encounter with an ant hill," Maggie replied.

"Oh dear. Terrible reaction?"

"To say the least. One of the worst I've seen. I cleansed the skin and applied a salve. I gave instructions and sent the jar with him."

They rocked for a few moments before Maggie spoke again.

"He seemed more pleasant this time and actually apologized for the other day."

"Did you accept his apology?"

"I did. He seemed sincere and I appreciate that. His attitude still galls me, but I understand your point about trying to help him see the error of his views towards the Negroes."

Dr. Towne smiled. "And thus, you've taken your first step into the diplomatic realm of wartime interactions. Well done, Maggie."

Chapter 16

October 1862

Elora

"Polk!" the captain hollered as Elora strode past his tent. Dark circles shadowed his eyes as he ran his hand through his hair.

Elora hurried over to him, wondering what had him in such a state.

"I've just received word of an ambush a few miles from here. Seems a few stray Rebs took out several of our men. I need you to check into this and bring me any information you can glean," he commanded. "And Polk...."

"Sir?"

"Take care."

After giving her the coordinates, he plunked onto his desk chair and stared at several maps.

Over the past few months, Elora had been able to steal away from her duties as aide-de-camp, change into the dress, and scout around the outskirts of towns for information about confederate movements. It never ceased to astound her how much people trusted her and the depth of information they provided. A hint of guilt pervaded her soul for her actions since she too was a southerner, but a southerner who believed in the country as a whole. She pushed away thoughts of childhood friends who may be in harm's way, then again, she had family and friends fighting on the Union side as well. One thing was certain, war made for the most uncomfortable and unprecedented circumstances, intensifying Elora's desire for peace.

The travesties of war were weighing heavily on her psyche. She was busier than ever trying to maintain two personas, neither of which were her. Her captain had entrusted her with more than most aides for which she was thankful. And yet, she found spying more fulfilling and exciting. The people with whom she spoke were incredibly gullible, judging her to be one of them based on her accent and words. It was entirely too simple.

If she planned her route carefully, she'd have an opportunity to assist her fellow soldiers while also gathering information from any confederates she encountered. She packed the dress in her saddle bags just in case. Hopefully, Elora a.k.a. Laura Kirk, would make an appearance on this mission.

Hours later, Elora was on her way back to the captain with news of an unexpected shift in the Confederates' route. Stopping in a heavily wooded area, she dismounted, and shimmied out of the dress she'd worn to get information from a group of Rebs. After slipping back into her uniform, she mounted Jasper, and started on her way when she heard muffled groans coming from a clump of trees nearby.

Fearful of what she might discover, she approached stealthily until she could ascertain the situation. Prodding Jasper closer, Elora peered through the branches where she caught a glimpse of the source of the sound. Three soldiers in blue surrounded a soldier in gray, one on each side holding his arms while the other barked commands.

"Tell us who you're spyin' for," the taller man hollered, kicking the prisoner in the gut.

The man in gray choked as the man's boot met his stomach.

"Can't hear you Rebel!" he yelled.

"Stop kicking me and maybe I'll be able to answer you," he spat.

The Union man leaned over, his face inches from the confederate prisoner's.

"Stupid rebel, I oughta kick the crap out of you until you're dead," he growled. "Now tell me who you're with or I'll kill you slow."

"I already told you, I'm on your side. I gave you the code word. Check with your commanding officer. He'll confirm what I'm saying is true."

"How stupid do I look rebel? I know a conman when I see one. No doubt, you acquired that code word from a weak soldier. You probably beat it outta him and now I'm going to return the favor." The Union soldier drew back his fist and landed a hit across the man's jaw sending blood spurting across his uniform.

Elora started to turn around and leave the men to continue their interrogation when she noticed something familiar about the man in gray. A long scar ran down the right side of his face. She blinked a few times trying to process the scene but there was no denying it. The wavy hair, the scar, the blue eyes; this wasn't any soldier, this was Seth!

Her heart stuck in her throat as she pondered what to do. She and Seth were outnumbered but she was an aide to the captain of her regiment and wearing blue. They'd listen to her. Without another thought she spurred Jasper forward and rode into the area where the men stood.

"What seems to be the problem?" she asked in her gruffest voice, pulling Jasper up behind the soldier who had hit Seth.

He glanced at her, scrutinizing her uniform. "Who are you?" he grumbled.

"That's Lieutenant. What are you doing with this man?"

"He's a Confederate spy," he said, his mouth crinkling into a sneer as he spat on the ground.

"He's obviously a rebel but what makes you believe he's spying for them?" She tried to stay as neutral as possible even though her heart was pounding so hard against her ribcage, she was certain they could hear it in the next county. All she wanted was to free Seth and get him to safety. Then she could find out what had transpired.

"He claims to be on our side. Says he's the spymaster for Colonel Pennington but I don't buy his lies."

The men holding Seth's arms glared at her.

"Isn't there a specific code word to reveal whether he's one of ours?"

"Yeah, he gave us the code word but his accent don' agree with it so I took the liberty of interrogating him." His eyes sparkled as he said it.

"Maybe that's what makes him a successful spy." Looking at Seth, she issued an order. "On your feet Rebel."

The two men helped him up, blood dripping from a swollen lip and a gash across his forehead. Elora was trying to figure out why Seth was wearing gray. He'd made it abundantly clear the last time she saw him he'd be fighting for the Union. What had happened to make him change his mind?

Seth spit a wad of blood on the ground before shifting his blue gaze to meet hers.

"Who are you with?" she asked.

"Colonel Pennington with the Pennsylvania Cavalry."

"What's the word?" Elora asked, struggling to keep her emotions intact. Seth's haggard demeanor ripped at her heart.

"Celatum," he replied flatly.

Elora nodded her head and pursed her lips. "Let him go."

"Are you crazy? This man's a spy!"

"He is a spy, for the Union," she said, stressing the last word. "I'm the aide for Captain Dixon and familiar with the spy network."

"But he's wearing gray and talks like a southerner!" the soldier retorted.

Elora's limbs began to tremble with anger. "I said he's one of us. Release him now!" she demanded through gritted teeth. "Unless you want me to speak with your commanding officer about insubordination!"

The stabbing glare she gave must have convinced him because he nodded to his fellow soldiers who promptly let go of Seth's arms. Seth turned quickly and socked one man in the gut before spinning around and belting the other in the jaw. The two soldiers writhed in pain on the ground as the other started for Seth.

Elora drew her weapon and fired a shot in the air causing the soldier to stumble backwards.

"Don't even consider it or I'll take you down myself. You're lucky I don't allow him to teach you a lesson for your ignorant behavior. As it is, I'll let you return to your camp. But if I run across any more of your antics in the future, I'll save the army some time with the reprimands and shoot you myself."

The man spat on the ground and gave a nod to the others to follow him. They stomped off without looking back, apparently glad to have escaped without repercussion.

Elora alighted from the saddle and ran to Seth's side. "Are you alright?" she asked in her normal voice.

Seth shot a look in her direction. "Excuse me, Sir?"

Licking her lips, Elora inhaled. Should she reveal her identity or let Seth believe she was another Union officer trying to keep the men in line? It was probably best to keep her identity a secret. No doubt, Seth would have a fit and insist she return home.

"I wanted to make sure you aren't hurt too badly. Do you require medical assistance?" she queried, returning to her gruff male voice.

"No, I'm fine," he said rubbing his jaw. "Those idiots wouldn't believe a word I said. I'm glad you came along when you did."

Seth reached out his hand and Elora gave it a hearty shake.

"Where's your horse?" she asked, looking around.

Seth's brows furrowed. "How do you know I have a horse?"

"You mentioned it," she said, scrambling for an excuse.

"I did no such thing," he replied, taking a step back.

"Obviously they knocked you around pretty good. You said you were with the Cavalry, didn't you?"

"I suppose my mind is rattled. I haven't slept. I'm sure you've been there."

Elora nodded. "I've gone days with hardly any shut-eye. It definitely messes with your ability to think clearly. So, do you have a horse or are you on foot?"

Seth brought his fingers to his lips and blew. The whistle echoed through the trees followed by rustling. Phantom stepped from the wooded area and approached Seth. He reached up and patted the horse's head.

"Nice looking animal," Elora said.

"Thanks. We've been together for years. Trust him more than most men," Seth said, swinging into the saddle with a grimace. "Thanks again for your help."

"Think nothing of it. Always glad to be of service to a fellow soldier."

"Which way you headed?" Seth asked, gathering up the reins.

"West," she said, mounting Jasper.

"I'm going north. Good luck, Lieutenant."

"Same to you," she said and watched him gallop off.

Elora cued Jasper forward, contemplating her meeting with Seth. He was a spymaster? It seemed he was a bit too good at his Confederate persona being the soldiers who'd detained him wouldn't believe him when he gave proof of his alliance to the Union. Her stomach fluttered when she realized her own secret identity had withstood the ultimate test. She'd known Seth for most of her life and although he almost recognized her when she let her real voice slip, he never made the connection. She chuckled to herself, rather proud of her ability to not only fool the men with whom she served but one of the dearest people she'd ever known.

Nudging Jasper into a canter, she loped across the open field toward her destination. Within one day she'd tricked a group of Confederates into believing she was one of them and fooled a trio of Union soldiers that she was a man. She was beginning to feel like a chameleon, able to alter her appearance and personality on a whim.

Chapter 17

October 1862

Elora

Elora pushed Jasper into a full gallop toward the encampment. She needed to get the new information she'd garnered about the ambush to the captain so he could reroute their troops. Stopping to help Seth had delayed her. As she neared a creek, she slowed Jasper to a walk. He dipped his velvety muzzle into the water and took a few swallows before shaking his head, splattering water around. Elora patted his sweaty neck and prodded him forward. Halfway across the creek, Jasper stopped and started pawing at the water.

"Oh no you don't!" she hollered. She squeezed her heels into his flank, sending him bolting forward to the other side. Thank goodness. The last thing she needed was for him to roll in the creek with her astride.

Once they made it up the small incline back to flat ground, Elora sent him back into a gallop. The wind whipped against her face as her mind jumped from one thought to another, adrenaline coursing through her limbs. As she neared the site, she noticed a steel gray horse emerge from over the hill. It was the captain.

She slowed Jasper to a walk as she approached him.

"Polk, glad to see you. We received word that a confederate unit is making its way southward. We need to counter them."

"Your reports are wrong sir," she replied. "I have it on good advice the unit is heading up river toward the township. They mean to make their way north toward Pennsylvania."

He furrowed his brow. "Are you absolutely certain?"

"Have I steered you wrong before?" she asked.

"No. Everything you've told us has been accurate."

"Please trust me on this," she pleaded. "I know it to be true."

Nodding his head, the captain stared off. "Alright. Let's take this to the colonel. But be prepared, he may want your source."

Elora followed him back to camp all the while trying to prepare her answers about her secret alter ego. She'd been able to keep her 'source' secret from the captain because he trusted her, as a soldier. What if she couldn't convince the colonel and he decided she was a spy for the south? If he sent her to the brig, they might discover her gender which wouldn't bode well for her survival. Bile rose in her throat, burning her chest. She'd made it this far without discovery so why the sudden doubt in her ability to maintain her role as a man? Elora dismissed the thought from her mind. Obviously, she was rattled about the encounter with Seth and was worried the same misunderstanding could happen to her.

She took in a deep breath as the colonel's tent came into view. As if sensing her trepidation, the captain turned to her. "Don't look so forlorn, Polk. He doesn't bite."

Elora snorted at his statement which released the tension

from her shoulders. "Let's hope not," she replied. Thankfully, the ride had dried out her mouth and throat. She'd been in a rush to get back to camp and hadn't stopped for a drink, making her voice brusquer than usual which she hoped would work in her favor. Whenever she was overly stressed her tone had a tendency to rise a bit. It hadn't been a problem with the captain and the other men because she'd been comfortable with them. But the colonel was an entirely different situation.

They rode to the colonel's tent, dismounted, and walked inside. He was a stern looking man with a full gray beard, silver hair to his shoulders, and a large build. His demeanor exuded a no-nonsense sort of power that said, 'don't mess with me, I don't tolerate fools.'

"Captain," he said in a deep baritone voice.

"Sir, I've got some news regarding the location of the Confederate unit we've been tracking. Lieutenant Polk has brought a report that could thwart the enemy's efforts."

The colonel turned stern gray eyes her direction, making Elora's insides shrivel.

"Go on, Lieutenant," he said.

Mustering her courage, Elora squared her shoulders. "I have word from a reliable source that the rebels are heading toward Pennsylvania, sir."

"What source?" he asked, his eyes forming slits.

"A woman, sir. She's a union sympathizer. She garners information from fellow southerners and gets it to me." Elora felt her heartbeat click up a notch. What if he didn't believe her or demanded to meet her source?

"Sir, this woman has provided a great deal of accurate information that has benefitted our efforts. I can vouch for the lieutenant's source," the captain said.

The colonel's eyebrows furrowed. "Are you willing to stake your commission on that?"

The captain glanced at Elora who gave him a nod.

"Yes, Sir."

The colonel rubbed the scraggly hair at his chin before responding. "Very well. Give me the details and we'll see what needs to be done."

Elora exhaled, relieved he was willing to listen to and trust his men. They gathered around his table as she recounted the information she'd gleaned during her last outing dressed as a woman. When the meeting concluded and orders were given, Elora and the captain put their horses up, went to the captain's quarters, and sat at his desk to continue planning.

Exhaustion blurred her vision. She'd been up for nearly eighteen hours and had managed to gather information as her alter ego, help Seth, report back to her unit, and assist in a new plan for attack. Her back ached from sitting so straight and riding for miles. The bandaging that flattened her chest was not only scratchy but was beginning to dig into her ribs. It must have shifted during her ride. Still, she had to keep up her appearance as a man, regardless of how uncomfortable or tired she felt. All these thoughts raced through her mind along with concern for Seth, the upcoming battle plans, and the fact she'd never really noticed how blue the captain's eyes were before now.

What on earth had possessed her to do this? If she hadn't enlisted, she'd be curled up in the comfort of a soft bed in her dorm room. Even though she believed in what she was doing, deep in her soul she was a southerner and conflicted over her role. She wanted nothing more than to preserve the Union and providing secrets from the enemy was a good way to help. Despite her need to serve, there was a tinge of guilt that accompanied it. After all, many of her family and friends were fighting for the south. If her role left them maimed or dead, she'd carry the guilt for the rest of her life. The only thing she wanted was freedom for every person, regardless of their color. Dividing the country wouldn't make that happen.

"Polk?" the captain said, knocking on the desk to get her attention.

"Sorry, sir. My mind wandered off."

"Thinking about home?"

Elora stiffened. How could he possibly know? Diverting her gaze, she blew a breath across her lips.

"My apologies," she replied, rolling her shoulders as she leaned forward. "I didn't mean to ignore what you were saying."

The right side of his mouth curled as he shook his head. "No need to apologize, Polk. Just because we're men doesn't mean we don't think of home. We just don't talk about it."

"Understood," she said flatly. "You got a wife waiting?" Her heartbeat increased as soon as the words crossed her lips. Why was she asking such a question?

"My wife passed three years ago. Died from the fever," he said, sorrow flashing across his sea blue eyes.

"My condolences."

"What about you Polk? Got a girlfriend or a wife?"

"No sir, never really had time for that with my studies and all."

"Probably for the best. Leaving your heart behind to fight a war isn't easy. Dwelling on home and family can distract you. We've got to focus and stay sharp if we want to preserve this country and see our loved ones again."

"Agreed." Elora yawned and straightened in her chair. "Let's get back to work so we can win this thing and go home."

An hour later, Elora was in her tent unwrapping the binding from her breasts, a sigh of relief escaping her lips. It was well past two in the morning, and she was beyond exhaustion. She knew she should rewrap her chest but was too tired and needed a break, even if it was only for a couple of hours. She slipped on a night shirt and started for her cot when a rustling noise near the front of the tent grabbed her attention.

Her breath caught. Who was out there? Elora pulled the blanket from her bed, wrapped it around her shoulders to hide her femininity, and tiptoed toward the sound. Nearing the tent opening, she gasped when a blur of gray fur flew beneath the flap, across the ground, and out the back side of her quarters. Her heart thumped against her ribcage as she took several deep breaths.

Her limbs still quivering from the furry interloper, Elora flopped onto the cot, rested her head on the pillow, and closed her eyes. As her heartrate slowed, visions of Seth paraded through Elora's thoughts. Had he made it back to his regiment without further interference? Her blood boiled when she thought of the soldiers who'd so thoughtlessly abused him. How could they disregard protocol so flippantly? This was no way to win a war.

Then her mind shifted to the captain and her heart fluttered. Something in his gaze and the personal information he'd shared about his wife tugged at her heart. Quickly, she dismissed the thoughts. Now was not the time to have romantic feelings, especially for a man who viewed her as a comrade in arms. And why was she suddenly drawn to the captain? She'd been working alongside him for over a year. What had changed? *It's only a passing fancy*, she told herself, *probably nothing more than admiration for a respectable officer.*

She concentrated on thoughts of home, of a blue heron taking flight from the marsh as warm breezes tousled her hair and billowed her skirt. How she missed wearing a dress. Even her corset was preferable to the bandaging she used to restrain her womanly curves. Yawning, she rolled over and waited for sleep to escort her to a peaceful slumber, free from war and secret identities.

Chapter 18

October 1862

Seth

Seth's sides hurt and his jaw throbbed from the beating he'd taken earlier. Every time he took in a breath a stabbing pain raced through his chest, making him believe he might have a few broken ribs. What he wouldn't give to get his hands on each of the soldiers who'd done this. Rage pulsed through his body making his limbs tremble and his head ache. He couldn't recall the last time he wanted to beat someone to a pulp with this much intensity. His stomach grumbled from lack of sustenance although his true hunger was for revenge.

When he returned to camp, he went straight to Colonel Pennington's tent and dismounted.

"Was starting to worry about you, Daniels," he said, taking a sip from a tin cup. Seth knew it was probably more than coffee at this time of day.

Seth took a seat and slumped against the back of the chair, removing his hat, and running a hand through his sandy locks.

"Good grief man, what the heck happened to you?" Pennington asked, narrowing his eyes.

"Ran into some trouble." Seth gruffed with a sideways glance.

"As in Rebs?" The colonel's jaw clenched as he squared his shoulders.

"As in fellow Union soldiers."

"What regiment?"

"Don't know, wasn't able to discern that at the time," he replied, squeezing his fingers into a fist. "They were too busy trying to kill me."

"Why?"

"I was dressed in gray. Had just gleaned some important information about the Confederates making their way to Pennsylvania. I'd gotten off Phantom to change into my blues when three Union soldiers came out of the woods."

"Did you give them the code?"

"I did but they accused me of stealing it from a Union soldier and using it to fool them. Said my southern accent gave me away."

Seth watched as the colonel's back stiffened and the vein in his forehead pulsed.

"Honestly thought I wasn't going to make it, sir."

Seth went on to share the experience beginning with the Union soldiers who'd beaten him and the other soldier who intervened.

"Fortunately, the soldier who rode up on the scene believed my story and accepted the code word. He threatened the men with reprisal if they didn't release me," Seth said.

"Did you get the soldier's name and unit?"

"No sir. All I know is he was a lieutenant."

With a nod, the colonel looked at Seth. "If you ever find out who these men are, let me know immediately. No one messes with my spymaster and forgoes the consequences."

"Thank you, sir."

"What information did you get before the unfortunate encounter?"

Seth spent the next hour relaying the coordinates and plans he obtained from his source.

"That accent may have gotten you kicked around but it sure does work well at prying secrets from the enemy," Pennington said with a wicked grin.

"Let's hope the information works in our favor. We can't let this war cross into Pennsylvania," Seth said, his heart palpitating at the idea his family was safely ensconced within the state.

"Not to worry, we'll stop them." The colonel's words exuded confidence settling some of Seth's trepidation. He could handle facing the horrors of war but the idea of his family being directly impacted shook him to his core. He'd do what was necessary to keep them safe.

"You've had a long day and tomorrow promises to be even longer. Get some shut-eye."

Seth stood, thankful for the command to get some sleep. No doubt, he'd be sore in the morning, and he didn't look forward to it. He walked Phantom to the paddock, untacked and rubbed him down, before giving him a helping of grain and a few flakes of hay. As he walked to his tent, he could feel the muscles in his back and shoulders tightening. He wished he had some of the ointment Maggie created for these occasions. The idea of her hands rubbing his shoulders and back snagged at his chest. He missed her more than he realized.

He removed his coat and boots and flopped down on his cot. Closing his eyes, his thoughts returned to Maggie, her auburn tendrils flowing across her shoulders. And then his mind flipped back to the soldier who'd come to his aid earlier.

Something in the man's eyes had struck him as vaguely familiar even though he knew it couldn't be. The only northern men he was acquainted with were those in his unit and the ones he'd met in Reverend Milner's parish. Perhaps the stranger was related to one of them explaining the sense of familiarity he'd felt. Convinced that was the situation, Seth rolled over and promptly fell asleep.

Chapter 19

January 2, 1863

Maggie

Maggie dressed in her warmest wool frock and wrapped a knit shawl around her shoulders before slipping on her bonnet and tying the bow beneath her chin. The New Year had begun with the war still raging and no sign of peace. She was weary from the fighting and the divisiveness of the country, but most of all she wanted to be reunited with Seth. Slipping on her woolen mitts, she checked her appearance in the looking glass and headed downstairs.

This was a monumental day. She and so many others had worked for years to see this event come to fruition. President Abraham Lincoln had finally freed the slaves. Granted, it was only in the southern states since the constitution allowed for slavery. While not the perfect scenario it was a step in the right direction. If only Seth could be here with her. She lamented not being able to share this joyous moment with him. Maggie and so many others had fought and dreamed of this and now it was being enacted, and by the President! At least she'd be sharing the occasion with Dr. Towne, Ellen Murray, Willa, and Letty.

Ellen Murray, close friend of Dr. Towne, had arrived a few months earlier to teach the Negroes at the newly founded Penn School. They'd chosen the name in honor of William Penn, a quaker for whom Dr. Towne's home state of Pennsylvania had been named. He was an avid proponent for human dignity and thus the perfect choice for the school's title.

A flutter of excitement tickled her insides as she stepped into the wintry air where Dr. Towne and Miss Murray chatted with Willa and Letty. The commencement of the celebration would take place at nearby Camp Saxton, the encampment for the First South Carolina Volunteers.

"Good morning, Maggie," Dr. Towne said with a broad smile.

"G'morning," she replied, a bit of Irish tinting her words.

"Shall we go?" Miss Murray asked.

With a nod, Maggie boarded the wagon with Willa and Letty on either side of her. Dr. Towne and Miss Murray rode on the front bench.

Although brisk, it was a glorious day beneath blue skies with a gentle wind gracefully shuttering the moss dangling from towering trees. As they approached Camp Saxton, the site for the festivities, the smell of barbeque wafted through the air making Maggie's mouth water. Her heart swelled when she saw hundreds of Negro men, women, and children gathered. They halted the carriage and disembarked. The five women promenaded toward a stand erected beneath a grove of trees as the horns and drums of the Eighth Maine Regiment band rang out.

The atmosphere buzzed with excitement as the music blared, with people laughing and chatting in the background. Once everyone congregated, the Reverend Fowlers, chaplain of the First South Carolina Volunteers, stepped up to the stand and waved everyone quiet.

Maggie's heart pounded as joy broadened her smile. Willa and Letty stood on either side of her, grasping her hands, with Dr. Towne and Miss Murry to the right of Willa. Tears crested in Maggie's eyes as the reverend directed everyone to bow their heads for prayer. After that, Dr. Brisbane, who had once been a slave holder but was now a staunch abolitionist, began his speech.

By the grace of God, having been fully convinced that slavery, perpetual, involuntary servitude, is a condition of wrong to man, and on the part of the master, of sin against God, I feel it a duty to myself as well as to society, to make known in a public manner, that I most heartily repent of all part that I have heretofore voluntarily taken in supporting this unholy system of wrong and oppression.

Applause and shouts of joy echoed as he finished. Dr. Brisbane proceeded to read the President's Proclamation which brought louder shouts, clapping, and a host of Hallelujahs. There wasn't a dry eye anywhere in the crowd, and for the first time since the war had started, Maggie felt hopeful. Joy radiated from broad smiles and even Letty seemed unusually chipper and lighthearted amongst the gathering of both Negroes and whites for the momentous occasion. The chill in the air was vanquished as hope and thanksgiving radiated warmth throughout the crowd.

Several other men made speeches before the throng of onlookers took part in the meal. A cluster of roughly constructed tables were lined with rows of tinware. Officers of the regiment served beef and sweetened water to the mass of Negroes who seemed to enjoy the food and their newly proclaimed freedom. As happy as Maggie was about the situation, her heart was heavy over the fact she'd not been able to experience it with Seth by her side.

Tears threatened to fall as she wondered where he was and if he was warm and healthy. Horror stories of soldiers without proper attire in the colder climates and a lack of adequate food haunted Maggie diminishing her appetite. Seth had enlisted to keep the country intact, something he truly believed in. However, he was also opposed to the institution of slavery. Even though the south seceded due to economics and states' rights the foundation of their dispute was rooted by the desire to hold slaves. Now that the war was about ending slavery, Maggie knew Seth would be more vehement about his service than before.

Willa walked up to Maggie and draped her arm around her shoulders.

"He be fine and hopefully comin' home soon."

Maggie leaned her head on Willa's shoulder and sighed. "How did you know what I was thinking?" she asked.

"Anyone can see you is hurtin' and I know how much ending slavery means to you. Ain't nothin' else could be bothering you but missing your husband," she said, giving Maggie's shoulders a squeeze before releasing her.

Looking at Willa, Maggie grinned. "I miss him terribly. I only hope he's safe and not freezing to death on some faraway battlefield."

"You always said he be a resourceful man. Trust in that and his need to come home to you and the children."

Willa's words lifted the worry plaguing Maggie's heart. If only she could be certain of his safety, she could relax but the perilous nature of the war and the impact that freeing the slaves would have on the outcome was distressing. Knowing that many of the Union soldiers viewed the Negroes as nothing more than chattel made her wonder if the northern forces would themselves be divided over the recent proclamation. Then what would happen? Would the war be prolonged and how many sides would there be?

Maggie scanned the crowd and noticed a tall man making his way toward her. As he drew nearer, she realized it was Major Brunson.

"Mrs. Daniels," he said, tipping his hat. "I suspected you would be here."

Maggie lifted her chin. "I must say I'm surprised to see you, Major."

"Why is that?"

"Because you made your views of the Negroes clear. You believe them to be inferior."

The major looked away, his lips forming a tight line. "Indeed." Looking back at Maggie, his expression softened. "Now that the President has freed the slaves in the south, I have no choice but to consider their welfare."

"I see," she replied. "So, you still hold the same opinion but are willing to accept the proclamation by the President?"

"Mrs. Daniels, I'm doing my best to uphold the constitution of this country which allows for slavery. The president who is my commander-in-chief has issued a statement declaring the enslaved in the southern regions to be free. My personal opinions are immaterial although I am conflicted."

Straightening her stature, Maggie did her best to control her tone. "Perhaps you should consider the moral viewpoint instead of a document forcing you to uphold the rights of all individuals." Maggie swept her hand through the air. "Look at these people. They are living, thinking, feeling human beings who deserve the same opportunities and rights to a happy life. Anyone who sees them as less than that has no scruples."

The major licked his lips. "Mrs. Daniels, I appreciate your

candor but please understand that accepting a new way of thinking takes time."

"It shouldn't take very long. Any compassionate, intelligent person can see that."

With a nod, he walked away. While annoyed by the major's stubbornness regarding the Negroes, a small part of her was glad he was trying to correct his misconceptions.

Maggie watched the newly liberated men and women as they laughed and ate. The scene was exhilarating. Jubilation rippled through the crowd as they finished their meals and dispersed to their homes and the comfort of knowing they were finally free. For now, she'd have to enjoy this huge leap toward equality and sweep her fears and doubts for the future to the corners of her troubled mind.

The major became a regular visitor at The Oaks, often staying for dinner. One evening after the dishes were cleared, the major joined Maggie and Dr. Towne in the front parlor.

"I see you have a chess set," he said, with a nod at the game perched atop a table beneath the far window. A cloak of dust suggested it hadn't been touched in some time.

"I believe it belonged to the previous owners of the home," Dr. Towne replied. "It was there when we arrived."

"Do you play?" the major questioned.

Dr. Towne smiled. "Not in a while and the work here doesn't allow for recreation such as that."

"How about you, Mrs. Daniels?"

"Goodness, no."

"I imagine a woman of your intellect would be astute at the game. I'd be happy to instruct you."

Maggie chewed her lower lip. The major was putting forth an effort to be hospitable. Since the day of the incident in town, he'd been attentive to her and was obviously trying to alter his antiquated perspectives regarding the Negroes. Perhaps if she spent a bit more time with him, she could coax him into seeing the freedmen as equals.

"That would be lovely, Major. Thank you."

A broad smile crinkled his eyes. "Would you like to start now?"

Maggie nodded and joined him at the small table. His instruction was informative, and Maggie took to the game quickly. After two hours of play, Maggie yawned.

"Why don't we stop here? I can see you're tired," the major said, standing.

"Afraid I'll beat you?" Maggie teased as another yawn escaped her lips.

"Considering how well you've played, I'd say that's a possibility," he chuckled.

"I have an early morning and should retire," Maggie replied, flattered by his compliment.

"Dr. Towne, thank you for a delicious meal and a delightful evening."

"It's always a pleasure to have you join us."

"Goodnight, Major," Maggie said as the doctor escorted him to the door.

Maggie blew out the lamp near the chess board, a warmth spreading through her chest. Her time with the major had been a temporary respite from the reality of war and she found herself looking forward to their next round of chess.

Chapter 20

March 1863

Maggie

The March chill nipped at Maggie's nose and fingers as she pummeled herbs in the marble bowl. Her right shoulder ached as she worked the basil leaves into a paste. Papers reported bloody conflicts and dismal conditions in Virginia and Maryland. Deep snow, lack of warm clothing, and a diminished food supply for the soldiers was wreaking havoc on their efforts. The published scenarios were grim at best. Even worse, she'd not heard from Seth in weeks, and it weighed on her heart. For years, he'd traversed the northern region during the frigid winter months conducting Negroes to freedom and yet it hadn't been as dire as the current circumstances.

If Seth's regiment was in the thick of the frosty conditions, she prayed he had what he needed to survive. So many had already sacrificed their lives in this war, a conflict the men had boasted wouldn't last more than a few months. And here they were in the second year of it. Rations were meager at times and the overall morale in this young country was sinking like a ship with a gaping hole trying to make its way across stormy seas.

Letters from Mrs. Polk and Mrs. Milner expressed the longing of Jane and Joshua to have both of their parents back with them again. While their pining ripped at Maggie's heart, she knew they were safe and well cared for. Her work was vitally important to the Penn School, and she needed to continue.

Nevertheless, her concern for Seth, the guilt of leaving her children in the care of others, and the ongoing battle to stay positive for those around her was fraying Maggie's resolve. It was during these cold months with frost sparkling on window panes that Maggie desired Seth most. She longed to curl up in his arms cocooned beneath a quilt with the heat of his body warming hers. She missed knowing her children were down the hall sleeping soundly in their rooms. It had been so long since she'd heard their voices or felt Seth's gentle touch. Sniffling, Maggie rubbed a tear from her cheek. She startled when someone called her name.

"Sorry, didn't mean to frighten you," Major Brunson said, stepping into the shed.

"I was deep in thought and didn't hear you approach," she replied. Maggie inhaled deeply and straightened her shoulders in an effort to hide her heartache.

The major rolled his lips as his eyes glinted with delight.

"What is so amusing, if you don't mind my asking." Annoyance tinted Maggie's words over his obvious mirth, especially when she felt so forlorn. How was it men could be so oblivious to a woman's melancholy?

He reached up and tapped his left cheek. "You've a bit of something, greenish, on your face."

Maggie reached up and wiped her cheek with the hem of her apron. Looking at the green smear on the already stained cotton, she chuckled. "What can I say? I'm a messy worker." A smile lifted her cheeks washing away the temporary annoyance. "Is there something I can do for you, Major?"

His visits were beginning to charm Maggie out of her initial contempt for him. Despite having forgiven him for his lack of response when she and the Negro woman had been attacked, she was still working on helping him to see the newly freed slaves as human beings and not chattel. His views were starting to ebb, and she hoped with more time he'd eventually succumb to her way of thinking. Even though they held differing views, the major had been good company in Seth's absence, listening to Maggie's opinions as well as teaching her to play chess.

"What brings you out here this afternoon? Surely you didn't come all this way to tell me I have green goop on my face."

"Of course not," he said, diverting his gaze from hers. "I have a request...." His words trailed off.

Her smile broadened. She found it charming when the major's awkwardness took hold as he attempted to interact without causing offense.

With a deep breath, he continued. "I came to ask if you'd be willing to teach me how to dance." He paused and looked down at his hands. "I'm embarrassed to say I never learned how. I'm expected to attend an event next week at Halston Plantation in Yemassee that will require such skills." His face colored as his eyes met Maggie's.

Resting her hand on her mouth, Maggie bit her lower lip to suppress the laugh threatening to burst forth.

"No need to stifle your amusement, Mrs. Daniels. I realize a man of my rank and standing should be well schooled in these things; however, I'm a bit uncoordinated when it comes to dancing and chose to avoid the task whenever possible. Now it seems I have no choice." He cleared his throat and looked away.

"I'm certain you can't be all that clumsy," Maggie replied, trying to be sensitive.

"Oh, I assure you I am. I once knocked over a priceless vase and shattered a window in one lesson."

Maggie gasped. "How were you able to accomplish that during a dance lesson?"

"It's rather embarrassing, actually. I was learning the waltz and managed to trip on the edge of the rug, knocking my instructor backwards. I reached out to steady her throwing myself off balance. I stumbled backwards into the plant stand knocking off my mother's favorite vase which flew through the upstairs window. Even worse, I hadn't let go of my instructor and inadvertently, pulled her down on top of me. Needless to say, I've never been so humiliated. She of course was mortified by the entire situation and quickly scurried from atop me. I apologized profusely but to no avail. She dismissed me as a student that afternoon."

Maggie could contain her laughter no longer. Tears clung to her eyelids as her shoulders shook with amusement. "I'm sorry, Major. I don't mean to make you feel badly, but it is a comical story."

A grin formed on the major's face as he let out a chuckle. "While it was anything but funny at the time, it is laughable now. Will you help me? I promise to do my best to avoid tripping you or destroying any property."

"What sort of gathering will you be attending?"

He blew a breath across his lips, obviously uncomfortable with the upcoming event. "It's a dinner for the commanding officers in the region with dancing afterwards."

"And there will be ladies present?" Maggie asked, shocked that women would be in attendance. Generally, only wives or fiancées would attend such functions.

"The General's niece is in town, and he has *informed* me I

will be escorting her to the dinner. He's been very supportive of my work in this region, and this could help with future commissions. I cannot afford to pass up this opportunity."

His eyes pleaded with Maggie, weakening her resolve. She was a married woman and wasn't comfortable being in contact with a single man, especially one she'd held in low regard for so long. Then she recalled what Dr. Towne had told her about doing their best to get along with the soldiers who were in charge. Being agreeable would make the situation more comfortable. Under normal circumstances propriety would have been of the utmost importance. But this was war where such things were of little concern. All the same, she'd make sure someone was present in order to maintain decorum.

"I suppose if Dr. Towne is there, it would be alright."

He stepped forward and grasped Maggie's hand, her skin tingling at his touch.

"Thank you so much, Mrs. Daniels. I truly appreciate your willingness to assist me in this endeavor."

"I'm happy to help," she replied, although she wasn't certain she was completely comfortable with the situation. Her husband was off fighting, and she was going to help an unmarried man learn to waltz. No doubt, Dr. Towne would be pleased with Maggie's willingness to assist the major despite their differing views. The education and care of the newly freed slaves seemed like more of a political show than a humanitarian effort on the part of the soldiers. Nevertheless, this would give her another opportunity to remedy his erroneous views.

"Thank you again," he said, releasing her hand and rushing from the shed.

Rubbing her fingers, she watched as he mounted his horse and rode away leaving Maggie to ponder whether she'd agreed too readily to his proposal.

. . .

The major arrived at seven the following evening. Willa agreed to sit with them at Maggie's request since Dr. Towne had paperwork to complete in her office. Ellen Murray was helping a group in their cottage down the road and Letty was resting from a pulled muscle in her back.

Maggie greeted the major who immediately removed his weapon and coat. He glanced at Willa who sat on the settee knitting.

"Good evening, Miss Willa. How are you?"

Willa looked up, a grin plumping her cheeks. "I's good. And yourself?"

"Very well," he replied.

Willa gave a knowing glance to Maggie who stood next to the major. Maggie was thrilled he'd addressed Willa in a digni-fied manner, something he wouldn't have done when she'd met him. She relaxed a bit, wondering if his altered manner toward a Negro was because of Maggie's agreement to help with his dancing or to avoid an argument. Either way, she was happy to see him putting forth an effort even if he didn't completely believe in his actions yet.

"Shall we begin?" Maggie asked, her insides fluttering like a young girl getting ready for her first dance with a gentleman.

"I'm ready when you are," he replied.

Maggie showed him where to place his hands although she kept a suitable space between them.

"Keep in mind, you can hold her closer than we are right now, but you still need to maintain a slight distance to preserve decorum."

"Alright," he replied, tugging at his shirt collar.

Maggie smiled. "You'll be fine. Trust me."

"I trust *you*, Mrs. Daniels, it's my feet I'm not so sure about."

"I'll lead until you get the rhythm of the steps down, then we'll change roles. Ready?"

He nodded, staring at his feet.

Maggie moved one foot forward instructing him to move his back. She moved slowly, explaining each motion step by step. He faltered several times, stepping forward when he should have stepped back and on one occasion moved sideways instead of forward. Judging by the perspiration moistening his brow, Maggie could tell he was nervous. It was nearly an hour before he was able to achieve a basic series of moves.

"I think this is a good start, Major," Maggie said, stepping back with a smile. "Tomorrow we'll review the steps and work more on your posture."

"How is it I can go into battle, ride a horse, even climb a tree, but cannot master something as simple as a four-step dance?"

Maggie shook her head. "Everyone has something they struggle with. I wonder if your hesitation is due to some underlying discomfort being in the presence of ladies."

The major rolled his lips and looked away. "Mrs. Daniels, you have great perception. I am in fact nervous around females but never made the connection between the two. You are quite astute in your observations."

"In time you'll meet a woman with whom you feel comfortable, and all of the anxiety will melt away." Maggie grinned.

"Perhaps," he said softly, a forlorn expression veiling his countenance. He grabbed his jacket and weapon and made a low bow.

"Until tomorrow, Mrs. Daniels."

"Until then," she replied.

"Good evening, Miss Willa," he said with a nod before walking out the door.

Maggie watched as he mounted his horse and rode off into the darkness. Turning to Willa, she giggled. "He's an interesting man, is he not?"

Willa shook her head. "Interesting be a good word to describe him, that's for sure," she said, standing. "I best be gettin' back to check on Letty. She was grumblin' when I left about how ridiculous the major was for asking such a thing of you."

"You know how Letty blusters when she doesn't feel well. I'm sure she's just aggravated by her back."

"Don't make no excuses for her. You know she's always been on the grumpy side, sore back or not," Willa said with a huff and a playful smile.

"I'll walk you back to your cabin," Maggie offered.

"I don' need no escort. I'm perfectly capable of finding my way home," she said. "You get some rest. I'll see you at breakfast."

"Goodnight, Willa," Maggie said.

"G'night".

Maggie stood on the porch with her shawl wrapped tightly around her shoulders watching Willa lumber down the path to her and Letty's cottage. When her friend was out of sight, Maggie stepped into the drafty hallway of the house. She'd enjoyed her time with the major, but it increased her longing for Seth. She missed dancing with him in the parlor, his arms holding her snuggly as he guided her with ease about the room in a series of twirls and dips. Maggie yearned to have him home with the kids running through the yard. Not having a letter from him in months frayed her fortitude. Why hadn't he written? Was he injured, deep in battle, or worse? A lump formed in her throat and her eyes moistened.

Trudging up the stairs, she paused at her bedroom door as a thought popped into her head. Maybe the major could find out where Seth was. After all, he had connections. Renewed energy pulsed through Maggie's veins as she slipped into her room.

When the major arrived tomorrow evening, she'd broach the subject with him. It was the least he could do after she'd endured an hour of being bumped about and having her toes stepped on several times. Changing into her nightgown, Maggie's mind wandered to the major's comments about being uncomfortable around women. He was such an astute and confident man with a great deal to offer and yet he was as timid as a mouse when it came to the fairer sex. Maybe he'd had an unfortunate experience with a lady, leaving him insecure. Whatever the reason, Maggie felt certain she could help. All he needed was a little encouragement. If she was able to alter his views about the Negroes surely, she could build his confidence with women.

Chapter 21

March 1863

Maggie

The following evening, Major Brunson arrived promptly at seven for his next dance lesson. Willa had joined them once again. She knitted while Maggie reviewed the steps they'd learned the previous day. Much to her surprise, he did rather well, only stepping on her feet a couple of times.

"I practiced when I got back to my quarters last night and again this morning before breakfast," he said with the pride of a school boy who just received a perfect test score.

"It shows. You're much smoother than you were last night. We'll practice foot placement a few more times and then move on from there."

He rested his hands on Maggie's shoulder and waist, keeping the appropriate distance between them as they began to move. Willa glanced up anytime Maggie yelped over a misstep or when the major bumped into something. She'd shake her head and resume her knitting while Maggie tried to distract the major from her friend's obvious amusement.

Things seemed to be going smoothly until Maggie

suggested he lead. The major managed to make one ungainly round about the room before he stepped forward instead of back, knocking Maggie off balance. He scrambled to stabilize her, lost his footing in the process, tumbled over a small walnut table, and landed with a thump. Maggie rushed to his side and offered to help him up. Shaking his head, he accepted her outstretched hand and rose to his feet.

"How embarrassing," he mumbled, his face flushing as he gave a sideways glance at Willa who lowered her head, her knitting needles working at a furious pace. "My apologies, Mrs. Daniels."

"No need to be ashamed. There was no harm done and no windows broken," Maggie said, the right side of her mouth curling. "We still have a few more days of practice."

The major chuckled as he resumed the dance. His steps were more deliberate and carefully placed. By the end of the lesson, he was beginning to flow more and stumble less.

The mantel clock chimed eight alerting them to the late hour. The major bid goodnight to Willa and stepped onto the porch with Maggie close behind.

"Major, may I ask a favor?"

He stood straighter, a smile creasing his cheeks. "Mrs. Daniels, after all you've endured with my roguish ways and inept dance skills, a favor is the least I can do for you."

Maggie took in a deep breath while twisting her wedding band. "I've not heard from my husband in more than three months. I was wondering if you might be able to locate his regiment and find out if he's in good health?"

"I'll make a few inquiries," the major said.

"Thank you," she muttered as a sob rushed from her lips, her shoulders shaking as she buried her face in her hands. The major drew her to him and wrapped his arms around her. Leaning into him, she cried all the tears that had built up since

Seth left. When the tears ran dry, she pulled away and wiped her eyes.

"My apologies, Major, for unburdening myself on you like that," she said, sniffling.

"Please don't apologize, Mrs. Daniels. You've no need to put on a brave front for me. I know your strength. I'm honored you feel comfortable enough to trust me with your distress."

"All the same, I'm a married woman and you're a single gentleman."

His grin widened to a smile. "There was a time you viewed me as a scoundrel. It does my heart good to hear you refer to me as a gentleman. I consider it high praise coming from you."

"Thank you," she replied with a simper. "I'm pleased with your efforts to improve your attitude, and your dancing."

"I shall see you tomorrow evening," he said, his eyes sparkling. "Goodnight, Mrs. Daniels."

"Goodnight," she replied, watching him mount his horse and ride away.

Maggie stepped inside as Willa gathered her knitting and placed it in her bag.

"Everything okay with you, Miss Maggie?" she queried.

"Of course, why do you ask?"

Willa planted her hands on her hips. "Don' pull that innocent act with me. I can see your eyes is red and I knows you well enough to know when somethin' is up. You gonna tell me about it?"

"I'm missing Seth is all," she mumbled.

"I know you is," Willa said, as she headed for the door. "Be careful, Miss Maggie. It's easy to get in trouble when your heart is heavy."

Maggie cocked her head. "What do you mean?"

"The major is having a hard time keeping his feelings in

check. You might've kept some distance between you for dancing but the distance to his heart is getting closer."

"Don't be ridiculous," Maggie retorted. "The major is an acquaintance, nothing else."

"Maybe for you but it be more for him." Willa said, patting Maggie's arm as she headed into the night.

Closing the door, Maggie leaned against it. For a moment, she pondered her friend's words but quickly dismissed them. Willa was just being overprotective. The major would never do anything untoward. At least that's what Maggie told herself as she ascended the stairs and prepared for bed.

Maggie spent the next three evenings working with the major on his dance steps and much to their delight, he was catching on. Unfortunately, he hadn't been able to locate Seth's regiment. Then again, it had only been a couple of days and Maggie held out hope he'd find something soon. Until that time, she focused on her work and prayed for peace.

The night before the dance, Maggie spent a little extra time working with the major who seemed to be regressing a bit in his skills. When they stumbled for the fourth time, she stopped and took a step back.

"Major, is something troubling you this evening? You seem distracted."

Inhaling, he met Maggie's stare. "As this event draws closer, I fear my nerves are taking hold. This is our last rehearsal before tomorrow evening. A good showing could open doors for my career. I don't want to make any mistakes."

"You won't make any if you do exactly as I've instructed you."

"It's easy in this parlor with you guiding my steps but tomorrow will be an entirely different scenario. There will be dignitaries and officers of high standing, and..." he hesitated, "ladies." He glanced at Willa who continued stitching without acknowledging the conversation.

"Why are you so frightened of women? We're supposed to be the weaker sex," Maggie said, arching her brows.

"As I've told you, I've always been a bit...shy around the ladies. I never know what to say."

"You haven't had any problem speaking with me."

"But you're married and not...." His words dropped off.

"Available?" she asked.

"Exactly. Nothing I say matters because I'm not pursuing you romantically."

Maggie gave a quick glance toward Willa who'd dropped her head before their eyes met. Even though her friend was pretending not to listen, Maggie knew better.

"Major, you're a soldier and have seen battle. Surely, a few dances and light conversation with a woman won't be the end of you."

"Let's just say I find the enemy less intimidating."

"How about this. When you dance with the General's niece, pretend you're with me in this parlor. You seem relaxed here."

Pursing his lips, he nodded. "Actually, it's not a bad idea. Thank you, Mrs. Daniels for your frankness and your time." He bowed low and brought her hand to his lips, placing a kiss upon it. "I shall visit the day after tomorrow to share the outcome of the evening."

"I look forward to hearing about it," Maggie replied, escorting him onto the porch. She watched him mount his steed and ride away. After closing the door, Maggie sat in the chair across from Willa.

"That man is a conundrum," Maggie said, shaking her head.

"That man be in love with you," Willa replied with a smirk.

"He's merely a friend, albeit an unexpected one. I must admit I've grown rather fond of him these past few days. He seemed so arrogant the first time I encountered him. But now, he's softer and more empathetic."

Willa shook her head. "That's cause he gots feelings for you."

Maggie stiffened. "Why do you keep saying that? You heard him say he's nervous around women. And don't try to deny you were listening. You might act like you're absorbed in your knitting but I know better."

Willa snorted. "Don't get all high and mighty with me. I been watchin' that man. He looks at you like a freshly baked cake. His whole face lights up when you starts humming and take that first step. I's telling you, the man has feelings for you and it's more than friendship. Be careful, Miss Maggie."

"Careful of what? The major wouldn't harm me."

"Not you, but you did ask him to check on Mr. Seth. If he feels strongly enough 'bout you he might try and get rid of the person standing in his way."

"Your imagination is running wild," Maggie huffed. "I'll see you in the morning."

"See you tomorrow," Willa said, gathering her things and walking to the door where she paused. "Miss Maggie, please take heed of what I said. Matters of the heart are nothing to poke fun at. The major almost say as much when he said he'd rather face the enemy than a lady."

Willa stepped into the cool night air, lumbered across the porch, and down the stairs. Maggie secured the door, extinguished the oil lamps, and headed for her room. After changing for bed, she perched on the edge of the mattress ruminating on what Willa had said. She had to be mistaken. The major hadn't shown any romantic inclinations toward her, but the idea he could possibly cause harm to Seth rankled Maggie's courage. With a sigh, she dismissed the idea. Her friend was probably just overreacting.

Content with her rationalization, Maggie rested her head against the pillow, her mind drifting to Seth. She missed him so much her chest ached. If only she knew he was safe, she could relax a bit. Until then she'd have to grapple with the unknown.

The following morning after breakfast, Maggie went straight to work in the shed. She was boiling herbal stalks for a remedy when the floor beneath her feet shuddered as hoof beats pounded down the drive. She rushed to the doorway to see the major striding toward her. Her heart seized. Why was he here today? He wasn't supposed to visit until tomorrow. A lump caught in her throat as her body trembled with trepidation. Had he located Seth? Was he okay? Did he come to deliver bad news? Her vision blurred and her head swam with possibilities, none of them good.

As the major neared the shed, Maggie felt like she might faint.

"Is everything alright, Major?" she called out. "We weren't expecting to see you today."

He stopped at the entrance, removed his hat, and ducked his head before speaking.

"I've got some upsetting news."

Bile filled Maggie's mouth and her knees began to quiver as she gripped the door jamb. "What news?" Her voice faded as she tried to swallow. "Is it about...my husband?"

"It's nothing as serious as all that. I didn't mean to upset you, Mrs. Daniels." Sliding his hand beneath her elbow, he guided her to a chair by the work counter. "I only wanted to tell you I received word from the General this morning. His niece has fallen ill."

Maggie exhaled. Seth was safe, or so she hoped. Relieved the dilemma was nothing more than the lack of a dance partner, Maggie took in a few deep breaths until her heart beat slowed.

"You look a bit pale, should I call for the doctor?" he asked, his eyes veiled with concern.

"I'm quite alright," she replied, sitting straighter.

"My apologies for giving you such a shock. It's just..." he paused. "The General insists I bring a lady with me this evening."

"Doesn't he realize there are few ladies in the area for you to escort to such a function?" Maggie said.

"One would think, and yet he's adamant. Making a good impression would be favorable for my career."

"What are you going to do?" she asked, wondering why he'd come to her for advice. Unless he was thinking of taking Dr. Towne or Miss Murray and wanted Maggie's opinion before asking one of them.

"As you said, there aren't exactly swarms of young women flowing through the streets of Beaufort." He scuffed the floor with the toe of his boot. "Mrs. Daniels, would you consider going with me? I'm less likely to make a fool of myself with someone I know so well. I'm comfortable in your presence and already know how to dance with you."

His eyes pleaded with hers as he waited for a response.

"I'm not entirely sure it's proper for me to accompany you being that I'm married."

"I will make your marital status known and that a suitable escort was not available on such short notice."

Maggie was torn. The idea of an evening of dancing was tempting but something about it felt wrong, as if she were being disloyal to her husband. Then again, it was an innocent request, not one that would belittle her marital status or portray her in a negative light. Even better, some of the men in attendance might be able to find out if Seth was safe.

"I think an evening away would be lovely. I'll happily accompany you, Major."

"Splendid," he replied, his eyes glimmering. "Be at the ferry dock about four o'clock. We'll board the carriage in town and travel to Halston Plantation from there."

"I'm afraid I haven't anything fancy to wear. All I have are work dresses."

The major took in a deep breath as he rubbed the stubble on his chin. "I know a woman about your size and believe she may have something you can borrow, that is, if you don't mind."

"That would be fine."

"I'll have a dress sent here before noon," he said with a nod. "I must be on my way. Thank you again Mrs. Daniels for agreeing to help me with this matter."

Maggie watched him walk back to his horse and ride away. Returning to her work, she pondered something he'd said. He knew a woman with a nice dress about Maggie's size. Why not take her to the dance? she thought. Willa's words echoed through Maggie's head as she rested the pestle in the bowl. No, she chided herself, his invitation was innocent and only meant to advance his career. The major had no romantic interest in her, of that she was certain.

As promised, a gown was delivered to the plantation house by midday. Dr. Towne had come by for lunch at the same time the package arrived.

"What's all this?" she queried.

"The major asked me to accompany him to the dinner at Halston Plantation this evening. The woman who was supposed to go with him fell ill. Apparently, the General insisted he bring someone to the event."

The doctor tapped her finger against her lip. "So, he asked you to go with him?"

"It's perfectly acceptable for me to go," Maggie replied defensively.

"Of course, it is," she said, a slight smile forming.

"Then why do you seem so amused?"

"Because I find it interesting how you've gone from loathing the major to accompanying him to dinner."

Maggie sighed. For a moment, she feared the doctor was going to make the same claims as Willa. "He's not as awful as I originally thought. His perspective seems to be altering, although not as completely as I'd like. Getting to know him better has opened my eyes to his qualities. With a bit more influence I believe he will abandon his deplorable views."

"Most people are good at the core, but life's experiences shape us, sometimes in unpleasant ways," the doctor said. "It's important to get to know someone before making snap judgements. We can shape people better with kindness than animosity."

Maggie nodded. "The major sent a dress for me to wear. I was getting ready to try it on."

"Please come down once you've changed. It's been such a long time since I've seen anything vaguely fashionable."

Maggie hurried up the stairs to her room. She placed the box on her bed, removed the lid, and gazed at the shimmering deep blue taffeta that glimmered in varying shades depending on how the light hit it. Lifting it from the box, Maggie held it in front of her and peered at her image in the looking glass. It had been ages since she'd seen anything this fine. Her mind wondered back to her first dance with Seth when she donned the emerald silk gown that later became her wedding dress.

Tears flowed as she bowed her head and hugged the frock to her chest. She missed Seth terribly. Where was he and what was he doing at this moment? Her throat tightened. She was preparing for a grand evening of dinner and dancing while her husband was somewhere battling for the preservation of their country. Her kids were safe but missing their parents. How could she enjoy herself when others were suffering?

Then she remembered the dignitaries and high-ranking officials who would be in attendance. If they could locate Seth, it would be worth it. Pacified with her rationale, she held the dress up once more and admired the azure hue as it gleamed against her milky skin.

Chapter 22

March 1863

Maggie

A full moon rose over the marsh, the water sparkling like sapphires as the carriage rocked and jostled over sandy roads. Maggie sat across from the major, fidgeting with her wedding ring beneath her glove. She kept telling herself she was doing this for Seth, well, for information about him. Her stomach cramped. Regardless of her intentions, she was uncomfortable traveling alone with the major. Even though propriety had all but disappeared with the war, she still held to certain conventional rules between men and women.

The dress was a bit snug, but the overall appearance was lovely. If she ate lightly, she'd make it through the evening. Her hair was swept into a roll at the nape of her neck with a lace cap crowning her head. Ellen Murray loaned her a cameo brooch for the swooping neckline and Dr. Towne gave her a set of pearl earrings to wear. Staring out the carriage window, Maggie watched as the landscape whizzed past. Every so often she caught a glimpse of the major staring at her. When she looked in his direction, he diverted his gaze to the floor and fidgeted with his gloves.

"Are you alright, Major?" she asked.

His head shot up as he shifted in his seat. "Just a bit nervous, I suppose."

"You'll be fine," Maggie giggled. "I'll not let you trip."

His jaw relaxed as he let out a laugh. "I'm more concerned about falling into something and making a fool of myself."

Sometime later, the carriage arrived at a palatial mansion, its windows glowing with candlelight. Exiting the carriage, the major handed Maggie from within. She did her best to hide her feet since the only shoes she had to wear were her everyday work boots. Although worn, she was able to polish them to a slight sheen.

The major hesitated. "Mrs. Daniels," he said. "Would it be...would you consider..."

"What is it, Major?"

"Just for this evening, when others are out of earshot, could you address me by my first name?"

Shocked at his question, Maggie cocked her head. "I suppose. Why do you ask?"

"The night is stressful enough without more formalities." He paused. "I consider you a friend. I believe it will help me relax when it comes time to dance."

"If you think it will help. What is your first name?" She chortled. "I'm not sure I've ever known you as anything but Major Brunson."

"James," he replied, his smile broadening.

"Alright, James. But I insist you do the same and call me Maggie.

"Agreed."

"Shall we go inside?"

He gave a nod and offered his arm. Maggie slipped her gloved hand into the crook of his elbow and walked beside him. Her taffeta skirt rustled as they promenaded down a long brick walkway and up a set of marble stairs. Once inside, the major's stature altered to one of authority. He spoke with confidence, making introductions as they made their way through a throng of blue uniforms and silken gowns.

The mansion was resplendent with fine furnishings, imported rugs, and framed landscapes lining the walls. This was nothing like the homes in Beaufort that had been ransacked by their union occupants. Artwork had been shredded and furniture broken for fire wood. The soldiers seemed to enjoy vandalizing property and did so flagrantly. Even the churches had been desecrated when officers housed their horses in them. Somehow, this mansion had been left in its original splendor. It was pleasant being in a grand house once again. Maggie hadn't seen anything this opulent since Rose Hall.

"Major Brunson," a booming voice called. "Glad you made it." A large man with mutton chops and a thick neck approached, his gloved hand outstretched.

"General Milford," he said, shaking his hand. "It's an honor to be here, sir."

"My niece was terribly upset that she was unable to attend. She'd been looking forward to meeting you," he said. "I see you were able to find another lovely young lady to accompany you this evening."

"Indeed, sir," the major replied. "This is *Mrs.* Maggie Daniels. She works with Dr. Towne on St. Helena."

The General's bushy eyebrows lifted. "You're married," he said. "Where is your husband?"

"Fighting with the Pennsylvania Cavalry," she responded with a curtsy.

"I see," he said. "Glad to hear he's on the right side."

"Yes, sir," she replied. She considered asking if he knew

anything of Seth's regiment but thought better of it. She'd wait until the major was occupied elsewhere.

"Brunson, please join me in the other room. We need to discuss some things."

"If you'll excuse me, Mrs. Daniels," he said with a slight bow.

"Of course," she said. The two men cut through the crowd and joined a small group of officers at the far end of the entryway before slipping into one of the side rooms.

Maggie sauntered to the front parlor where a crowd of people were gathered. Not in the mood for chitchat, she made her way onto the porch at the rear of the house. Leaning against the spindled railing, she took in the spectacular view as moonlight shimmered across the choppy current. The familiar Lowcountry scent of brackish water filled her senses. At the opposite end of the porch two Union officers conversed, one a colonel. A light wind cascaded over the water carrying their voices as they spoke.

"This entire war has gotten out of hand," the stout man said. "What was Lincoln thinking?"

"Who knows?" the other man replied with a snort of derision. "But I can tell you my men and I won't be fighting to free darkies."

"Agreed. I'll fight to preserve the country but I'm not going against the wishes of our founding fathers. If slavery was so reprehensible they would've abolished it."

"Heck, most of them owned slaves."

Maggie's insides shriveled. How could these men be so insensitive not to mention disobeying orders from the president? All this time she believed the major's attitude was uncommon and yet these officers were speaking with the same disregard. Disgusting, Maggie thought as she returned to the parlor.

Scanning the room, Maggie looked for the major, but he wasn't there. Her stomach swirled. At that moment, she wanted to flee. She didn't know anyone and what she'd overheard was disconcerting. Was Seth facing the same attitudes with his regiment? If he was, it wouldn't bode well for him.

Maggie wandered to the main entry where the major was speaking with two other officers. He glanced up, catching her gaze, and smiled. When she didn't return the smile, he said something to the two men and came toward her.

"What's the matter?" he asked, concern masking his expression.

Rubbing her upper arms, Maggie exhaled. "Nothing really. It's just these men...."

The major's cheeks turned a deep shade of crimson as his jaw tensed. "Has someone said something inappropriate?" he asked, rage glimmering in his stare.

"Depends on what you consider inappropriate," she huffed. "I thought they would be more enlightened."

Puzzlement wrinkled his brow. "Enlightened how?"

"As in against slavery," she replied. "How can people be so ignorant?"

Blowing out a breath, the major paused before speaking. "Maggie, not everyone is as free thinking as you."

As he said it, she crossed her arms over her chest and narrowed her eyes. Her mouth opened as she prepared a scathing retort when he held up his hand.

"Please don't be upset with me," he said. "You know I speak the truth. Slavery has been a viable and customary institution for centuries. It will take time for some to alter their opinions."

Maggie stiffened. "The idea that anybody ever considered owning another human as acceptable shows a lack of intelligence and morality."

She regretted the fierceness of her statement as soon as she saw the wounded expression on his face. Then again, there was no excuse for his views either. Squaring her shoulders, she prepared for his rebuttal. Except it didn't come.

Before he could reply, a slender, fair skinned Negro stepped into the hall and rang a bell.

"Dinner is served," he announced before disappearing into the dining room.

The guests made their way to the room where a long mahogany table anchored the space. Portions of beef, potatoes, and carrots steamed from gleaming china plates as each person took their seat. Maggie's mouth watered. It had been some time since she'd had steak. Generally, they ate chicken or whatever could be caught from the river.

The major pulled out Maggie's chair before sitting next to her, the tension lingering between them. Not in the mood for conversation, Maggie nibbled at her meal listening to those around her talk about battles and how the war couldn't last much longer. If only that were true. More than anything, she wanted to be back home with Seth and the kids. She spent most of the meal thinking of her husband and how wonderful it would be to have him sitting next to her instead of the major.

As the plates were being cleared, music wafted in from the parlor.

"Sounds like the dancing is about to begin," Brunson said.

"Then we should join the others," she replied.

Placing his hand at her elbow, he gently guided her to the parlor where several couples began to twirl about the room. In the far corner three Negroes played fiddles. Maggie's heart pounded as fury surged through her veins. These soldiers had no problem dancing to the music of these colored men yet some wouldn't fight to ensure their independence.

Maggie looked at the major. His throat bobbed as his cheeks flushed. Be nice to him, she told herself. He'd made a great deal of progress with his outlook even if it wasn't where she'd like it to be. If she could win him over perhaps, he could influence others to alter their perspectives as well. Da always said kindness spread much faster and farther than bitterness.

"Shall we dance?" Maggie asked.

He started at her words. "Um, yes, I suppose."

"James," she said softly. "You'll be fine, trust me."

His stare locked onto hers as he took her hand and led her to the dancefloor. They danced several waltzes with a few polkas in between. After a few rounds, Maggie began to loosen up, the tension melting from her nerves. She was enjoying herself for the first time since coming south.

By the time the evening came to a close, Maggie's toes were cramped, and the balls of her feet ached from dancing in her boots. From what she could tell, the gathering had been a success for the major. No one seemed offended by him bringing a married woman to the event. Apparently, others had done the same when visiting places without their spouses.

Many of the high-ranking officers and dignitaries from Washington were quite impressed with the major and spoke highly of his accomplishments. Based on some of the conversations Maggie overheard, he was getting credit for the progress being made on the islands. He accepted the compliments even though Maggie knew the healthcare and education of the newly freed slaves was due to the efforts of Dr. Towne and Ellen Murray. Regardless, the Port Royal Experiment, as the program was called, was solid and appeared to be helping the freedmen acclimate to their independence. Despite the praise for the program, Maggie stewed over some of the officers who still held very low opinions of the blacks considering them inconsequential. Interestingly, the major hadn't joined in on those conversations. He'd nodded his head but didn't contribute to the topic nor did he offer any insight into the plight of the freedmen and women. She considered that growth no matter how small.

Maggie was relieved when they finally climbed into the carriage and started for Beaufort. The major sat across from her, his hat resting in his lap as he stared out the window. Moonbeams filtered through the space, illuminating his chiseled features, his demeanor downcast.

"James, is everything alright? You seem preoccupied," Maggie said. "The evening was a great success. Your dancing seemed to impress the senator who spoke to you about an introduction to his daughter."

He turned to look at her, his expression sullen as if he'd lost a battle or a loved one.

"I'm fine, thank you. I was only mulling over something the general said." He inhaled. "He hinted at a possible promotion based on my work in Beaufort."

"That's wonderful news." Maggie declared.

"Indeed," he replied. "It's a boon for my career. I come from a long line of soldiers, as far back as my great-grandfather."

"Are any of your family still alive?" she asked.

"Both of my parents, two brothers, a sister, and my paternal grandfather." He fidgeted with his hands.

"Then why so forlorn? Certainly, they'll be pleased with this news."

"They'll be incredibly proud. However, if I get this commission..." He hesitated. "I'll be relocated."

"Oh," Maggie said softly, surprised at the pang in her chest at the idea of him leaving. She'd grown fond of him and looked forward to his visits. He distracted her from her worries about Seth. "You don't wish to go into battle."

He shook his head. "That's not it. I was bred to fight. Oddly, battle doesn't frighten me."

"Then what is it?"

"You'll think me silly."

"Nonsense, say what it is that's troubling you. Perhaps I can help."

He looked down at his hands, once again shaking his head. "I'm quite certain you cannot help me."

Silence permeated the atmosphere except for the rattling of the wheels and the jolting of the carriage over rough roads. Finally, the major spoke.

"I've grown fond of the Lowcountry. Quite enamored as a matter of fact. The idea of leaving the area is...disconcerting." His eyes glimmered in the darkened interior of the carriage as his stare met hers.

"There's nothing disconcerting about that. I was whole-heartedly in love with my native Ireland. But the famine struck, and my father had no choice but to send me away. I never thought I'd love another place as much and yet I adore the Lowcountry even more. So, you see, it's not silly to fall in love with a place. People do so every day."

"You have such a positive outlook on life, Maggie. I envy you that."

"You give me too much credit," she said, her cheeks warming.

"I could never give you too much praise," he replied, shifting his gaze to the window.

"There were many lovely ladies in attendance tonight. I noticed a few watching you specifically," Maggie said, hoping to quell the sadness in her heart over him leaving.

"Hmm...," he replied, his voice low. "I hadn't noticed."

They rode in silence for the remainder of the journey. Maggie fought to keep her eyelids from shuttering closed. Between the dancing, and the long ride to and from Halston Plantation, she felt as if her limbs were filled with jelly. Despite her yearning for Seth, she'd had a lovely evening. It was exciting wearing a fine gown again and getting to sip champagne.

The carriage made its way down the main road of Beaufort and halted at the ferry dock. She hadn't even thought about how to get back to the island at such a late hour. The ferry usually didn't run past 9:00 at night.

Hopping from the carriage, the major stood to the side and grasped Maggie's gloved hand. She leaned out, the major steadying her with his other hand while helping her to the ground. As her boot touched the dock she started to slide. Before she could blink, the major's arms were about her, his firm yet gentle grip reminding her of Seth.

"Thank you," she whispered, noticing the tender twinkle in his gaze.

Releasing her, the major introduced the older black man standing at the water's edge with the ferry. "Mrs. Daniels, this is Jones. I paid him to convey you home since the ferry doesn't normally run at this hour. He knows these waters like his own heart and can maneuver the sand bars and undercurrent better than the fish."

"I know Mr. Jones. He's ferried me across this river many times. But we've never been formally introduced," Maggie said. "It's nice to officially make your acquaintance."

"Yes ma'am," he replied.

The major took Maggie by the arm, helped her onto the ferry, and stepped up behind her.

"James, it's terribly late. There's no need to see me home.

Dr. Towne said she'd have a wagon waiting on the island when I arrived."

"I insist on escorting you across the river," he said, his chest puffing as he glanced at Jones.

"Me too," Jones said. "Ain't right for a colored man to be alone with a white woman after dark."

The major gave a nod sending a ripple of anger through Maggie's chest.

"If you both insist then I have no other recourse." Looking at the ferryman, she stood straighter. "Mr. Jones, I've ridden across this river many times with you and would have no problem doing so after dark."

The major started to say something when she gave him a withering glance letting him know she meant what she'd said and not to contradict her. He looked away; his jaw clenched as his mouth formed a thin line.

Maggie lowered herself onto a wooden box at the center of the vessel as Jones pushed the ferry from the dock with a long stick, maneuvering the waters with the grace of a gondolier beneath the full moon. The major stood like a sentinel watching the small wake rippling from the sides of the flat-bottomed vessel. His attitude toward Jones bothered her. Based on his recent behaviors, Maggie had been pleased with his progress in dismissing his antiquated mindset. Yet, he seemed agitated with her declaration that she would ride alone with Jones.

When the ferry docked on the other side, the major helped Maggie onto the shore. She turned to Jones and reached out her hand.

"Thank you, Jones, for working so late."

With a quick glance at the major, Jones kept his hand at his side. Maggie's annoyance with the major's attitude was growing.

"Goodnight," she said, starting toward a wagon waiting a few feet away. An older Negro dressed in overalls and a plaid shirt perched on the bench seat.

"Perhaps I should go with you," the major offered, scrutinizing the man.

"Major, I find your insinuations reprehensible. Would you have the same concerns if he were white?"

"Actually, I would never allow a lady to ride unescorted with a man, Negro or otherwise."

"Didn't bother you for the ride to Halston," she retorted.

"That was different. I wouldn't take advantage of the situation."

"But he would?" She planted her hands on her hips, her blood boiling. "I'll have you know the man in the wagon is Henry. He works for Dr. Towne and has driven me many places before without incident," she blustered.

A smile curled the major's lips.

"May I ask what you find so amusing?" she declared, anger accenting her words.

"Has anyone ever told you how beautiful you are when aggravated?"

"Major, how dare you say such a thing?"

"James, please. And I said nothing inappropriate. Your convictions are admirable, Maggie. I admire the depth of your principles."

He offered his hand to help her into the wagon, which she allowed even though she was irritated with him for his insolence toward Jones and Henry.

"Thank you for an enlightening evening," he said with a bow.

"Thank you, *Major,* for escorting me across the river," she replied curtly.

"Please don't be cross with me," he said. "Your guidance

these last few months has helped me to see things in a different light. But old habits take time to quell."

"I'm not upset with you, only disappointed in your misguided opinions. I assure you my interactions with white men have been much more negative than any Negro."

He stared at the ground for a moment before speaking. "I'm sorry for that."

"Don't be," she retorted. "I survived despite my dreadful encounters."

"Thank you, Henry, for seeing Mrs. Daniels home," he said to the driver.

Maggie exhaled as the wagon lurched forward leaving the major at the dock. Even though she knew change took time, she was exasperated by his poor attitude. Surely by now, he could see the error of his ways.

A short while later, the carriage tottered down the drive to the plantation house. Lanterns blazed on the front porch and from inside the two-story structure, casting eerie shadows across the yard.

"Thank you, Henry, for driving me home," she said, climbing down from the wagon.

"Happy to do so," he replied with a tip of his hat.

Maggie paused at the base of the porch steps, taking in the twinkling stars overhead. Overall, the evening had been pleasant despite her stiff legs and aching feet. If only she could have garnered information about Seth's regiment from the officers at the gathering. Unfortunately, she never got the opportunity.

Maggie trudged inside, grabbed one of the lanterns, and extinguished the rest. Shuffling up the stairs to her room, she changed into her night clothes, and climbed into bed. Even though she was exhausted, her mind raced from the pleasure of dancing again to her discontent regarding the attitudes of the soldiers she'd overheard at the gathering. At least the major was trying to correct his distorted ideals. He could be so agreeable at times and infuriating at others. Never had she felt so conflicted about a person. Sleep fingered Maggie's limbs as her lids fluttered shut. Her dreams were filled with scenes of the evening's dance except instead of the major, she waltzed with Seth.

Chapter 23

June 1863

Maggie

"Maggie," Dr. Towne called out. She entered Maggie's small work space with a petite black woman neatly dressed in a plain cotton frock, her head wrapped in a cloth, and dark piercing eyes. Something in her small stature exuded confidence with an aura that demanded respect. "This is Harriett Tubman. She's come for some supplies."

Goosebumps prickled Maggie's skin. While Maggie had heard of the legendary woman and her stalwart efforts to free the enslaved via the Underground Railroad, their paths had never crossed. And now she was finally in the presence of Moses, as Mrs. Tubman was affectionately known. Maggie was shocked that a woman so petite could be so powerful.

"It's...wonderful to meet you. I'm Maggie Daniels," she stuttered, offering her hand. Mrs. Tubman returned the handshake, the right side of her mouth curling.

"You any relation to the Ghost?"

Maggie's heart pinged at the sound of Seth's Railroad persona.

"Mr. Daniels is my husband," Maggie replied. Sorrow tugged at her heart. Where was he and more importantly, was he alright?

"I've heard 'bout you as well. The two of you done a lot of good work."

"Thank you," Maggie said, her cheeks warming at the compliment. This woman had always been a hero in her eyes.

"Please pack whatever Mrs. Tubman requires," Dr. Towne said. "If you'll excuse me, I have a group of students awaiting my arrival." With a bow of her head, she exited the small space.

Mrs. Tubman handed her a list of what she needed. Maggie pulled things from shelves and packed them into a large basket, excitement pulsing through her limbs. Harriet Tubman was almost mythical on the Underground Railroad. She'd successfully freed dozens of the enslaved in only thirteen trips without losing a single soul. She was also renowned for her ability to disguise herself. One story told of her walking past her former master without being recognized. More than anything, Maggie wanted to sit and discuss how she'd been so successful. But now wasn't the time.

"These things are mostly for wounds. Are you helping with the injured?" Maggie asked.

"Can't say right now but they'll be needed soon."

"Do you want me to write down instructions for their use?"

"Just tell me," Harriet replied boldly. "Can't read."

This bolstered Maggie's admiration. It was astounding what Harriett had endured and accomplished without the ability to read. Maggie explained in detail how each remedy was to be applied. Mrs. Tubman gave a nod then walked out the door with the basket of ointments and salves, boarded a wagon, and headed down the drive in a cloud of dust.

Standing in the doorway, Maggie pondered the secretive nature of Harriett's plans. The Underground Railroad was still functioning but had been greatly hindered due to the war. Perhaps that's what Harriet needed the supplies for. Then why not disclose her intentions, especially if she knew Maggie had been part of the Railroad? Regardless, Maggie was thrilled to have met one of the great heroes of the enslaved. Someday, she hoped, people would speak of Harriett Tubman with awe.

The afternoon was busy for Maggie as she mixed liniments for sore muscles and tended to the vegetable garden. The sun had softened to a deep glowing gold as it prepared to hand day over to night. Caked in sweat and dirt, Maggie closed the door to the shed and trudged to the house to wash up for supper. The major would arrive soon, and she was determined to find out if he knew anything of Mrs. Tubman's endeavors.

After dinner, Maggie and the major sat on the porch rocking while Dr. Towne and Miss Murray strolled about the yard discussing plans for the school.

"I met Mrs. Tubman this morning," Maggie said.

"A formidable woman," he replied.

"I'm glad you feel that way. I was curious, do you know what she's doing in the area?"

He rocked quietly before answering. "I can tell you now that things have been set in motion," he said, looking at Maggie. "Mrs. Tubman has been gathering information from the colored folks for several months. With the information she's provided, Colonel Montgomery will be leading an attack on the Combahee River about ten miles north of here where the Salkehatchie and Little Salkehatchie rivers meet."

"When?" Maggie asked, stilling the rocker.

"As we speak," he replied, a roguish grin curling his lips.

Maggie resumed her rocking mulling over what the major had shared. No wonder Mrs. Tubman had wanted so many salves and remedies. There'd be a large number of injured men.

"Do you feel the battle will be a success for the Union?"

"Without doubt," he replied with a nod.

"You don't believe the fighting will make it this far, do you?"

His eyes twinkled in the twilight as his gaze fixed on hers. "Not a chance. This battle will be fought on the river and isn't likely to spread from its intended location. I've seen some of the plans and they're quite brilliant. Victory is almost guaranteed. With the information Mrs. Tubman has garnered there's little chance of defeat."

Maggie swallowed hard. Anytime skirmishes neared their area she got a bit nervous. Although the south was outnumbered, and in many cases out-gunned, they'd fought hard and won many of the battles. Nothing was failsafe in war.

"Hopefully, this will be the closest the fighting gets to us," she said quietly.

"There will be one more blow to this area very soon."

"What's that?" she asked, puzzled by the obvious joy radiating from his eyes.

"The Bluffton Boys started this mess and need to be taught a lesson for their indiscretions." He paused. "Several officers have decided to burn the town of Bluffton. We need to send a message that their rebellious ways will not go unpunished."

Maggie gasped, her hand covering her mouth.

"Certainly, you don't deny these men the retribution they deserve for starting the war?"

"I'm aware of their role in this conflict. It's just..." She hesitated, unsure how to broach the subject with a man who seemed almost jubilant over the upcoming devastation to the town she called home.

"What is it, Maggie?"

"My cottage is in Bluffton. I understand the outrage you and your fellow officers must feel toward the people of this area, but that doesn't make the destruction of my home or those of my neighbors any less distressing." Her chest was heavy as she chewed her lower lip and brushed a tear from her cheek. The idea of the Polk's mansion and her family's cottage being burned to the ground was painful. Not to mention the danger to the workers who'd stayed behind.

The major stopped rocking and faced her. "Where is your home?"

"On the Polk's land, Rose Hall Plantation."

He took in a deep breath and rubbed his jaw. "How far from the township is this place?"

"Just west of town," she gasped, clutching her chest. "Many of our workers are still there. These are wonderful people. They don't deserve to be misplaced."

"Don't you mean the slaves that were left behind?" he asked, sarcasm dripping from his words.

Anger straightened Maggie's back as she responded. "There is not a single slave on that plantation! Every worker is free and paid for their services. They stayed behind because it's their home and they didn't wish to leave!"

"Seems an unlikely endeavor, if you don't mind my saying so."

"Are you accusing me of being dishonest, *Major*?" Maggie's tone was sharp enough to slice bread.

He flinched as she emphasized his rank instead of using his first name. "I'd never suggest something so demeaning. But it would be incredibly dangerous to run a plantation in the manner you've indicated."

"True, the Polks put themselves at great risk but that didn't deter them from doing what was right. They've contributed to the care and welfare of many enslaved individuals over the years and don't deserve to have their home destroyed due to the ignorance of others."

The major took in a deep breath. "Very well. I'll send word

to leave Rose Hall untouched. The last thing I want is for you and your family to pay the price for the rebellion. Obviously, you and yours do not share the belief of those who lit the flame of this war."

"Thank you, James," she said, the tension in her muscles beginning to ebb. "I appreciate your assistance in this matter." She only hoped he had the power to follow through on his promise and that their homestead would survive.

Chapter 24

June 1863

Maggie

As the major had predicted, the Combahee River Raid was a huge victory for the Union Army. Not only were the three Union gunboats able to wreak havoc on the area, but Harriett Tubman lived up to her reputation, and her nickname of Moses, freeing seven hundred slaves on the same night. Furthermore, the burning of Bluffton happened a couple of days later, reducing the town's original sixty structures to a mere ten. Thankfully, the major was true to his word and kept Rose Hall safe. Not a single building or person was harmed, giving Maggie a slight sense of relief.

She continued to work long hours each day to thwart the heaviness in her heart. She missed her husband and their children desperately and longed for them to be together again. Maggie wrote to Jane and Joshua as often as possible and enjoyed the letters they sent; however, she'd not heard from Seth in some time. She kept telling herself he was safe but with the fighting intensifying throughout the country, she worried for his well-being.

. . .

A couple of weeks had passed since the Combahee River Raid and the burning of Bluffton. Daybreak crested over the horizon in vibrant hues of lavender and gold as Maggie rose early to run several errands. Thankfully, the temperature was mild on St. Helena Island this summer morning with a strong breeze billowing off the river keeping the humidity at bay.

After making several deliveries and checking on a few locals in need of care, Maggie turned the wagon toward Mr. Henderson's place. Mr. Henderson was one of the newly freed slaves who repaired leather and also created beautiful bridles and halters. He'd been owned by Mr. Jarvis of Frogmore Hall. While Mr. Jarvis had never physically abused Mr. Henderson, he required 90% of his earnings whenever he sold any of his leather work. Mr. Henderson was elated to finally be in complete control of his income.

Since the Union army had arrived in Beaufort, the cavalry men had done business with Mr. Henderson and raved about the quality of his workmanship. Maggie had also noticed he'd taken a shine to Letty, but her friend would have nothing to do with him. Every time he dropped things off at The Oaks she'd scowl and make herself scarce. Poor Mr. Henderson wasn't so easily dissuaded. He kept coming back and Letty kept doing her best to avoid him. It amused Maggie to watch the cat and mouse escapades between the two. If only Letty would consider him, she might finally find the happiness necessary to soften her sardonic nature.

Maggie pulled the horse to a halt and disembarked from the wagon as Mr. Henderson emerged from his small shop. Several leather bridles hung from a hook outside the door of the building, paint flaking from its exterior. A horse grazed in a neighboring pasture and trees whispered their secrets as the wind rustled through the leaves.

"Good afternoon, Miss Maggie," Mr. Henderson called,

wiping his hands on his apron. "You be here to collect dat harness for de doctor?"

"Yes, sir," Maggie replied.

He scooted inside and reappeared moments later with the freshly oiled harness.

"How Miss Letty getting' on?" he queried, a sparkle glinting in his eyes.

"She's well. You should come by for a visit," Maggie suggested. Her friend would have a fit if she knew Maggie was playing cupid.

Mr. Henderson glanced at the sandy ground, the right side of his mouth curling. "Not so sure she be wantin' to see me."

"Nonsense, we all enjoy your visits. Come by any time you're in the area," Maggie said.

"Dat's mighty kind of you." He handed her the harness, a broad smile lifting his cheeks. "Tell the doc I be addin' this to the bill that'll come out at the end of de month."

With a nod, Maggie placed the harness in the wagon, climbed onto the bench seat, and prodded the horse forward. For a man who'd been held in slavery his entire life, Mr. Henderson was sharp with numbers and ran his business proficiently. His adjustment to freedom had been much smoother than that of the field workers.

Maggie made one more stop at Mrs. Buckley's place to pick up some canning jars before heading back to the plantation. She jostled over the pitted road, the summer sun chasing away the cooler temps from earlier. The Lowcountry humidity had kicked in making it feel as if she was being brought to a boil in a stew pot, every inch of her body soaked with sweat.

Thankfully, she'd stopped wearing gloves months ago as there was no need for gentility under the current circumstances. The work in which she engaged wore heavily on her hands. Growing the vegetables and herbs needed for her remedies in addition to the arduous task of mixing the concoctions and canning vegetables had left rough calluses on her palms and fingertips.

Most of the time she worked on her own but occasionally Willa and Letty helped when they weren't instructing the freed women in herbal remedies. Understandably, the Negroes seemed more comfortable learning from Willa and Letty. Maggie was glad to see them sharing their knowledge with others and encouraging them to be more independent.

Maggie turned the horse down the sandy path beneath a canopy of moss draped branches leading to The Oaks. Dust swirled as the horse trotted toward the barn where Henry met her.

"Hey, Miss Maggie. You get that harness?" he asked, running a handkerchief across his glistening brow.

"It's in the back of the wagon," she replied, handing him the horse.

"Thank you for gettin' it. Saved me a trip."

"Glad to help," she said, grabbing the canning jars from the wagon.

Maggie ambled along the path to her shed with the box of jars. Perspiration trickled across her forehead, stinging her eyes as she squinted in the sunlight.

Plunking the jars onto her work table, she reached for her apron when she heard the shuffling of feet approaching. Willa stood at the door, huffing from the exertion of hauling her rotund figure around in the oven-like heat.

"Miss Maggie, I was at the house when the mail arrived. I saw this letter addressed to you and thought I oughtta bring it immediately." Willa puffed.

Maggie glanced at the envelope instantly recognizing the handwriting. It was Da's. Her heart skipped a beat as fear for her children's health filled her chest. Tearing the envelope open, she exhaled when she saw another one inside with the words "Soldiers Letter" in a familiar script. Maggie's fingers trembled knowing it was permissible for soldiers to send letters without postage so long as the recipient paid the stamp price. This had to be from Seth.

Willa slipped away giving her some privacy. Maggie ran her hand across the letter as if it were made of velvet. She could hardly contain her excitement as she gently unfolded it, tears cascading across her cheeks.

My dearest Maggie,

I apologize for the length of time since my last letter but I've hardly had opportunity to sleep much less write. My regiment continues its pursuits with great success. We've won most of the battles in which we've been engaged. Our losses have been heavy at times but not to the extent of other groups. As of now, I am still scouting which keeps me from the heaviest fighting although I do not know how much longer that will last. The war is intensifying instead of resolving. It feels as if it will never end.

The only thing that gets me through is thoughts of you. I miss your smile and the way the light turns your curls into shimmering copper. I long for your touch and to hold you in my arms as we fall asleep. I ache for you, Maggie, in a way I cannot begin to express in words. Know that you occupy my every thought and I love you more than life itself. Give the kids hugs and kisses for me.

Lovingly yours,

Seth

Maggie reread the letter several times before collapsing into the chair next to her worktable. Holding the letter to her chest, she closed her eyes as tears washed her face in a combination of gratitude and sorrow. She was thankful to know Seth was alright, but guilt gripped her chest for deceiving him about being on St. Helena. No doubt, she'd have gone mad by now had she remained at the Milners. She missed him so much it physically hurt.

Maggie slipped the letter into her pocket, sweeping the tears from her eyes. There was no time for blubbering. The best thing she could do was get back to work. Immersing herself in her duties occupied her thoughts allowing her to escape the remorse of her dishonesty and the agony of missing her husband. Yet something else brewed in the pit of her stomach, something she wasn't ready to admit even to herself.

Chapter 25

July 1863

Elora

Gettysburg

Smoke and sulphur saturated the air, stinging Elora's nostrils. She galloped across a ridge, trying to reach the far side where her unit was engaged in battle. Despite her warning about the impending invasion, the confederates had made it to the small Pennsylvania town of Gettysburg. It felt as if the world were coming to an end with the screams of men being blown to bits, the stench of flesh decaying in the sweltering conditions, and the grotesque, contorted expressions of the dead. Forcing air into her lungs, Elora fought to maintain her presence of mind. This was no time to falter. Her own survival and that of her fellow soldiers depended on her ability to focus. She had to ignore the fear and revulsion.

Elora couldn't remember the last time she'd slept or eaten anything. Adrenaline pulsed through her veins making her feel as if she was a ghost of herself, a mere shell with no insides or feelings. Emotions were all but gone. Except for her feelings toward Captain Dixon. She pushed them aside. No time for that now.

Jasper crested the hill where smoke billowed in the distance. It looked as if a cloud had fallen from the sky, hovering over the ground below. Realizing she was an open target; Elora quickly maneuvered her horse over the rocky landscape and headed for the woods. She ducked into the shadowy hilltop, laying low against Jasper's mane as she navigated through the wooded terrain. When she reached an opening in the trees, she sat straighter. A fiery sensation cut through her shoulder sending her tumbling to the ground.

Her back hit a rock, shooting pain through her ribcage, and knocking the air from her lungs. The burning in her shoulder intensified like the sting of a thousand hornets. Grabbing at the wound, she sucked in a breath and saw her hand was covered in blood. She fought to steady her breathing but every time she inhaled a stabbing pain ripped through her core. Tears trickled across her dirt caked face as she processed the magnitude of her situation. Everything had happened so suddenly she hadn't time to consider where the shooter was or how many rebels were in close proximity. Now more than ever she needed to focus and find a way to escape.

Panic squeezed her chest, hindering her ability to think clearly. Gazing up through the trees, she searched for a scrap of blue but all she could see was the smokey remnants of gunpowder snaking through the branches.

Her mind fogged over and her vision blurred. No, she told herself, you can't give up. She tried to steady her breathing and lift her torso into a sitting position, but her body wouldn't respond. It was as if she was held down by a boulder. She was going to die here and never see her family again. A sob strangled her, sending another bolt of pain tearing through her chest.

Out of nowhere, two soldiers ran up to her, grabbed her shoulders, and yanked her up. She screamed as they drug her over tree roots and rocks until they reached an opening where another soldier, his sleeves rolled up and arms coated in blood, was furiously bandaging one of several wounded men. Apparently, she was in a makeshift triage. Elora blinked several times and despite the agony racking her body she was relieved to see she'd been rescued by Union soldiers. But her relief was short-lived when she realized the doctor would be working on her soon, meaning he'd have to remove her clothes to treat her injury. She needed to get to her feet and flee.

Once again, Elora tried to sit up but one of the other men gently pushed her back to the ground.

"Stay still soldier," he said gruffly, "Doc will be with you as soon as he can."

He walked away to check another soldier. She had to get away quickly. But how? Looking around, she noticed an overgrown trail that led to the woods. If she could make her way into the wooded area maybe she could find an isolated spot to work on her wound.

More men were brought over and lined up according to the severity of their injuries. In spite of the anguish ravaging Elora's body, she was thankful to see others were in worse shape which meant she'd be moved further down the line for treatment. Until she noticed one of the severely wounded soldiers was her captain.

Fresh tears christened her eyes. He was lying there motionless, his breathing shallow as a blackish crimson stain spread across his chest. Her heart felt as if it might explode, her emotions erupting in waves of despair. After months of suppressing her feelings for the captain, she realized the depth of her adoration bubbling beneath the surface like lava in a volcano.

"That's Captain Dixon," one of the men called out, kneeling at his side.

Another man rushed over and pressed his fingers against

the captain's neck. Shaking his head, he stood. "Not much we can do for him."

The two men raced off amidst the bedlam leaving the captain to perish.

Elora wanted to scream for them to come back and tend to him. Maybe with medical attention he could survive. He was a strong man and deserved a chance. If only she could help but her injury prevented it. Squeezing her eyes shut, she swallowed the bile burning her throat. She couldn't watch him die, not like this. The turmoil swirling through her mind gave her the burst of adrenaline she needed. The commotion around her as soldiers pulled bloodied men to the site while others raced around bandaging and treating wounds gave her the perfect opportunity to sneak away.

Elora lifted her knees slightly and dug her heels into the ground, pushing her body a few inches. Thankfully, the chaotic surroundings prevented anyone from taking notice. She continued doing this until she was able to lean up on her good arm and prop herself against a tree. Taking a few shallow breaths in an effort to ward off the throbbing in her shoulder, Elora struggled to her feet. The trees and brush spun with the force of a tornado almost catapulting her to the ground like an acorn.

Somehow, she was able to grab onto a low-lying branch, the sound of cannon fire and gunshots echoing around her, as she steadied herself. She hobbled further into the wooded area, glancing back to make sure no one had taken notice of her retreat. With one last glance, Elora took in the sight of her captain, his body still as death. Swiping at the tear cascading down her grimy cheek, she nearly lost her balance.

Adrenaline coursed through her limbs giving her the strength to take a few steps. Then her vision swirled, and she crumpled to her knees unable to rise again. She had to get away before they discovered her secret. Prostrate, she felt a hand on her shoulder.

"I'm fine," she muttered, wincing. "Just let me rest for a minute."

"Soldier, you're badly injured, let me help you before you bleed out."

Her heart thrummed at the man's words. She knew that voice. Looking up, Elora gasped as she gazed into the steely blue eyes of one of her dearest friends.

"Seth," she whispered, clutching his hand. "Get me out of here, now!"

Seth cocked his head, bewilderment furrowing his brow.

"Excuse me?" he said, leaning closer, his eyes searching hers.

"I don't have time to explain but I need you to get me away from here, and fast," Elora croaked.

"How do you know me?"

"For goodness' sake, Seth, it's me, Elora!"

Seth's eyes widened in horror as he looked her up and down until the recognition registered in his gaze. Without hesitation, he lifted her up and ran through the woods until they reached an opening near a farm house. Every step jarred her body, barbs of pain stabbing at her wound. Seth set her gently on the ground beneath a maple tree.

"I've got an idea. I'll be right back," he said, hurrying off.

Minutes later he returned, scooped her up, and made his way to a small red barn on the outskirts of the fighting. How he carried her that far without encountering another soldier was astounding. Once inside the barn, he placed her on a pile of straw in the far corner. Rushing back to the door, he peered outside before closing it and returning to her side.

"I'm not even going to ask what you're doing here," he paused, "and dressed like a man?"

"It's a long story," she said, grimacing as he unbuttoned her jacket and pulled it off. "What are you doing?"

"Tending to your wound. You've been shot and lost a great deal of blood. I don't know how you've maintained consciousness."

He pulled a knife from his pocket and began cutting away her shirt, when she grabbed his wrist.

"You can't do that," she groaned, her face flushing.

"Whyever not?" he asked.

"Because, I'm a...you're a..." She swallowed hard, her eyes filling with tears. "Man."

"Elora Polk, you've gotten yourself into one heck of a mess. You obviously took on something you should never have done. I need to clean the wound and treat it or you'll die."

His words were stern, and anger brewed in his eyes. She'd never seen him this intense.

"Let me take care of the wound," she whimpered. "You can't see me...undressed."

"You don't have anything I haven't seen before. This is no time for modesty. If you can fight like a man, then you can put aside propriety like a man."

She winced as she nodded her agreement. As gently as possible, he cut away her shirt and the binding flattening her chest. She looked away, as he inspected the damage in her shoulder from the gunshot, bile filling her mouth over the shame of being exposed combined with the agony of the wound. After two years of living with men, she was shocked at how much humility still remained. Apparently, Seth sensed her shame, removing his coat and covering her breasts as best he could before resuming his examination of her injured shoulder.

"Looks like the bullet went clean through without leaving any fragments. But there's a lot of dirt. I need to clean it up to avoid infection. This is going to hurt."

Seth pulled a flask from his pocket, unscrewed the lid, and handed it to her. "Take a swig," he said, glancing around the space. He walked over to the far corner and grabbed a rake.

"Hold onto this," he said, laying the wooden handle of the rake across Elora's lap.

She nodded her agreement, turned her head, and closed her eyes. Seth poured the whiskey onto the wound making Elora's body tense as she squeezed the handle with all her might, clamping her teeth shut to suppress the scream clamoring to escape.

"Sorry," he whispered as Elora's body crumpled against the straw. "Hang on, I've got a few more things to do."

Tears flooded Elora's face as Seth wiped away the blood and dirt. He reached into his satchel and removed a small jar of salve. After applying it to the wound he bandaged the shoulder. By the time he was done, Elora was soaked in sweat and panting.

Seth held his canteen to her mouth as she guzzled down the metallic tasting water. When she finished, he took a swig, poured some on a strip of cloth, and proceeded to wipe the dirt from her face.

"After dark, I'll try to find some food. When was the last time you ate?" he asked.

"Can't remember. How long has the battle been going?"

"Three days."

Elora closed her eyes. Three days since she'd eaten or slept for any length of time. All of a sudden, her mind began to drift, and all went dark.

She awoke the next morning feeling as if she'd been run over by a stage coach. Every muscle ached, her shoulder throbbed, and her stomach screamed in protest over its empty state. She looked around as light filtered through the crevices of the barn walls. Jasper and Phantom stood in the far corner munching hay but there was no sign of Seth. If it hadn't been for the excruciating pain and aching joints, she'd have thought it was all a dream. At that moment, the barn door creaked open, sending her heart racing until Seth slipped in and closed it back. He carried a basket and his satchel. Plunking down beside her, he pulled the canteen from his side and offered her a drink.

"Where'd you go?" she asked, her voice scratchy.

"To find food. You passed out last night, so I let you sleep. I brought the horses back here and went in search of food."

"Where'd you find Jasper?" she asked, reality slowly cutting through her mind's fog.

"Wasn't hard. Jasper was near where I found you." Seth started digging through the basket and pulled a loaf of bread, cured ham, a slab of cheese, and a bottle of whiskey from within.

Elora's eyes grew as her stomach grumbled. "Where did you get all of that?"

"Located an abandoned farmhouse down the road. I rummaged through their basement and discovered all kinds of things."

Elora's mouth watered at the sight of food. She never imagined how simple fare could become delicacies under such dismal circumstances. Seth doled out the portions and they sat in silence eating and washing it down with the whiskey. Elora had never been much of a drinker outside of an occasional glass of wine, but the war had altered things. So had impersonating a man. Was her change in perspective due to depicting a male role or wartime circumstances? She chuckled at the thought.

"What's so funny?" Seth asked.

"I was wondering whether my taste in food and drink has been influenced by my portrayal of the opposite sex or the war."

Seth shook his head. "Only you would think of such a thing. Speaking of which, what possessed you to dress as a man and join the army? I know your parents didn't condone this."

"Obviously, they know nothing about it," she said, lifting her chin in defiance.

"If you must know the reason behind my decision, I was tired of being fawned over and treated like a porcelain doll."

"And this is the way you chose to prove yourself? I've known you since you were eight years old. You've done some crazy things but nothing this foolish."

With a groan, Elora sat straighter, her brows furrowing. "How dare you accuse me of being foolish? I'll have you know I've accomplished a great deal in this war!"

"Including being shot," he reminded her, taking a bite of the bread.

"That was unfortunate," she mumbled.

Seth leaned forward; his expression grim. "You could've been killed, Elora, not to mention your true identity being revealed. How do you think your parents would have taken that?"

She swallowed hard, trying to control the emotions she'd pent up for so long.

"I was determined not to be injured or killed so they'd never know."

Seth wrinkled his forehead. "How'd that work out?"

"Stop it!" she fussed, anger burning her cheeks. "I did what I thought was best. No one ever took me seriously. I was just sweet little Elora who needed to be protected and pampered. I'm a strong, intelligent woman and deserve to make my own way in this world."

"When has anybody accused you of being weak or insignificant? On the contrary, you're full of spunk and vinegar and we've always had to keep you restrained to prevent you from getting hurt." He reached for her hand, but she yanked it back.

"That's my point. Life is filled with trauma and disappointments. I'm not a child, I'm a grown woman. I need to experience everything, the good and the bad. Otherwise, I'm nothing more than a pretty little shell of a person who walks and talks and stitches seat cushions." Elora slumped back against the pile of straw, a bolt of pain shooting through her chest as she wiped away her tears.

"No one has ever viewed you in that manner," he replied.

Elora's anger melted at his calm demeanor. Seth had been her closest confidant throughout her life. Her own brother moved away when she was young, and Seth had filled that role when he arrived at their plantation. He'd always treated her with respect and now she realized it was more than him being kind to a lady. Her time with the regiment had also broadened her views and strengthened her self-perception. Pride filled her chest. It seemed she was stronger and more capable than she'd ever imagined.

Seth reached for her hand again and this time she allowed it. "As a father, I'll do everything in my power to protect my children from the horrors of the world for as long as I can. Your parents did the same thing, and you'll do the same for your children someday."

Children. Elora had never focused on marriage, instead pursuing her own interests. Then the war came. Things were different now, and until this moment, she hadn't realized that she did want a family. But she wanted a family with the captain.

Choking back a sob, she closed her eyes in an effort to dam up her feelings, but they broke through in a flood of tears. Her body shook as she wept, making her shoulder ache. Seth sat quietly, holding her hand until her gasps began to subside.

"Want to talk about it?" he asked quietly.

"It's stupid," she whined.

"Try me, I'm pretty good with stupid."

Elora rolled her eyes. "I never saw myself married or with a family. I always thought I would go to college, travel the world, and someday take over the plantation."

"But that's changed now?"

With a sniffle, she nodded. "I've made a mess of my life." She hesitated. "I've fallen in love."

"How is that a bad thing?" he asked.

"I'm in love with my captain."

"Oh," Seth said, taking in a deep breath. "And he believes you to be a man."

"That's not it," she mumbled, the tears flowing freely. "He's gone. I saw his body at the triage where they took me after I'd been shot."

"Doesn't mean he was dead," Seth said, with a sympathetic expression.

"Blood was pouring from his chest, and he wasn't moving," she cried. "One of the men checked his pulse and said nothing could be done for him. There's no way he could have survived. I've seen men die from lesser wounds."

Seth moved to her side and pulled her close. She rested her head against his shoulder, gasping out sobs.

"They left him to die," she whimpered. "They didn't even try to save him."

"I'm so sorry, Elora. I truly am."

"The worst part is he never knew how I felt. My secret identity was working so well and then one day I noticed a look in his eyes and a gentleness in his demeanor. That's when I realized he'd captured my heart. Have you any idea how tortuous it is to be in love with someone and not be able to tell him?"

"As a matter of fact, I do. I thought Maggie hated me for the longest time. I wanted desperately to tell her how I felt but she was always pushing me away."

"But you finally told her and now you're married. The captain is dead, and I haven't any recourse," she said, sniffling.

Seth sat for a minute before offering a suggestion.

"You can't share your feelings with him now but there is something you can do to honor his memory."

"What's that?"

"When the war is over, visit his family. Tell them everything you observed in him and what he meant to you. They don't know you as a man so you can go to them as your true self. It doesn't bring him back, but it may give you some peace."

Elora looked into his deep blue eyes and smiled. "I like that idea. Perhaps I'll do that."

Seth offered Elora the bottle of whiskey and she took a long drawl.

"Get some rest," he said. "You have a lot of recovering to do before you can ride again."

"What about you? Won't your regiment wonder where you are?" It hadn't occurred to Elora until this moment that Seth had been with her for nearly twenty-four hours and his fellow soldiers may be searching for him.

"I'm the spymaster for the colonel. He's used to me being gone for days. I'll find a way to get word to him but not until I have you safely on your way."

"On my way, where?" she asked, narrowing her eyes.

"Back to your parents, but I suspect you'll fight me on that."

"I will. I'm needed here."

"What will you say about your absence when you reunite with your unit?"

"I'm not sure. I'll need to come up with a viable excuse as to why I disappeared from triage."

"Or you could let them believe you died and join my regiment," he said, raising his eyebrows.

"How?"

"I can put in a good word for you. That way I can keep an eye on you too."

"If I've learned nothing else while fighting, it's that being distracted by feelings can get you killed," she said. "I'll not put your life at risk."

"I'm usually scouting or spying so I won't be around that much. But I trust my men to look after one another."

"I've been spying too. Maybe I could help with that," she replied, taking another swig of whiskey.

"Spying? How?"

"I dress as a woman and speak with southern sympathizers. My accent makes them believe I'm one of them. It's how I was able to get information to the captain..." Her voice trailed off momentarily as a lump formed in her throat. "It's how I was able to warn him about the confederates changing route and heading for Pennsylvania."

Seth gave a wicked grin and shook his head. "I carried the same information to my colonel."

Elora's eyes lit up at his words. "Then maybe this is the best way. I could spy as a woman like I've been doing and continue as a soldier with your unit."

Seth furrowed his brow. "Let me think about this before I agree to it. I really don't like lying to your parents or putting you in danger."

"It's too late for that. I've been in danger for well over a year. Either help me or I return to my regiment. I'll come up with some sort of excuse."

He blew out a breath. "Fine, I'll get you in with our group, somehow." Reaching into his pocket, he pulled out the garnet brooch. "I believe this belongs to you."

Elora grasped the sparkling jewel and smiled. "Annalissa insisted I wear this for good luck. She said Maggie had done the same. Looks like it worked."

Seth's brows arched. "Annalissa knows about this?"

"Yes," Elora shrugged. "Please don't be upset with her. She knew there was no talking me out of it."

"I'm not happy with her but I understand how stubborn you can be," he said with a wink. "We can't undo the situation so we may as well deal with it as best we can."

Relief washed over Elora. Seth seemed to be accepting her role. More importantly, he was willing to help her continue her efforts so she wouldn't have to return to her regiment and face the captain's absence.

Chapter 26

July 1863

Maggie

A stifling heat blanketed the evening as Major Brunson, Maggie, Dr. Towne, and Miss Murray gathered for supper. Dr. Towne discussed the latest goings-on with the school which seemed to hold more interest for the major as of late. It pleased Maggie to witness the alteration in his views of the freedmen from condescending to tolerance. He still had a long way to go before accepting them as equals but at least he was making headway.

It had been a typical Lowcountry summer with a host of difficulties ranging from swarms of flies and mosquitos to rashes and allergies. The major hadn't been to the plantation house as often to play chess due to obligations at his office. Maggie found herself missing his visits as he'd become a dear friend.

"Do you honestly believe they're absorbing all you and Miss Murray have been teaching them?" the major queried, taking a sip of wine.

"I do. These people are intelligent and hard working. I won't deny it was difficult in the beginning. They'd never been in a formal school situation and for some of the children it took some time to adjust to the structure. Miss Murray and I are quite pleased with their progress."

The major nodded. "I'm glad to hear it," he replied, swirling the wine in his glass, his gaze fixed on the sparkling red liquid. "Command will be pleased with the report."

"Is something the matter?" Dr. Towne asked.

"Not at all," he replied. "I have a great deal on my mind. I'm gathering information for my successor who will be here later in the month."

A hush fell over the table.

"You're leaving?" Maggie asked, her hand resting on her chest.

"I'm being promoted."

"Congratulations," Miss Murray and Dr. Towne chimed in unison.

"Thank you. I'm thrilled with the opportunity although I will miss this place." He glanced around the room before his eyes settled on Maggie.

"I'm happy for you," Maggie said with a forced smile. There was a tug at her heart. She'd miss their chess games and lengthy discussions.

Most days she felt as if she would crumble at any given moment with the heaviness she carried in her heart missing Seth and her children. The major's visits distracted her from those vulnerable feelings, especially in the evenings when she was weary from the day's work and her mind wandered to dark places.

When the dishes were cleared from the table, they all retired to the parlor where Dr. Towne and Miss Murray discussed plans for their students the following day, specifically a writing lesson. Maggie and the major sat at the small wooden table in front of the window. Maggie's fingers rested on her queen as she studied her options. She was so preoccupied by the major's announcement at dinner that she was having difficulty concentrating. She grinned when she saw her opportunity. Lifting her queen, she placed it next to his king.

"Checkmate," she said softly, her eyes meeting his.

"It would appear I did an excellent job teaching you to play. This is the third time in a row you've beaten me."

She sat straighter and smiled at him. "I don't believe for a moment you aren't *letting* me win," she replied.

"Maggie, there are two things I'm quite passionate about, chess and war. I do not compromise in either situation."

Satisfied with his answer, Maggie began organizing the pieces for their next game.

"I shall miss this," she said.

"Perhaps my replacement will indulge you."

"Unlikely. Keep in mind, it's taken me a great deal of effort to mold you into someone fit to be around," she said teasingly. "I doubt he'll be as obliging."

"Regardless of his nature, I've no doubt you will make him into a decent fellow with your stubborn ways and wit."

"You make me sound as if I'm some sort of shrew," she said, pursing her lips. "All I did was help you see the error of your ways and I'm proud of it."

His eyes met hers, holding her gaze for a moment. "It's getting rather late," he said, standing. "I should probably head back to town. Thank you for an enlightening evening."

Maggie stood as he bid goodnight and left, leaving the ladies in the parlor with a promise to return as soon as he was able.

Days later, the major arrived promptly at seven o'clock for dinner followed by a game of chess with Maggie. As he moved his queen toward Maggie's king, she knew the game was over.

"Checkmate," he whispered, glancing across the room at Willa who had fallen asleep on the settee, her head leaning against her chest as she snored softly with her knitting crumpled in her lap.

Maggie grinned as she watched one of her dearest friends snoozing peacefully.

"Let's go out onto the porch," Maggie whispered, rising from her chair.

The major followed closing the screen door quietly behind him. A soft breeze ruffled the curls resting on Maggie's neck as she peered at the stars twinkling against the inky night sky.

"I'm going to miss this place," he said, gazing at the marsh.

"It's magical here," she replied.

"I'll be missing more than the landscape," he said, touching her arm.

Maggie's eyes locked onto his, her heart thumping hard against her ribcage.

"I don't know how else to say this," he said. "I'm in love with you, Maggie."

Maggie took a step back her gaze shifting to the porch floor. His confession both repulsed and thrilled her. She'd spent a great deal of time in his company and had convinced herself it was to distract her from missing Seth. Now she was questioning everything. Did she care for him, and if so, had she inadvertently drawn him in? Chewing her lower lip, she looked up at him. "This isn't an appropriate conversation, Major."

He cringed when she referred to him by his title instead of his name. "I couldn't leave without making my sentiments known. I realize you don't return my affections," he paused, "but I had to let you know just in case..."

"My heart belongs to one man and that's my husband. You've become very dear to me as a friend, but nothing more." She felt her chest constrict as the words left her mouth. She loved Seth and him alone. She was certain of it. So why the churning in her gut and the shortness of breath?

Swallowing hard, the major looked away. "I'm sorry for my brazenness. I shouldn't have said such a thing." His gaze returned to her. "You're the most incredible woman I've ever known. I pray you have a happy life and that someday you can forgive my impertinence."

"I wish you all the best and hold no ill will toward you. Please know, I cannot reciprocate your feelings."

"I understand," he said, running his hand across his mouth. "I should be going. I'll not be back as it would be inappropriate to see you after such a confession."

"Don't punish yourself," she said, grasping his hand. "I consider you a cherished friend but understand that's all I can give."

"Thank you, Mrs. Daniels for your kindness in this matter."

He gave a slight bow, marched down the stairs, mounted his horse, and galloped down the drive.

Maggie exhaled as the screen door creaked open and Willa stepped out.

"Where's the major?"

"He left," Maggie said flatly, hoping to avert any questions. Willa could see straight through a fib. The last thing Maggie wanted was to confront her own feelings regarding the major and discover something might be there.

"You, okay?" Willa asked.

Maggie nodded.

"See you in the morning," Willa said, patting Maggie's arm.

She watched Willa lumber down the drive before stepping back inside. Her friend had been correct in her deductions regarding the major's feelings. Willa was the first to point out that he may be interested in Maggie as more than a friend. She should've listened to her and ceased further interactions with him outside of business. How could she have been so foolish?

Climbing the stairs, Maggie ruminated over the major's confession. Guilt infiltrated her soul as nausea rolled through her stomach. She refused to entertain any notion of attachment to him. The possibility she'd been unfaithful in her thoughts was more than she could stand.

Once in her room, she slipped into her cotton gown and brushed her auburn tresses. As she gazed in the mirror, Maggie began dissecting the time she'd spent in the major's company. His quick side glances when she was in the same room, the joy reflecting in his eyes when they waltzed, the shrewd grin he'd give when she won at chess; they all made sense now. What she'd viewed as friendship was adoration on his part. Except in the depths of her subconscious, she had been aware of his inclinations. She realized that now. It wrenched her heart to think she'd somehow acted in a manner that led him to fall in love. She hadn't meant to encourage him, or had she?

Doubt wriggled its way into her mind. She'd not felt this way since she believed she'd inadvertently seduced Seth away from Elora. Granted, it turned out Elora and Seth were never attached but Maggie didn't know that at the time. Had she repeated the same misguided behavior with the major?

After weaving her coppery locks into a long braid, Maggie walked to her bed, perched on the edge, and sighed. Defeated, she tried to drive away the discomfort permeating her soul. No matter how she viewed the situation, she felt certain she'd unintentionally enticed the major possibly with her own longing for Seth. At least she'd not have to face him again. In a few days he'd be gone and nothing more than a memory.

Too bad Elora wasn't here. She'd have made a good match for him. Shaking her head, Maggie admonished herself for being so silly. The last thing she needed to do was play matchmaker under such dreadful circumstances. Elora was safely ensconced in her missionary work out west, far from the fighting, for which Maggie was thankful.

Blowing out the candle on the night table, Maggie rested her head on the pillow. Despite the late hour, and the exhaustion pulsing through her limbs, she couldn't sleep. Seth entered her thoughts, his deep blue eyes sparkling and his hair curling at the base of his neck. Her heart pounded a bit harder when she imagined him lying beside her, the warmth of his body encapsulating her in comfort. Tears dripped onto her pillow as she squeezed her eyes shut trying to block out the sorrow. She was so tired of being away from Seth and wondering when the war would finally end. Maggie missed her family and her life. She longed for normalcy. Eventually, her quiet sobs subsided as the nightmare of the ongoing conflict and separation from her family haunted her slumber.

Chapter 27

July 1863

Seth

S eth had spent nearly a week at the barn in Gettysburg tending to Elora. She'd always bear a scar from the injury but fortunately no major organs had been damaged. However, Elora hadn't looked him in the eye since he'd seen her without clothing. He'd treated her like a doctor would his patient. Despite the awkwardness of the situation, she seemed appreciative of his efforts.

Once Elora was strong enough to travel, they packed their things and rode to Seth's regiment to meet with his commanding officer. Now more than ever, he needed to keep her close so he could watch over her. He'd never forgive himself if anything happened to her. The Polks had saved his life once and he was determined to repay them by keeping their daughter safe. They'd taken him in when he ran away from his abusive father who'd tried to kill him. When Seth was found in the woods close to their plantation bleeding and near death, they nursed him back to health, and gave him shelter and work. Elora was only eight when he came to live at Rose Hall, and they'd become as close as blood siblings, a bond they held to this very day.

"Let's go over everything again so our story sounds credible when we meet with Colonel Pennington," Seth said as they rode through a dense patch of woods.

"I'm Charles Polk from South Carolina. I lost most of my unit in Gettysburg and was wounded when you found me. You suggested I come with you and join the ranks of your regiment."

Seth glanced over at Elora and shook his head.

"What's the matter?" she asked, concern veiling her face.

"Can't get over how much you look like a man," he chuckled. "Your mother would have a fit if she saw you dressed like this."

"She'd have more of a fit if she knew the things I've seen while portraying a man. Your gender is disgusting when it comes to table manners, or lack thereof, not to mention toileting."

"Spoken like a true lady," he replied, spurring Phantom into a gallop as the woods cleared into a wide-open field.

Elora followed suit trailing behind him until an encampment sprouted over the horizon. Riding up to a large tent, they dismounted, and walked inside.

A hefty man with a forest of graying whiskers glanced over his spectacles as they entered. A slight smile crinkled his eyes as he stood from behind a table concealed beneath a series of maps.

"Daniels, I knew you'd make it. Had us a bit concerned after that bloodbath in Gettysburg."

"Sorry about that sir but I was tending to a fellow soldier," Seth replied, motioning toward Elora who stood ramrod straight. "This is Lieutenant Charles Polk. He took a bullet to the shoulder and nearly bled to death. His unit was wiped out, so I brought him with me."

The colonel raised one eyebrow. "And you trust this young man?" he asked.

"Yes sir. We knew each other in South Carolina. He's an excellent tracker. We used to hunt together."

"Another southerner fighting to preserve the Union. Interesting." The colonel took his seat and smoothed his beard. "If it weren't for Daniels' recommendation soldier, I'd not believe in your loyalty."

"I understand, sir," Elora replied.

"You're good at tracking, Polk?"

Elora glanced at Seth before answering. "Yes, sir."

The colonel ran his tongue across his teeth before speaking. "Daniels, take Polk with you for the next few weeks and get him acquainted with what you do. With the fighting intensifying we could use another scout."

"Yes, sir," Seth replied, relieved Elora would be with him so he could keep an eye on her. Most importantly, the colonel believed their story. Hopefully, Elora would be able to maintain her male persona. If her true identity were discovered, they'd both hang for it.

"Get him settled in your tent, Daniels. And get some rest. I've got something I need you to do first thing in the morning."

They gathered their horses, untacked them, and settled them for the night. Once they were in Seth's tent, Elora smacked Seth's arm.

"Why'd you tell him I was good at tracking? I've never hunted in my life!"

"I had to come up with something to keep you from the front lines."

Elora's face reddened. "I've been fighting and spying in this war for a long time. I don't need you to protect me now."

"I wasn't trying to protect you. Your skills as a spy will come in handy, especially with your female identity. I don't like what you're doing but I also know how capable you are."

For the next few weeks, Seth and Elora scouted together. They made a formidable team. With his scouting savvy and knowledge of southern attitudes along with Elora's feminine attributes, they were immensely successful at gathering secrets. They'd just returned from a mission when Seth was summoned to Pennington's tent.

"Have a seat, Daniels," he said, motioning to the chair in front of his desk.

Seth removed his hat and sat.

"You and Polk have done a good job," the colonel said. "The last bit of information will serve us well."

"Glad to be of service, sir."

"I have another mission for you."

"Yes, sir," Seth replied, sitting straighter in his chair.

"I'm sending you to St. Helena Island off the coast of Beaufort," he said.

A slight smile curled Seth's lips at the idea of going home. If only Maggie could be with him.

"I know the area well," Seth said, trying to contain his excitement. "Will Polk be going with me?" He hoped she'd be able to accompany him. Maybe they'd have a chance to check on Rose Hall and see how it was faring. He'd write Maggie once he got there and give her all the latest news on the area.

"Polk will be assigned elsewhere. You're going to be accompanying another officer, Lt. Colonel James Brunson," he replied.

"What's our mission?" Seth asked, confused by the request to work with an officer he'd never met.

"This is a humanitarian assignment," the colonel said. "You'll leave in the morning. Brunson will fill you in on what's required."

"Why me?"

"He requested you," the colonel replied flatly, letting Seth know not to question him further.

He dismissed Seth who walked back to his tent, puzzled by the sudden alteration in his regular duties. He didn't like the idea of leaving Elora even though he knew she was capable of handling the spying on her own. She was formidable in her duties, and he admired her for it. Still, he wanted to protect her at all costs.

"Everything alright?" Elora asked, sitting up on her cot.

Seth nodded as he started going through his trunk. "Being sent to St. Helena on a humanitarian mission."

"Humanitarian mission?" she asked, quirking a brow.

"A Lt. Colonel Brunson requested I accompany him. Don't know the guy."

"Maybe he wants you to go because you're familiar with the area," Elora said. "How wonderful to be able to go home. Do you think you'll have time to check on our folks at the plantation?" Excitement radiated in her stare.

"I hope so. I want to make sure everyone is safe and have what they need. Those blockades are really hurting the south."

"Did the colonel say anything about me?"

"Says he has a mission for you." He sat next to Elora on the cot and blew out a long breath. "Promise you'll be careful and not take any unnecessary chances."

"Stop treating me like a woman," she responded, her voice firm.

"You are a woman, and not any woman, but one whom I love. Please don't make me regret bringing you here."

Her attitude softened as she gripped his hand. "I'll do my best to avoid getting killed, captured, or hurt."

"I'm counting on it," he said, standing.

Seth spent the next hour gathering his things and penning a letter to Maggie letting her know where he was heading. He'd been more proficient in writing as of late and wanted to remain consistent. Writing letters seemed to reduce the distance between them. When he finished it, he folded it into an envelope, and addressed it to the Milner's farm with 'Soldier's Letter' written on the outside.

Early next morning he posted the letter and rode Phantom to the meeting point where he'd rendezvous with Brunson. He was looking forward to discovering more about this humanitarian mission and why he was selected for it.

Chapter 28

Early August 1863

Maggie

Maggie sat on the front porch of the house sipping fresh lemonade while reading a letter from Lt. Colonel Brunson. She hadn't heard from him since he'd left and was surprised he'd written to her. Thankfully, he didn't renew his sentiments from the last time they met. It was still an uncomfortable situation and she continued to blame herself for his misplaced attraction.

The letter was brief, merely saying he would be in the area within the next day or two and wished to pay a visit to the doctor and possibly have a game of chess with Maggie. A slight flutter tickled her heart at the thought of seeing him again. She'd missed their evening engagements over the chess board.

Maggie rested the correspondence in her lap as she gazed out over the water. An egret took flight from the dense marsh grasses, its lanky legs trailing behind as it soared upward. Mulling over the Lt. Colonel's letter, Maggie decided she would decline the chess game. It was too awkward being in his presence, especially knowing how he felt about her. She couldn't dissuade him from seeing Dr. Towne, but she'd make herself unavailable while he was there.

She'd also received a letter from Seth for which she was grateful. Learning he'd been at Gettysburg almost broke her spirit. So many had perished in that gruesome three-day battle, and it haunted her. She was relieved he'd survived but mourned for those who didn't make it out alive.

Maggie sipped the tart drink, thankful for the breezes wafting in from the water. Granted, all it did was circulate the already stifling hot air, but the movement made the balmy summer heat more bearable. Rocking, she leaned her head against the back of the wooden rocker, letting her mind drift to brighter days. She closed her eyes and pictured her children gamboling about the yard in front of their cottage while Seth fished from the dock behind their home. Tears stung her eyes at the memory. Would they ever experience such simple joys again?

Filling her lungs with the salty scent of the marsh, Maggie stood in a stretch. No need wallowing in what ifs. There was work to be done. The gardens were in desperate need of weeding after the heavy rains a few days prior. Considering the date of the letter, Lt. Colonel Brunson could arrive at any time. Dr. Towne was at the school house so Maggie would have to wait until dinner to inform her of his impending visit.

Maggie fastened the sun bonnet on her head, grabbed a basket, and headed down the stairs of the porch. Grass crunched beneath her leather ankle boots as she traipsed across the yard where rows of vegetables grew alongside her work shed. She set about tugging weeds and plucking a few late tomatoes and stalks of okra which were abundant at this time of year. Pearls of sweat trickled down her neck and forehead, stinging her eyes. Mopping the perspiration from her brow with a hankie, she nearly jumped from her skin when a hand reached out and touched her shoulder.

"Maggie?"

Lt. Colonel Brunson's voice sounded strange as she swung around. "James, you startled me...."

She sucked in a breath. It wasn't Brunson. Her mind struggled to accept what her eyes were seeing. It was Seth. But how? Throwing her arms about his neck, she melted into his embrace as he lifted her off the ground and spun her around.

"You're here," was all she could get out before he placed her gently on the ground, his lips pressed against hers. All of a sudden everything in the world ceased to exist. The only thing was Seth. She smiled up at him as he took a step back, surprise furrowing his brow.

"What are you doing here?" she asked.

"I might ask you the same thing," he said, his gaze locking onto hers.

Stumbling for the words to say, Maggie chewed her lower lip. "I, um, well, it's a long story," she managed to say, glancing toward the ground. Her chest tightened. She felt like a bear caught in a trap, her mind searching for an explanation that would pacify her husband. When she met his stare, she saw the sparkle in his eyes and the slight curl of his lips. "Must we discuss this now?"

He pulled her close, his gaze penetrating her soul. "Right now, all I want is you."

He kissed her long and hard, taking her breath away. Sweat dripped across her forehead and down her neck.

"Come inside for some lemonade," she said, grasping his hand.

With butterflies swirling in her stomach, she led Seth inside. Violet was in the kitchen sorting through the larder when they entered.

"Violet, this is my husband, Seth," she declared, out of breath. "May we have some lemonade?" Maggie could hardly contain her excitement. Seth was actually here. She hadn't seen him in what felt like an eternity.

Violet's eyebrows arched. "Dis a nice surprise, Miss Maggie. De lemonade be in de pitcher on de table," she said with a quick nod in that direction. A mischievous grin dimpled her cheeks. "I best get down de road to Miss Jinkens' place."

Maggie cocked her head in confusion. "I thought you were there yesterday. Did you forget something?"

Violet snorted and shook her head. "I didn't forget nothin'. I be back in 'bout an hour or so," she said, removing her apron and affixing a hat to her salt and pepper gray hair. "Ain't nobody 'spected to be round until later." She winked and left the room.

Maggie poured two glasses of lemonade and handed one to Seth. He put it back on the table and took Maggie's hand.

"Where's your room?" he asked, his lips brushing her hand, making her insides quiver.

"Upstairs," she replied.

The seductive grin on his face nudged Maggie forward. Gripping his hand, she led him up the stairs to her room and closed the door.

Maggie delighted in the comfort of Seth's skin against hers as he held her close. After being separated by war for almost two years, his touch had been a distant memory. Now he was here.

Rolling over, Maggie planted a kiss on Seth's lips. "I've missed you," she muttered, her body more relaxed than it had been in months.

"I think of you every day," he replied, his lips grazing hers.

"I still can't believe you're here." She smiled.

Seth leaned up on one elbow. "What *are* you doing here?" he asked.

Taking in a deep breath, Maggie fingered the edge of the sheet as she contemplated her response. She hadn't considered Seth discovering her whereabouts and wasn't prepared for his questions. "Dr. Towne asked me to join her. She's been tasked, along with her friend Ellen Murray, with educating the freed slaves. We not only provide an education but medical care as well."

Seth's expression darkened. "When were you going to tell me?"

"I didn't want to worry you. You need to be alert and not concerned about my welfare."

"I'm always concerned about you, Maggie. I love you."

"Which is why I decided not to let you know where I was," she replied. "It's safe here and I've been able to provide a great deal of support."

Seth hesitated. "You still should've told me."

"I'm sorry if I've upset you, that was never my intention. But I couldn't sit around the Milner's farm and fret. I needed to stay busy, and this has allowed me to do that." Her Irish spirit was beginning to take hold. "By the way, how did you know to come here?"

"Lt. Colonel Brunson told me to pay a visit to the new school on the island for the freedmen," he replied.

Her chest tightened at the mention of Brunson's name. Why had he done all this? Seth swung his legs over the edge of the bed and began dressing.

"Do you have to be somewhere?" she queried, pulling the sheet over her chest as she sat up.

"I need to check in with headquarters not to mention the

woman downstairs said she'd be back in an hour so we'd better get dressed."

Maggie slipped from bed and put on her undergarments and frock while Seth pulled on his boots. She understood why he was disgruntled but it wasn't like she'd gone into battle.

"And another thing, Maggie." Seth grasped her shoulders, his gaze locking onto her emerald green eyes. "Why did you call me James when I found you in the garden?"

"Ja...," she stuttered. "I mean Lt. Colonel Brunson sent a letter saying he would be coming for a visit. I assumed it was him. It never occurred to me you would be the one to arrive."

Seth inhaled and looked toward the window where the gauzy curtains danced on marsh breezes. "I don't understand. Lt. Colonel Brunson requested I accompany him to Beaufort on a humanitarian mission and then I find you here. Is there something I should know about the two of you?"

Maggie took a step back, her heart pounding. "What are you inferring?"

Seth licked his lips. "I'm pulled from my duties to come here with an officer I don't know. I arrive to find my wife, who is supposed to be in Pennsylvania, working in a garden and saying another man's name when I touched her shoulder."

Without thinking, Maggie's hand landed across his cheek with a loud thwack. "How dare you insinuate such a thing? I've been immersed in my work here, which by the way, is not as dangerous as what I did on the Railroad. Yes, I know *Lt. Colonel Brunson*, but as a friend and nothing more." Maggie took in a breath, guilt flooding her chest as she tried to dismiss the undercurrent of feelings for James coursing through her veins. She kept telling herself he was only a friend, regardless of how he felt. "The only thing that has consumed my every thought is you," she said boldly. "How could you believe anything else?"

Seth stiffened as he rubbed his cheek. "Maybe I'm a bit hesitant to believe anything you say since you were less than honest about your whereabouts these past two years. If you lied to me about that, how can I believe anything else you tell me?"

Maggie's head was spinning. What was happening? She felt as if someone was tearing her heart out with a dull knife. "You had no problem *reuniting* with me and now you accuse me of being an adulterer?"

"I don't know what to think right now," he replied, running his fingers through his sandy locks.

Maggie's anger softened as she grasped Seth's hand, "You are the only man I've ever loved. Please believe me."

Seth withdrew his hand and took a step back. "I need to report to headquarters."

Without another word, he left the room. Maggie's knees gave way as she crumpled onto the bed and sobbed into her pillow. She'd spent the past two years pining for her husband and now he was questioning her faithfulness. Dark thoughts raced through her mind. Had James staged this scenario to sabotage her relationship with her husband? And if so, was it revenge or a means to clear the way for himself? Regardless, she'd have a word with the Lt. Colonel when she saw him next and demand he remedy the situation.

Sitting up, Maggie wiped the sorrow dripping from her cheeks. Her muscles felt like mush and her stomach was in knots. Something in the depths of her soul was niggling at her conscience. Something she couldn't face. She loved Seth, there was no doubt about that. Her connection with James was merely friendship. At least in her mind they were only friends.

Maggie pressed the heels of her hands to her eyes. Was her bond with James more than she realized? And if so, had she led him to believe there was something between them? Maggie shook the idea from her mind. It was preposterous, she told herself. Besides, now wasn't the time to dwell on such things. First, she needed to find her husband and convince him she'd remained faithful in his absence. She'd deal with the rest after she worked things out with Seth. The question was, would he be willing to listen?

Chapter 29

Early August 1863

Seth

Seth mounted Phantom and raced down the sandy road. He wasn't sure where he was going but he had to get away. His mind and heart warred with each other as he pushed Phantom to a full gallop. Dark images of his beloved wife engaging with another man plunged into his thoughts while his heart buoyed with the hope she'd never do such a thing.

Instead of heading to the dock to catch the ferry, he rode Phantom toward the trails he'd traveled years before while on missions to help escapees. There was a peaceful spot he remembered overlooking the river and he headed toward it. The trees parted as he neared the location, slowed Phantom to a walk, and dismounted. Rambling to the edge of the water, he took in the serenity of his surroundings. Pelicans dipped into the glittering water scooping up a snack before soaring into the great blue expanse above. A strong breeze billowed through his hair as he took in the salty scent of the Lowcountry.

Seth's chest ached as he ruminated on the argument with Maggie, his stomach twisting as he contemplated her words.

They'd had minor disagreements in the past but none as acrimonious as this. Rubbing his cheek where she'd slapped him, he dropped his head in shame. He'd deserved it. How could he think such a thing more or less accuse her of infidelity? Then again, she wouldn't be the first woman to stray into the arms of another while her husband was at war.

He needed to apologize and beg her forgiveness. No doubt, she'd be furious when he returned, and rightfully so. Maybe he needed to let her settle a bit before going back. Lowering himself onto the sandy ground, he ran his hands through his hair. Remorse infiltrated his soul. Obviously, the war had taken its toll on his ability to think logically.

As he leaned against the massive trunk of a century old oak, he closed his eyes allowing the tears to flow. He'd endured so much in the war from nearly being beaten to death to discovering Elora portraying a soldier to watching comrades being blown to bits before his very eyes. It had changed him. Now he questioned whether it had changed him in a negative way. To accuse Maggie of having an affair was something he never would have considered before the war. Now he'd said things he could never take back and it stabbed at his heart.

Burying his face in his hands he wished he could undo what had happened and start again. But that wasn't possible. He took in a deep breath and stared out over the waterways snaking through fields of marsh grass. Somehow, he had to make this right. But not today. He needed time to think things through and let Maggie calm down.

Seth hoisted himself onto Phantom and rode to the dock, caught the ferry, and headed toward the two-story Federal style mansion serving as headquarters on the main street of Beaufort.

Taking the steps two at a time, Seth entered the once grand mansion. Dings and holes marred the plaster walls and the lackluster furnishings showed the neglect of being regularly polished. Seth's boots echoed on the bare heart-pine floors as he approached what would have been a front parlor and rapped on the doorjamb.

Lt. Colonel Brunson looked up from a table where he was reviewing several maps. Two doors framed the fireplace with a large mirror crowning the mantel. The floors were scuffed from boots scraping across them and the windows were dull from lack of washing. The house definitely showed wear.

"Daniels, come in," Brunson said, motioning toward a chair next to the table.

Seth took a seat, removed his hat, and waited.

"I'm surprised to see you here," the Lt. Colonel said. "I thought you'd still be with your wife."

"Why'd you bring me here?" he asked.

Brunson leaned forward and rested his elbows on the table.

"What do you mean?"

"Why did you ask me to accompany you here?" Seth repeated. Anger brewed in his chest, taking hold of the hurt. Even though the man outranked him, he wanted to know his intentions.

"I brought you here to help with a mission," he replied, his gaze steady as Seth searched for any indication of deception.

"Why? You don't even know me."

Brunson shifted in his chair. "If you must know...." He paused when a soldier bolted through the door, out of breath.

"Sir, we have news from Charleston," the young man declared, handing a crumpled paper to the Lt. Colonel.

"If you'll excuse me, Daniels," he said, reading through the correspondence. His face paled as he scribbled a response and handed it back to the young soldier. "Take this to Major Greggs immediately."

"Yes sir," he said, turning on his heels and rushing from the room.

"Daniels, I'm sorry but this requires my immediate attention. We can continue this discussion another time but for now I must get to Charleston."

Seth gave a nod as Brunson hurried from the room leaving him with more questions than answers. Standing, Seth exited the building, mounted his steed, and wandered down the dusty main street. He was shocked by the altered state of the once lovely downtown area of Beaufort. Phantom plodded along as Seth watched Union soldiers hanging out of upper windows surveying the traffic on the street below while others gathered in corners of storefronts, drinking, spitting tobacco, and calling out an occasional obscenity when a woman passed.

Loneliness and despair consumed him. What had possessed him to put off his apology to Maggie? Cowardice, he thought. He didn't want to face the pain he'd inflicted on her. Regardless, he needed to make amends with his wife, and it couldn't wait another moment. Turning Phantom around, he rode toward the ferry but found it missing.

"Excuse me," he called to an older black man passing by. "Could you tell me when the ferry will return?"

"Not 'til morning," he replied. "Jones had to make some repairs."

Seth's heart sank. There was no other way to the island unless he could find someone with a boat. But he couldn't risk leaving Phantom. At this point in the war, many would steal a horse without remorse and Phantom was a fine creature. Resigned to the fact he was stuck in town, Seth returned to headquarters where he settled Phantom in the stables for the night. After speaking with the officer on duty, Seth decided to sleep in the hayloft, so he'd be close to his horse. With his appetite long gone, he retired for the evening.

Seth fluffed the loose hay into a comfortable place to sleep, removed his boots, and reclined onto the prickly tufts. He stared at the ceiling, wondering what Maggie was thinking. Would she believe he'd run off? She had no idea he was stuck on the mainland. His chest ached at the idea she might be suffering from his words. Rolling over onto his side, he willed himself to sleep. First thing in the morning he'd go back to the island and beg her forgiveness even if he had to swim across the river to get there.

Chapter 30

Early August 1863

Maggie

Too upset to face anyone or answer questions about why Seth had left so abruptly, Maggie skipped supper, choosing to stay in her room. She'd spent the entire day listening for the sound of Phantom's hoofbeats pounding down the drive, but they never came. Her eyes were as dry as the desert after crying a river of tears. How could Seth have thought she'd be unfaithful? He was the only man she'd ever loved.

The worst part was Seth running off. She'd been elated when he showed up. Now more than ever, she longed to have him lying next to her, his breath tickling the back of her neck as he held her close.

A fresh flow of tears trickled across her cheeks as she perched on the edge of the unmade bed where she and Seth had spent the afternoon. Why hadn't he come back? She was certain he'd return and apologize for his unfounded accusations. Guilt tugged at her conscience. Perhaps there was something more to her relationship with James than she realized. She hadn't admitted this to herself before now, but she did feel a slight pull toward him. Yet she knew in her soul Seth was the only man she wanted. The war was bad enough, but the emotional turmoil swirling through her mind was unbearable.

Surely, Seth would return tomorrow so they could work through this misunderstanding. But what if he didn't? She couldn't stand the thought of animosity lingering between them. Thank goodness Jane and Joshua weren't here to witness what had transpired. They'd never understand a disagreement of this magnitude. She and Seth had quarreled but they'd never fought like this.

Exhausted from the ebb and flow of emotions for the day, Maggie nuzzled her head against the pillow hoping Seth would come bounding up the stairs and make amends. But the only sounds were the sullen cries of cicadas and a hoot owl. Maggie tossed and turned until sleep escorted her to dreamland where the wounds of her country and her marriage were healed.

Chapter 31

Early August 1863

Seth

Seth stirred from a restless slumber. Visions of Maggie's hand making contact with his face had haunted his dreams. He sat up and glanced around the hayloft. Still dark. The only sounds were the shifting of hooves on straw and a few early morning songbirds. Too wired to sleep, he decided to get up. Slipping on his boots, he climbed down the ladder, and checked on Phantom.

A soft nicker came from Phantom's stall.

"Hey old pal," he whispered, walking to the stall, and stroking his horse's velvety muzzle. "I've really made a mess of things. As soon as the sun comes up and the ferry arrives, we're going back to the island and beg Maggie's forgiveness."

As if his steed understood, he bobbed his head several times and pawed the ground. Seth threw a flake of hay into the space and watched as Phantom chomped down mouthfuls.

Seth stepped outside, the early morning air a refreshing break from the stifling confines of the barn. Hoofbeats shattered the quietude as Lt. Colonel Brunson rode up and dismounted, his face flushed and his horse's nostrils flaring. Indignation rushed through Seth's chest at the sight of him. Taking in a deep breath, he reminded himself that the colonel outranked him and not to let the anger brewing in his heart boil over. Even though things had ended badly with Maggie, he needed to get the Lt. Colonel's side before reacting.

"This is unexpected," Brunson said, removing his hat. "I was just getting ready to send someone on the ferry to fetch you."

"Why would you send word by the ferry?" Seth asked, his eyes narrowing.

"I assumed you'd be back on the island with your wife," he huffed.

Seth noticed the dark circles beneath Brunson's eyes and the tightness in his jaw. Something was wrong.

"What's the matter?" Seth asked, pushing his annoyance aside.

"I've received word of a plot by the Rebels to intercept the railroad south of Charleston. We need as many reinforcements as possible, immediately."

"I know the route well and will get there as fast as I can."

"Good luck to you, Daniels," he said as he remounted his horse and rode away.

Seth tacked Phantom, swung into the saddle, and started down the street when the ferry dock came into view. He needed to see Maggie before he left. His heart felt like it was being squeezed in a vice. The ferry would take nearly an hour to get across the river and then another hour back. That didn't leave much time to try to settle things with her. And this was a discussion that couldn't be rushed.

But if the Confederates blocked the railroad and made it to the Beaufort area, it would be dangerous for all who resided here, and he'd not put his wife at risk. As much as he needed to reconcile with Maggie, he knew it was better to thwart the enemy's attempt to disrupt the railway. He'd return afterwards and beg her forgiveness. At this point her safety was of the utmost importance. Apologies could wait, the war would not.

Chapter 32

Early August 1863

Maggie

Maggie rose in a stretch as the sun peered through her window casting shadows of orange and gold across the worn floorboards of her room. She'd hardly slept for the misery pervading her soul. Her back was stiff and her eyes were dry and slightly blurred. She trudged to the wardrobe and chose a fresh green frock. After dressing, she ran a brush through her hair and pinned up her wavy locks. Checking her image in the looking glass, she was pleased with her appearance. She wanted to look nice for Seth when he came back to apologize, if he did. She shook the doubt from her mind. Of course, he'd come back. They loved each other and nothing could come between them, not even a misunderstanding such as this.

Her heart thumped with each footfall on the stairs as she made her way to the dining room for breakfast. Dr. Towne and Miss Murray sat at the table, chatting over coffee.

"Good morning, Maggie," Dr. Towne greeted. "Violet said your husband was visiting. Is he still here?"

Maggie bit her lower lip. She hadn't thought about what

she'd say when faced with questions about Seth's visit. She swallowed the apple-sized lump lodged in her throat and poured a cup of coffee. Joining them at the table, she stared at the steaming brew.

"He needed to go to town," was all she could muster as an excuse. She prayed they wouldn't query further as she wasn't the type to be dishonest nor could she conjure up a believable story to appease their curiosity.

Dr. Towne arched her brows as she glanced across the table at Miss Murray.

"Is everything alright?" Miss Murray asked.

Drawing in a breath, Maggie's voice cracked as a sob burst from her lips and tears cascaded across her cheeks. "We had a terrible argument and he left," she muttered, Irish tinting her words.

Miss Murray moved closer and rested a hand on her shoulder. "My dear, the war is a difficult place for two people in love. Your husband, no doubt, has seen and experienced things that may have changed his view of the world. Give him some time to acclimate to the new manner in which he sees things. Surely, this was a misunderstanding and his feelings for you have not altered."

Maggie nodded. Miss Murray's words made sense except the reason for the fight wasn't due to the stress of battle. It was another man. She dried her eyes with a hankie and looked up to find Dr. Towne gazing at her with a knowing expression. Maggie's stomach churned. The doctor had watched Maggie and James spend time together. And now he'd brought her husband to visit. All of a sudden, everything clicked. No wonder Seth felt betrayed. The entire scenario did appear questionable. Considering what Miss Murray had said, Maggie now understood why Seth may have misinterpreted the situation. Even Maggie was questioning her relationship with

James. She had to make this right. Determination pulsed through her veins as her Irish spirit surfaced.

"Dr. Towne, would you mind if I went to Beaufort this morning? I need to find my husband."

"Take all the time you need. I'm certain Willa and Letty won't mind helping with the remedies."

"Thank you," Maggie said, rushing from the table.

She raced up the steps, tied on her bonnet, hurried back downstairs, and out the door. The sandy path crunched beneath her boots as she ran to the stables where Henry was sweeping up tufts of hay from the morning feeding. They only had two horses in the barn, Mandy and Jack. Jack was the better one for riding and she asked Henry to ready him for her.

Minutes later, Jack was tacked up and ready to go.

"Thanks Henry," she said with a weak smile.

Henry helped her onto the saddle. "Be careful, Miss Maggie."

"I will," she replied, nudging Jack forward. When they got to the end of the lane, she spurred him into a gallop. She needed to get to the ferry before it launched, otherwise it would be more than an hour before it returned, and she couldn't bear the thought of having to wait that long. Then again, she might find Seth on the ferry. Her heart lightened at the idea he could be riding her way. Perhaps they'd meet along the trail.

Excitement over the prospect of seeing her husband caused her stomach to flutter. As she rounded the corner toward the dock, her heart sank. Jones was waiting with no one else around. Slowing Jack to a trot, Maggie rode up to the dock, dismounted, and greeted Jones.

"You takin' dat horse wid you?" he asked.

"Yes, Jones. I have a lot of ground to cover, and he'll make it quicker for me." She led the horse onto the flat-bottomed vessel, keeping a firm hold as he tossed his head. Jack was generally a docile steed but like most horses, was easily riled when the rider was anxious. Her rush to get to the ferry had obviously transferred to him as nervousness causing him to sidestep as they boarded. Granted, some horses were skittish about traveling on the ferry across the river. Stroking his muzzle, she whispered to him until he settled. Jones pushed the ferry out from shore.

"Has anyone come across the river this morning, Jones?"

"No ma'am. You's my first passenger for the day," he replied, watching the water as a flock of seagulls soared overhead and a school of dolphins swam alongside the ferry's wake.

"Did you transport a tall gentleman with an ebony horse yesterday?"

"Yes ma'am. He seemed in a hurry like you is dis mornin'."

"Did he happen to say where he was heading?"

"No ma'am. Most de soldiers don't speak to me 'cept to give me orders."

Maggie exhaled as she stared at the shoreline across the river. It felt as if they were moving at the pace of a turtle when she needed to move more like a gazelle. If she could have jumped in the water and swam across, she'd have done so.

After what seemed an eternity, the ferry bumped to a stop. Once Jones secured it, Maggie thanked him and led Jack up the sandy incline to the main road. She found a mounting block and swung onto the saddle. Jack picked up a brisk walk and plodded through town. Soldiers milled about, some tipping their hats as she rode past while others ignored her altogether.

Maggie surveyed her surroundings, hoping to catch a glimpse of Seth or Phantom. By the time she reached the end of the main road, her heart was thumping so hard her chest ached. Tears christened her eyelids as she looked around. Nothing. She swung Jack around and started down the road behind the buildings fronting the main road. As Jack plodded along, she wiped tears from her cheeks. He has to be here, she thought. Jones said he'd transported him the day before.

She halted and scanned the area. Where would Seth have gone? Her eyes rested on the back of the building where James had been housed before being reassigned. She nudged Jack forward and stopped behind the Federal style home where the Verdier family had spent their summers. Dismounting, she tied Jack to the hitching post and scurried up the back stairs.

The house reeked of cigar smoke and whiskey but overall, its interior remained intact. So many of the other houses had been vandalized with the artwork slashed and the furnishings burned for warmth during the colder months. This one seemed to be faring better although its wallpaper was peeling, and the floors were in need of a good polishing to rid them of the scuff marks from soldier's boots.

Maggie approached the first interior door where a man with a full beard and receding hairline sat at a desk making notations in a journal. He looked up when she rapped on the doorjamb, his shoulders squaring when he realized she was a woman.

"Good morning," he said, standing. "What can I do for you?"

Maggie wrung her hands. "I was hoping you could help me locate someone."

He walked over to her, his boots echoing with each step.

"Who are you trying to find, Miss...?"

"*Mrs.* Daniels," she replied. "I'm trying to find my husband, Seth Daniels."

"Is he stationed here?"

"No," she said softly, glancing at the floor. "He's here on a temporary mission and came out to see me yesterday. He left rather abruptly." It was humiliating having to search for her husband. She could only imagine what the man before her must be thinking.

"Did he give a reason for *taking off?*" he asked with a shrewd smile.

Fury burned within Maggie's chest. He was mocking her. No doubt, he thought Seth had gone looking for comfort beyond his wife's embrace and it enraged her. Before Maggie could reply, a young man bolted through the back door.

"Major," he puffed not acknowledging Maggie's presence. "I've word from Charleston."

"Outstanding," he declared before turning back to Maggie. "If you'll excuse me ma'am, I've work to do."

The young soldier darted into the office. As the major started to close the door, Maggie reached out and stopped it.

"Please, if you could just tell me..."

"I don't mean to be disrespectful, Mrs. Daniels but your husband is probably passed out drunk somewhere in town. Many men seek solace after having an argument with their wives. He'll come back once he's sobered up and you two can make amends."

"What about Lt. Colonel Brunson?"

"Left this morning," he replied curtly as he closed the door.

Maggie's limbs shook at his innuendo and refusal to assist her. She wanted to scream that her husband wasn't a philandering drunk, and their relationship was solid and built on trust. And then it struck her with the force of a hammer hitting a nail. Trust. It was one of the strongest aspects of their relationship and she'd weakened it by hiding her work at the school on St. Helena from him. While she hadn't lied outright, she'd been dishonest through omission. The situation with the Lt. Colonel only complicated things.

Maggie plodded to the door and down the back stairs, where she plunked onto the bottom step. Burying her face in her hands, she wept. This was entirely her fault. Now Seth was gone, and she had no way to remedy the situation. What if he were injured or worse, killed during battle? She'd never forgive herself if their relationship ended on such a sour note.

Alarm siphoned her breath making her lightheaded. How could she have been such a fool? She never should have befriended James. Now more than ever she could see the error of her ways. The worst part was she may have sent her husband back into battle without being able to explain what actually happened. She took in several deep breaths in an effort to calm her racing pulse. Sniffling, she wiped the tears from her face and slowly stood. Everything spun for a moment before she steadied her quavering legs and walked over to Jack who waited patiently at the hitching post.

As she led him down the street, a wagon rattled past with a group of soldiers hollering out propositions. She ignored them all, lost in a fog of despair. When she reached the dock, she was surprised to find Jones getting ready to launch.

"Have you room for me?" she called out.

"Come on, Miss Maggie. Dere's always room for you."

His sentiment warmed her heart. A few months before, she'd made a remedy for a terrible gash he'd sustained on his hand when the ferry rope had ripped across his palm. Jones was a dear soul with better knowledge of the area waterways than the fish inhabiting them.

An hour later, Maggie left Jack with Henry and changed into her work dress. She trudged to the shed where she found Willa mixing an ointment for poison ivy. When Maggie stepped into the space, Willa looked up, a smile plumping her cheeks.

"Where's Letty?" Maggie asked, looking around.

"She gone to help Mrs. Harper with some things," she said,

stirring ingredients in a large bowl. "How was your trip to town?"

Maggie inhaled before answering. "Unsuccessful," she replied, pinning on her apron.

Willa leaned the wooden spoon against the side of the bowl, wiped her hands on her apron, and glared at Maggie. "What's goin' on?" she asked in a tone of voice that told Maggie she wouldn't accept any excuses or nonsense.

Maggie sat on the stool by the work table and rubbed her eyes with the heels of her hands. "Seth was here and we had an argument. He left yesterday afternoon in a huff, and I haven't seen him since."

Willa reached out and squeezed Maggie's hand. "I'm sorry for that. Ain't nothing worse than being at odds with people you love."

"I went to town this morning hoping to find him but couldn't," she said, sucking in a breath. "If anything happens to him on the battlefield, I'll not be able to live with myself."

"Don' go beatin' yourself up over this. He knows you love him just like you know he loves you. Married people have spats and that's just what this is, a spat. You both been under a lot of pressure these last couple years so it's only natural you gonna fight when you finally see each other. Give it time. I bet you'll get a letter with an apology real soon."

"A letter," Maggie muttered some of the worry fading from her mind. "I can write to him and explain everything."

"Then you best get to writin'. I'll take care of things here."

Willa's words soothed Maggie a bit. Her friend always had a way of clarifying things in a manner that calmed a weary soul. Maggie started for the door but stopped.

"No," she declared, returning to the work bench. "I need to work, it's what settles my nerves. I'll write to him later this evening and post it first thing tomorrow."

Maggie gathered the ingredients to start another batch of poison ivy ointment. They never seemed to have enough of it. As she mixed the ingredients, she felt the tension melting from her shoulders. It was good to be working alongside Willa again. Even though staying busy helped occupy Maggie's mind, her subconscious dwelled on the letter she'd compose when the day's work was done.

Chapter 33

September 1863

Elora

Elora rode Jasper at a full gallop toward the river, her skirts flapping behind her. She'd been in the southern region for well over a month, going back and forth between soldier and spy. Presently, dressed as a woman, she was comfortable in her old territory where she knew the trails and waterways like her own mind.

Bitterness smoldered in her heart over the captain's death. Now more than ever, she was determined to enact revenge. If the south hadn't waged war, Captain Dixon would still be alive. Then again, Elora wouldn't have known him. That would have been better than the pain and resentment she felt over his death. Had she known who shot him, she would have hunted the man down and killed him. As it was, she'd do everything in her power to thwart the enemy's progress. Keeping active, gave her an outlet for her grief.

As she approached a burned-out house, she slowed Jasper to a walk. The smoldering stench of ash wavered in the air as puffs of smoke snaked from the rubble. Elora knew this place. She'd attended a party here when she was only ten. The home had been filled with lovely furnishings and colorful rugs. The sprawling front porch afforded views of elaborately designed gardens bedecked with roses, crepe myrtles, soaring magnolias, and a long avenue of oaks. Brick slave cabins were located to the left of the main house. The marsh ran alongside the place with a massive live oak tree at the edge. Elora and her friend used to sit on the lowest branch with their feet dangling above the water. While she enjoyed her time at the plantation, she was always sickened by the slaves who were forced to serve them.

From an early age, Elora knew slavery was an abomination and that her family plantation held no one in bondage. However, she'd been carefully schooled to keep that from others, including her own grandparents, in order to preserve their way of life. She was also cautious not to reveal the role they played as a safe house for the Underground Railroad. Nevertheless, as the daughter of a prominent doctor she had certain societal expectations to attend gatherings and associate with girls deemed to be of her rank. That had been the most difficult part of her life, having to pretend she was like the others when deep down she loathed their view of slavery and the degradation of the Negroes.

Looking around, she pondered where her friend was now. Was she alive or had she become a victim of the army's cruelty? Elora had heard tales of the Union Army burning down houses and torturing women and children to death. War made monsters of men, bringing to light the wickedness brewing in the depths of their souls.

Elora rode Jasper to a sprawling magnolia at the edge of the water and inhaled. The heady scent of pluff mud and marsh grass filled her lungs and comforted her spirit. Even though she was far from her own home, it was still the Lowcountry giving her a sense of peace amidst the war-torn south.

In the distance, Elora heard someone cry out. She took in a deep breath and rode toward the sound, the screams growing louder as she approached. Dismounting, she looped Jasper's reins over a low-lying branch and made her way toward the cries for mercy. Her skin prickled as the pleas increased, wondering what she was about to witness. She pulled her pistol from the holster in her skirt pocket and traipsed deeper into the woods.

Hiding behind the broad girth of an ancient oak, she caught a glimpse of the scene. A group of black soldiers with weapons aimed, surrounded two rotund white men dressed in Confederate gray. The white men had nooses around their necks, each sitting on the back of a horse. The black soldiers taunted the prisoners, who continued to grovel and plead for their lives. Elora's eyes widened when she recognized the two white men. Curtis and Coyle Houston were red faced and blubbering. A black soldier stood at the head of each horse awaiting orders. As she scanned the other faces, her heartbeat quickened as she realized several of the black soldiers were some of the Houston's former slaves.

The Houston slaves were well known to everyone. Poorly dressed, sickly looking, and most of the men bore scars on the face and arms from torturous beatings. Even worse, when Curtis and Coyle were drunk, which was most every night, they'd abuse different slaves for sport. The women were used for pleasure whenever the notion struck them. And their callousness wasn't reserved for the Negroes. More than one white woman in town had been accosted by them yet no charges were ever filed for their indiscretions. The senior Mr. Houston either terrorized the victims or paid for their silence. As for the slaves, they had no rights in the eyes of the law and the Houston family capitalized on the situation. They were some of the most deplorable people in town.

The right side of Elora's lip curled as she watched Curtis and Coyle begging for mercy after years of inflicting so much cruelty on the men they'd owned. At that moment, Curtis's stupidity took hold. Apparently, he decided begging wasn't getting him anywhere, so he reverted to his slave owner tactics.

"Let us go this instant! Don't think for a minute we won't hunt you down and whip you within an inch of your life!" he hollered.

"Shut up!" Coyle yelled at his twin brother. "Release me, and I won't tell anyone about this. I promise!" His voice cracked as sweat trickled down his reddened cheeks.

"You fool!" Curtis hollered back. "These animals are dumb as dirt and won't do nothin' to us. Just gotta remind 'em who's in charge." Curtis's words came out strong, but his labored breathing and pained expression betrayed the depth of his fright.

"Mr. Curtis and Mr. Coyle, I believe we've heard enough," one of the black soldiers said, his shoulders squared as he looked at the man holding the horses. "It's my understanding you treated many of these men cruelly."

"Ain't nothin' wrong with that! Had to keep 'em in line so they'd get their work done. Lazy creatures," Curtis muttered under his breath.

Coyle's eyes widened as he looked from his brother to the soldier in charge.

"You whipped and beat them," the soldier continued. "Are you saying you're not sorry for your brutality?"

"I'm sorry," Coyle yelled, his voice quavering. "If you let me go, I'll make it worth your while. I have money."

"Nobody in the south has money anymore," the soldier replied. "Only one way to pay for what you boys have done." He gave a nod and the men holding the horses released them with a smack on their haunches. The horses bolted forward leaving Curtis and Coyle wriggling from the tree branch, their pudgy faces turning a deep shade of crimson and their eyes bulging.

The black soldiers stood in silence until the only sound was the creaking of the ropes swinging from the branches as the bodies swayed back and forth. Elora watched the life drain from two of the most notoriously brutal men she'd ever known. She remained hidden as the soldiers walked off leaving Curtis and Coyle dangling from the tree. A fitting end to a dynasty of bombastic, ruthless men.

When the soldiers had dispersed, Elora made her way back to Jasper, swung onto the saddle, and rode toward her destination where she hoped to garner some information for her regiment. An odd sense of satisfaction filled her chest. She'd known the Houstons her entire life yet felt no remorse for seeing them hang.

Chapter 34

Fall 1863

Seth

Months passed and Seth had yet to write to Maggie. He just couldn't find the words to explain his actions. At least his work kept him busy. Idleness would have driven him to insanity. He galloped back to the encampment after scouting for the afternoon. As soon as he arrived, he was summoned to the Colonel's tent.

"Daniels," Pennington said gruffly. "We have a situation that requires immediate attention."

"Sir?"

"A Union soldier is being held in a prison at the border of Washington, D.C. He's been selling secrets to the confederacy."

"Do we know his source?"

"We know he's a civilian, but I'll need your skills to locate the traitor," he said, his eyes simmering with rage. "The soldier won't give us what we need."

"When do I leave?"

"Immediately," he said, sliding a paper across his desk. "This is where the soldier is being held. Ride there and interrogate him," the colonel ordered, leaning forward. "And when you find his source, *deal* with him."

"How would you have me do that, sir?"

"As you see fit," he growled.

"Yes, sir."

Seth went to his tent and gathered what he'd need for the mission. As he pulled an extra shirt from his trunk, a lock of Maggie's hair tied in a ribbon toppled to the floor. She'd given it to him the day he left to join his regiment. If only he could wrap his arms around her and plead for forgiveness. But there wasn't time to think of such things. He had a job to do. When he returned, he'd write the letter no matter what. He'd waited too long already but wanted the words to be flawless. Now he realized he'd never find the perfect way to express himself. All that mattered was that he wrote it. Tacking up Phantom, he swung into the saddle and rode off ready to face his next assignment.

Days later, Seth arrived in Washington and went straight to the prison where the traitorous soldier was being held. A sprawling brick building loomed before him, its barred windows and drab exterior showing signs of neglect. Entering the run-down structure, he was met with the stench of dysentery and urine. The guard at the door looked Seth up and down before speaking.

"Somethin' I can help you with?" His gruff voice matched the scowl on his scarred face.

"I'm here to interrogate a soldier brought in for selling secrets."

With a nod, he spit on the ground. "I'll bring him to ya."

The guard disappeared for a few moments before reappearing with a scrawny fellow dressed in ragged attire, a swollen purple bruise circling his left eye. The guard led the prisoner and Seth to a cramped room. Once inside, the guard shoved the soldier to the dirt ground.

"Tell 'em what you know traitor, or I'll beat the answers outta you myself."

Obviously, they'd already attempted to extract information if his black eye, split lip, and bruised cheek were any indication.

"Thank you, Corporal, I can take it from here," Seth said. If he could reason with the young soldier perhaps, he'd get what he needed without taking too much time. It was hard to tell how much information this man had released to the enemy. Seth needed to act fast to save lives.

"Suit yourself," the guard said, spitting on the ground as he exited.

Seth sat on a rickety wooden chair, the only piece of furniture in the room. Reaching into his satchel, he removed a flask and handed it to the prisoner.

The man eyed him with suspicion. "Is it poison?" he muttered.

"Whiskey. Go ahead and take a swig. You're no good to me dead."

The prisoner grasped the flask and took a long drawl. Wiping his mouth with his tattered sleeve, he handed it back.

"I've been informed you've been conspiring with the enemy. Is this true?"

The young man sneered. "The Feds are the enemy now."

"So, you're against maintaining the union?"

"Course not! But when that emancipation proclamation came about, I couldn't support the Union no longer. Just ain't right. Them darkies is too stupid to live on their own. They need whites to manage their lives, or they'll wreak havoc."

Seth sucked in a breath. He wanted to wring the guy's neck. This wasn't the first Union soldier he'd encountered with these views. All were willing to fight for the preservation of the country, but a small faction believed the Negroes were meant to be enslaved which meant they weren't willing to fight for their emancipation. Nonetheless, the sooner he could reason with this man, the faster he could stop whoever was behind the betrayal.

"Tell me where you've been getting your information and I'll make sure they go easy on you."

"Do I look stupid? Ain't no way they gonna do anything but hang me," he groused.

"Then do the right thing and tell me what you know. You'll be saving lives."

"Like I care about a bunch of slave lovin' fools."

Seth's limbs quivered as his temper pulsed through his veins and quickened his heartbeat.

"You got a mother?" Seth asked, hoping an emotional approach might work.

"Leave her out of this!" he yelled. "She's a good woman and ain't never done nobody no harm!"

"But she hates the Negroes," Seth said. He hoped to get to the bottom of the man's prejudice. If he could figure out the easiest way to his conscience, he'd have a better chance of getting to the truth.

"Naw, my ma likes everybody. She might be a fool that way, but she's got a big heart."

"What's she going to think when she finds out her son is a traitor?" he asked, raising his eyebrows as he turned the flask over in his hands.

Gulping, the man looked away, his foot bouncing like a ship on stormy seas. He closed his eyes and chewed his lower lip. His anguish was palpable. "It'd break her heart," he sighed. "Her pa fought in the Revolutionary War. She believes in this country which is why my brother and I signed up when the war started."

"And now you're turning against the country your grandfather fought to establish because you don't think the slaves should be freed?"

"They oughtn't! If they were meant to be free the Constitution would've said so," he said, his rage resurfacing.

"Is your brother still alive?"

"Far as I know," he replied.

"Does he share your views?"

The young man shrugged.

"Did it occur to you that the secrets you've been selling could result in his death?"

"I suppose," he mumbled.

"So, you'd leave your mother with no sons to care for her when she's old. As you said earlier, you'll be hanged for this. If your spying results in your brother's death you will have taken your mother's heart and destroyed it."

Seth watched the man's jaw clench as he considered his words.

"Hadn't thought of it that way," he said, rubbing his forehead.

"Tell me the name of your source and spare your mother the loss of both her sons. It'll be bad enough when she learns you've been hung for treason."

The young soldier blew out a breath. "Any way you can keep her from knowin' about that?"

"I can try. I'll write to her personally and let her know you did the right thing in the end. Perhaps that will give her some peace."

"There's a man outside of Philadelphia. Only thing he cares about is making money. He's always playing cards with a bunch of Union officers. Supposedly, he gets them liquored up and gathers any information he can and then sells it to the Rebs."

"What's your role in this?"

"He pays me to deliver the information and collect the money," the soldier grumbled.

"How much do you get?"

"Five percent."

"That's not much to betray your country," Seth huffed.

"Been sendin' it home to my ma. She's havin' a hard time."

"Give me the name and address of your source and I'll write a nice letter to your mother about how you cooperated."

He ran his tongue across his teeth. "You got something to write on?"

Seth reached into his satchel and removed a piece of paper and pencil. "Go ahead."

The young man did his duty supplying the name and address of the gentleman who'd been selling secrets to the confederacy. Then Seth got the name and address of the man's mother so he could send a letter explaining how her son did the right thing in the end. Seth bid the young man goodbye, knowing he'd never see him again. But he'd keep his promise and write to his mother. Placing his hat on his head, Seth exhaled. How was it he could pen a letter to a complete stranger explaining the treasonous acts of her son but couldn't find the words to apologize to the woman he loved more than his own life?

Over the next few days, Seth made his way to Philadelphia. It had been years since he'd been to the city; before he and Maggie were married. His muscles tensed at the thought of his wife. Their acrimonious parting still plagued him. For now, he needed to focus on the task at hand and not be deterred by his personal issues. He had a traitor to find and that took priority.

Phantom plodded through the streets of Philadelphia as carriages and pedestrians shuffled about. Things here seemed ordinary as if there wasn't a war raging in the southern states.

Aside from Gettysburg, there hadn't been any major battles in the northern regions for which Seth was thankful.

Stopping at headquarters, Seth requested an escort. He had no idea what awaited and wanted backup in case things got violent. Two soldiers were assigned to accompany him to the address he'd obtained from the young soldier. They rode to the outskirts of the township, where he found a line of brick row houses, neatly kept. Wrought iron fences bordered the yards with autumnal trees dressed in shades of gold, red, and orange. Seth glanced at the addresses until he found number 21.

"This is the place," he said, dismounting and tying Phantom to the post out front.

The two soldiers followed suit and marched up the brick steps behind him. Using the heavy brass knocker, Seth banged three times. A petite young woman wearing a black dress and white cap opened the front door. Her dark eyes were downcast and her expression forlorn.

"May I help you?" she asked timidly.

"I'm looking for Mr. Farris. Is he home?" Seth said.

The young woman stepped back, allowing the men to enter. "I'll let him know he has visitors," she said, before scurrying down the hall like a frightened rabbit.

The home was exquisitely furnished with mahogany and walnut pieces, a gallery of artwork, and multicolored rugs. Layers of silk curtains framed the windows. The décor was as fine as he'd ever seen, making him seethe with rage. This man was making money by selling secrets to the enemy. He was a coward and a scoundrel. Seth clenched his teeth as he heard footfalls echoing down the hall. A stately gentleman wearing a well-tailored dove gray suit appeared. He exuded a dignified air with his silvery mutton chops and hair, and his brown eyes glinted when he smiled. Something in his gaze was familiar although Seth couldn't figure out what it was. He'd never met the man before; of that he was certain. He would've remembered him.

"Gentlemen," he said as he approached. "What can I do for you today?" Arrogance oozed from his words making Seth despise him all the more.

"I'm Lieutenant Daniels with the Pennsylvania Cavalry. Am I speaking with Mr. Farris?"

"You are," he replied.

"We need to talk with you in private."

"Follow me," he said, leading them to his office at the back of the house.

The young maid who'd answered the door reappeared as Seth and his two comrades sat down.

"Adeline, please make sure no one disturbs us," Mr. Farris commanded, taking a seat.

"Yes, sir," she replied, her eyes focused on the floor as she left the room.

Farris leaned forward, rested his elbows on the desk and folded his hands. "How may I help you?" he asked, seemingly unfazed by the fact three Union soldiers were seated before him. Apparently, he had no fear of being caught in his underhanded activities.

"Mr. Farris, we've come to collect some information regarding your connection with southern regiments."

The man stiffened and leaned back in his chair. "Why would you think I possessed knowledge of the confederates? I detest their rebellious ways." He smiled again and the familiarity of his expression caught Seth's attention.

"We have reason to believe you have knowledge of their activities. In fact, we have evidence you've been assisting them." Seth watched the man's demeanor closely as it altered from arrogance to anger.

"How dare you come to my house with these fraudulent accusations?" he declared, bolting up from his chair.

The two soldiers rushed around the desk, sandwiching Mr. Farris between them. His face turned a deep shade of crimson.

"Get out of my house now! I'll have you court-marshalled for this," he growled.

"I don't think you will," Seth said.

The soldiers placed their hands on Mr. Farris's shoulders and forced him back into his seat.

"I know powerful people in the Union. Leave my house this instant and maybe I won't have you thrown in prison!"

Seth leaned across the desk, his face inches from Farris's. "A young soldier is being held in Washington as we speak. He's charged with treason and named you as his source. Given what you just said about friends in important places I'm going to assume he told me the truth."

"I don't believe you," Farris grumbled. His dark brown eyes locked on Seth's.

Once again, Seth felt a sense of recognition but couldn't pinpoint the reason.

"You don't have to believe me," Seth responded. "We'll take a trip to Washington and let you answer questions there. I have orders to obtain and interrogate you. We can do this here or at headquarters. It's up to you."

Mr. Farris struggled to free himself from the soldiers holding him in his chair, rage glinting in his stare. "I'll not be intimidated by a miscreant such as yourself! Especially in my own home!"

"My patience is running thin, Mr. Farris. I suggest you comply, or I'll ask these men to help with your decision."

"You brute! Don't you dare threaten me!" Mr. Farris bellowed. "I meant what I said about having friends with the authority to end your career."

"If that's the way you want to play this," Seth replied, removing a piece of paper from his pocket, and laying it on the desk in front of Farris. "This is the extradition order from the General directing me to bring you to headquarters in Washington. Do your friends outrank him?"

Mr. Farris's smug expression melted from his face as he scanned the paper and gulped. "What do you want to know?" he asked, his body slumping in defeat.

"Everything."

"If I disclose what I know what will you do for me?"

A negotiator to the end. The man was a snake.

"I'll decide once I hear what you have to say," Seth said.

Mr. Farris cursed under his breath. "I can pay you, handsomely, all of you," he said. "I'll tell you what you need to know and then I'll disappear."

Seth shook his head as the right side of his mouth curled. "No deal. You give me the information I asked for or I take you to Washington and you can answer in a federal prison." Seth looked around the room at its swagged draperies and leather covered furnishings. "I can assure you the accommodations are not as comfortable as these."

"I demand to speak with an attorney!"

"Not an option." Seth leaned over the desk once more and through clenched teeth repeated his earlier demand. "Tell me what you know, or I'll have these two beat it out of you. If you survive, I'll haul you off to prison."

A hint of fear glimmered in Mr. Farris's eyes. After several moments of tense silence, he exhaled. "Fine, but I expect leniency for my cooperation."

Reluctantly, Mr. Farris shared all the details of his transactions, most of which were conducted over poker games in his front parlor. By the time he'd finished, he'd managed to indict several Union officials as well as those avoiding service. In addition to his perfidious endeavors, Mr. Farris had been paying others to serve in his place. While it wasn't against the law to send someone in your stead, it wasn't openly acceptable.

"Now that you have your precious confession, can we make a deal?" he asked.

"I appreciate all you've shared but until we confirm what you've said is true, I'm afraid you'll have to bunk behind bars."

"You lying jerk! You told me you'd work with me!"

"I did no such thing. You made an offer and I listened, nothing more."

Seth gave a nod to the two soldiers detaining him, indicating it was time to leave. Mr. Farris resumed his struggle, his face reddening as he tried to free himself. Something in his expression niggled at Seth's mind.

"One more question, Mr. Farris," Seth said. "Have we met before?"

"Not likely. I'd have remembered you," he sneered.

Seth stepped closer, scrutinizing the man's face. "I'm certain I know you," Seth muttered when something in his memory clicked. Jane had the exact same eyes and jawline as this man. Searching his memory, he tried to recall what Maggie had told him about his adopted daughter's heritage.

"Have you ever played cards with a Mr. Stevenson?" Seth queried.

"The man was the worst player I've ever seen," Farris grunted, rolling his eyes. "Don't tell me you're related to him although it would explain a lot."

"For someone who acts as if he's superior, you're not very bright. You've been insulting me since I arrived and I'm the one holding your life in my hands."

Clenching his jaw, Mr. Farris looked away.

"I believe Mr. Stevenson's daughter was in your employ," Seth continued.

"Worthless little thing. Had to dismiss her. She was too lazy and too stupid to instruct my children."

A rage like nothing he'd ever felt rushed through Seth's limbs making them quake. He stepped up to Mr. Farris, his nose nearly touching his.

"You didn't find her too worthless to have relations with," he growled.

Mr. Farris's face paled although his cockiness reflected in his stare. "Are you her keeper? Lover perhaps? She is a temptress. A man can only resist seduction for so long, even from a worthless tramp."

Seth landed a fist to Farris's mouth sending blood spraying from his lip. "She was my wife's cousin. We adopted her daughter, *your* child, after she died."

A wicked grin formed on Farris's face, revealing blood-soaked teeth. "You can't prove a thing," he said. "Now, take me to headquarters. I'll negotiate some sort of deal for my release. I have money and rights. There's nothing you can do to me. As for that little tramp you spoke of, what happens beneath my roof is my business."

"You took advantage of Susannah in the worst way and then threw her to the streets to fend for herself and her child. Your child," Seth growled through gritted teeth. "She died a pauper." Turning to the soldiers, Seth nodded them toward the door.

As they escorted Mr. Farris into the hall, an older woman came screeching from the front parlor.

"Where are you taking him?" she screamed. "I demand you release him!"

"Dearest, it's only a misunderstanding," Farris yelled over his shoulder. "Don't let your blood pressure rise. No need having a fainting spell. I'll be back once this is cleared up."

The woman watched in horror as Seth and the soldiers

pushed Mr. Farris through the back door to a wooded area behind the property.

"What are you doing?" Farris demanded, still trying to squirm free from the soldiers' grip. "You said you were taking me to headquarters. Why are we in the woods?" His voice raised an octave with each declaration.

Seth looked at the two soldiers. "You heard what he said inside."

"Yes, sir, I did," the shorter man replied.

"Ain't nothing but a scoundrel and a traitor," the other soldier responded.

"He's also a rapist," Seth added. "He took advantage of a young woman in his employ some years ago. When she became pregnant, he sent her to the streets. She had no money and no one to help her or her daughter."

"I didn't rape anyone. The little whore offered herself to me and then ran off when she got pregnant. That baby could have been anybody's!"

The two soldiers tightened their grip on his arms, squeezing a yelp from him.

"I happen to know differently," Seth said. "I suspect if I ask the young maid who opened the door for us, she'd have a similar story. Shall I ask her?" Seth queried.

"What's wrong with having a little fun with the help? They're flattered by the attention. Not many maids catch the eye of a gentleman such as myself," he said, haughtily.

"I may have forgotten to tell you one thing," Seth said, stepping closer.

Farris sucked in a breath as Seth leaned in. He noticed the trembling in Farris's arms and the beads of sweat peppering his brow.

"The general told me to deal with you as I saw fit."

The color drained from Farris's face, his throat bobbing as he swallowed. "What do you mean by that?" he stammered.

Seth glanced at the two soldiers and grinned. "How would you guys like to handle this?"

"A traitor and a rapist? Only one thing to do with the likes of him," the shorter man said.

"Then I'll leave you to it," Seth replied with a sly grin as he turned to walk away. "Get him to the jail before dark. But make sure he's still breathing. The general may have more questions for him once he gets to Washington."

"You can't do this!" Mr. Farris yelled. "I'll have you arrested for mistreatment! I know my rights!"

"We'll afford you the same rights you provided Susannah Stevenson when she was in your service," Seth replied.

"Wait!" Farris squealed. "I'm sorry! Please don't do this! I'll do whatever you want!"

"Of course, you will," Seth said. He gave a nod to the two men holding Farris.

The first punch landed in Farris's gut relieving him of his midday meal. The second one met his jaw sending him to the ground. From there, the two soldiers proceeded to pummel him with their fists, bloodying his nose and upper lip.

Seth watched a few moments more as Farris writhed in pain, raising his arms over his head in an effort to ward off the attack.

"Stop," Farris groaned. "I can't take any more." His face was swelling and his breath came in rapid pulses.

Seth stepped closer and leaned down. "Is that what Miss Stevenson said when you forced yourself on her?"

A tear trickled down Farris's face mixing with the blood from his nose. Squeezing his eyes shut, he croaked, "I'm sorry."

"That we can agree on," Seth replied, kicking him in the groin.

A scream erupted from Farris as he curled into a fetal position.

"Clean him up before you take him in fellas," Seth said. "And if anyone asks, he resisted arrest."

Turning, Seth walked out of the woods toward the front of the house. A sense of satisfaction filled his chest as he mounted Phantom and headed to headquarters in town to report the information he'd gleaned.

Chapter 35

Christmas 1863

Elora

Sun glinted across iridescent slopes as snow covered the ground on Christmas Day. Dressed as a woman, Elora rode Jasper across a shimmering field of white, the icy particles crunching beneath his hooves. Her breath curled in miniature clouds as her mind drifted to Christmases past. She could still feel the warmth of the hearth at her childhood home as a buffet of eggs, bacon, grits, and biscuits were laid out on the sideboard. The memory was like ambrosia to her soul as she reflected on the doorways wreathed in fresh evergreen boughs adding the fragrant scent of pine to the delectable aroma of coffee. Even though Elora had never been much of a coffee drinker, always preferring hot tea, life as a soldier had altered that. Now she required a strong cup of java to get her going in the morning. The bitterness of the brew served in the encampment no longer mattered to her. She'd drink anything closely resembling the flavor so long as it was hot and perked her up.

A shiver rattled her body. Her female winter attire was scant compared to her uniform. At one point she considered using her uniform coat for warmth but quickly realized the error of her thinking. She couldn't garner secrets from southern supporters while dressed in Union blue. At least her frock was made of wool, and she'd managed to acquire a flannel petticoat for warmth.

Jasper plodded along the snowy tundra of the Virginia countryside when Elora heard voices coming from the other side of a barn. Unsure who was there, she steered Jasper into the wooded area nearby when she heard a man cry out in pain. Her heart thudded against her chest as she quickened Jasper's pace. Tufts of snow smacked against her already chilled shoulders as she maneuvered through the trees. Halting Jasper in an area where she could see without revealing her presence, Elora sucked in a breath at the sight.

At the side of the barn were two soldiers, one in blue, the other in gray. From what she could tell, the Confederate had sustained a wound in his right arm. Blood stained the tattered sleeve of his uniform and reddened the snow where he lay. The Union soldier stood over him and reached into his pocket. She braced herself for what was about to happen next, unable to look away despite the murderous act unfolding before her.

He pulled a cloth from his pocket, knelt down next to the Confederate, and tended to the man's wound. The man cried out in pain making Elora flinch. She watched in amazement as the Union soldier opened his satchel and removed some bread and a flask. Taking a seat beside the soldier in gray, he doled out the bread and drink. She listened as the two men shared stories of childhood Christmases, many of their traditions similar in nature despite the current divide between north and south. When the food and drink were gone, the Union soldier helped the Confederate to his feet. They shook hands, wished each other a Merry Christmas, and went on their way.

Elora pondered the scene. How could they be so kind to one another one moment and then try to kill each other the next? If Christmas could bring about so much compassion and comradery, why couldn't that same compassion be extended every other day of the year? Astounding, she thought, how Christmas Day could bring peace to the most hardened of enemies. Enemies that were more alike than not.

Once the men disappeared, Elora continued her trek. She had a meeting with one of her more reliable sources, a man with a Georgia regiment who'd provided a great deal of valuable information in the past.

When she arrived at the designated location, Elora was surprised to find two men waiting. Her stomach churned. She considered turning back but feared it would lead to a chase she may not be able to outmaneuver. Thus far, her source, Major Davenport, had been solid so she shouldn't have any reservations, unless he'd become suspicious of her. Just in case, she reached into her skirt pocket and grasped her pistol.

"Mornin' Miss Kirk," Davenport called out, using her spy name.

"Sir," she replied with a nod, squaring her shoulders in an effort to appear bolder than she felt. Having portrayed a man for so long, she'd learned how to exude confidence through body language. "Who have you brought with you?"

"This is my commander, Colonel Bridgestone. He wanted to speak with you."

Elora swallowed hard. Had he figured out she was a spy? Her stomach roiled at the thought she might be entering a trap.

"How can I help you?" she asked, using her best southern accent.

"The major tells me you've been quite helpful to our cause."

"I'm only doing my part."

"Humph," he grunted. "Most women are mending uniforms or keeping up the homestead. Riding around stealing Union secrets and sharing them with us is a bit brazen, is it not?"

Elora smiled coquettishly as a Lowcountry drawl flowed from her lips. "Why Major, not every woman was meant to stay at home and tend to domestic duties. Some of us have too much adventure in our souls for such things. I need more from life than motherhood and baking," she purred with a simper.

If there was one thing Elora knew about southern men it was how much they appreciated a pretty face and a little mystery in a woman. Propriety was at the forefront of a southern gentleman's upbringing and they'd not likely cross that line even when confronted with a little flirtation.

The Colonel blew out a long breath. He glanced at the major who gave a nod of approval.

"We have reason to believe there's a Union soldier who has been infiltrating our ranks and taking information to his regiment. We've lost several skirmishes due to this."

"What can I do?" Elora asked, puzzled by the request. Why would this man involve her? Why not use one of his own spymasters?

"The major tells me you have an uncanny manner about you and that your skills are unmatched. I need you to find this man who has been sharing our secrets."

"With all due respect, Colonel, why ask me? Don't you have a spymaster to help with such things? I've only worked with Major Davenport on a few occasions. While I doubt my involvement has been overly significant, I do hope it's been helpful."

The Colonel rubbed his scraggly beard. "You've given just

enough to aid us. While we've not been able to outmaneuver the Yankees yet, your information is greatly appreciated. My spymaster has not been as *competent*."

Elora smiled in her mind. She'd done just that, given them just enough to appear helpful but nothing so detailed it would result in a victory for them. She'd gained the major's trust and now reveled in her duplicity. Men were so easily led by the perceived innocence of a woman when she played her role well.

"I appreciate your candor, Colonel," she replied with a smile. "Who is this soldier you want me to locate?"

"He's with a Pennsylvania unit, a Lieutenant Polk. Supposedly, he's a distant relative of the South Carolina Polks. I'm certain you've heard of Mr. Jefferson Polk, one of the main supporters of secession."

"I'm aware of the family," Elora replied, trying to hide her amusement over the discussion of her own grandfather.

"Needless to say, there's some speculation Lt. Polk is using his family connections to gain information and then share it with the enemy."

"And you want me to find one man in an army of Union soldiers? You must think very highly of me."

"You have a strong reputation with my men. I've also been told you tended to a few who'd been injured for which I'm grateful," he said. "Your work has shown me how effective and persuasive you can be, and we need your help, Miss Kirk. With your ability to infiltrate enemy lines and gather the information you've provided thus far; I believe you can accomplish this."

A smile parted her lips. "I'll be happy to search out this Lieutenant Polk."

The major tipped his hat. "I'm much obliged to you, Miss Kirk. I hope we'll be in touch very soon."

"I suspect we will," she replied. "I'll do my best to locate him and get word to you as soon as I do."

Major Davenport gave Elora a nod as he and his commanding officer disappeared into the woods. Nudging Jasper into a trot, Elora chuckled at the irony of being tasked with finding her alter ego.

Chapter 36

January 1864

Maggie

It had been months since Maggie had seen Seth. Her resolve was worn to a frazzle robbing her of sleep and diminishing her appetite. She'd sent a couple of letters but had no idea if they'd reached him or if he was even safe. Dr. Towne kept her busy which helped maintain her sanity.

It was the second week of January and winter was upon them, greatly increasing coughs and other cold weather illnesses. Since gardening was out of season, Maggie spent the time knitting scarves and hats for anyone in need of warm clothing. She was sitting in the front parlor before a roaring fire with a half-finished scarf in her lap when the clip-clopping of a horse caught her attention. She glanced at the mantel clock. It was time for mail delivery. Wrapping her shawl tightly around herself, she stepped out onto the porch. Much to her surprise, it wasn't the postman but a Union soldier.

He stopped at the base of the stairs and tipped his hat.

"Good day, Ma'am. I'm looking for Mrs. Daniels."

Grabbing the porch rail, Maggie steadied herself as her knees weakened and her breath caught. Had something happened to Seth? Why else would a soldier be looking for her? She opened her mouth to speak but the words wouldn't form. Mustering all her courage, she took a wobbly step forward. "I'm Mrs. Daniels," she said, her mouth dry.

"I have a message for you," he said, pulling a note from his pocket.

Grasping the envelope, she muttered, "Thank you."

"Good day, ma'am," he replied before wheeling his horse around and galloping down the drive.

Maggie collapsed onto the porch rocker staring at the parchment, her hands shaking as she held it. Tears crested in her eyes and her heart pounded with the force of a raging river after a flood. Was it bad news? Was Seth injured, or worse, dead?

She swallowed the fear caught in her throat and opened the letter. Blinking back tears, she scanned the words, her heart beat increasing.

Dearest Maggie,

When you receive this note, ride out to the old blue shack where we used to stop on our way north with cargo.

Lovingly yours,

Seth

He was alive and close by, she thought, releasing the breath she'd been holding. Without hesitation, Maggie ran inside to the desk, pulled a sheet of paper from the drawer, and dipped the pen in the ink bottle, her hands trembling with excitement. She scribbled a message to Dr. Town letting her know she'd be gone for the night. Leaving the note where she knew the doctor would find it, Maggie darted upstairs, grabbed a bonnet and wool cape, and hurried to the stables.

"Henry," she called as she rushed into the barn.

Dropping a bale of hay to the ground, Henry hurried over.

"Everything okay, Miss Maggie?" he queried breathlessly.

"Everything is wonderful. Could you tack up Jack for me?"

"No problem," he replied, walking down the aisle.

Maggie fidgeted with her fingers and paced while she waited. What was taking so long? Chewing her lower lip, Maggie felt as if she might explode if the stable hand didn't hurry up. Moments later, the clip-clopping of hooves jarred her from her racing thoughts as Henry led the chestnut gelding toward her.

He helped her onto the saddle and patted the horse's neck. "Have a safe ride, Miss Maggie," he said with a nod.

"Thank you, Henry," she replied.

At the end of the lane, Maggie spurred Jack into a full gallop toward the ferry. Relief washed over her as she approached the dock. Jones was on this side of the river waiting. Maggie dismounted and rushed onto the flatbottomed boat.

"You looks to be in a rush today, Miss Maggie."

"I am," she replied, anticipation twisting her insides.

Jones wasted no time getting started for which Maggie was grateful. Winter's breath blew across the choppy waters nipping at Maggie's cheeks and nose. Every inch of her skin tingled. Between the cold air and the urgency of her quest, Maggie could hardly stay still. Seth was alive and had sent for her. Perhaps he'd forgiven her deception. For the first time since their argument, she felt hopeful.

An hour later she was galloping toward the little blue shack in the woods where they'd hidden escapees when slave hunters were close at hand. It was one of many spots they'd made use of during their journeys northward with the Underground Railroad.

Frigid air whipped against her cheeks, blowing the bonnet from her head with only the ribbons tied beneath her chin to prevent it from flying off. Her eyes stung and her feet were numb from the frosty temperatures as she leaned forward in the saddle pushing Jack faster. As the underbrush thickened, she slowed him to a walk and meandered covertly through the woods until the dilapidated blue shanty came into view. Much to her surprise, it was still standing and hadn't been burned or knocked down during battle. She took Jack to a small, make-shift paddock nestled in a grove of trees where Phantom nibbled at some hay. Jack nickered a soft greeting as she removed the saddle and bridle and turned him loose in the paddock.

Maggie scanned her surroundings as she made her way to the shack and rapped on the door.

Nothing.

She leaned her ear against it, listening for sounds of movement.

Still nothing.

A chill rankled her body. Phantom was in the paddock, so where was Seth? A horrifying thought raced through her mind. What if someone had discovered this place and killed her husband? She quickly dismissed the idea. The person would have taken Phantom. Still, something was off. Seth wouldn't have summoned her and not been here to greet her. She felt a sudden urge to flee.

Turning abruptly, she ran into Seth who stood behind her. His steely blue eyes met hers as he pulled her to him. They gazed at each other for a few moments. When Maggie opened her mouth to speak, Seth placed his finger gently on her lips and smiled.

"Later," he said, leaning in to kiss her.

She returned the kiss with the same passion. Stepping back, she looked up at him and ran her hand along the side of his face. "Where were you? I was worried," she whispered.

"Double checked the area to make sure we'd be safe," he

replied, kissing her again. "It's freezing out here. Let's go inside."

He took her hand and led her into the shack which wasn't much warmer than outside but at least it prevented the wind from biting through her dress. A couple of quilts were arranged on the floor where he'd obviously been sleeping, and an oil lamp burned in the far corner.

"How long have you been here?" she asked, glancing around the space.

"A day," he said, pulling her back to him. He kissed her long and hard making her knees tremble. Seth grabbed one of the quilts and wrapped it around her before they sat down.

"I'm so sorry about our argument the last time we met," she said, her gaze locking onto his.

A sparkle flickered in his eye. "I was at fault, Maggie, not you. I never should've said the things I did. I know you'd never do anything untoward, and I was wrong to infer such a thing." He ran his hand through his hair. "I was a fool and I've berated myself ever since. I was going to come back the next day but was called to Charleston to help with a raid on the railroad. After that I was sent to Philadelphia to deal with a man selling secrets to the Confederacy."

"I should have told you of my plans to help Dr. Towne with the school. It was wrong of me to hide it." Maggie reached up and touched the stubble sprouting from his chin. "I love you Seth and would never do anything to hurt you. You've occupied my every thought since you left." Tears welled in her eyes.

"Not a moment goes by when you aren't on my mind," he whispered, tipping her chin toward him. "Let's not waste any more time." He leaned in and brushed her lips with a kiss erasing all the hurt and anguish that had plagued her for months.

. . .

Beneath the quilts, the warmth of Seth's skin against hers chased away winter's chill. For the first time since the war began, Maggie slept soundly dreaming of her children romping around the yard while she and Seth swayed in the rockers on the porch.

The following morning, they tacked up the horses and prepared to leave. Seth wrapped his arm around Maggie's waist and drew her to him. "I love you, Maggie Daniels." Adoration streamed from his deep blue eyes flooding her heart with joy.

"I love you," she replied, kissing him.

He helped her onto the saddle before swinging up onto his.

"Take the old route back, no one uses it anymore," he said, gathering his reins.

"Stay safe," she replied, a lump forming in her throat. They'd spent a wonderful night together and she prayed it wouldn't be the last.

The right side of his lip curled as he winked and trotted away. Maggie took the route Seth had mentioned and made it back to St. Helena by afternoon. As Jack plodded along, Maggie scrutinized all that had transpired in the past few months. Even though her insecurities about her marriage had been swept away, her thoughts wandered to James. Somehow the feelings she'd had for him seemed dimmer. Relief washed over her. Perhaps it wasn't affection she'd experienced for the Lt. Colonel but a longing for her husband.

Guilt plucked at her heart. Why was she even thinking about him after spending the night with Seth? Stop it, she thought. You love your husband. Now more than ever, she was certain her feelings for James had been misplaced, at least that's what she told herself. Once his views toward the Negroes had altered and she got to know him better, Maggie had come to enjoy his attention. James was a personable man. Any woman would find him suitable. So why was she dwelling on this? It was only friendship, nothing more. Maggie sighed as she rode along the path. If only she could reconcile her feelings for James like she had the misunderstanding with Seth.

An hour later, after leaving Jack with Henry, Maggie meandered down the sandy lane to the house, her heart full and her worry rekindled. Emotionally drained, Maggie made her way to her room, tossed her bonnet on the dresser, and plopped onto her bed. Having made amends with her husband gave her a modicum of peace.

Maggie's mind drifted back to the night before. The warmth of Seth's body against hers and the comfort of his arms wrapped around her lingered on her skin. If only they could be together again. She was tired of all the fighting and disruption that had fragmented their lives. How much longer would it be before the war ended so she could be reunited with her husband and her family? Exhaling, she dismissed the pang of foreboding fingering her thoughts. Now more than ever, she needed to stay busy for the sake of her sanity.

Chapter 37

January 1864

Seth

Contentment permeated Seth's soul as he rode toward the South Carolina border. After reconciling with Maggie, he felt rejuvenated and peaceful. If only the country could come to a truce so he and Maggie could return home and resume their lives with their children. Joshua and Jane's images flashed through his head bringing a smile to his face as pride washed over him. They were intelligent and kind-hearted individuals and he longed to tuck them in at night with a bedtime story. Granted, Jane was well on her way to becoming a young lady and soon would no longer partake of childhood endeavors.

Inhaling sharply, Seth deliberated over his encounter with Jane's biological father, Mr. Farris. Even though he felt the man deserved anything he got, leaving him to the vices of angry soldiers needled at Seth's conscience. Violence was never the answer unless it was the only means for survival, but the war had altered his perspective in some ways. He'd experienced things he could never extract from his mind; the things of which nightmares were made. For a brief moment, while he was with Maggie, he'd considered unburdening himself but thought better of it. Their time together was precious, and he didn't wish to sully it with guilt for his misdeeds. When the war ended, he'd share the encounter with his wife. Then again, there were some things that should be buried deep, and this was one of them.

Seth spurred Phantom into a gallop in an effort to outrun the indelible mark the war had left on his soul. He made his way toward the designated meeting point with one of his unit's soldiers. He planned on doing a bit of reconnaissance in the area before returning to the encampment. There was an old, abandoned farmhouse about ten miles north. If he kept up a good pace, he could make it there by nightfall and resume his journey in the morning.

By the time Seth arrived at his destination, the sun was sliding behind the horizon. His stomach rumbled reminding him he hadn't eaten since that morning. Although the barn on the property was long gone, the paddock fencing was secure. He untacked Phantom, filled the water trough, and set him loose in the open pasture. Phantom snorted and lifted his back hooves in a buck before galloping around. Finally, the ebony steed stopped and pawed at the ground before rolling in the freshly scratched earth. Once he was thoroughly covered in the dusty soil, he hefted himself back up and gave a full-body shake removing the excess dirt.

Seth grinned at Phantom's joyful antics before ambling toward the back door of the dilapidated farmhouse. Its back porch sagged, and white paint peeled from the siding like the bark of a birch tree. He stepped inside the darkened space, letting his eyes adjust before making his way to the front parlor. Twilight cast ghostly shadows along the walls opposite the glassless window panes. He tossed his saddle bag onto an old chair, the stuffing protruding from tears in the faded fabric.

A sense of sadness pervaded the house. Seth pondered what the family was like who had resided in the home before the war broke out. Did they farm their own land, or had they enslaved their workers? There were no signs of slave cabins, making him believe they worked the land themselves. Remnants of a happy home remained with a few paintings on the walls and tattered calico curtains framing the windows. A frayed braided rug and a few wooden blocks sat next to a child's rocker by the hearth. The war had separated families, exiled people from their homes, and destroyed a way of life that should have been abolished long before the first shots rang out at Fort Sumter.

His ruminations were interrupted by the sound of movement coming from the second floor. Unholstering his weapon, he stood as still as a statue trying to determine if it was a predator of the four-legged or two-legged type. Seth's skin prickled as the hair on the back of his neck stood on end. He hovered at the base of the stairs honing in on the noise.

A floorboard above creaked, letting him know it was a human being. Sucking in his breath, he held steady, his pistol cocked, and waited for the person to make their way down the stairs. His body stiffened as adrenaline pulsed through his limbs.

Whoever was up there had obviously heard him enter and seemed determined to stay hidden. Seth contemplated leaving but thought better of it. By the time he readied Phantom, the stranger could ambush him. He couldn't risk it. His best course of action was to confront whoever was hiding on the second floor.

Instead of going upstairs, Seth decided to ferret the person out. He went back to the hearth where a fire poker rested against the wall. Grabbing it, he slammed it against the floor with all his might sending an ear-splitting clang reverberating through the room. From there he hid in the small indention at the base of the stairs and waited.

Light footfalls echoed across the upstairs floor and down the stairs just as he'd hoped. Seth brought the pistol to his chest and prepared to fire. With the sound of each footstep, he tensed until he could see the booted feet of a soldier. What he couldn't determine was whether he was Blue or Gray. Holding his breath, Seth watched the soldier round the newel post and walk his direction.

Seth exhaled when he saw the blue of the soldier's coat. He stepped from the shadowy nook where he'd been hiding with his gun ready, just in case. As Seth came into view, the other soldier took aim.

"My goodness, Seth! You scared me half to death!" the other soldier hollered, lowering the pistol.

Shaking his head, Seth lowered his weapon. "Elora, what are you doing here?"

"I might ask you the same thing," she said.

"I knew the place was abandoned and decided to stay the night," he replied.

"As did I," she said, removing the cap from her cropped hair.

Seth walked over to her and pulled her into a hug. "I'm glad it's you," he said stepping back. "Is there anything to eat around here?"

"I was getting ready to look when you arrived."

"Maybe between the two of us we can scrape something up."

Elora lit an old lantern that was sitting on the floor in the back room where they found several jars of pickles. From there they scavenged the grounds and discovered the remnants of an old garden with a few withered vegetables.

"Looks like pickles for supper," Seth said with a sigh.

"Better than nothing," Elora replied.

They returned to the house, grabbed a couple jars of pickles, took their meager feast to the parlor, and sat upon the floor.

"How long have you been here?" Seth asked, pickle juice running down his arm as he bit into the sour vegetable with a grimace.

"Arrived this afternoon. I'm going back and forth between regiments," she said, biting into a pickle. "Got some interesting information. Right now, the Major with the 5th Georgia Cavalry is relying on me. He thinks I'm spying for them."

Seth shook his head. "I'm astounded at this ruse you've perpetuated. You've always been extremely bull-headed and independent, but I never imagined you accomplishing all of this."

"You say bull-headed as if it was a bad thing," she chuckled. "I must admit, I'm a bit surprised at my success. Never thought I'd end up being a spy *and* a soldier."

"Still don't understand what possessed you to join the army."

Elora shrugged. "I always felt as if my life was insignificant. Don't misunderstand me, I appreciate all my parents have done but it wasn't enough. I needed to do something substantial, not just get married and have children." She slumped back against the wall.

"You're a brave woman," Seth said, grasping Elora's hand.

"Haven't done too badly as a man either," she laughed.

"Maybe it was all that pirate play we did when you were growing up."

Elora shrugged. "Maybe."

"Funny, I don't remember you ever talking about marriage," Seth said, biting into another pickle.

"Never thought about it," Elora replied, her gaze fixed on the small rocker with the blocks scattered around. She quieted as if she'd slipped into a dream.

"What is it?" Seth asked.

Elora popped out of her stupor. "What do you mean?"

"Something's up. Don't try to fool me. We've known each other too long for that."

"And yet you didn't recognize me the day I rescued you from those scoundrels who tried beating you to death," she said with a knowing grin.

Rolling his eyes, Seth nudged her shoulder with his. "Tell me what's troubling you. You can't do battle if your mind is preoccupied."

Elora licked her lips and took in a deep breath. "I can't stop thinking about missed opportunities."

"As in?"

"My captain," she whispered. "I know I'm being ridiculous. It's not like there was any hope of a relationship, and yet..."

"It's not ridiculous. Obviously, you loved him and that's not easy to dismiss. There's not a day that Maggie isn't on my mind. Some days are harder than others. I have to keep those feelings at bay so I can do what is necessary to stay alive and win this war."

Elora buried her face in her hands, her sobs shaking her body. Seth wrapped his arm around her shoulders and pulled her close.

"My heart hurts so badly I fear it may stop beating from the weight of my sorrow," she murmured.

Leaning over, Seth kissed the top of her head. "With time you'll be able to give your heart to another, someone who knows the real you, not your fake male persona. Even if the captain had survived, do you truly believe he could've accepted you as a woman after knowing you as a man."

Elora sniffled. "You really think he'd not be able to forgive my deceit?"

"I'd have a hard time falling for a woman I'd only known as a man," Seth replied.

"Doesn't matter anyway. He's gone," she croaked, fresh tears falling. "It hurts that he died without knowing someone loved him. If only I could have tended to him, maybe he'd still be alive."

"You said the doctor wasn't able to help him. If that's the case, I doubt there's anything you could've done, not to mention, you were severely wounded."

"I've learned enough from watching my father over the years to render aid. I may have been able to help."

"Elora, the man is gone and there's nothing you could have done to prevent his death. You'll love again," he reassured her. "But hopefully when you do, it will be as a woman."

Elora gave a slight smile, dried her tears with the cuff of her shirt, and shoved her shoulder against Seth's. "You're incorrigible."

"You wouldn't have me any other way."

"True," she said, snuggling back against him. "Have you heard from Maggie?"

"In a sense," he said, his lips curling into a smile as his mind revisited their tryst.

Elora sat up straighter. "What do you mean by that?"

"I was with her last night."

"Are you delusional? There's no way you could travel from Pennsylvania back to South Carolina in a day," she said, furrowing her brow.

"We rendezvoused at the old blue shed," he replied, a spark in his eye.

"She's *here* in South Carolina?" Elora declared.

"Yup. She's been on St. Helena Island for almost two years. Dr. Towne was tasked with opening a school for the freed slaves. She asked Maggie to come with her and help."

"And when were you planning on sharing this bit of news with me?"

Seth laughed. "I just shared it."

"You know what I mean," she replied. "Why are you just now telling me?"

"I only discovered it myself a few months ago."

Shock veiled Elora's expression as she tilted her head. "She didn't tell you?"

"Nope. My commanding officer sent me on a humanitarian mission with a Lt. Colonel Brunson who'd befriended Maggie while stationed in Beaufort. Brunson made a few inquiries about my location and then requested I travel south with him. Apparently, he didn't realize Maggie had kept her whereabouts secret from me."

Elora's hand flew up to her open mouth.

"Needless to say, I was shocked when I found her on St. Helena," Seth added.

"How did she react?"

"As surprised as I was." He inhaled deeply and rested his head against the wall.

"What happened?" Elora asked.

"Our reunion wasn't as pleasant as we would have liked it to be. I was upset she hadn't told me about working with Dr. Towne and then there was the situation with the Lt. Colonel."

"What do you mean, the *situation* with the Lt. Colonel?" she asked, straightening.

"I may have inferred she'd engaged in wrongdoing."

Elora gasped. "Seth Daniels, how could you do such a thing? Maggie would never do anything inappropriate."

"I know that now, but I wasn't thinking straight. She'd been dishonest about her location and my mind went to a dark place."

Elora shook her head. "Shame on you for thinking it."

"It was a terrible misunderstanding and we've promised never to let anything like that come between us again."

Elora nudged Seth's arm with her elbow. "I'm glad. I'd hate to make you walk the plank," she said in her best pirate voice.

"You'd have to catch me first," he replied with a mischievous grin.

"Don't underestimate me," she said. "I'm a lot stronger and swifter than I used to be and apparently, quite gifted as a spy."

"Meaning?"

"Meaning, I've been tasked as a spy to locate my soldier persona, Lt. Polk, and bring his location to Confederate Colonel Bridgestone."

Shaking his head, Seth laughed. "You never cease to amaze me."

"I love you, Seth," Elora said, grasping his hand.

"Love you too, Elora. Or should I call you Miss Kirk?"

With a yawn, Elora leaned against the wall and closed her eyes. "You can call me tired. Let's get some shut-eye."

"Sounds like a good idea," he replied, slumping against the wall.

It wasn't the most ideal place to snooze, but as soldiers they knew the importance of staying alert. At least they had each other should unwanted visitors arrive. No matter how cautious one might be, the war was always close at hand and there was never a time to let down one's guard.

Chapter 38

April 1864

Seth

It had been a long winter and Seth was thankful to have spent most of his time in the south where the temperatures were warmer, and snow rarely fell. Weariness from three years of war saturated his soul. He'd not seen his children in a couple of years or Maggie for several months. Visions of Joshua and Jane, their eyes glinting with wonder, as Maggie regaled them with Irish fairy tales clutched at his heart. He could still hear their giggles as they tossed flour at each other during their baking escapades. His wife's inner beauty radiated in all she did whether tending to the garden, fishing off the dock, or reading bedtime stories to their children. Memories of his last reunion with Maggie at the small shack made him yearn to run his fingers through her auburn tresses and snuggle with her beneath a quilt until the sun peeked over the horizon.

Word that Mr. Farris had hung for his treasonous endeavors had reached Seth for which he felt no remorse. The man had lived a life of cruelty and dishonor making his demise fitting. The only decent thing to come of him was Jane. Seth's eyes stung at the thought of how changed she and his son,

Joshua, must be after so many years. Would they recognize him when he returned home? His once clean-shaven face was covered in a full beard and his sandy brown curls were tied in a pony tail. No doubt, his appearance was one of a disheveled wanderer. He made a mental note to get a shave and haircut before returning home when the conflict was over, whenever that would be. At this point, the war ending felt more like a fantasy than reality.

Battles across the Virginia countryside had been brutal, much like the carnage of Gettysburg and Antietam. The loss of life was astronomical, leaving hardly any family untouched by grief. Thankfully, he and Elora had survived having seen little front-line battle. Spying carried its own set of risks which at times could be more dangerous than facing the enemy head on.

Donning his Confederate gray, Seth steered Phantom through the woods for a rendezvous with a Confederate colonel from whom he'd been reaping secrets over the past few months. He rode at a leisurely pace, taking in the budding trees and fresh scents of springtime's rebirth. As Phantom plodded along, Seth was grateful for the momentary respite until the tranquility was shattered by the sound of gunfire. He spurred Phantom into a gallop, ducking and shifting to avoid being unseated by tree branches as he raced toward the shots.

As he approached the clearing, Seth slowed Phantom to a walk and scanned the area. He spotted a flash of blue moving through a copse of trees to his left. Dismounting, he drew his weapon and maneuvered through the underbrush where he'd seen the movement. Blood pulsed through his veins with the force of a waterfall, each step making his heart pound harder. He raised his weapon, preparing to shoot.

Inching around a large oak, he caught a glimpse of a union soldier, who also had his gun cocked and ready to fire.

"Psst," Seth muttered, catching the man's attention. Before

the soldier could react, Seth whispered the code word. The man lowered his weapon and hobbled over to Seth; a bloody tourniquet wrapped about his thigh. Seth's chest constricted as the soldier got closer.

"Brunson," Seth whispered.

"Daniels," he moaned, collapsing against the tree trunk. "Glad to see you. There's a group of Rebs closing in."

"We need to get you out of here. Where's your horse?"

"I'm on foot," Brunson breathed. "Managed to hold the men back. Was lucky to make it to the woods." Looking down at the blood-soaked tourniquet on his leg, he grimaced. "Losing too much blood to get much further."

From what Seth could tell, Brunson's analysis was correct. His skin was pale, and his breathing labored.

"My horse is nearby," Seth said. "I'll bring him over and you can ride to the nearest encampment."

Brunson nodded as Seth reached beneath his left arm and steadied him. Before they could move, three men in shabby gray uniforms burst through the trees with rifles drawn. At that moment, Brunson pressed the barrel of his pistol against Seth's head.

"Take another step and I'll blow his brains out," Brunson growled.

Shock radiated through Seth's limbs, momentarily para- lyzing him. What was Brunson doing?

"Stupid Yankee!" one of the men in gray hollered. "What makes you think you can take out one of our men and still be able to kill the three of us?"

Without speaking a word, Brunson cocked his gun.

A shot rang out, temporarily deafening Seth as Brunson collapsed to the ground. The three confederates ran over, surrounding Brunson who lay on the ground bleeding profusely from the right side of his chest.

"You okay?" the tallest man said to Seth.

"Fine, thanks," he replied, watching Brunson's life seep into the ground. His shallow breathing suggested his time was limited. If there was any hope of saving him, Seth needed to get rid of these confederates.

"What are you doing out here on your own, soldier?" the stocky one asked Seth.

"On my way to meet with Colonel Allen."

"He's camped about a mile from here," the tall one replied. "You go on and we'll dispose of this Yankee," he commanded, spittle flying from his weathered lips.

Seth shook his head. "This guy was getting ready to kill me. I'd like to repay the favor," he said with a sly grin. "You saved my life. The least I can do is finish him. Go on, I've got this."

"Much obliged," the stocky man replied.

The three confederates hurried away leaving him alone with Brunson. Once the soldiers were safely out of earshot, Seth leaned over the Lt. Colonel to evaluate the situation. Blood oozed from his chest and his skin was sallow.

"Brunson," Seth whispered.

The Lt. Colonel's eyes fluttered open. "Why are you still here, Daniels?"

"That was a foolish move. What were you thinking?" Seth asked, ignoring Brunson's question. "We could have found a way to get both of us out alive."

"You and I both know that wasn't going to happen," he choked. "I did what needed to be done."

"I don't understand you. There was no need to sacrifice yourself like that. You hardly know me."

Brunson went into a coughing fit as he tried to speak, blood trickling from the right side of his mouth.

"Maggie loves you. I couldn't bear the idea of anything causing her pain. If those men suspected we knew each other they'd have killed you too, especially if they discovered you're a spy."

"You're in love with my wife," Seth said flatly.

The Lt. Colonel closed his eyes and managed to nod. "For some time," he gasped. Opening his eyes, he stared at Seth. "But her heart belongs to you."

Seth clenched his jaw as he looked away. He'd been correct in his assumption about Brunson's feelings for Maggie. What he hadn't expected was the depth of the man's affection and his loyalty to Maggie's heart. A mixture of contempt and compassion flooded Seth's chest.

"Is there someone I can contact for you?" Seth asked, knowing Brunson's time was short.

"Aside from my parents and siblings, I'm alone in this world," he sputtered. "My career is all I have." He coughed again, spewing blood all over his chin.

"I'll make sure your family and command know about your heroism and sacrifice."

Brunson looked at Seth and muttered, "I'd rather go out like this than face a life without her. She's the most incredible person I've ever known."

Seth nodded. "Is there anything you wish for me to tell her?"

"No," he wheezed, his voice barely audible. "I'm sorry for saying what I have. Although tempted, I never acted on my feelings."

"I know," Seth replied. "But Maggie still cares about you. If there's something you need me to tell her, I'll...." Seth paused for a moment, weighing his words carefully. "I'll do so." Although Seth wasn't comfortable with this conversation, he felt he owed a dying man, a fellow soldier who'd saved his life, this one last request.

"Tell her," Brunson wheezed, "having known her gentle nature made me a better man."

With a gasp, the Lt. Colonel exhaled one last breath, his eyes fixed on the sky above. Gently closing Brunson's eyelids, Seth leaned back on his heels and bowed his head. This was a good man, a brave soldier, and it pained him to witness his death. Any lingering resentment or animosity over Brunson's feelings about Maggie melted away. All that remained was a sense of respect and regret. While thankful to still be alive, Seth felt a pang of guilt like a punch in the gut. There was no way to transport him back to a Union encampment, especially with Rebel soldiers scouring the area. He needed to find a way to bury him here.

Seth's shoulders and upper arms burned as he scratched out a shallow grave using a large section of branch he found beneath the oak where Brunson died. He placed the Lt. Colonel's body within the earth's embrace and covered him with dirt and nature's debris, making a conscious effort to remember the location. He would try to return after the war and provide him with a proper burial. Once Brunson was entombed, Seth said a prayer, collected Brunson's personal belongings, found Phantom, and rode to his original destination to meet with the Confederate commander.

Even though they'd made amends, Seth felt even worse about his accusations to his wife months prior. Why had he ever doubted her commitment to him? He considered writing Maggie to tell her about the Lt. Colonel but decided against it. He needed to deliver this message in person. Ruminating on what Brunson had said about Maggie, Seth smiled. He was correct in his statement. Maggie was an incredible person. How Seth had managed to find and marry such a woman left him perplexed. But she was his, heart and soul, and he longed to be with her.

In the meantime, Seth had a mission to fulfill, one that would be the most perilous of his time with the army. He'd considered enlisting Elora's help but thought better of it. Although she was capable, he wouldn't put her at additional risk. He owed her parents that much. This was a mission he'd have to handle on his own, no matter the danger.

Chapter 39

Late spring 1864

Elora

Elora sat at the edge of the river, watching the current trickle over rocks and fallen logs. Dipping her bare feet into the cooling embrace of the water, she looked up. Trees overhead whispered secrets as their leaves fluttered on warm spring breezes. She was in the northern part of her home state of South Carolina. Despite being born here, she'd not traveled much within its borders, only so far as the plantations she'd visited in the coastal regions.

Filling her lungs with the fresh forest air, Elora rolled her shoulders in an effort to loosen the tension knotting her muscles. Up until the war, her life had been charmed. Part of her felt guilty for the privileged existence she'd enjoyed while so many others had suffered. Even though she'd never endured cruelty, hunger, or abandonment, something was missing from her existence, something she'd never allowed to the forefront of her consciousness.

Captain Dixon's face popped into her head, the gleam in his eyes and the curl of his lips making her heart palpitate. Something about him had altered her perspective about love.

She'd taken Seth's advice and pushed him from her mind. It didn't take away the remorse she felt for not trying to help him or the rage she harbored for his death. Lowering her head, she cried for the loss of a man who continued to hold her heart, the lost innocence of her youth, and all the lives that had been destroyed by the war.

Elora lifted her head, wiped away the sorrow streaming down her cheeks, and got to her feet. There was no use dwelling on past disappointments. She'd proven to herself that she was more than just a pretty face and well-schooled female. She was cunning, brave, resourceful, and it had saved lives. Her view of the world was much altered with the violence she'd encountered and witnessed over the past few years, but it made her stronger and more perceptive. For that she was grateful.

Slipping on her socks and boots, Elora trudged up the embankment where Jasper grazed peacefully in a small patch of grass. It was time to meet her Union cohort at a section of road known as Fiddler's Elbow. Something churned in the pit of her stomach as if this meeting was doomed. She shrugged off her apprehension and mounted Jasper.

Dressed in her uniform, she'd share the information gleaned from her Confederate source with her Union contact. After that, she'd change back into her dress and her role as Miss Kirk and follow the Confederate commander's order to search for Lt. Polk, the soldier they believed was betraying them. She chuckled at the idea she'd been tasked to find her male persona. It was the easiest assignment she'd been given thus far. However, Elora wouldn't complete the mission to bring her alter ego to the commander for punishment. No, she'd ride away with the satisfaction that she'd successfully fooled a trained military man with her feminine charms and southern ways all the while doubling as a Union soldier.

Chapter 40

November 1864

Seth

November brought frigid temperatures and shortened days, making the war efforts more difficult. Weary from years of fighting and scouting, Seth traversed the coastal region of Georgia, a place with which he was quite familiar. The sun bid farewell as the moon rose in a clear sky illuminating the shadows in an eerie glow. As he made his way through the wooded area about fifteen miles outside of Savannah, he was distracted by something in the underbrush to his right. A shiver rattled his spine. He couldn't ascertain whether his unease was due to the wintry air or the precarious feeling niggling at his brain. Nonetheless, he nudged Phantom forward, keeping a watchful eye on whatever was hovering in the bushes.

As Phantom plodded along, Seth ruminated over an account he'd heard from another soldier about a recent incident in Georgia. Union General Jefferson Davis, General Reb, as he was known since he shared the same name with the Confederate President, had led his troops toward Savannah along with hundreds of Negro refugees. Although fighting for the north, his actions were akin to those who viewed the Negroes as second-class citizens. According to reports, he'd tired of them slowing his men as they marched toward Savannah to join Sherman's efforts. Determined to dispose of the unwanted followers, the General commanded his troops across a make-shift pontoon bridge with orders for the Negroes to wait until given the go ahead to cross.

When the last of the troops made it to the other side, they were ordered to dismantle the bridge. Confusion rose amongst the Negroes as they watched their means of escape demolished. Being left behind meant returning to slavery or death should the confederates find them. In a panic, several plunged into the water trying to swim to the other side. Many drowned while attempting to navigate the raging rapids. The ones who made it across were shot by Union soldiers as they crawled up the river bank.

Seth's blood boiled at the account. He wanted to see the general punished for his crimes even though he knew it wasn't likely. Hoping to help any of the freed men and women still in the area, Seth set out in search of survivors. It would take some creative maneuvering to continue with his assigned mission while getting the remaining Negroes on the path to freedom, far from the indifference of military personnel who viewed them as nothing more than chattel and a hindrance to their military ambitions. The hatred and prejudice of some of the northern soldiers he'd encountered was almost as rampant as what he'd known in the southern regions.

As Seth neared a copse of poines, his skin prickled. He felt Phantom's body tense as the horse tossed his head several times. Something was amiss. Holding his breath, Seth reached for his weapon. The quietude was shattered when a loud pop rang out accompanied by a burst of light. A searing pain tore through Seth's chest toppling him from the saddle. The air was knocked from his lungs as his head and back smacked against the forest floor. Seth gripped the gushing wound with his right hand while feeling around for his gun with the other.

The crunching of leaves alerted him that someone was approaching. He was vulnerable and needed to act fast. As adrenaline pumped through his body, Seth latched onto the handle of his pistol, pointed, and pulled the trigger. He watched the soldier in gray who'd been running towards him crumple to the ground a few inches from where he lay.

Seth managed to lean up on one arm, groaning as pain ripped through his torso. Bits of brain matter and bone swam in a crimson halo expanding around the other soldier's skull. There was no denying he was dead. Lucky shot, he thought. Forcing himself to a sitting position, Seth shook his head in an effort to revive his senses. His surroundings spun with the force of a whirlpool. He needed to get back in the saddle and leave before any other confederates arrived. But the pain was intense, more than any other wound he'd ever endured. He glanced down at the stain blooming through his coat, blood gushing from the hole. The bullet may have nicked an artery which meant he'd bleed out in a matter of minutes. He had to do something fast, or he wouldn't make it. Adrenaline, along with images of Maggie, gave Seth the strength to try.

Moving closer to the dead soldier, Seth mustered all his strength and tugged at the sleeves of the man's coat until it slipped off. He pressed the woolen jacket to the hole in his chest, hoping to slow the blood flow. Exhausted from his efforts, he slumped against the massive tree trunk.

Everything seemed to be moving in slow motion. A coppery taste filled his mouth and his head wobbled. Maybe if he rested for a minute, he could get on Phantom and ride to an encampment for help. Feeling as week as a newborn calf, Seth did his best to take in air. He puckered his dry lips and let out a breathy whistle. Phantom plodded over and nuzzled Seth's shoulder.

"That's my pal," he croaked. "Give me a minute and we'll be on our way."

Staring up at the multitude of stars sparkling like diamonds in a canopy of black, Seth remembered a night years before when he and Maggie sat on the edge of the dock behind their cottage gazing at the starlit night. She was snuggled close, the soft curves of her body warming his as she leaned against him. A smile curled the right side of his mouth at the memory. Images of Joshua and Jane joined the procession of recollections parading through his mind. How he longed to hear the sound of Jane's giggles and see Joshua's scrunched face when he was asked to eat any sort of vegetable. But most of all, he yearned to feel Maggie's heart beating in rhythm with his as they lay beside each other in bed. He'd miss them all, he thought, as the stars above blurred, and his mind shifted to darkness.

Chapter 41

November 1864

Maggie

Melancholy wrapped around Maggie like a blanket as she strolled to the edge of the marsh and shifted her gaze to the sky. She was tired of the war, tired of being without Seth, and tired of being separated from her children. Her soul ached for some semblance of normalcy.

Sitting on the ground, she leaned back on her hands and stared at the glittering sky above. Thousands of points of light twinkled against the inky backdrop of night, the moon shimmering across the water and shadowing the marsh grasses. She wondered what Seth was doing at that moment. A chill slipped down her spine making her shudder.

Maggie shook off the disquiet weighting her chest. Things were going smoothly at Penn School. Willa and Letty had settled into the community and would probably remain after the fighting ceased, if it ever did. Although Maggie's work was purposeful, her presence wasn't as necessary as it had been when she first arrived. Perhaps it was time to head home and be with her kids. They'd been inadvertently orphaned for years with their father at war and their mother working to help the newly freed slaves.

More than anything, she yearned to return to Rose Hall with her family and the Polks. Regret squeezed her heart like a vice. She was pleased with her efforts at Penn School although she still questioned whether leaving Jane and Joshua for so long had been wise. Would they accept her when she returned or hold bitterness in their hearts over being abandoned for more than two years? How could they possibly understand the importance of helping others at the sacrifice of one's own comfort? They'd never known the horrors of slavery having been shielded from the barbaric institution while living at Rose Hall. But they were young and might not be willing to welcome her home after such a long absence regardless of her efforts to help others.

Maggie's eyelids moistened as she stared at the heavens. The hopelessness of not knowing when the conflict would end permeated her soul making it hard to breathe. She lay on the ground despite its hard, cold surface and wiped tears from her cheeks. As she watched the twinkling pinpoints above, something stirred in her spirit, something unpleasant. An ominous sensation pulsed through her limbs. Bolting upright, she grasped her chest as if someone had stabbed her heart. Maggie swallowed hard and fought back the dread filtering through her mind. Everything would be alright, she told herself, it was just a moment of weakness from the stress of the past few years and missing her family.

Chapter 42

March 1865

Elora

For months Elora had been switching back and forth from soldier to female spy. Exhaustion saturated her muscles as she rode toward the Colonel's tent, dressed in union blue. After providing valuable intelligence she'd obtained as a female in spring of '64, which resulted in several successful campaigns for her unit, Elora was promoted to Captain. Sick of the war with its dead bodies and constant battles, she wanted nothing more than to return home. These were the times when the idea of being pampered didn't seem as disagreeable as it had when she began this endeavor. She longed to sleep in her own bed, enjoy a delicious breakfast with real coffee, and stroll along the edge of the marsh without fear of being shot. But how could she return to a conventional existence after all she'd endured?

Elora regretted nothing she'd done. She was proud of her service and her ability to fool so many with her alternating identities. If nothing else, she'd discovered her inner strength as well as the joy of being female. It seemed as if she'd been in the trenches of battle forever with her former life nothing more than a distant memory. War had scarred her in permanent ways. Visions of men bleeding to death or being blown to pieces resided in her subconscious and haunted her dreams. Yet she'd saved so many and contributed to the preservation of the country she loved. The freeing of slaves in the south was an added benefit.

Elora had done so much in the past few years, too much to return to a simple life of luxury. What would she do at the end of the war, if it ever came? The Elora Polk that enlisted years before was gone. Her role had been significant even if no one would ever know about it, except for Seth. But these were thoughts for another time. For now, she needed to focus on her mission.

As she rode Jasper towards an old shack where she'd change into her dress to meet with the Confederate commander, her mind drifted to Seth. She'd not seen him in weeks and wondered where he was and what he was doing.

When she reached the run-down hovel, she slipped inside and changed. Shifting her skirts, she climbed onto the saddle, spurred Jasper to a gallop, and headed toward the Confederate encampment. Once she reached the commander's tent, Elora halted Jasper, dismounted, and walked inside.

"Good afternoon, sir," she said with a smile.

"Hello, Miss Kirk. Have you any news of Polk's whereabouts?"

"Actually, I'm rather close to finding him. I should have an exact location soon."

"Good work, Miss Kirk," he said, shifting in his seat. "It's a shame you aren't a man. We could've used you in the army."

A mischievous grin curled her lips. "I've been scandalous enough running around the countryside trying to help capture a Union spy. It's probably best I remain a helpless female."

The commander huffed. "You may be a lady, but you're far

from helpless. Your service to this unit has been exemplary. I look forward to your report when you find that dastardly spy."

"Thank you, sir," she replied. Pleased with the compliment, she left the commander, remounted Jasper, and headed for the shack where she would resume her role as a Union soldier.

As Elora rode back to her regiment dressed as Captain Polk, her thoughts returned to what her life would be like once the war was over. After years of service, she needed to do something meaningful. Being a woman greatly hindered her prospects. Even in her current roles, she gained more respect as a male officer than a female spy.

One thing was certain, once she returned home her parents would expect her to complete her education. What purpose would it serve to get a degree but not be able to use it? Being educated meant nothing in her world of tea parties and balls. Elora was conflicted. Part of her longed to live a simple life after years of hard service while the other part wanted to do something substantial.

In time, she'd be expected to marry and contribute to the community in ways deemed proper by societal standards, in other words have children and run a household. Tears stung Elora's eyes. The idea of settling down was odious now. Her heart belonged to Captain Dixon and no other man would ever be able to fill that part of her soul.

Sighing, Elora decided her family would have to accept her role as an independent woman. Maybe she'd do something shocking like tour Europe unaccompanied or start her own business. Her shoulders slumped as she blew out a breath. What could she possibly do that was as meaningful as this? Then again, the war may never end, and she could be soldiering and spying for the rest of her life.

Elora's stomach knotted. She couldn't keep this up forever. Eventually, her mother and father would discover her deception. It was shocking she'd made it this far without being exposed. Visions of her parents' reactions rattled her fortitude. They'd be hurt and furious at the same time. While they'd forgive her anything, they'd never believe her again.

If only Captain Dixon had survived, maybe they could have done something daring together. Of course, even if he did forgive her ruse, he'd never be able to trust her. It didn't matter anyway. He was gone. Shaking off the unease of her parents' reactions to her future choices and her sorrow over a life without the captain, Elora rode on, determination straightening her back. When the war ended, she'd choose her own path, regardless of the world's narrow expectations for women.

Chapter 43

Maggie

April 1865

Jack plodded along the dirt road, swishing his tail, as Maggie inhaled the fragrant aroma of spring jasmine and the salty marsh air. Live oak branches swayed, sending shadows dancing across the lane like marionettes. This had been her home for nearly three years now. Things were running as smoothly as possible despite the battles raging in the areas around them. It was difficult to fathom the brutality of the war when it hadn't crossed the threshold of her little piece of the world.

Maggie had received several letters from the kids and Mrs. Milner, but nothing from Seth. The idea that he may be near the fighting was stressful; however, she'd become accustomed to the helplessness of not hearing from him or being aware of his situation. In her mind, no news meant he was probably alive and entrenched in his duties.

She turned Jack down the drive towards The Oaks. She'd grown fond of the place despite missing her family. Word on the streets of town was that the war couldn't last much longer due to the winnowing away of the confederacy's weapons, man power, and basic necessities like food rations and medical supplies.

Once Jack was handed off to Henry, Maggie traipsed to the house, her heart tinged with melancholy. Climbing the front steps, she was deep in thought when the sound of wagon wheels startled her from her stupor. As she turned to see who was caroming down the drive a soft breeze tickled her neck whisking a loose strand of hair against her cheek.

A lanky, dark-skinned man halted the wagon and climbed down from the bench seat, a wide brimmed hat shading his face. He lumbered to the rear of the wagon and helped a gaunt white man down from the back. Once the man's legs met the ground, the Negro reached into the wagon, removed a cane, and handed it to him. The white man was a grisly looking fellow, dressed in a tattered blue uniform, unshaven with long hair, and a skeletal physique. He took a few wobbly steps, staring at the ground as he hobbled alongside the Negro who walked patiently beside him.

Maggie wondered why they were at the plantation house. Dr. Towne rarely saw patients outside of the island community and the soldiers were always taken to nearby hospitals on the mainland. Perhaps this man was being sent here to convalesce although Maggie couldn't imagine why Dr. Towne hadn't alerted her to the situation.

As the men drew closer, the Negro looked up and smiled. There was a kindness in his gaze that gave her a sense of comfort. She'd never seen him before and yet something in his air and manner of walking was familiar. When the men reached the base of the stairs the disheveled white man glanced up, his deep blue gaze grabbing Maggie's heart.

"Seth!" she hollered, bolting down the stairs. She threw her arms around his neck, nearly knocking him off balance.

With his free arm, he pulled her close.

Maggie stepped back, scrutinizing her husband's unkempt appearance and emaciated frame. Tears threatened to fall as her eyes locked onto his, her heart pounding.

"What happened?" she muttered.

"It's a long story," he replied, a smile lifting his whiskered cheeks. "Let's go inside and I'll tell you about it."

Maggie's knees quivered as she led the tall Negro man and Seth up the stairs and into the parlor. Seth lowered himself onto the wing chair by the front window while the wagon driver removed his hat and stood near the door. Maggie stared at Seth, still trying to convince herself he was actually here. Any moment she feared she'd awaken from a dream to find herself alone in her room.

Seth leaned the cane against the window sill and gazed up at Maggie.

"I'd like to introduce, Brantley," he said, motioning to his escort. "This is my wife, Maggie."

The man gave a slight bow. "Pleasure to meets you, Mrs. Daniels."

"And you," she replied. "Please, won't you sit down?"

"You's sure 'bout that?" he asked, raising an eyebrow that sent a shudder through Maggie's core. He was so familiar to her. Maybe he was from the area.

"Of course," Maggie smiled. "Everyone is welcome here."

He glanced back at Seth who nodded. Brantley lumbered across the room to a small chair, his knees jutting up in the air as he sat. Maggie started to suggest he sit somewhere more comfortable and suitable to his tall stature but thought better of it. Obviously, he wasn't accustomed to being treated as an equal.

"Let me get some lemonade and we can talk," she said, hurrying from the room.

Maggie bolted into the kitchen, making Violet jump.

"Miss Maggie, you scared de life from me!" Violet declared, grabbing her chest. "What's got into ya?"

"My husband has arrived," she said breathlessly. "I was wondering if you have any lemonade?"

"Your husband here?" she said, planting her hands on her hips. "What's you doin' in dis kitchen? You shoulda rung da bell and I'd have brought it to you. Get back out there dis minute!"

"Thank you, Miss Violet," Maggie said as a broad smile swept across her face. "There's another gent here too so we'll need three glasses."

Maggie returned to the parlor and cleared a spot on the center table for the tray of refreshments, her hands trembling with excitement. Moments later, Miss Violet walked in with a pitcher of lemonade and three glasses. She set the tray on the table and sucked in a breath when her eyes rested on Brantley. Straightening, she adjusted her apron.

Noticing Violet's reaction, Maggie grinned. "Miss Violet, this is Mr. Brantley. Mr. Brantley, this is our cook, Miss Violet."

The right side of his mouth curled. "Nice to meets you. But I's just Brantley, there's no mister to it," he said with a wink.

Maggie's stomach tightened. Why was this man so familiar? She was certain they'd never met. Perhaps he resembled someone who'd helped with the Underground Railroad or been one of the escapees she'd escorted to freedom.

"Nice to meet you," Violet said, with a sheepish grin and a quick curtsey. "I was gettin' ready to fix some sandwiches for lunch. Is you stayin?"

He glanced at Seth who nodded. "He's staying," Seth replied in a hoarse voice.

Miss Violet left the room, her ebony cheeks plumping as she walked away. Maggie served the lemonade and sat on the chair next to her husband's, grasping his bony hand in hers.

"Tell me what happened," she said, her gaze fixed on him.

He shifted in his seat before taking a long sip of the tart drink. "It happened last November," he began.

Maggie listened, immersed in Seth's story as he recounted everything that led up to being shot.

"I knew I was in trouble when I saw blood pouring from my chest and realized it was near my heart. I was determined to get back on Phantom and ride for help. Did my best to put pressure on the wound but there was too much blood loss and I passed out." He paused to take another sip.

"Where is Phantom?"

"At the stables behind headquarters on the mainland. I'm not able to care for him right now and found a reliable man to do so."

Maggie swallowed the lump in her throat. He was so frail. There was a sickly pallor to his skin which stretched tightly over his cheekbones.

"If it hadn't been for Brantley, I'd have bled to death," Seth said. "According to him, when he found me, my pulse was weak, and I'd lost a great deal of blood." Turning to Brantley, he gave a nod. "Tell her what you did."

"I checked the injury. Saw his time was short and managed to remove the bullet. Had a small sewing kit with me, stitched him up, and bandaged the wound. His horse was still there so I secured Mr. Seth on my saddle and led his horse with us to the surgeon's camp."

"Thank you for saving my husband, Mr. Brantley," Maggie said, her voice cracking with emotion. The idea that she'd almost lost him rankled her nerves.

"Didn't do much," he replied, his gaze dropping to the floor.

"I disagree," Seth chimed in.

"What you did was astounding," Maggie declared. "Where did you learn how to treat wounds? Are you a doctor?"

"No ma'am, but I's owned by one. Used to watch everything he done. When the war come, I's lucky enough to serve under a Union commander. He treat me pretty good and let me do some stuff I learned when I's owned by the doctor."

"So, you were enslaved by a southern physician?"

"Yes ma'am. Started out as his driver. We's in a bad accident one night. The carriage I's drivin' turned over when the rains wash away the road. The gentleman travelin' wid him was cut up mighty bad. The doctor was hurt too and needed help treating the man as well as tendin' to his own injuries. He was so impressed with what I done dat he teach me some things so I be able to take care of his slaves. He own four hundred of 'em."

"What happened to the doctor?" Maggie asked, intrigued by Brantley's history.

"He gone off to serve with the Confederacy. Took me with him." Brantley exhaled. "One night when he's sleeping, I snuck off. Took me a few days but I finds a Union regiment and join them. Course, a Negro couldn't be a soldier den but I's useful to them all the same."

"That's an incredible story."

"I reckon so," he said, shrugging his shoulders. "Don' know if my massa still alive or not."

"Would you care if he was?" she asked. Having heard so many different accounts along the Underground Railroad, Maggie was always surprised at the affection some held for their enslavers.

"Yes ma'am. I don' like bein' owned but he treat me good enough. Like I said, he teach me 'bout medicine so I can help people."

"Mr. Brantley, I'm ever so thankful for your efforts. You saved my husband's life."

A slight smile curled his lips as he shook his head. "Ain't no mister, just Brantley."

Something in his broad smile and manner of speaking tugged at Maggie's heart. And then it struck her like a cannonball.

"Have you any family?" she asked, straightening in her chair.

"Had a son and a wife once, but I's sold off and never seen 'em again," he said, his demeanor altering as sorrow darkened his eyes.

"How long ago was that?"

"Couldn't say exactly, it been so many years. My wife was the cook for the big house." His countenance softened. "She made the best apple pie you ever did eat."

"Tell me about your son." Maggie's heart beat quickened as she awaited his response.

"He a good boy but we masssa was a cruel man. Beat my boy for cryin' after he give him the plantation brand. He not but five years old. I can still smell he flesh burnin' and hear he screams when de massa press dat red hot iron against he skin." His eyes watered. "Dey sell me to the doctor right after dat and I never see him or my wife again."

Brantley wiped at his eyes. Obviously, the pain of his past was as raw today as it was years before. He rolled up his sleeve revealing the scarred letters, LP. "I's glad to have a nicer home with the doctor but my time with my first massa be with me forever."

Maggie swallowed hard. "What was your son's name?"

A broad smile wrinkled his eyes. "Sellers."

Maggie's hand flew to her mouth as tears stung her eyes. She knew something about this man was familiar and now she knew why. He had the same lanky frame, warm smile, and sparkle in his gaze. The brand confirmed her suspicions. Sellers had been her dearest friend and confidant at her uncle's farm. If it hadn't been for his sacrifice, she wouldn't be here now.

"Sorry if my story shock you, ma'am," he said, worry furrowing his brow.

Maggie glanced at Seth who squeezed her hand and gave a reassuring grin. She realized he was letting her know she needed to tell Brantley the truth.

"Mister...sorry, Brantley, I have something I need to share with you." Maggie's heart thudded within her chest as a tear trickled down her cheek. Here before her was the father of one of her dearest friends. How on earth was she going to share the heartbreaking news that his son was dead because of her?

All of a sudden, the idea of telling him about Sellers seemed like a poor decision. It had taken her years to smother the guilt she'd held for his death. Deep down she knew it hadn't been her fault yet somehow, she couldn't reconcile that belief between her heart and her head.

"You know where my family be?" Brantley placed the empty glass of lemonade on the side table and leaned forward, anticipation dancing in his stare.

"I never met your wife, but I knew your son." Maggie chewed her lower lip and twisted her fingers in her lap. Brantley's hopeful expression wilted.

"What happened?" he asked, his voice barely a whisper.

"I'm sorry to tell you, but your wife passed from the fever before I met Sellers."

"She still a slave?"

Maggie shook her head. "They escaped to Pennsylvania where she worked for my uncle. I heard she was the finest cook in the area."

Tears welled in his dark eyes. "And my son?"

"I'm so sorry," Maggie said, sorrow streaming down her cheeks.

Brantley's mouth formed a thin line. "Tell me 'bout my boy."

Maggie looked at her husband.

"Go ahead," Seth replied with a nod.

Inhaling, Maggie wiped her cheek with a quivering hand. This was one of the most painful confessions she'd ever made.

"Sellers tended to the cows at my uncle's farm. He was one of the dearest people I've ever known, always happy, hardworking, and loyal."

"He was treated good?" he asked.

Maggie nodded. "Sellers was surrounded by wonderful people. He was like a brother to me," Maggie sniffled, wringing her hands. "My uncle was a cruel man..."

Brantley stiffened. "What happen to my boy?"

"You need to understand what transpired the day my uncle, um, when I..." Maggie paused, trying to find the right words to break the news to Brantley as gently as possible. Seth gave Maggie's hand a squeeze sending a spark of courage through her limbs. Despite his withered appearance, there was still strength in his grip. She had to do this, no matter how painful.

Maggie proceeded to give an abbreviated version of the abuse she endured under her uncle's oppressive rule. "What began as cruel words and demeaning statements morphed into physical attacks. When I realized he'd likely kill me the next time he was angry, I decided to run. I hid in the hay loft of the cattle barn until I could escape at the first light of day." Gulping down the pain of her uncle's mistreatment, Maggie continued. "I was trying to leave when Sellers arrived to feed the cows." Her chest tightened at the image of her friend whistling as he pushed the hay cart down the barn aisle. If only she could go back. Even so, would she have had the courage to do things differently? As if sensing her angst, Seth ran his thumb across her knuckles and gave her a reassuring nod.

"Sellers knew you was there?"

"Not at first. I tried to keep my presence hidden from him, but he caught a glimpse of me behind the hay bales when my uncle came to the barn and confronted him." Maggie licked her lips which felt as dry as a drought-laden field. "When he wouldn't reveal my location, my uncle shot him."

"My son died for you?" Brantley asked, his voice barely audible.

"He did," she gasped. "I'm so sorry. I loved him with all my heart and if I could've stopped my uncle..."

"Why you not show yourself?" he asked, anger rising in his tone.

"I was so afraid. He had the gun and had beaten me so badly the night before." Maggie's body began to shake. Seth leaned over and wrapped his arm around his wife's quivering shoulders.

"Brantley, you can't fault a woman for being terrified of a man who'd been abusing her. She truly loved your son and would never have done anything to cause him harm."

Brantley stood, his full six feet towering over Maggie. "I understand you was scared but my boy shouldn't have paid the price. We Negroes been beat and brutalized for centuries and we been forced to take it." Looking at Seth, he took in a breath. "I's glad to be of service to you Mr. Daniels but I can't accept this, not right now. If you folks'll excuse me, I needs to be on my way."

Seth rose, wobbling a bit as he squared his shoulders. "Do you have any sisters?"

"Three. They's all taken away when I's just a boy." A mix of rage and pain flashed across Brantley's face.

"If one of the other slaves had threatened to kill them, what would you have done?"

"I'd have stopped him!" Brantley bellowed. "No way I gonna lets nobody hurt my sisters..." his voice trailed off.

Seth pulled Maggie to a standing position and draped his arm about her shoulders. "My wife loved your son. But she was terrified and rightfully so. Her uncle had beaten and tormented her for over a year. Your son was a hero in my opinion. He loved Maggie enough to die for her. Just like you would have done for your own sisters."

Shaking his head, Brantley put on his hat and started for the door. Maggie raced to his side, her flushed cheeks glistening with tears.

"Please forgive me," she sobbed. "There's not a moment I don't regret not coming forward. I was a coward but that doesn't change how I felt about Sellers. I know he loved me as I loved him. We were family."

Brantley's jaw clenched. "No Negro can be family wid a white person."

"You're wrong," she declared. "He taught me how to fish and I taught him how to skate on ice. We worked side by side every day. There's nothing I wouldn't have done for him."

"'Cept give your life for his."

His statement knocked the breath from her lungs. "There aren't enough words to express the misery and remorse I've carried since he died. But I knew him well enough to know he sacrificed himself for me willingly and he'd want you to be proud of his heroism. Hate me if you must but please know your son was a brave and caring soul to the very end." She paused, "I think...no, I know he'd tell you not to be angry with me."

Brantley's lips formed a thin line as he glanced toward the door. With a long sigh, he looked back at Maggie. "I get what you's saying. I know my boy was special. He have a soft heart. That why the animals take to him. Haven't seen him in almost twenty years and always hoped I'd find him and my wife. This a bit much for me, Mrs. Daniels. Maybe someday I can forgive this but not now."

Maggie nodded, unable to speak. She understood why he was upset. If anything happened to Jane or Joshua, she'd be inconsolable.

Without another word, Brantley opened the screen door and marched to the wagon. Moments later, she heard the clattering of wheels going down the drive. Maggie buried her face in Seth's chest, the feel of his emaciated frame against her cheeks, as she cried for Sellers. After years of torment and finally accepting she hadn't been at fault for his demise, the wound was reopened.

"Maggie," Seth whispered in her ear. "Let's sit down."

She could tell he was still weak and walked with him to the settee. Her anguish over Brantley's reaction to his son's death dissipated as she gazed at the fragile state of her husband.

"Forgive me for being so insensitive," she whispered, grasping his hand. "Can I get you anything?"

He leaned in, his lips brushing hers. "No apologies. I'm sorry Brantley was so harsh. Give him time. He's a reasonable man. I'm certain he's just in shock over the news."

"I don't blame him," she muttered. "Tell me more about what happened to you. I suspect there are some things you haven't shared yet."

Seth ran his tongue across his teeth. "Can we discuss it later? I'm exhausted."

"Of course," Maggie said, kissing him again.

The following morning, Maggie awoke, her back aching after tossing and turning throughout the night. She dressed as quietly as possible to avoid waking her husband. He needed his rest. Closing the door behind her, she made her way downstairs to the dining room buffet for a cup of coffee.

By the time she'd gone to bed the night before, Seth was already asleep. Between knowing her husband almost died and Brantley's refusal to forgive her regarding his son's demise, slumber had evaded her. She felt certain Seth's demeanor would improve once he regained his strength; however, her role in Seller's death was not something she could easily dismiss. She'd mentally punished herself over the years for not doing more to save him. It was only recently she'd realized the situation in the cattle barn that morning had been beyond her control. Stepping forward most likely would have resulted in both of them being killed. Still, the guilt lingered.

Sitting in the front parlor, Maggie swirled the coffee in her cup when hoofbeats interrupted her thoughts. "Now what?" she muttered, walking toward the window. Much to her surprise, she saw Brantley halt his horse and dismount. Her heartbeat quickened. Was he back to reprimand her further for not saving his son?

She watched as he climbed the stairs and knocked. Inhaling, Maggie gathered her courage and opened the door.

"Good morning, Brantley. Please come in," she said, stepping aside as the towering figure entered the room. Her hands shook as she motioned for him to take a seat. "Would you like some coffee?"

"No ma'am. Won't be stayin'."

She chewed her lower lip preparing for him to state his purpose in coming. "What can I do for you?" she queried, her stomach wrenching.

"Came to thank you for tellin' me 'bout my boy bein' a hero," he replied, removing his hat.

Maggie tilted her head, shocked by this unexpected declaration.

"But I thought…"

"I done some thinkin' and know this weren't your fault, Mrs. Daniels. I didn't know my son very well. He was only five when I's sold off. All dese years I wonder what kind of man he be, or if he's still a slave. I rather him die a free man on he own terms than at the hand of de massa."

Maggie looked away as tears crested in her eyes. "His death haunts me every day."

"From what you told me, he make up his own mind. He musta cared a lot 'bout you."

"We loved each other," Maggie whispered. "He said I was like a sister to him."

"I's glad you's alive. Mr. Seth told me 'bout you and the youngins. He also say you help slaves get to freedom. In a way, by savin' your life, my son help free lots of people through you."

A lump formed in Maggie's throat. She'd never thought of it that way. The pain still gripped her heart at the memory of Sellers' sacrifice but now his father was offering forgiveness. While it wouldn't heal the wound left by Sellers' death, it softened the pain a bit.

"I'd like to know 'bout my boy when you have time."

"It would be my pleasure," she replied.

Miss Violet entered the room, her apron fresh and her hair neater than usual.

"I heard voices and came out to check on who be here," Miss Violet said, her eyes twinkling. "Miss Maggie, why you not call me to bring some coffee?"

"Brantley only stopped by for a brief visit. He declined the offer of coffee," Maggie smiled. She'd never seen Violet so effervescent.

A grin spread across Brantley's face as he fiddled with the brim of his hat. "I suppose one cup won't hurt nothin'."

"Miss Maggie, you mind helping me?" Violet asked.

"Of course," she replied. "Brantley, please sit down. We won't be long."

Once they were in the kitchen, Violet turned to Maggie.

"Dat man got him a woman?" she asked.

"Not that I'm aware of," Maggie chuckled.

"Dat good news," Violet said, smiling. "Dat real good news."

Shaking her head, Maggie helped Violet prepare a tray with coffee, mugs, and a plate of biscuits. It seemed Brantley had caught Violet's eye which meant they'd likely be seeing more of him in the coming weeks. Violet wasn't one to walk away from something once she set her sights on it.

Chapter 44

April 1865

Seth

Humming an upbeat tune, Violet cleared the breakfast dishes and returned to the kitchen leaving Seth and Maggie at the dining room table. Brantley had left a few minutes earlier with a promise to come back for dinner.

Maggie reached across the table and grasped Seth's hand. "I'm glad you joined us for breakfast. You were asleep when I went to bed last night and I didn't want to wake you. Tell me more about what happened after you were shot and Brantley found you."

Seth's head swam with doubt. How would his wife accept that he wasn't the strong man he used to be? Would she still love him as a weakened version of himself? The idea had plagued him throughout his convalescence. Taking in a deep breath, he gathered his courage and continued the story of his health issues.

"There were complications with my recovery. According to the doctor, I may never fully regain my strength."

Seth watched fresh tears pool in Maggie's eyes. She won't

be able to handle this, he thought. The look on her face was more agonizing than the months of battling infection. She'd have been better off if he'd perished under that tree. Then she could remarry without guilt.

"How bad is it?" she sniffled.

"Won't know for a while. The doctors in the field hospitals do their best but they don't have time for in depth analysis. If it hadn't been for Brantley, I'd be dead. According to him, by the time he got me to the doctors, I was incoherent. An infection resulted from the crude measures used in the field hospital resulting in damage to my heart. The doctors didn't believe I'd recover."

"But you did," she murmured, glancing at the cane leaning against the wall.

"I've been told I'm susceptible to heart failure if I engage in any sort of strenuous activity. Needless to say, my days of soldiering are over."

Maggie squeezed his hand. "None of that matters now," she said. "I'll take care of you."

Seth's stomach lurched. This is exactly what he didn't want from her, pity. He could see it in her eyes. She loved him, of that he was sure, but now she saw him as an invalid, not the man she'd known. If only Brantley had never found him. Death was a better alternative than the pitiful creature he'd become.

Chapter 45

April 1865

Elora

Lying on her cot, Elora sighed. Her joints ached. She'd ridden several miles the day before. The lack of sufficient rest combined with meager food offerings were affecting her strength. If it was this bad for the Union army with all their resources, she knew it must be devastating for the confederates.

Hoofbeats pounded through the encampment. Elora bolted from bed and raced out of her tent to see one of the couriers galloping toward the Colonel's quarters. Eager to know what was happening, she ran to join the others who were congregating at the commander's tent. The courier alighted to the ground, his chest heaving as he ran to the colonel who stood in the opening of his tent.

"Word from Virginia, sir," he breathed, handing him a crumpled piece of paper.

Elora's heart pounded and her fingers tingled. No doubt, another bloody battle was close by, and they'd be racing to meet the enemy. The scenario was like a recurring nightmare with no end in sight. Her soul was drained of emotion. She couldn't remember the last time she slept soundly without fear of attack.

Unfolding the parchment, the colonel scanned the page, rubbing his full beard with his free hand. When he finished, he refolded it, squared his shoulders, and took in a deep breath. A slight smile lifted the ends of his mustache.

"Men," he called out. "Lee has surrendered! The war is over!"

A thunderous chorus of cheers and hoorahs resounded across the encampment as others rushed to see what was happening. Soldiers slapped each other on the backs or threw their hats in the air while Elora stood like a statue trying to absorb the colonel's words. The war was over, she thought. No more fighting, no more bloodied bodies, no more pretending to be a man. She was going home to her family. It was almost too much to comprehend.

"What's the matter Polk?" a soldier hollered as he smacked her between the shoulders. "Aren't you thrilled about the news? We're going home!"

Jolted from her thoughts, she punched him in the arm and smiled.

"Of course, I'm happy. Just stunned it's finally over."

"What're you gonna do first when you get home, Polk?" he asked, his eyes dancing with excitement.

"Take a long, hot bath, and sleep," she replied in her gruffest tone of voice. Much to her relief, she only had to maintain her male persona a little while longer.

"Ha! You sound like a girl!" He shook his head, still grinning. "First thing I'm gonna do is go see my lady," he replied with a wink.

Elora nodded as the man walked over to another group who were enthusiastically sharing stories of what they'd do when they returned to their respective homes. The exhilaration pulsing through the crowd was dizzying.

"Polk!" the colonel called out, motioning her to his tent.

She followed him inside as he took a seat at his desk.

"Didn't have a chance to let you know about this earlier but the information you provided on your last mission resulted in the capture of that confederate commander. I know the war is officially over, but I'm recommending you for a commendation. Good work."

"Thank you, sir. It's been an honor to serve under you," she replied. She'd never see that commendation and wondered what the Colonel would think when they found no record of the man she'd portrayed during the war.

The colonel spoke again, jolting her from her ruminations. "I'm glad Daniels brought you to us. You've been an invaluable member of this unit."

"Speaking of Daniels, sir, where is he?" she asked. Elora hadn't seen Seth in a while and wondered where he was and if he'd heard about Lee's surrender?

Concern shaded the colonel's face. "He was seriously wounded in Georgia. Had to be sent home. The injuries were of a nature that he was unable to resume his duties."

Elora nodded, trying to keep her knees from folding under her. Seth had been injured? And badly enough he couldn't return to battle?

"You're dismissed, Polk. Enjoy the celebration with the rest of the men. You've earned it."

Apprehension burned in Elora's chest. Following the colonel's orders, she joined the others even though she wanted to return to her tent and prepare to go home. More than anything she wanted to know about Seth. Was he in Pennsylvania or convalescing on St. Helena with Maggie? At the moment, she needed to celebrate with the men otherwise they'd be suspicious, and she couldn't risk being discovered now.

Hours later when things settled a bit, she went back to her tent, her thoughts swirling like a cyclone. Plunking down on her bunk, she looked around her quarters. It was a simple canvas cocoon with her cot, a small chair, and a lantern. This had been luxury compared to the times she'd slept in the woods, on wet ground, or in abandoned buildings with rats scurrying about.

In a few days she'd be returning to the comfort of a house with a soft bed, home cooked meals, and quiet. No gun shots or the boom of cannon fire. Even though she'd have to return to Pennsylvania before heading home, the luxuries she'd enjoyed her entire life would be restored. For months she'd yearned to return to these everyday comforts but now that it was in the immediate future, she didn't desire them as much as she thought she would.

So much had transpired since Elora left the campus of Oberlin College. She'd successfully portrayed a male soldier without discovery, watched men crumple to the ground in agony when she shot them, and carried secrets from southerners to union officials as a woman. She was no longer the pampered plantation owner's daughter. Now she was... different.

Elora exhaled. There was no way to erase all she'd seen and done. It was forever etched on her soul. Her thoughts skipped through her brain like a stone across water. What would she tell her parents about her 'missionary work?' And what would she do once she was home? Continue on the path that had been paved for her since birth? Finish college, marry, have children? The only man she'd ever consider was gone. Hope drained from her heart. Suddenly, her future seemed dismal and without purpose. Unless she followed her instincts and set out on her own as she'd done when she joined the army.

Rubbing her eyes with the heels of her hands, she exhaled. The world she'd known was completely different. The slaves had been freed in the south, yet the constitution still allowed for the abominable institution of slavery. How would that play out now? Would they be enslaved again?

More importantly, what was the nature and extent of Seth's injuries? To be permanently discharged from fighting meant something serious had happened. Had he lost a limb? Or worse, was he paralyzed? Elora swallowed hard. She'd have to wait to find out.

All these things whirled through her mind. Then Captain Dixon's handsome face flashed in her head bringing tears to her eyes. She should be celebrating with him right now but instead she was mourning him. Elora sat straighter and admonished herself for allowing her thoughts to wander to dark places. The war was over and that's all that mattered. Whatever the future held, she'd deal with it. If she could survive a war, portraying a man, spying as a woman, and all the horrors she'd experienced in the past four years, she could face whatever awaited when she returned home.

Chapter 46

Spring 1865

Maggie

The carriage bounced over rutted roads, jostling Maggie to and fro like a ship on stormy seas. Although sad to say goodbye to Dr. Towne, Miss Murray, Willa, and Letty, she was glad the war was finally over and that she and Seth were on their way to the Milner's to gather the children. She was even more anxious to return home to their cottage at Rose Hall Plantation and resume their lives. More than ever, she needed her Da. Things had been stressful since Seth's return and her Da's bear hugs and whispers of wisdom always made the darkest situations lighter.

Maggie glanced over at Seth who sat silently, staring out the window. She was worried about him. He seemed preoccupied the past couple of weeks, justifiably so considering the scope of his health issues. It seemed the more Maggie tended to him, the more distant he became. The only things that had boosted his spirits were the announcement of the war's end and talk of seeing the children.

Having spent the entire war in the confines of the Sea Islands, Maggie was shocked at the devastation and ruin along the route to Pennsylvania. Charred timbers and lonesome brick chimneys were all that remained of once beautiful homes. Dead and decaying bodies littered ditches and hillsides. The scenery relayed the depth of the carnage in ways that would haunt Maggie's mind for years to come. Perhaps they should stay in Pennsylvania with the Milners for a while in order to shield the children from witnessing the horror left behind.

Her body shuddered at the thought of what Seth had experienced during his service with the Union. Since his return, Maggie had learned about some of his clandestine exploits as a spymaster and was thankful he'd shielded her from the knowledge at the time. She'd have worried herself senseless had she known the hazardous nature of his duties.

The idea of being reunited with Jane and Joshua brought tears to her eyes. It had been so long since she'd seen them, and she imagined how they must have grown in her absence. A twinge of regret tugged at her heart. Would they be glad to see her or angry over her prolonged absence. And what about Seth? How would they respond to his weakened state? At least she and Seth would be together when they reunited with them. Perhaps that would soften any hard feelings the kids might be harboring toward her.

In her Da's last letter, he'd explained that Dr. Polk and Rev. Milner would be on their way home from their respective duties with the Union army making for a grand reunion once everyone arrived. There was no word from Elora yet. Early in the war, Mrs. Milner had written about Elora taking time from school to help missionaries in the western part of the country. Maggie was thankful Elora had avoided all the unpleasantness of the conflict and looked forward to hearing tales of her grand adventures over the past few years.

Maggie gazed out the window at the passing landscape budding with hope. How apropos that the rebirth of the nation would coincide with spring's season of renewal. So many had made the ultimate sacrifice and were unable to celebrate the peace taking hold of the battle-scarred country. Lt. Colonel Brunson's image flashed through Maggie's mind, momentarily seizing her heart.

Seth had disclosed the circumstances of Brunson's death, and she was glad he hadn't died alone. Visions of his clumsy attempts at learning to waltz and his intense expression as he concentrated on his next move at chess, floated like clouds through her memory. Lt. Colonel Brunson, James, had begun as an adversary but had quickly become a dear and respected friend.

Guilt fluttered through her stomach like a thousand butter-flies. James gave his life for Seth's and for that Maggie would always be grateful. But was she the reason he was dead? Had her intentions toward him been as innocent as she wanted to believe? She couldn't deny her feelings for him although they'd never match those she held for her husband. No man could capture her heart as Seth had. Yet, there was something linger-ing, something she couldn't quite process regarding her time with James. Shoving those thoughts from her mind, she buried them deep within the recesses of her memory. Now was not the time to be thinking about another man, not when her husband needed her.

Maggie glanced at Seth, his thin body swaying with the carriage. "What are you thinking about?" she asked.

Seth startled. His dull blue eyes met her gaze.

"Nothing," he replied. "Only watching the devastation left behind." He turned back to the window.

Maggie opened her mouth to offer words of comfort but stopped. What could she possibly say to a man who nearly died in the war and was now witnessing the remnants of what once was? Instead, she changed the topic to one familiar to them both.

"What do you think will happen with the emancipation of the enslaved now that the war is over?" Maggie asked.

"I assume they'll live as free people."

"Will they? President Lincoln only freed those in the rebellion states."

"Hopefully, it will become law throughout the country," he replied.

"Which means the Railroad will no longer be needed," Maggie said with a slight smile. The idea that all people could live as free citizens was exciting. She'd seen too many lose their lives in the pursuit of freedom.

Seth continued staring out the window, his shoulders slumping. "Wouldn't matter to me. My ability to do that sort of thing is over."

Maggie reached out and touched his arm. "You'll regain your strength and be as fit as you were before."

"Don't coddle me," he snapped with a seething gaze. "I don't need you hovering over me."

"I'm sorry," she whispered, withdrawing her hand as if she'd been burned.

She watched as he turned back to the window, his silence crushing her heart. Closing her eyes, Maggie rested her head against the seat and let the rocking of the carriage soothe her. Her husband had been through a great deal and needed time to readjust to civilian life. Somehow, he'd learn to cope with his health restraints. Perhaps Dr. Polk would be able to help. But what if he couldn't? Desperate for any shred of hope, Maggie convinced herself things would be better once they were home at Rose Hall.

Chapter 47

May 1865

Elora

A hint of melancholy imbued Elora's mood as she packed the few meager possessions she'd hauled with her over the past few years. Jasper was saddled and ready to go. Elora bid farewell to her remaining comrades, mounted her steed, and rode away. Once she made it a fair distance, she slipped into a heavily wooded area and changed into her dress. No sense pretending any longer. Her life as a woman had resumed. Leaving her uniform bundled at the base of a tree, Elora pinned Annalissa's brooch to her collar and resumed her journey, forever abandoning her identity as Captain Polk. Granted, Captain Polk and Miss Kirk would always be a part of her, living and breathing in the depths of her memories.

Elora spent a great deal of time agonizing over her return. How would she explain her missionary work which never occurred? More importantly, should she sell Jasper and pay for a carriage to transport her to the Milner's farm in Pennsylvania? Her chest tightened as she patted Jasper's neck. She could never part with him. He'd been her constant companion for four years and delivered her from danger multiple times. Now she understood the depth of Seth's connection with Phantom. No, Jasper would remain in her care for the rest of his years. She owed him that.

Jasper plodded along, rocking Elora back and forth. She was taking her time on this journey. For too many years everything had been rushed and filled with panic. Now she could slow her pace and concoct the story she'd share with her family. With any luck, no one would question her accounts. Only Seth would know the truth. Hopefully, he was at the Milner's place recuperating, and she'd see him upon her return.

Elora's future pursuits continued to vex her. The idea of college seemed trivial now. And yet, she'd be expected to resume her studies without question. The freedom to make her own decisions would revert back to which color thread to use for embroidery and what book to read next. Her stomach flopped. How could she possibly return to such mundane occupations after years of soldiering and spying?

Blowing out a long breath, Elora shook her head at her foolishness. She'd been able to join a regiment, fight as a man in the fiercest of battles, extract secrets from confederate officers, and survive a war. If she'd accomplished all that, she could find a way to live her life as she saw fit. The only problem was figuring out what she wanted to do. At least she was finally at peace with the loss of Captain Dixon. She'd always carry his memory in her heart but now was the time to move on and start anew.

Days later, Elora rode down the dirt drive of the Milner's home. She'd prepared her story for the barrage of questions her parents would no doubt be asking. As the stone house came into view, a sob erupted from Elora's lips. It was exactly as it was the last time she'd seen it.

Elora rode around the side of the house to the barn. Thankfully, no one was around. She untacked Jasper and bedded him down in a stall with a few flakes of hay and fresh water. She checked the other stalls for Phantom. Her heart dropped when she didn't find him. Seth wasn't here. Was he with Maggie on St. Helena or had he succumbed to his injuries? Bile burned her throat. She couldn't stomach a life without him in it.

Now more than ever she wanted to see her mother. She longed for her embrace and soothing words. Elora had been through so much over the past four years, first losing the captain and now possibly Seth. If only her mother could smooth away the pain and heartache of adulthood like she had the little scrapes and scratches of Elora's youth.

Her pace quickened until she was running toward the back door of the farmhouse. She bolted inside and glanced around the space. A kettle hung over the fire in the hearth as the smell of baking cookies tickled her nose. It was teatime. As much as she wanted to see everyone she decided to stay in the kitchen and surprise them. The Milners were an informal family who gathered around the kitchen table for meals and afternoon tea which meant they'd likely be there any minute.

Darla, the Milner's housekeeper, was the first to arrive, hurrying into the room from the back stairs. She gasped when she saw Elora sitting at the table. Holding her finger to her lips, Elora shook her head.

"My dear child," Darla whispered. "When did you arrive?"

"A few minutes ago. I assume tea is about to be served?"

"As soon as I steep the leaves and pull the cookies from the oven."

"I'll set the table," Elora offered.

A slow smile spread across Darla's face as she gave Elora a

wink. Once everything was prepared, Darla headed for the front parlor to announce that tea was ready. Butterflies danced in Elora's stomach as she waited.

Dr. Polk's voice carried down the hallway sending bumps skittering across Elora's skin. She'd missed her father. There'd been nights during the war that she wanted nothing more than to curl up in his arms and forget the world existed. Should she hide in the pantry and surprise them or stay at the table?

Before she could decide, Mrs. Polk stepped into the kitchen. "Darla, when you get a chance...." Mrs. Polk grasped her chest. "Elora! You're home!" she cried, rushing to her daughter's side.

Elora stood from the table and embraced her mother letting the scent of roses fill her senses. After years of battle and alter egos, it felt good to be wrapped in her mother's arms like she had as a child after a tumble from a fence or being awakened by a nightmare.

Reverend and Mrs. Milner along with Dr. Polk stood in the doorway watching as Elora and her mother clung to each other sobbing.

When the tears subsided, everyone sat around the table with steaming cups of tea and a plate of freshly baked cookies. Elora closed her eyes, relishing the sweetness of the molasses confection as it crumbled across her tongue. She hadn't enjoyed any food this much since the beef served one Christmas at the encampment near Maryland. Elora had shivered through the entire meal but delighted in the savory flavor of the meat. Generally, they were served beans and bread making the beef the best Christmas gift they could've received.

Elora glanced around the table. "Where are Jane and Joshua?"

"Down the road at the Cole's farm," Mrs. Polk said. "They'll be thrilled to find you here when they return."

"What about Maggie and Seth?" Elora asked, biting her lip.

"Should be here any day," Mrs. Milner replied.

Elora blew a long breath across her lips. That's why Phantom wasn't in the stables. They weren't here yet. Most importantly, Seth was alive.

"Tell us about your mission work," Rev. Milner said, taking a sip of tea. "I understand you joined one of the church groups on campus and then traveled West."

A hint of guilt clutched Elora's conscience. She hated lying, especially to the Reverend.

"It was an amazing experience," she started. "Our group assisted in the establishment of a Presbyterian church."

"How exciting," Mrs. Milner declared. "Was there a building in place or did you meet in tents?"

Elora wove an elaborate tale of congregating in tents until a permanent structure was completed. She knew little about the frontier except what she'd read before undertaking her role as a soldier.

"Iowa was beautiful," Elora said.

"Iowa?" Mrs. Polk asked. "I thought you said you were in Oregon."

"Did I say Iowa? I don't know why I said such a thing," Elora chuckled nervously. "I must've been thinking about one of the ladies I worked with. She was from Iowa. I meant to say that Oregon was beautiful." Her shoulders tensed as she waited for further queries.

"I must admit I was rather concerned when your mother wrote of your decision to embark on this endeavor," Dr. Polk said, leaning forward with a scrutinizing stare. "Did you encounter any Indians along the way?"

Swallowing hard, Elora did her best to veil the anxiety welling in her chest. Her father had always been good at reading her expressions.

"Actually, no. We were told we'd been quite fortunate to escape any attacks."

"I've never been out West," her father continued. "What was it like?"

"Well, um," she stuttered, "very green and lush. And much colder than home."

"When did you leave Oregon?" he asked, leaning back in his chair. "I'm surprised we didn't get a letter letting us know you'd be coming."

"Since my mission group was coordinated through the college, I needed to stop at the campus first to take care of some things. I arrived there a few days ago," Elora said, wondering when this line of questioning would end. She was running out of answers. "There wasn't time to write, and I didn't want to delay so I came straight here."

"You must have just missed Annalissa," Mrs. Milner said. "She left a few days ago and should arrive any time now."

Mrs. Polk reached across the table and grasped Elora's hand. "I know your studies have been delayed, and I can't say I was happy about your decision to go West, but I am proud of your sacrifice."

Elora forced a grin. If only she knew the extent of her sacrifice, her mother would have a fit.

Once the questions about her mission work subsided, her unease began to melt away, at least for the moment. Knowing Seth was alive helped too. Elora spent the remainder of the day happily ensconced with her family followed by a relaxing nap in a soft bed, something she'd foregone the past few years.

She awoke to delectable scents wafting up from the kitchen below. Freshening up, Elora padded down the stairs to the front parlor where her mother, Mrs. Milner, Jane, and Joshua were gathered.

"Miss Elora!" Joshua squealed, bolting across the room, and

throwing his arms about her waist. Turning back to Mrs. Polk, he smiled broadly. "Is this the surprise you told me about?"

"It is," she replied.

"My goodness, how you've grown," Elora said, holding Joshua at arm's length.

"Almost as tall as you!" he declared, his eyes twinkling.

Jane waited patiently behind her brother; her dark hair pulled neatly into a bun at the nape of her neck. She was a young lady now with womanly curves and a graceful air.

"Jane," Elora said, embracing her. "What a fine young woman you've become."

Jane stepped back. "I've missed you," she said with a simper. "How was your time with the mission group?"

"Busy and exhausting but let's not discuss that now," Elora replied. "I want to hear how you've occupied your time in my absence."

Elora perched on the settee, her stays digging into her ribcage. Blasted corset. By far, this was the most difficult part of reestablishing herself as a woman. Elora and Jane chatted until Darla called the family for dinner. After a filling meal of chicken, roasted potatoes, and carrots, everyone gathered in the front parlor for coffee and lively discussion. As yawns spread across the room, all bid goodnight except for Elora and her father

"I heard horrid things about the war, Father. How did you manage?" she asked once the others had gone to bed.

Shifting in his seat, Dr. Polk took in a deep breath. "Things were difficult, but this isn't a subject for a young lady."

Anger burned in Elora's veins. For a moment she considered telling her father she was anything but delicate and that she'd fought in the war for the last four years. There was nothing he could do about it now. Then again, upsetting him wouldn't alter his views. Taking in a deep breath, she composed herself. "Father, I appreciate you wanting to shield me from unpleasant things, but I'm a woman now. I've been West and seen my share of horror. Please don't treat me like a child." Her words were firm and direct.

Raising one brow, Dr. Polk pursed his lips. "It seems my little girl left in innocence and has returned a seasoned woman. What would you like to know?"

Chapter 48

May 1865

Maggie

Maggie could hardly contain her excitement as the carriage made its way down the drive to the Milner's home. Her limbs quivered and her heart pounded as the driver pulled the horses to a halt. She let herself out and turned to help Seth, but he waved her away. Before he made it out of the carriage, Joshua came bounding through the front door of the stone house and bolted toward his father.

"Papa! You're finally home!" he squealed.

Seth wrapped his arms around his son and pulled him close. Tears trickled across Maggie's cheeks at the sight. Joshua was much taller, and his wavy red locks were past his shoulders. Breaking free from his father's embrace, he hurled himself at Maggie. All her worries about Joshua being angry with her melted away as she held her son.

"I missed you, Mama," he muttered, burying his face against her bodice like he'd done when he was little.

"I missed you to the moon and back," Maggie replied, squeezing him tightly. In all his excitement, it seemed Joshua hadn't noticed the thin state of his father's physique for which Maggie was thankful.

Jane, however, wasn't as oblivious. She waited on the front stoop watching them intently. Maggie's breath caught. Jane looked more like her mother Susannah than ever before.

Joshua clambered to the boot of the carriage, insisting he help the driver with the bags. Grasping his hand in hers, Maggie led Seth toward their daughter who stared at her father's labored gait. When they reached the porch, Maggie gathered Jane in a hug, kissing her cheek.

"My dearest, Jane, how you've grown. You're more beautiful than I remember."

With tears streaming down her cheeks, Jane looked up at Maggie. "I've missed you, Mama." Then turning toward her father, she took in a deep breath. "Are you alright, Papa?"

Maggie watched her husband's cheeks color as he gazed at his daughter. "I was injured but I'm going to be fine."

Embracing her father, Jane shot a quick glance at her mother. Maggie's heart sank. She could tell by her daughter's expression she didn't believe all was well with Seth.

"Jane, stop hogging Papa and let me have another turn," Joshua hollered.

Maggie laughed. At least some things hadn't changed. Joshua was as impetuous as ever and not about to let anyone get more attention than he.

They went inside where laughter echoed from the kitchen at the back of the house. Walking down the hall, they entered the room where Darla and Mrs. Milner were cooking while Dr. Polk and Rev. Milner reclined at the table. Gray tinted the reverend's temples and Dr. Polk's visage had weathered, but otherwise they looked the same.

Dr. Polk rose from the table and embraced Maggie. "So

good to see you. Mrs. Polk informed me you've been in the Lowcountry for the past few years."

"I've been working with Dr. Towne and Miss Murray. They started a school for the freedmen. I kept the garden and mixed remedies and salves."

"Sounds like the perfect fit."

"I'm glad I was able to help but it's wonderful to be back with family." She grinned.

"I agree with you completely," he said.

"Where's Da?" Maggie asked, glancing around the space.

"Right here," he replied, stepping in the back door. His Irish brogue made Maggie's heart flutter. As he pulled her into a bear hug, she inhaled deeply, taking in his special scent of pipe tobacco and cotton.

"Missed you, Da," she muttered into his shoulder. "Where were you?"

"Had to take care of a lamb who cut his leg this morning."

"Always tending to the lost sheep of this world," she said, releasing him. "I'm glad to know you haven't changed."

They all gathered round the heart pine table as several conversations buzzed about the room like a swarm of bees.

"You're here!" Elora declared as she and Annalissa entered.

Maggie ran to her dear friend and embraced her. Stepping back, she studied Elora. Something was different. Was it her hair or her carriage? Apparently, her mission work had altered her in some manner. Whatever it was, Maggie would hear about it later.

"How long have you been back?" Maggie asked.

"Two days," Elora responded. "Annalissa arrived yesterday afternoon."

The greetings and welcome homes continued until everyone was seated at the harvest table sipping tea and chattering about everything from the state of the roads to how the country would heal now that the fighting had ended. Most importantly, it was good to be back with family and dear friends. If only Seth's health would improve, Maggie's world would be complete.

Chapter 49

May 1865

Elora

Elora watched everyone laugh and converse. Exhaustion from the transformation of soldier and spy to a lady of means had drained her emotionally. Although she missed the adrenaline rush of contributing to the war efforts, she was thrilled to be sleeping on a soft mattress with cottony sheets and plenty of food to eat. Even better was knowing Seth was alive despite his peaked appearance.

She approached him and smiled. When his pale eyes met hers, she bit her lower lip trying to contain her emotions. Now wasn't the time to make a fuss. Wrapping her arms around him, she could feel Seth's ribs. Elora took a step back and gazed up at him.

"Missed you," she muttered.

"Missed you too," he replied.

"I want to hear about it later," she whispered.

With a nod, he took a seat at the table. Elora watched her father's eyes lock onto Seth. Obviously, he was just as concerned.

As she glanced around the table, her imagination drifted to

a scene where the captain was sitting with her. He spoke with her father about their plans for the future as she held his hand in hers. Elora's stomach knotted. Stop it, she told herself.

The evening was filled with good food, laughter to the point of tears, and reminiscences of times before the war, except for Seth who sat solemnly picking at his dinner. A short time later, Seth and the children bid goodnight and went upstairs. Elora understood the early bedtime for the kids, but it seemed strange for Seth. Then again, his fatigue had been apparent to her, making Elora wonder why no one had addressed it.

Before long, Elora's eyelids began to flutter, and she excused herself. She headed to her room, slipped into her night gown with its embroidered hem and smocked neckline, and sat before the vanity mirror to brush her shoulder length locks. Her mother had questioned the reason for her bobbed hair style. She'd explained it was easier to manage when working. Although she lamented lying to her parents, she regretted nothing about her service even with the deception shrouding it.

A soft rap at the door caught her attention.

"Come in," she called.

Seth peeked his head into her room, a sly smile lifting his cheeks. Slight lines eclipsed his eyes and creased his mouth, telling of the things he'd seen and done.

"I thought you went to bed," she said, turning on the vanity stool to face him as he sat in a chair by the door.

"Couldn't sleep." He leaned forward, resting his elbows on his knees.

"I understand," she sighed. And she did. Even though it was wonderful to be sleeping in a comfortable bed without fear of attack, battle scenes paraded through her mind keeping her awake for hours.

"I know you do," he replied. "We haven't had a chance to speak in private since I returned. How are you doing?"

"Alright," she shrugged.

"Liar," he said, narrowing his eyes. "I wanted to check on you. You seemed...distracted downstairs."

Guilt fingered her chest. She should be asking if he was alright not the other way around. Fidgeting with her fingers, Elora inhaled deeply before responding. Seth was the only person she could talk to about this.

"It's all so strange. I'm ever so glad to be home again and yet sometimes I miss the encampment."

Seth nodded. "Transitioning from military to civilian life is rough. I can only imagine how difficult it is for you since you can't share your experience with others."

"And that's what you wanted to discuss?" she asked.

"Not exactly. I can tell there's something else bothering you."

His words were like a punch to the gut knocking the breath from her lungs. The subject was one she wished to bury yet the more she pushed the captain's memory from her mind, the more it festered in her heart.

"I can't stop thinking about Captain Dixon. I came home alive and healthy but he..." her voice trailed off as she wiped a tear from her cheek.

"Have you thought any more about visiting his family? They'd probably appreciate hearing about his service, and sacrifice."

"I have. In fact, I was able to get an address for his parents' home in Boston." Elora said. "But I don't know if I have the courage to make the trip. What will I say to them?"

"Tell them the truth."

"What if they ask how I knew him? I can't very well share my duplicity."

"Then say you're Captain Polk's sister and that he didn't make it home. It's not a lie. Captain Polk died when the war ended."

Elora mulled over what he said. Perhaps if she spoke with Dixon's family, she could put her feelings to rest and start healing from the loss of the only man she'd ever loved.

"I'll go with you, if you'd like," Seth offered, his gaze meeting hers.

"Thank you but I need to do this on my own," she said. "I'll send a letter to his parents tomorrow."

Seth shifted in the chair, a groan escaping his lips as he gripped his side.

"What about you?" Elora asked. "You're not well."

Turning his gaze toward the window, Seth exhaled. "It's been tough. After I was shot, Brantley left me at the hospital where my condition worsened."

"Who's Brantley?"

"That's another tale in itself. The abbreviated version is he found me bleeding out. He was with a Union regiment that happened to be in the area. Thankfully, he had medical training from his former master which he used to save my life."

"That's incredible!" she exclaimed. "I'm so glad he was there."

"I almost died." Seth sighed. "According to the doctors, an infection developed near my heart. Between that and the blood loss, they told me I'd never be the same."

Elora straightened. "I don't believe that for a moment. I've known you most of my life. You came to us half-dead from infection and blood loss after your father tried to kill you. You'd ridden for days in that condition. You survived that without complications, and you'll do the same now." Her words were firm as her gaze fixed on his slumped shoulders and weary expression.

"This is different. It's my heart," he replied, defeat dripping from his words.

"Has my father examined you?"

"Not yet, but I doubt—"

"Until father has pronounced your condition permanent, I'll not hear another word about it," she declared.

"I'll let you carry the hope. I'm too worn out."

Seth stood slowly and walked over to Elora. Scooping her into his arms, he held her close. "I love you Captain Elora Polk," he whispered, kissing the top of her head.

"I love you too," she replied, thankful for his presence. He'd supported her throughout her life, and it was a comfort to be able to return the favor.

After Seth left, Elora grabbed the garnet brooch, padded down the hall to Annalissa's room, and knocked.

"Come in," she called.

Elora entered the shadowy space. Annalissa was propped up in bed reading by lamp light. Closing her book, Annalissa patted the mattress. "Come sit with me," she said, her cheeks dimpling.

Elora slid next to her friend and handed her the brooch. "Thank you," she murmured.

Annalissa took the trinket and stared at it. "You're home which means it brought you luck."

"You could say that," she replied, her thoughts drifting back to her heartache.

"What's the matter." Annalissa asked, grasping Elora's hand.

Elora proceeded to share an abbreviated version of her time at war, being shot and saved by Seth, and her affections for a man who was dead.

Annalissa listened to the tale occasionally nodding or gasping when Elora spoke of her injuries.

"Sounds like my mother's brooch brought you good fortune in many ways," Annalissa said softly. "I'm sorry your captain didn't survive but I know in time you'll find your way."

Elora embraced her friend, bid goodnight, and shuffled back to her room. Curling beneath the covers, Elora drifted into a peaceful sleep far from battles and loss.

Chapter 50

August 1865

Elora

Elora was finally on her way to visit the Dixon's in Boston. Her letter had been brief, only saying that she wanted to speak to them about their son's service in the war. She needed to put the captain's memory to rest and this seemed like a fitting way to say goodbye. After days of travel, the carriage stopped in front of an elegant brownstone in the heart of the city. Elora had rehearsed what she'd say for weeks, hoping she wouldn't falter when she finally met Captain Dixon's parents.

The driver opened the door and handed her from within. Straightening her skirts, she glanced around. A row of brick structures with ornate ironclad staircases and colorful blooms sprouting from window boxes lined the street.

Gathering all her courage, Elora climbed the steps. She stood at the front door for a few moments before lifting the brass knocker and banging it several times. Footsteps echoed from within, and the door swung open.

"Good day, may I help you?" An older gent towered before her, his black livery highlighting his silvery hair.

Elora presented her calling card. "I'm Miss Elora Polk and I've come to speak with Mr. and Mrs. Dixon. They're expecting me."

The butler gave a slight bow and motioned her inside. Elora entered, taking in the grandeur of the place. Tile floors in geometric designs extended down a narrow hall with a long Persian rug topping them. An array of pastoral scenes housed in gilded frames graced the damask covered walls. A matronly woman sashayed toward her, the silk hem of her royal blue dress swishing like a cat's tail with each step. Her chestnut hair was tinged with gray, accentuating her mahogany eyes.

"Good day to you," she said warmly. "I'm Mrs. Dixon."

Elora gave a slight curtsey. "I'm Elora Polk."

"So glad you arrived safely. Please, follow me."

Elora followed the elegant woman into a sumptuously clad parlor. Velvet draperies puddled onto the gleaming wood floors and brocade covered furnishings surrounded a marble topped center table. Mrs. Dixon motioned for Elora to sit on one of the chairs while she perched on the settee.

"Thank you for allowing me to visit," Elora began. "I wanted to speak with you about your son, Captain Samuel Dixon."

Elora braced for a sorrowful reaction but before Mrs. Dixon could speak a gentleman entered the room.

"Who wants to speak with me?"

Grasping her chest, Elora nearly toppled from the chair. Her heart raced and the room began to spin. Tears stung her eyes as the gentleman rushed to her side. It was him. Captain Dixon was alive and standing before her.

"Are you alright, Miss?" he asked, his gaze boring through to her soul.

At that moment, Elora noticed the left arm of his sack coat pinned at his side.

"My apologies," she muttered. "You took me by surprise. I was under the impression you were…" her words trailed off in a whisper as she scanned his face to make sure she was seeing correctly.

"I was what?" he queried.

"I'd been led to believe you were killed at Gettysburg."

A laugh rolled from his lips making his eyes dance. "Don't believe everything you hear, Miss?"

"Polk. Elora Polk."

He cocked his head and smiled. "Are you related to Lt. Polk?"

Elora swallowed hard. "He was…my brother. He died at Gettysburg," she responded, the half-truth rolling off her tongue.

"I was wounded there," he replied, giving a nod to his left side. "Lost my arm and nearly my life. That's probably why you thought I was dead. The records aren't always accurate."

"Thank goodness," she muttered unable to shift her gaze from his handsome face.

"You seem to have had a shock. May I get you some tea, or perhaps a sherry?"

"Samuel!" his mother declared. "It's too early in the day to consume alcohol. You've been coarse since returning from the army and I'll not have you insulting guests, especially a lady." Her brows arched as her gaze connected with his.

"I'm sorry, Mother. And my apologies to you, Miss Polk," he said. "Sometimes I forget myself."

The right side of Elora's mouth curled as her chest warmed. She was having trouble reconciling what her eyes had witnessed on the battle field at Gettysburg and the man standing before her now. Her emotions dipped and soared like a pelican over marsh waters searching for fish. She was caught between utter astonishment that he was alive and the desire to throw herself into his arms and declare her adoration.

"No offense taken," Elora managed to utter, fidgeting with her skirts. "My brother could be the same way at times."

Samuel took a seat on the tufted parlor chair to her left. The butler entered and placed a silver tea service in front of them. Mrs. Dixon poured tea into a porcelain cup bedecked with delicate pink roses.

"Would you care for cream or sugar?" she asked.

"Sugar, please."

Mrs. Dixon handed Elora the cup and fixed two more.

"So, tell us why you've come to call," Mrs. Dixon said, lifting the cup to her lips.

"My brother, Lt. Polk, wrote several letters about serving under Captain Dixon who was killed at Gettysburg, or so he thought. He told of his admiration for the captain and I thought it might give you comfort to know your son had been highly esteemed by his men."

Samuel cocked his head. "But your brother was killed at Gettysburg. How was he able to write about it?"

"Did I say my brother wrote the letter?" Elora coughed, swallowing her tea the wrong way. "My apologies, I sometimes muddle what I'm trying to say. I meant my brother often wrote about you before he was killed. It was a fellow soldier who sent word to my parents about his death, and yours, at the Gettysburg battle."

"Your brother was a brave man," Samuel said, his voice taking on a serious tone. "He saved many of our men. I was saddened by his death and even more upset that his body was never recovered."

"Our family was devastated that we were unable to give him a proper burial in the family plot."

For nearly an hour, Elora listened as Samuel shared stories

about Lt. Polk's heroism. Enraptured by his every word, she found herself succumbing to his charms. This was a side of Captain Dixon she'd not experienced on the battlefield and she was enamored with it.

"I miss your brother," he said, placing his empty cup on the table.

"He misses you too," Elora replied.

Samuel's eyebrows furrowed. "Pardon me?"

Realizing her faux-pas, Elora scrambled for a response. "What I meant is that he, um, would have missed you as well, had he survived." Elora's cheeks colored. She was babbling like a love-sick school girl.

"Miss Polk, would you like to stay for lunch?" Mrs. Dixon asked.

"That would be lovely, thank you."

After a meal of ham, sweet potatoes, and peas, Samuel escorted Elora to the entryway, his mother lingering nearby to maintain propriety.

Opening the door, Samuel spoke in a hushed tone, "Miss Polk, may I call on you?"

"I'd like that very much," she replied. "I'm staying at the Tremont Hotel in town. I'll be heading home day after tomorrow."

"Perhaps you can join us for supper this evening?" Mrs. Dixon called, her eyes dancing.

"I'd like that very much," Elora said. With a curtsey, she ambled down the brick stairs to the carriage. Her heart pounded with the force of an avalanche. Could her dreams of being with Samuel actually come to fruition? She could feel the joy dissolving years of heartache from her soul like sugar in a teacup.

Elora extended her stay in Boston a week, spending every day with Samuel. She met his father, a stout man with dimpled cheeks and the same sparkling eyes as his son. In order to maintain decorum, Mr. and Mrs. Dixon were always in their company. The feelings Elora had harbored for so long were burgeoning into something much deeper. She desperately wanted to ask Samuel about his missing arm and how he'd survived what she assumed had been a fatal injury but was hesitant to do so. There was no way to broach the subject without raising suspicions about her knowledge not to mention most soldiers didn't like to discuss such things. After all, she'd only met him as her true self days earlier. His parents' constant presence also limited certain topics.

One evening, Elora and Samuel were able to catch a brief moment alone, his mother making some excuse about needing Mr. Dixon to help with something in the library. Holding her hand in his, Samuel brushed Elora's lips with a kiss. Her heart danced. What she'd believed to be impossible was actually happening. Her beloved Captain Dixon was alive and well and seemed to be falling for her.

"I cannot explain it, Miss Polk," he whispered, staring down at her. "I feel as if I've known you for years."

"I feel the same way." Remorse over her deception plucked at her conscience. It was obvious an attachment was forming between them. What should she do? Pursuing a relationship based on a lie was no way to begin what she hoped would be a lifetime commitment. Shame shifted her gaze, catching his attention.

"Did I say something wrong?" he asked.

He was so perceptive. She'd never be able to keep up this charade forever. How would she explain her relationship with a man who had served with her make-believe brother to her parents? All of a sudden, her corset seemed to tighten, and she feared she might faint.

Instinctively, Samuel wrapped his arm about her waste,

steadying her. "Are you alright?" Concern veiled his eyes. "Have I been too forward?"

"Not at all," she replied. "Mr. Dixon…"

"Please, call me Samuel."

His eyes locked on hers. She'd faced cannons, gunfire, and death, yet none of it had been as terrifying as the dilemma before her now.

Swallowing hard, she squared her shoulders and inhaled. "Samuel, there's something I need to say that might end any further contact between us."

His features softened as he brushed her cheek with his right hand. "Nothing you say could ever drive me away."

Elora gathered all her courage and looked him in the eye. "I'm not who you think I am."

His brows furrowed. "You're not Elora Polk?"

"I am Elora Polk, but there's more to it."

Taking a step back, Samuel cocked his head. "I don't understand."

"I'm Lieutenant Polk." Elora blew out a breath as her shoulders slumped. She'd finally said it. If nothing else, she could take comfort knowing she'd told the truth, even if he sent her away.

Samuel shook his head. "What do you mean *you're* Lt. Polk?"

She stepped closer, her face only inches from his. "Lt. Polk reporting for duty!" she said in her male voice.

Samuel's eyes widened as he studied her face. "But how?" he mumbled. "Polk was killed at Gettysburg. His body was never recovered."

"I pretended to be a man and enlisted in the army. Later, I spied for the Union by dressing as a woman. I gathered information from Confederate soldiers who believed me to be a fellow Rebel." Tensing, she waited for his response.

Samuel's head tipped back as a roar of laughter bellowed from his lips. "This is unbelievable!" he declared, jovially. "You really are Lt. Polk."

"Indeed." Elora took a step back unsure how to react to his response.

"And you came here to meet my parents because you believed I was dead. Why did you think such a thing?"

"I saw them bring your body to the triage at Gettysburg. There was so much blood and you were..." she gasped out a sob. "You were still as death. One of the soldier's checked your pulse and declared there was nothing to be done. There's no way you could have survived, or so I thought."

"The gunshot nearly blew my arm off. They had no choice but to remove it which of course ended my military career. The surgeon told me it was a miracle I survived due to the amount of blood loss," he said. "What about you? When we never found your body, we assumed you'd been killed."

"I was wounded in the shoulder. While I was lying there waiting for medical attention, I realized my secret would be discovered when they removed my uniform, so I managed to sneak off."

Samuel pursed his lips and looked away.

"I understand if you're angry and never want to see me again, but please know I care about you," she said, reaching for his hand. Instead of withdrawing it, he slipped it around her waist and pulled her close.

"How can I be angry with the most amazing woman I've ever known?"

"But I lied about who I was."

"And served your country, bravely."

She glanced down.

Gently, he lifted her chin and met her gaze. "I never understood it before but something about you always tugged at my heart. I realize we've only known each other in this context for a week, but I must confess, I'm in love with you, Elora Polk."

She searched his face for signs that he might be toying with her but found none. A smile curled her lips.

"I've loved you for some time, Samuel Dixon."

He leaned in, punctuating their declarations with a long kiss stealing the breath from her lungs.

Straightening, he caressed her cheek. "May I call on you in South Carolina?"

"I would hunt you down if you didn't," she replied boldly. "But please say nothing of what I've shared. My parents are unaware of my involvement in the war."

"I'll take your secret to the grave," he replied, kissing her once again.

Their courtship was brief, with only Seth knowing the roots of their relationship. Within three months they were engaged, and a year later they were married at Rose Hall. It seemed Elora's life was turning out better than she ever imagined.

Chapter 51

December 1867

Maggie

Sun dappled the brick path leading to Maggie's front porch as winter's icy breath caressed the cottage. It was a typical December day in the Lowcountry with oranges weighting the tree at the side of the house, budding camellias of all hues, and deer foraging for food in the yard beyond. Seth was out with some of the workers harvesting oysters while Maggie stitched the hem of her daughter's gown. Jane would be attending a gathering at a neighboring plantation with several other young ladies and gents from the area. Joshua would be in attendance as well.

Jane was engaged to Everett Jensen, a young man whose family had moved south after the war. His father was a barrister and Everett was determined to follow in his footsteps. Maggie and Seth were pleased with the match and looked forward to the wedding ceremony that would be held at Rose Hall in the spring.

Joshua was growing tall like his father and had inherited Seth's manner of dealing with animals. He was planning on attending veterinary school once he finished his studies at home.

Seth's health was much improved. Dr. Polk had consulted with a doctor from Charleston regarding his condition. With exercise and diet, Seth managed to regain most of his strength although he still had to restrict some of his activities. Nevertheless, he'd adjusted to his limitations and regained his positive demeanor. He did what he could and rested when necessary. Seth was determined to be around for his daughter's wedding and the grandchildren that would follow.

"Hey, Ma!" Joshua called as he scaled the porch steps. "Would it be alright if I rode to the party with Hank Jones?"

"What's wrong with riding with your sister and Mr. Jensen?"

Joshua's upper lip curled. "Cause they get all mushy and say the dumbest things."

Maggie chuckled. "I'm afraid you'll have to endure it. Your sister cannot accompany Mr. Jensen without an escort."

"What about you?" he asked.

"I'll be here enjoying an evening of quietude," she replied.

"Come on, Ma," he pleaded. "Just this once let them ride together without a chaperone. They're going to be married soon."

"Joshua Daniels you will escort your sister and I'll not hear another word about it," Maggie said.

"Alright," he moaned, stepping into the cottage.

Shaking her head, Maggie grinned as she resumed stitching the hem of Jane's dress. Life at the plantation was better than ever. The 13th Amendment had passed in December of 1865 forever abolishing slavery. This had ended the Underground Railroad's efforts and allowed the workers at the plantation to live openly without having to pretend they were enslaved.

Even better, Willa and Letty remained on St. Helena Island with Dr. Towne and Miss Murray allowing Maggie to visit them often.

Evening tide chased the sun below the horizon, speckling the inky sky in pinpricks of light. With a shawl wrapped about her shoulders, Maggie swayed in the wooden rocker. Seth stepped onto the porch and sat in the rocker next to her.

The rungs creaked in unison as they tottered in the frosty air.

"I'm surprised to find you out here in the cold," Seth said.

"Sometimes I enjoy the frigid air. It reminds me of Ireland," she smiled, glancing his direction.

"Without the subzero temperatures and snow," he chuckled.

"Indeed, I don't miss that part," she replied, Irish peppering her words.

"After all these years, you can still speak with that accent."

"Aye, you don' like how I speak?" she replied in a heavy brogue.

Reaching over, he grasped her hand and brought it to his lips. "On the contrary. I find it alluring."

A smile spread across her face, as she stood up, the rocker continuing to sway.

"It's chilly out here," she said, leaning over to kiss him. "Why don't we go inside and warm up a bit?"

Standing, Seth swept her close. "I think that's a splendid idea, Mrs. Daniels."

They entered the cottage, embraced by the warmth of the hearth and the love that encapsulated their lives. Despite times of trouble, sorrow, abuse, and even a war, they'd survived, their love seeing them and their families through to happier days. And for that, Maggie was eternally grateful.

Humming her favorite Irish tune, Maggie followed her husband into their room, closed the door, and reveled in the beauty of her life.

Epilogue

Spring 2018

A slender woman dressed in a long skirt and lace collared top with a nametag that read *JoAnn, Rose Hall Docent*, stood at the base of the winding staircase. Her white hair glimmered in the overhead light and her deep blue eyes danced as she regaled the tour group with facts about the Gothic Revival mansion. Oil paintings of the Polk family, including Dr. Polk and his wife Diane, hung on the far wall of the expansive entryway. A framed cabinet card photo of Elora Polk Dixon sat on a mahogany half-moon table below her parents' portraits.

The tour guide stepped toward the family pictures and began her scripted account of the Polk family history including Dr. Polk's service as a physician with the Union army in Washington D.C. during the civil war and his famous daughter, Elora.

"It was Elora Polk Dixon who left her mark on the world," JoAnn said. "After marrying Captain Samuel Dixon here at the plantation, they returned to Boston where they lived most of the year. Every summer they returned to the Lowcountry and stayed with the Polks. Samuel was a brilliant accountant. Initially, Elora taught at an all-girls academy until she took up writing. Her military service haunted her and the only relief she found was keeping a journal.

"Three years into the marriage, Elora gave birth to a son, Alexander, and two years after that another son, Eli. As many of you know, Elora Polk Dixon went on to write several novels to great acclaim, one of which featured a female protagonist posing as a soldier while spying for the Union army. Her ability to describe battle scenes was uncanny for a woman who'd never seen combat thus earning her many accolades for her writing. Interestingly, her journal entries were discovered posthumously revealing her most popular novel, *Shadows of the War*, to be autobiographical instead of fictional."

Several tour guests smiled, moving closer to the table to glimpse Elora's photo.

"Any questions before we head into Dr. Polk's office?" JoAnn asked.

A lean woman wearing black raised her hand.

"Do you have any ghosts?" she asked, her dark eyes sparkling as a grin lifted her plum-colored lips.

"Actually, we have two." She smiled. "The most prominent one is a lady who's said to have died here after traveling by coach from Pennsylvania to visit family in South Carolina. She fell ill during the journey and was brought to Rose Hall so Dr. Polk might help her. Sadly, the doctor was out of town, and she passed a few days later. Legend says the mysterious woman is buried somewhere on the plantation. Many tour guests have reported seeing the image of a woman dressed in a long gray gown hovering on the staircase."

"And the other spirit?" the woman asked.

JoAnn's smile faded. "She's a bit bolder. Some say she must have been an unhappy person in life as they get an uneasy feeling when she's around. At times she can be aggressive throwing items from tables or shelves."

Many of the tour guests began looking around the room, concern creasing their faces.

"Not to worry, the other spirit mostly haunts the small cottage next to the house that functions as a short-term rental." JoAnn reassured them. "Shall we continue the tour?"

Several heads nodded as the tour guests followed JoAnn into Dr. Polk's office. As the last of the group disappeared into the next room, a translucent figure with flowing red hair and piercing green eyes appeared at the base of the staircase. Her gray dress puddled about her feet and the right side of her mouth quirked into a half smile as she scanned the space before vanishing from sight.

Author Notes

First and foremost, I want to thank everyone for taking this journey with me through a dark period of our country's history. By no means is this story meant to take a political stance regarding which side was right or wrong. I merely wanted to share some aspects of the Civil War that aren't commonly discussed. *Shadows of the War* is meant to focus on the characters' lives with the civil war serving as the backdrop.

While some elements in this story are based on actual events (burning of Bluffton, Combahee River Raid, Dr. Laura Towne, Ellen Murray, and the founding of the Penn School) much of it is fictional. I am not an expert on historic battles or those who led them nor am I knowledgeable in military tactics or the detailed workings of a spymaster. I took artistic liberties with the research I gleaned of these elements in order to make everything fit with the story.

I am intrigued by those women who stepped outside of the typical role designated for females of the time period, risking life and forgoing comfort to be of service. Harriett Tubman, in my opinion, is one the greatest heroes in American history. Not only did she have to contend with the era's perspective toward females but her ethnicity as well. I don't have to give background on this astounding individual as her fame is well known. Her role in the Combahee River Raid in June of 1863 was nothing shy of miraculous. This is a well-known story in the Lowcountry and should be taught in every history class across America.

Next on my list of heroes are Dr. Laura Towne and Ellen Murray. These two women left the comforts of their northern homes to tend to and educate the newly freed slaves in the war torn south. They endured the humid, bug ridden Lowcountry as well as living with soldiers who at times were not always gentlemanly in their behavior. Dr. Towne and Miss Murray loved what they did and remained in the Lowcountry well after the war ended.

Many women enlisted in the armed forces disguised as men or serving as spies. One woman in particular, Loreta Janeta Valezquez who was the inspiration for Elora's character in this book, served as both soldier and spy. Although Loreta fought and spied for the Confederacy, Elora did so for the Union Army.

I enjoyed doing the research for this novel and hope it inspires the reader to delve deeper into the intricacies and perils of the Civil War. I'm including a list of interesting books for those who would like to read more about this time period.

Suggested reading:

·*Letters and Diary of Dr. Laura Towne Give history of Dr. Laura Towne 1862-1884* by Laura M. Towne and Rupert Sargent Holland

·*April 1865: The Month That Saved America* by Jay Winik

·*Stealing Secrets: How a Few Daring Women Deceived Generals, Impacted Battles, and Altered the Course of the Civil War* by H. Donald Winkler

·*A Woman Doctor's Civil War: Esther Hill Hawk's Diary* edited by Gerald Schwartz

Acknowledgments

Acknowledgements

To my husband, Darryl, thank you for your love, support, patience, and your willingness to listen to my stories and provide valuable input. I love you!

To my mom, Karen Oates, thanks for reading, editing, and cheering me on! Love you!

To my writing coach, Charlotte Rains-Dixon, thank you for always helping and encouraging me to be a better writer. You are the best!

To my cover designer, Rena Violet, thank you for creating another incredible cover! You are truly amazing!

To my 'other mother', Millie Boyce, thanks for always being there and encouraging me! Love you!

To the businesses who carry my books, Nevermore Books, Beaufort Bookstore, MacIntosh Books, The Lowcountry Store, Grayco, Lowcountry Living Room, and Main Street Reads-thank you for your support!

To my friends and family who cheer me on, Joan Jones,

Aimee Tidwell, Darlene Stokes, Lynn Bristow, Diane Morrison, Michelle Dufour, Mary Beth Klinar, Kay Keeler, Richard Norris, Jo and Ralph Beaver, Teresa Partin, Chris Crooke, Charlie Frost, Peggy Callahan, Catherine Horry, Janell McClure, Sarah Hetzler, Kelly Taylor, Bernie Ladd, Jonathon Haupt, and Janet McCauley -thank you for your ongoing support! Love you all!

To all my readers- I appreciate each and every one of you! Thank you for reading my books! Your kind words and continued support mean a lot!

Most importantly, thanks be to God! With Him all things are possible!

In Memorium:

Thanks to all those who supported me over the years but have gone on to Heaven, Harvey and Catherine Oates, Michael Wiegel, David Clark, Sam Poovey, Rachell Poovey Navratil, Tom Boyce, John Keith, Phyllis Sooy, Cathy Benson, and Becky Baldwin. Love you always!

About the Author

Kim Poovey is a storyteller and author of historical fiction and haunted tales. She has traveled the Southeast for more than 20 years presenting on 19th century fashion, mourning practices, and other Victorian era topics. In 2011 she portrayed Mrs. Stanton, wife of Secretary of War Stanton (Kevin Kline), in the Robert Redford film, *The Conspirator*. Her published works include *Truer Words, Through Button Eyes; Memoirs of an Edwardian Teddy Bear* (out of print), *Dickens' Mice, The Tails Behind the Tale, The Haunting of Monroe Manse* (book 1 in the Dreamist series), *The Haunting of Edgefield Manor* (Book 2 in the Dreamist series), *The Haunting of Borden House* (book 3 in the Dreamist series), *Shadows of the Moss* (first in the trilogy), and *Shadows of the War* (book 2 in the Shadows trilogy). Kim has also written for several magazines to include Beaufort Lifestyles, Bluffton Breeze, Citizen's Companion, and the Civil War Times. Kim lives in a haunted 1890s Victorian cottage in the South Carolina Lowcountry with her husband, Darryl, and their furry children.

Also by Kim Poovey

Truer Words

Through Button Eyes; Memoirs of an Edwardian Teddy Bear (out of print)

Dickens Mice; The Tails Behind the Tale

Shadows Trilogy (in order)

Shadows of the Moss

Shadows of the War

Dreamist Series (in order)

The Haunting of Monroe Manse

The Haunting of Edgefield Manor

The Haunting of Borden House